DAMNATION OF ADAM BLESSING

Adam Blessing had been an overweight orphan, a nuisance to those who knew him. Now in his twenties, he has re-created himself as an upscale autograph dealer. But the old wounds run deep. He obsesses about his rich childhood friend, Billy, and begins to drink too much. He chases after Billy's estranged girlfriend, Charity. He antagonizes Dorothy, the woman who cares for him, and deludes himself with dreams of success. All Adam wants is to be respected–whatever it takes. It's time to re-create himself again, only this time he'll need to take more drastic measures.

ALONE AT NIGHT

Slater Burr is happily married to Jenny, half his age and his perfect match. But Slater has a secret. He has gotten away with murder. His first wife, Carrie, wouldn't give him a divorce so he ran her down in cold blood outside the country club. Fortunately young Buzzy Cloward was drunk enough that Slater was able to maneuver him into the car to take the blame. Buzzy went to prison. Now Buzzy is back. And all of Slater's careful plans are beginning to unravel. It's all Slater can do to stay one step ahead of the rumors– and one step ahead of Carrie's sardonic laughter.

VIN PACKER BIBLIOGRAPHY

Spring Fire (1952)
Dark Intruder (1952)
Look Back to Love (1953)
Come Destroy Me (1954)
Whisper His Sin (1954)
The Thrill Kids (1955)
The Young and Violent (1956)
Dark Don't Catch Me (1956)
3-Day Terror (1957)
5:45 to Suburbia (1958)
The Evil Friendship (1958)
The Twisted Ones (1959)
The Girl on the Bestseller List (1960)
The Damnation of Adam Blessing (1961)
Something in the Shadows (1961)
Intimate Victims (1962)
Alone at Night (1963)
The Hare in March (1966)
Don't Rely on Gemini (1969)

As Ann Aldrich

We Walk Alone (1955)
We, Too, Must Love (1958)
Carol in a Thousand Cities [editor] (1960)
We Two Won't Last (1963)
Take a Lesbian to Lunch (1972)

As M. J. Meaker

Sudden Endings (1964) [published in pb as by Vin Packer]
Hometown (1967)

As Marijane Meaker

Game of Survival (1968)
Shockproof Sydney Skate (1972)
Highsmith: A Romance of the 1950's (2003)

As M. E. Kerr

Dinky Hocker Shoots Smack (1972)
If I Love You, Am I Trapped Forever (1973)
The Son of Someone Famous (1974)
Is That You, Miss Blue? (1975)
Love is a Missing Person (1975)
I'll Love You When You're More Like Me (1977)
Gentlehands (1978)
Little Little (1981)
What I Really Think of You (1982)
Me Me Me Me Me: Not a Novel (1983)
Him She Loves? (1984)
I Stay Near You: One Story in Three (1985)
Night Kites (1986)
Fell (1987)
M. E. Kerr Introduces Fell (1988)
Fell Back (1989)
Fell Down (1991)
Linger (1993)
Deliver Us from Evie (1994)
"Hello" I Lied (1997)
Blood on the Forehead: What I Know About Writing (1998)
What Became of Her (2000)
Slap Your Sides (2001)
Snakes Don't Miss Their Mothers (2003)

As Mary James

Shoebag (1991)
The Shuteyes (1993)
Frankenlouse (1994)
Shoebag Returns (1996)

Damnation of Adam Blessing

Alone at Night

by Vin Packer

STARK
HOUSE

Stark House Press • Eureka California

THE DAMNATION OF ADAM BLESSING / ALONE AT NIGHT

Published by Stark House Press
2200 O Street
Eureka, CA 95501
griffinskye@cox.net
www.starkhousepress.com

ISBN: 0-9749438-6-x

Text set in Kennerly Old Style and Dogma
Cover design and layout by Mark Shepard, shepdesign.home.comcast.net

First Stark House Press Edition: July 2005

0 9 8 7 6 5 4 3 2 1

Table of Contents

GOLD MEDAL DAYS

By Vin Packer

I didn't even have a telephone the afternoon I got my first call from Dick Carroll, an editor with Gold Medal Books. It was 1951, and New York City was still feeling the effects of World War II's aftermath. I had found an apartment I could afford, so long as I shared it with three sorority sisters, all of us fresh from the University of Missouri. We had a two-bedroom up in Washington Heights, but we took our phone calls in the basement, on the super's line.

"Our of your roommates has been telling me about you," said Dick. "I hear you want to be a writer. How do you feel about being a reader in the meantime?"

Missouri grads were held in high esteem at Fawcett Publications. Ralph Duigh, the editorial director, had graduated from the Journalism school there.

I hoped I'd fare better on West 44th Street, in the Fawcett Building, than I had other places. Beginning at Dutton Publishing, and ending finally with The Proctological Review and The Journal of Gaestroenterology, I'd been fired from eight jobs in a little over a year... employers did not fancy my habit of writing on the side, while the filing piled up, and the letters I'd typed were filled with errors.

I reported to Fawcett on a Monday, where I was introduced to a tall, blue-eyed man with brown hair and a thick Irish accent. You'd have imagined Dick was right off the boat from Ireland, instead of right off the train from Greenwich, Connecticut. He was filled with the old blarney, too, and would in a few years be featured in Rona Jaffe's first novel, *The Best Of Everything*. She was one of his assistants, then, one of the regulars at the little table in the restaurant in the Fawcett Building. where a gang gathered every night after work to drink and talk, most of the drinks landing up on Dick's bill.

He was forever ordering another round when no one was finished with the first drink, then at the end of the month complaining bitterly that the bar padded his check.

Ah, but he was a happy fellow, mostly. He'd been dug up from the depths of despair out in Hollywood, to come East and help Bill Lengel "revolutionize the publishing industry."

At last, the writer was getting a good break. No longer would hardcover publishers rake off the huge shares of paperback royalties; Gold Medal was publishing paperback originals, and paying very nice advances... a typical paperback printing was 400,000 copies. As a new Gold Medal writer, you might get $2000 down and $2000 on delivery of your manuscript... You were paid on print order, a penny a copy... it was a very sweet deal.

So I became a reader, for a very short time. Bill Lengel received a complaint from a major writer of the day, who'd had his book rejected by me. I'd said in the letter the plot was "tired," thus angering a brand name Gold Medal would have liked including on its list.

Lengel fired me as proof to the writer I had no judgment or tact (true, true) and the writer was treated to a long dinner at The Algonquin next door, the result of which was a contract.

In those beginning days, Lengel was the chief. Dick was under him.

I decided to freelance full time, because I'd sold a short story to "Ladies Home Journal" for $750. That was three months' salary in those days. The story I'd sold was set in a boarding school, and when it came out, Dick called and said to meet him for drinks immediately.

"How about a boarding school novel?" said Dick. "We are having tremendous luck with a novel called *Women's Barracks* by Teresk Torres."

Fawcett was getting their first hint of how well a theme of lesbianism sold.

I said I'd rather try fiction set in a sorority, since that experience was newer to me.

I outlined and wrote a chapter of a book called *Sorority Girl*. Dick advanced me two thousand against thirty-five hundred, and I was in business.

Dick changed the title to *Spring Fire* because James Michner had a best seller called *Fires of* Spring.

A year later, Roger Fawcett, the seldom seen CEO appeared in his office long enough to shake my hand and announce that I'd outsold *God's Little Acre* an the paperback bestseller list.

Vi Packer was launched.

I'd chosen the pseudonym because I'd had a dinner one night with a man whose first name was Vincent, and a woman whose last was Packer.

I had a lot of pseudonyms because I was my own agent, handling a dozen clients, all me.

The other pseudonyms began to slip away as Packer took over. I switched to homicide, solely because I'd heard that Anthony Boucher reviewed paperbacks in the Sunday *Times*, as did James Sandoe in the Sunday *Tribune*. I wanted to be reviewed.

Thanks to both Sandoe's and Boucher's encouragement, I stayed in the field around twelve years, producing some twenty-two books, ten of them suspense novels.

What I most liked writing were fictionalized versions of real crime.

I started in that direction at the suggestion of Boucher, who called my attention to a case in Australia, two girls killing the mother of one.

I sent for all the trial papers, and felt my hair rise as I read the diary of one: *Thousands die every day. Why not mother?*

There was the title leaping out at me. *Why Not Mother?*

But of coarse, I didn't reckon with Dick Carroll's passionate sense of the commercial.

"What you put inside the book is your business," he would tell me, "but the outside is mine."

By then he was the editor in charge, and Lengel was in retirement.

Dick was doing well. Writers like Cornell Woolrich, Richard Prather and John McDonald were aboard. Sales were good. Spirits high. "Spirits" were always high when Dick was on the scene, tossing back his scotch, telling his bawdy Irish jokes, thinking up titles to replace yours.

Why Not Mother? became *The Evil Friendship.*

When I made a novel of the Fraden/Wepman matricide some years later, my title *One to Destroy* (...is murder by the law), was changed to *Whisper His Sin.*

Now and then, Dick would give in to me. I did the Emmett Till Mississippi Wolf Whistle case, and he let me keep my title *Dark Don't Catch Me.* (Dark don't catch me in this town...)

But more than often, I was in tears as I caught a cab, on 44th and 6th, certain weekday evenings after Dick took the 7:45 to suburbia. I would have just learned the new title of my book... and read the cover copy.

Favorite phrases having little to do with the inside of my books, really, were: "sexual awakening," "sexual passions," "sexual guilt," "this startling novel," "terrible secrets revealed," "secrets. that shattered," and "another tempestuous tale by the author of *Spring Fire.*"

One Christmas I made spaghetti sauce (my recipe) with a friend, for Christmas gifts. We put a label on the jar: "Another tempestuous dish by the author of *Spring Fire.*"

Those years were good ones, despite the lack of autonomy when it came to covers. I was able to launch myself as a fulltime freelancer only because of Gold Medal. I could not have afforded the career of writing if I had had to depend on the average hardcover advance.

When I finally did go on to hardcover, I abandoned Packer for the most part. I was myself for awhile... and then in the 70's I had a complete sea change and became M.E. Kerr, a young adult writer.

Although I do have a suspense series featuring a detective's son, John Fell (*Fell, Fell Back, Fell Down*) Ms. Kerr does not usually wander onto Ms. Packer's old turf.

I have so many memories of the 50's in New York City, when Alfred Hitchcock's profile was just appearing on TV to the jaunty theme music, Rod Serling was inviting you to come to *The Twilight Zone,* and a lot of us were thinking we ought to go to the coast if we wanted to stay freelancers: television was the coming thing, wasn't it?

"In the sixties." Dick would say, "hardcover books will start to fade away, as they have in Europe. In the seventies, there'll just be paper... you're in at the beginning of a revolution!"

And then he'd say what he always said, "Waiter? All the way around again! Make mine a double!"

Damnation of Adam Blessing

by Vin Packer

PART ONE

1

"I dreamed again last night that I was Billy."
FROM ADAM BLESSING'S JOURNAL

Mrs. Auerbach was drunk again.

In the five years that Adam Blessing had worked for her, he had seen her drunk only once or twice a week. Things were getting worse lately; she was seldom sober. This Saturday afternoon in early May was her sixth consecutive day on the bottle. As usual she arrived at The Autograph Mart a moment or so before closing.

Adam had been calling her since noon about the customer for "The Lucy Baker Album."

"Where the customer is, Adam?" she asked, huffing and puffing her way across the floor of the basement shop.

Her habit was to eat a whole roll of peppermint life savers as she made her way from her apartment on Second Avenue and Fifty-seventh Street. It was a distance of three city blocks in a straight line, as straight as Mrs. Auerbach could manage.

"The customer," he said flatly, "is gone! He was in three times last week, twice this week. He won't be back."

"Goodt! He doesn't want it enough! I don't want to sell it to him anyway! That is a law, Adam!"

"Yes, ma'am," said Adam. "Why don't we just make it a law that we don't sell anything to anyone?"

The old woman ignored the sarcasm. With considerable effort she lowered herself to the folding chair before the card table which was her desk. She blew at some dust on top of old papers there. "Collectors do not interest me, Adam." She pulled a bottle of rum out of the wire wastebasket under the card table, and set it in front of her. "A customer must love what he buys from me, enough to come back a hundred times if he has to! To collectors I don't sell! Adam, they are worse than parasites, these collectors! They are saprophytes, who off the dead live!" She unscrewed the cap of the rum bottle. "Well, that collector is not going to live off Lucy Baker!" she said, and she punctuated it with a long swallow of rum.

Adam said, "We aren't going to live off her either."

Mrs. Auerbach was fat and in her late sixties. She always wore sweaters and skirts, even in the hot months, and silk stockings with ankle socks over them, and low black oxfords which were always polished. Her garters never reached above her knees. They were rolled to a stop an inch below her skirt. Her hair was a peculiar orange shade from the self-administered rinses. She wore it long, past her shoulder blades, and when she thought about it, she tied it in place with a piece of rough, brown wrapping cord. Today, she had not thought about it. She kept blowing at it from the sides of her wrinkled mouth, trying to keep it out of her eyes. Often when Adam was confronted with her dishevelment, he was reminded of the way she never dotted her *i*'s or crossed her *t*'s–bald proof of her absent-minded carelessness.

"So!" she said, setting the bottle back on the card table with a thud. "The City wins, no, Adam?"

Adam knew it was starting–another of Mrs. Auerbach's harangues against the city of New York. They were going to tear down the apartment house where she had lived for over thirty years. Already she was the only tenant remaining in the building; the gas and electricity had been turned off a week ago. Adam knew this was one of the reasons she was drinking so heavily lately. He sneaked a look at his wrist watch. Five past five. His date with Dorothy Schackleford was for six-fifteen at the Roosevelt Hotel.

"Mrs. Auerbach–" he tried, but she waved his words away with her pudgy hand.

She said: "I saw you. You are rushing so much all the time! All the time watching your clock, ah, Adam? Hasn't that been the trouble with the business, your rushing? In this business, no one rushes and makes one dime! You rush like the City rushes!"

"You never even arrive here until five o'clock, Mrs. Auerbach. Don't forget that."

"I once thought I would make you my beneficiary. You are young, you could carry on the business, but no! You rush too much! I leave the whole shooting match to the Universal Committee on Conversation!"

"Conservation!" Adam corrected her.

It was her favorite threat, to cut him out of her will. Adam wondered if she even had a will. It was a five o'clock threat, when she wanted him to sit and drink rum with her, and listen to her curse Commercialism, Collectors, Waste, Progress and the City. Her mood could just as easily swing, in a matter of minutes. Then she would offer Adam the autograph album which had belonged to Goethe's son, or she would announce to Adam that she was planning to adopt him legally as her son and heir, or she would inform him that it was the U.C.C. she was cutting from her will, because they were doing nothing about topsoil research. She was magniloquent in both moods, either offering Adam the world, or offering to pull it out from under him. There was no in-between, such as an offer of an extra five-dollar raise. Adam was still making the measly seventy-five dollars a week he had been earning for the past two years.

"Everything to the Universal Committee on Conservation!" she babbled on. "They want to preserve, Adam! You don't want to preserve! What do you care if some unprincipled saprophyte walks in to buy 'The Lucy Baker Album?' You would sell it in a blink of the eye!"

Adam sighed and walked across to his desk, starting to clear away the day's work. He said, "You know nothing about the man who wanted to buy that album."

"Where he is? Not here. Ah? He wants to buy, but he has no time to wait! I would sell it to him under no circumstances!"

"You're stubborn," said Adam. "Just stubborn!"

"What?"

"Nothing."

"Yah, nothing! I heard you under your breath! You and the City! Same birds!" She took another swallow of rum. "'Remember well and bear in mind, that a true friend is hard to find.'"

It was a verse from "The Lucy Baker Album."

"So is a good living hard to find," said Adam.

"Quit the whole shooting match if you don't like it! Anyway, you're fired! I fired you a hundred times, and you don't get it through your head!"

"All we sell any more," Adam said, "is autographs. We haven't sold an autograph album in seven months!"

"Sell all the autographs you want to," said Mrs. Auerbach, holding the rum bottle to the light to see its level. "Who cares for an old slip of paper with Button Gwinnett scrawled on it? Ah? Yah, worth money, but who cares for it? And all the other signers of your Declaration to Independence! Some independence when the City comes to wreck your home!"

"'The Lucy Baker Album' could have paid for a whole remodeling job here," Adam grumbled.

Mrs. Auerbach chuckled. "I hate to sell the albums, Adam. The autograph books–there's where my heart is. The *Stammbuchs,* with all their sweet sentiments! There's the heart in this business, and you would sell it!

Sell Button Gwinnett's *schlimm* signature, but leave me my heart!"

"Never mind," said Adam. "Sunday I'll look in the *Times* for something. Some other work!"

Mrs. Auerbach did not raise her eyes from the rum bottle. She had heard that before. She knew how Adam loved The Mart. For Adam too, the autograph books were the most interesting part of the business. He loved to study the handwriting of the people who wrote in them; handwriting analysis had become his hobby. He enjoyed imagining the friendships, love affairs, and family relationships, and more than often he could pick out the most sinister dips and loops written in some of the saccharine and homely verses; as well as the contrary in some of the most dull and proper entries. Adam had never had a knack for making friends; love was a word which still sounded clumsy and joyless on his tongue. He had been raised in the Cayuga County Orphans' Home, in upstate New York, and the closest he had ever come to having a family was his hero-worship of a very wealthy man in the city. But this same man had a son of his own with whom Adam had never succeeded in getting along; the son, in fact, had been the blight of Adam's young years, always teasing him and showing him up. Adam had come away from upstate New York with a fierce embarrassment at having been an orphan. Often, with strangers, he invented a family; more than often he pretended to be the son of that rich man, using this masquerade only in the very unimportant moments–riding on a train or a bus, or having a drink beside someone in a bar. It was a little peculiarity of Adam's, and he did it without thinking, as though it were a perfectly normal thing to do. Usually he kept his own name, but there had been times when he went the limit, and said his name was Billy Bollin.

Mrs. Auerbach was the only person with whom he had ever discussed his past in detail, and honestly. She was old and warm and sentimental, in her better moments, and, he supposed, slightly daffy as well, but Adam could talk to her. When he had first come to New York and taken this job with her at The Mart, they had spent many long hours talking together. Mrs. Auerbach could carry on forever over a rum bottle, but never once had she told Adam anything about her past.

At twenty-four, Adam Blessing was a little under six feet, with strong muscles he had worked hard to develop, a pleasant manner, and a good appearance–which had also involved work. As a youngster he had been very fat, and far from neat; he had been slow in school, and the dolt of his classmates. The course he had run since leaving Auburn, New York had not been an easy one; it had been all uphill. He had enrolled in numerous adult education classes given in high schools around the city. He had taken speech and shorthand, a semester of German, art appreciation, music appreciation, ballroom dancing, economics, a course in business management and one in personality. He was not as shy as he used to be, and he was meticulous about combing his white-blond hair and parting it in a somewhat old-fashioned way on the far left side. He kept himself scrubbed clean, nails clipped, clothes pressed and immaculate. His face was not overly-endowed by Nature with perfect features, but he had a good nose and excellent teeth, which compensated for lips that were on the small side, and eyes that were a dull, yellowish brown, Adam could easily be taken for a school teacher, a seminary student, a teller in a bank; or for exactly what he was–Mrs. Auerbach's clerk.

This outward appearance of mild-mannered introversion was misleading. Adam Blessing was ambitious. His ambitions kept him awake nights, sent him on long walks through dawn-deserted city streets, and kept him writing letter after letter after letter to manufacturers, corporations, agencies and any number of private enterprises. He was a world of ideas without an axis on which to revolve. When his letters received any replies at all, they were simply polite acknowledgments; more frequently they were ignored. Adam imagined that they were probably laughed at, and often, just after he mailed one of his letters, his checks would smart with frustration and humiliation as he imagined the letter arriving, and being ridiculed. His ideas for a way to improve paper clips, for children's games, for advertising copy, for packaging pickles and olives in lighter containers, for promoting books and for publishing more readable newspapers–all of Adam's ideas were unrealized. He needed money; even ideas for making money cost money. That fact was his dead end.

Waking and sleeping, he dreamed of having money, but in those moments of stark reality when he was face to face with the glaring light of truth, he became resigned and somewhat bitter. He was Adam Blessing, no matter if he could see his reflection only hazily in the mirror behind the bar, no matter if the stranger beside him did put his beer down, shake his hand and say: "Glad to know you, Mr. Bollin."

After he had piled his correspondence neatly and rolled down the top of his desk, he glanced across at Mrs. Auerbach. She was humming a waltz. Some of the rum had dribbled down the front of her red sweater from the sides of her mouth, and her legs were spread in a careless fashion, so that Adam could see up to the long pink silk bloomers she wore; could see the jelly-fat-flabby thighs. He had seen her that way too many times to figure, but each time he was reminded of the only glimpse of his own mother which his memory retained. He was not even certain of how old he was, but he must have been very young, for it was some time before he had been taken to the Home. He was in a kitchen with her. She had been washing clothes at the sink on a hot day, and she had plopped herself down on a straight-backed wooden chair, in the same posture as Mrs. Auerbach's now. He had not been too young to feel a certain shame at being able to see up her skirt. She was not fat like Mrs. Auerbach. Adam could not remember her face. But he did remember something she said to him. Her tone was sarcastic. Adam liked to think that it was a sarcasm striped with a certain disappointment about something Adam had nothing to do with, but he could not be positive of that. He only knew for sure that she had looked at him and said, "And a lot *you* care!"

That was the only memory Adam had of a parent.

Mrs. Auerbach's mood had swung now. She was telling Adam that she was leaving him everything when she passed on. Adam was convinced she would leave it to dogs and cats, the Committee on Conservation, or perhaps some imaginary committee of her own, to fight the city of New York. He sometimes wondered what happened to an old woman's money when she had no beneficiary; but whatever did happen, and whoever did take over the business, Adam was sure he would be asked to stay on. In addition, he was sure his position would be a more important one. He knew as much about the stock at The Mart as Mrs. Auerbach did, and he had hundreds of ideas for making the place a success. Mrs. Auerbach was simply not interested in the business any more, despite her occasional harangues to the contrary. Whoever took over the business—and even in Adam's dreams he discounted himself, for he knew the old woman and her crazy ways—the new owner would need Adam. It would be a matter of time. Adam would be given more responsibility and more money, and while he would probably not get rich, he would have enough, he was sure...

Drunk or sober, Mrs. Auerbach embraced strangeness with the unreasoning enthusiasm of the certifiable eccentric. Adam knew that she often picked through city litter baskets for strange souvenirs—an old box, a hat band—once, the wheel of a baby carriage. It had been reported to Adam, by other shopkeepers along Fifty-seventh Street, that she kept thousands of dollars in used sardine tins in her icebox; and Adam was very used to seeing the jar of pepper she carried at all times, to ward off thieves.

About Mr. Auerbach—whoever he was, and if he ever had been—Adam knew nothing. Mrs. Auerbach mentioned no relatives, except to say she had lived a lovely life and it was done with some years ago; that now she and Adam were both orphans.

He walked across and sat down at the card table with Mrs. Auerbach, waving away her offer of the rum bottle. It was now twenty minutes past five. Adam's date was with an airline reservations telephone clerk he had met in his personality class.

"Mrs. Auerbach, I have to go soon. Really."

She was paging through the familiar autograph book, her favorite.

"This is the great poet Goethe's son's autograph book, Adam."

"Yes, ma'am, I know that by now."

"Yes, ma'am, you know, don't you? It's yours, but you think I should put it back in the safe. You don't believe it's yours, no?" She cackled and drank more rum. "My apartment was mine. Thirty years, Adam, yah? I believed it was mine, but no! The City's it was–all these years. Did the City pay the rent once? No, but the City's it is!"

"I'm sorry about that Mrs. Auerbach, I really am."

"But you're a hurry. Rush and rush, Adam, is that you? Like the City, rush and rush to get me out."

"I have a date, Mrs. Auerbach."

"Yes, but wait, Adam." She placed her hand on Adam's wrist. "The law is, this is yours. Take it." She put the worn autograph book in his hands. "It was Goethe's son's book, Adam. Oh, money it could bring you, and not a little. But more, Adam. Sentiment. Roots. Let it be your *Stammbuch,* Adam. Roots, I can't give you, but this is the next best thing. Yah, Adam?"

"Thank you," said Adam. "I'll put it back in the safe." She slapped her hand down on the book in his hand.

"Nein! This time, take it with you! It is yours, Adam!"

Adam said, "Yes, and thank you again. I'll keep it here in the safe."

"*Nein!*"

Adam held the book in his hand, uncertain of his next step. In all his years of receiving this "gift" from Mrs. Auerbach, she had never stopped him from putting it back in the safe; neither of them, Adam always thought, had ever taken her gesture with any seriousness. The book was worth thousands; it was one of The Mart's most valuable pieces of stock.

"'Hand to the patron the book, and hand it to friend and companion,'" Mrs. Auerbach recited. "I hope you will over and over read that, Adam. In Goethe's own handwriting."

Adam said, "This book is worth–"

"Money! Is that all you care for? Put it in your pocket and shut up your squealing and squeaking! I need some peace! You are like a collector with your money all the time! Put it in your pocket!"

Adam did as he was told.

"Go on, rush!" she said. "Shoo!"

"I could–help you home, Mrs. Auerbach."

Momentarily she regarded him coolly, letting his presumption hang in the silence. Adam had thought of walking her the few blocks to her apartment, then slipping back with the valuable book and locking it safely in The Mart. It was no good. "Since when did I need help home, Herr Blessing?"

He knew she was very angry.

"The law about 'The Lucy Baker Album stands!'" she announced, with a bang of the rum bottle on the table top for punctuation. "To that man who comes here for it, it is not for sale."

"Yes, ma'am."

"And there is filing piled up on your desk too!"

"I realize that, Mrs. Auerbach."

"Do you have correspondence on the Poe manuscript?"

"Yes, Mrs. Auerbach. I have it started."

"Go on! Next thing you'll want this overtime employees want, yah?"

"No," Adam said.

He kept the palm of his hand on his pocket where the album was. He knew he would keep it there all night, and that he would sleep with it under his pillow; not draw a free breath until it was back in The Mart on Monday. He could not even return it tomorrow, though he had a key. At 6:00 P.M. on Saturdays, Mrs. Auerbach's burglar alarm was wired to the keyhole, and centralized with the Palmer Protective Association. It was clocked that way until eight Monday morning.

"What are you waiting for, ah?" She sat erect now, with her plump legs crossed, the one dangling over the other, swinging–exposing her garter, her silk stockings, and her bright yellow ankle socks. As always, Adam could see his face in the shine on her shoes. He dismissed a crazy, sudden impulse to bend down and plant a kiss on that wild mop of orange hair.

As he turned, after saying good night, he heard her voice behind him snap: "Get in on time Monday morning, Herr Blessing!"

Outside, he climbed the winding stairs to Fifty-seventh Street. He sneaked a look at her, the naked electric light bulb dangling on a cord direct-ly above her head, the bottle of rum tipped to her mouth, and her feet tap-ping energetically to what Adam guessed was probably another waltz.

2

*"My youth was eaten away by Envy. Even in my sleeping dreams I imagined
that I was Marshall Bollin's son. Once when I was nine he said to me, 'Adam,
I'd be very proud if you were my boy.'... I wrote it down on a piece of paper and
put 'M.C. Bollin' after it, the way you'd copy a piece of poetry out of a book. I
put the date at the top, and over the date I wrote 'Spoken to Adam Blessing.'.*
FROM ADAM BLESSING'S JOURNAL

"You *are* Adam Blessing, aren't you?" the voice inquired. "Adam Blessing
from Auburn, New York?"

For some slow seconds everything stopped, the way a slow-motion cam-
era will grind to a halt on the pole-vaulter in mid-air, show him grimacing
and dangling there, suspended in time.

Musak provided a harmonica rendition of "Tangerine." At the table
across from Adam in the Roosevelt Grill, the waiter was wiping up a
spilled Manhattan.

Dorothy Schackleford, Adam's date, was holding out a souvenir for
Adam, an ashtray she had stolen from Alfredo's in Rome.

The voice came like a sudden clap of black thunder on an ordinary and
fair day... Adam had always known it would happen this way, when he
least expected it; so that the shock was still curling through his body as he
rose and faced Billy Bollin.... Time began again.

"Yes, it's Adam," reaching for Billy's outstretched hand. "Hello, Billy."

"Adam! Addie! My God, Addie!" Billy pounded him on the back.

"How are you, Billy?"

"I can't believe my eyes, Addie! God, Addie Blessing! Old Fatty Addie!
Look at you!" he said, holding Adam back, "Why, you're as thin as—" hes-
itating, searching for a simile.

"As you are," said Adam.

"Yes!"

"Yes."

"Well, my God, Addie Blessing!"

Billy had not changed. He still stood taller than Adam, and there was the
same tanned handsomeness about him, which offset his shock of bright red
hair. His jade-colored eyes sparkled with the same arrogant confidence, and
he wore the same sort of rich and casual clothes—a black and white shep-

herd's check jacket, coal-colored slacks, crisp white shirt, and a blue twill silk tie. He had dressed that way even as a young boy. Adam took it all in, right down to the gold cuff links with the simple soft-printed B embellishing their faces.

He introduced Billy to Dorothy Schackleford. He could tell by the crooked grin on his know-everything face that Billy had sized her up immediately. She was pretty but she was plain, and plainly impressed already by Billy Bollin. Her brown hair was fuzzy from a home permanent she had over-timed. There was a slight scorch mark on one of her white cotton gloves, resting atop her shiny black patent leather bag. Billy will patronize her, Adam thought, and Billy did.

"Oh," said Billy, "an ashtray from Alfredo's, ah? You've been to Rome!"

"Where I work we can go for practically nothing," said Dorothy. "I'm a clerk for Pan-Trans-America. I got this ashtray from Alfredo's for Adam, because he's given me some swell ones! The Sherry-Netherland, the Stork Club, the Twenty-One—all over, haven't you Adam? Where else, Adam?"

Adam blushed with embarrassment. "I don't remember."

"The El Morocco, that's another one! Gosh, I don't even know all the places. Adam's good at it, aren't you, Adam? I thought I'd die of fright while I was getting this into my bag, but I thought to myself: I've got to get one from Europe for Adam. Adam's never been, have you, Adam?"

Her round, red-cheeked face was glowing, and her nose was shining as well. Adam noticed for the first time that her lipstick was too purple, that she had shaped her lips into a vulgar cupid's bow.

Adam shook his head in reply to her remark, aware of the satisfaction the scene must be giving Billy. Here was Fatty Addie, thin now but not much different; grownup now, but still tagging at the heels of the rich—collecting ashtrays from the restaurants of the rich, sneaking around and pocketing evidence that he had been to them. Adam imagined Billy entertaining some of his friends with the story of this moment—imagined him beginning: "When I knew Addie, he was a fat kid from the county Home; in a way you might say Addie and I grew up together... only, of course, I wasn't an orphan. My old man is Marshall Case Bollin; the good Lord knows whose Addie's is, or was"—pause for a snide chuckle—"or if he had one!"

"Adam," Billy was saying now, "grew up with me. Didn't you, Addie?"

"You might say," Adam answered, "that we grew up together."

Billy regaled Dorothy Schackleford by telling her what a fat little boy Adam had been, how he was always eating or bawling or trailing after Billy's father. Dorothy giggled appreciatively, lighted one cigarette from the other before Adam could offer a light, and looked up admiringly at Billy in the manner of the female positive she had made a hit.

"But I've nearly forgotten my date!" said Billy suddenly.

Dorothy Schackleford was visibly disappointed at this announcement. Adam felt a wave of wild relief... until Billy added, "I'll go get her. She's in the back. We'll all have a round together!"

He pranced toward the rear of the room. Adam intended to announce to Dorothy that they would not go through with Billy's plan, but as he felt for his wallet to pay their bill, his hand brushed against the valuable *Stammbuch* given him an hour ago by Mrs. Auerbach. A crazy impulse captured him. He slid his wallet back in place and leaned forward, speaking in a low voice to Dorothy Schackleford.

"I am part owner of The Mart," he said quite clearly.

"Okay," she said, "I'm Brigitte Bardot."

"Listen to me, Dorothy, I'm serious. When he gets back I'm going to tell him I'm part owner of The Autograph Mart. It's practically true!"

"Adam, it isn't true. That old biddy pays you slave wages as it is!"

"Dorothy, won't you do me a favor?"

"I don't mind going along with a gag, Adam. I just don't want you to think it's 'practically true.'"

Adam said, "Listen, right here in my pocket," patting his suit jacket for emphasis, "I have an album she gave me which is worth close to $50,000. She gave it to me tonight."

"Goethe's son's album?" she said sarcastically . Adam had not remembered having spoken before about Mrs. Auerbach's drunken offers of the album, forgotten by her, or simply reneged in her sober moments–Adam was never sure which.

"All right," he said, "but tonight she forced me to take it!"

"You'll put it back in stock Monday."

"Maybe I will. Maybe I won't." He sounded unconvincing even to himself.

"You'll put it back in stock, and that's as close as you'll ever come to that much money from her!"

"I'm her beneficiary, Dorothy."

"Like I said, Adam, I'm Brigitte Bardot!"

Adam glanced toward the back of the room nervously. Then in a more urgent tone he said, "I'm asking you to do me this favor. It's important to me!"

"All right, Adam! And you don't live at the Y either, I suppose. You live at the Waldorf Towers!"

"That's right," said Adam, "I don't live at the Y."

"My gosh, you're dead serious, aren't you?"

"Dead serious," said Adam.

Dorothy looked at him with a puzzled expression on her plain counte-nance. Adam wished he had never noticed the purple lipstick or the cupid's bow. He knew he was seeing her through Billy's eyes; seeing everything through Billy's eyes now, the way he used to. Dorothy Schackleford shrugged and stood up. "Before this circus begins," she said, "I'm going to use the sand box."

Whenever she said that, she put her arms up close to her shoulders, curl-ing her fingers into her palms, imitating, Adam supposed, a cat on its hind legs. To frost the absurdity, she gave a mew, and whined: "Would Adam order pussy-cat another drinky-poo?"

Adam was just glad Billy was not witness to that moment.

Adam sat alone then, resigned to imminent embarrassment of some kind. For himself, he could carry it off, act the part–even produce the *Stammbuch.* Billy would believe him when he saw the *Stammbuch;* Billy knew what was and what was not worth money. Adam wished he was alone, wished he had had this dreaded encounter with Billy Bollin when he was by himself. With any other girl, Adam could have pretended he had given her the ash-trays from Those Restaurants because he *knew* it would impress her, and because he knew it was one way to get her into bed. His receiving the ash-tray from Alfredo's could even have been crossed off as an act of going along with her naiveté, for the same reason... Except that Dorothy Schack-leford was not the kind of girl one imagined a man panting after. She would embarrass him, that was all there was to it; she was the flaw in his pose. Adam remembered a time when he had embarrassed Dorothy Schackle-ford, before a gathering of *her* friends. He had gotten very drunk and he had criticized the presence of an imitation fireplace in one of her girlfriends' apartments; he had crowned the occasion by throwing up in the bathroom of the apartment. Dorothy Schackleford had told him she had never been so embarrassed in all her life. It had been their first date. She was really ashamed of him and angry. She had said she had not minded his getting sick so much as she had minded his attack on the fireplace. The fireplace, she had raged at him, had cost her girlfriend a good deal of money, and the fact that Adam could not appreciate a fine piece of furniture made her embar-rassed. Her girlfriend would think Adam had been brought up in a barn, she said. He might just as well have criticized the Metropolitan Museum for hanging an El Greco, as far as Dorothy Schackleford was concerned.

Embarrassment was an unpredictable enemy. It could react on individual conceits as personal and diversified as one's taste in underwear. Maybe, if Billy got to the table before Dorothy returned, Adam could give the impression she was just a girl who did typing for him occasionally, a spare-time job of hers, to earn a little extra money. Even as he thought it, he felt low, a feeling familiar to him from years back when Billy Bollin would make him react this same way. Yet he knew there was no way out; around Billy he was this sort of shabby person. In that way, Adam Blessing had not changed at all, and he had known it the instant he had heard Billy's voice call out his name.

Adam wondered what it was that would embarrass a Billy Bollin: perhaps that his fly had been open all through a Philharmonic concert; perhaps that he–but the next possibility remained unborn.

"Here we are, Addie!"

Certainly the almost-forgotten date would not embarrass Billy.

Adam stared at her as he stood up.

Billy said, "This is Charity Cadwallader."

Was that how it all began?

3

"More than anything in the world I wanted to be like Billy. I wanted to have what he had, and I believed that if I were ever to change places with him, I'd know better and wiser ways to enjoy his advantages. His father, for example—I would have been a good son to Marshall Bollin. I would have—but what's the use in mulling over the past! I must stop this constant mulling over of the past!

FROM ADAM BLESSING'S JOURNAL

Adam thought about her constantly. That Monday morning it was raining when he caught the crosstown bus. He had wrapped the *Stammbuch* in a brown paper bag and placed it under his coat to keep it dry. Before he had boarded the bus, he had bought the *Times,* as always, but he was unable to concentrate on the news. His thoughts went back to Saturday evening, as they had throughout the week end. He let them—hanging to a strap, pushed against the other passengers; he let himself go over it all again.

He remembered that brief moment in the lobby of the Roosevelt when he and Billy were waiting for the girls to come from the ladies' room. Billy had made the remark "It's a dreadful name—Charity—isn't it? But I adore her all the same!"

Adam had read in some psychology book that if the person became dear, the name became dear.

Billy had said: "Charity Cadwallader—it's like the name some novelist would give a rich girl, isn't it? Ah well, three-fourths of life is all clichés anyway."

"So she's rich, too," Adam had said.

"Very! She has the best kind of wealth, inherited."

"Just like you."

"Only more."

"Oh."

Billy had looked surprised; then he had laughed. "Good Lord, you actually sound disappointed. You weren't thinking of asking her for a—" but the girls had returned then.

The rain came harder and hit the panes of the bus in sharp needles. Adam wondered if she were sleeping still. Weren't all rich girls still asleep at quarter to eight in the morning? He thought of her long, black-as-night hair, spilled across a very white and soft pillow; and he remembered the simply-cut, elegant black suit she had worn Saturday night, and the infinitesimal gold watch on her wrist. She had worn tiny, pearl, pin-head earrings, and a smile which was polite, as though it disowned the penetrating green eyes that were watching Adam throughout their hour together.

Billy and Dorothy Schackleford had monopolized the conversation—Billy patronizing Dorothy almost as if say to Adam that he was not impressed by Adam's story of success; that his way of showing it was to encourage Dorothy in more of her ordinary and naïve palaver. Adam had found no opportunity to explain why the part-owner of the Fifty-seventh Street Autograph Mart was dating a girl like Dorothy, and Billy was making the most of the fact Adam had such a girl with him.

For some small space of time, Billy had succeeded in making Adam uncomfortable with this maneuver. Dorothy had a very unfeminine way of discussing various physical ailments in frank detail, and Adam had squirmed while she told of a stomach disorder she suffered in Rome. At one point, in the midst of one of Dorothy's sentences, Adam had broken in, slapping the *Stammbuch* to the table in a clumsy and tactless gesture. With a slight nervous break to his voice, which made the tone nearly shrill, he had exclaimed: "Look here, Billy, I guess you can figure what this is worth! It's mine, a little present I bought for myself from our stock at The Mart."

Billy had enthused in his predicative, condescending way, as though he were patting Adam's head. Then he had resumed the conversation with Dorothy, and Dorothy picked it up with more elaboration on what it was like to have "the trots."

It was somewhere in the middle of it all, that Adam became aware of Charity's eyes watching him. It was then that he stopped caring about Dorothy or Billy. It became a small matter that Billy was goading Dorothy into more banality, with the express purpose of humiliating Adam. He was nearly sure that Charity was not even listening and had not been. What she was thinking—even what she thought of Adam—he had no way of divining, but he was hypnotized by a certain mood of calm.

Afterwards, Adam had said to Dorothy Schackleford: "She was staring at me. Did you notice?"

"She was an awful dummy," Dorothy had answered. "She had absolutely *nothing* to say!"

As they were leaving the table, while Billy walked ahead and the girls went to the ladies' room, Adam had pocketed a slip of paper Charity had wadded up and tossed in the ashtray. When Adam looked at it later, he saw that it was simply a receipt for a watch repair job from a shop on Madison Avenue. Save for one thing, it was unimportant, but the one thing was interesting to Adam. Her signature. The tops of her *a*'s were all closely knotted, an indication of extreme secretiveness, evidenced again in the fact that the upstroke of her *d* was separated from the downstroke. The signature was not much to go on, but Adam had little else. That Monday morning he did not even have reason to believe that he would ever encounter Charity Cadwallader again.

There was a light burning in The Mart when Adam arrived, and the stale and too-sweet smell of Mrs. Auerbach's rum. Before Adam did anything else, he put the *Stammbuch* back in the safe. Then he walked across to the card table, threw an empty rum bottle in the wastebasket, and looked through the clutter of papers piled there. Sometimes in her drunkenness Mrs. Auerbach had a moment of lucidity when she would write Adam a note instructing him to do this or that, which invariably should have been done long ago, or already was done. Usually the latter, for Adam knew the working of The Mart thoroughly. Just occasionally her reminders were important, and often, nearly illegible. But instead of instructions that Monday morning, Adam found a piece of old yellow paper, across which at the top Mrs. Auerbach had printed LAST WILL AND TESTAMENT.

She must have been even more drunk when she wrote it than she had been when Adam left her. The printed words ran into one another, and the letters were of varying sizes:

I leave my business to my assistant Adam Blessing who must run it and not sell it. That is a law! All my money to him too, and the Stammbuch of Johann Wolfgang von Goethe's son. If I die, it is the City of New York who kills me. If Adam Blessing dies, all goes to the Universal Committee on Conversation. That is a law and God's will, so be it. Ada Auerbach, her signature. May, 1958.

Mrs. Auerbach's *a*'s were all closely knotted at the top, too. Adam had noticed that about her handwriting before, and he had often thought of the fact she seldom discussed her past. But this morning it was simply another reminder of Charity Cadwallader.

For a moment while he held the yellow paper in his hand, Adam wished the old woman really was dead. But Adam knew full well *his* sort of luck. Mrs. Auerbach would live another twenty years, and write a different will each year, and Adam would probably be still making the same salary. He thought of his copy of the *Times* which he had not yet looked at, and he promised himself that when he did look at it, he would go through the Help Wanted advertisements. He felt suddenly angry at Mrs. Auerbach. The will, like her gift of the *Stammbuch,* was another one of her meaningless gestures, forgotten even now as she snored through the morning rain, resting her huge fat self for another bout with the bottle, another of her harangues at five o'clock when Adam wanted to go home after a hard day's work. On an impulse which even Adam recognized as pointless, he folded the yellow paper and put it in his pocket.

Some rain had come in through the mail slot, so that when Adam picked up the morning's delivery, he found the ink smeared on several envelopes. On one, addressed to Adam, he noticed the *M*'s in "Mr." and "Mart," the high first stroke of the letter-mark of the arrogant social climber. He guessed that it was from that Mr. Clay on East Seventy-second Street, the customer who was so interested in owning a set of the autographs of Virginia's first families. When he looked at the return address on the envelope, his hands rushed to tear it open. It was from Billy.

Dear Addie:
You never told me where you lived, so I'm writing you at your business. When I returned to my apartment Saturday, I received a cable informing me that my father is very ill in Switzerland. I had been planning to go abroad for a year in September, but I must now leave immediately. Tuesday, in fact.

Some friends from Naples are taking my place in September, but it will be empty until then. I remember your mentioning that you were looking for a bigger apartment. Perhaps you could use mine until September, rent-free, of course. You would be doing me a favor, for I do not like to leave it empty, and you could forward my mail and pass on to phone-callers my situation. It is a large apartment with a garden. Would you call me the moment you get this, at EX 4-6161? It's a private listing, so don't lose this.

It was fun running into you last night.
                                        Yours,
                                        Billy.

A smile lingered on Adam's face after he folded the letter so that the phone number showed. He wondered what Billy would think if he knew that Adam's "place" was a barren-looking seventeen-dollar-a-week room in the Sixty-third Street YMCA. He could move into Billy's immediately, and he realized with a pleasant shock of surprise that Tuesday was tomorrow.

Adam tossed the rest of the mail on the card table, and walked, with a new spring to his step, toward the phone in the storeroom. He had the distinct feeling that he was on the threshold of a new way of life, that things were definitely taking a turn. He snapped on the light button in the storeroom. It was then, at precisely 8:22 that rainy morning at the beginning of May, that he saw Mrs. Auerbach hanging from a piece of rope. The chair she had kicked away from her was overturned on the storeroom floor.

4

"Getting thin took all my will power. I managed it, but not while the Bollins were living in Auburn. After they moved away. I was eighteen the summer of my new self. I was 145 lbs! So proud! The only one–or at least the first one I wanted to see me, was Marshall Bollin. I knew Billy was off in Europe, so I traveled the 90 miles to Rochester. I pretended to be just passing through. I called on Marshall Bollin, still my idol–though I had not seen him in three years... He not only did not recognize me (that could have been my new appearance) but even after I said my name, he did not recall me right away. When he did, he had only vague recollections. 'Weren't you from the Home?' he said... I wonder if I'll ever forget how I felt at that moment? But I'm at it again, aren't I? Dwelling in the past! Damn!

FROM ADAM BLESSING'S JOURNAL

On Tuesday morning the sun came out at last. Adam basked in it out in Billy's garden. The Mart was closed due to Mrs. Auerbach's death. Adam had made arrangements for her cremation yesterday, and in last evening's newspaper there was a U.P. human interest piece on her death. Adam soaked up the hot sun and reread the article, sipping a Bloody Mary. The headline said: VICTIM OF A CHANGING CITY.

She was an eccentric. It was no secret that she kept thousands of dollars in cash in her apartment; no secret that she kept daily rendezvous with a rum bottle. In this city of lacerated minds, she could easily have been the victim of a robbery. She could just as well have become another pedestrian fatality in traffic statistics, as she made her way home unsteadily each evening down Fifty-seventh Street, crossing Park, Lexington and Third Avenues. Many ways were possible for Ada Auerbach, age 67, to become a victim of this huge, busy, often cruel metropolis. And so she was its victim.

"If I die, it is the City of New York who kills me." These were the words she had written in a suicide note. Police were summoned to The Autograph Mart yesterday morning by Adam Blessing, age 24, who found her in the shop's storeroom. He told police...

Adam did not finish rereading the clipping. It gushed on about lonely city dwellers and their private universes, taking several pokes at the way the

City was tearing down residences to erect office buildings; and it teased the reader with descriptions of the sardine tins in Mrs. Auerbach's icebox, all of which contained a sum of $37, 000; and of Mrs. Auerbach's strange ways, as recounted by neighbors and neighborhood tradesmen.

Adam folded it and put it in the pocket of his shirt. Yesterday, an hour or so before Adam had moved his bags from the YMCA to Billy's, a lawyer had told Adam Mrs. Auerbach's will would probably hold up. He had sat up with Billy until all hours last night, but the more he discussed his plans with Billy, the more it seemed like all the other times he talked with Billy, as though none of it was true. When Billy went, Adam supposed, it would seem more real. At the moment, the only thing real was Adam's terrible hangover. It dulled the larger thoughts. The new world which Adam was about to realize seemed to be beginning as he had once read, in a poem, that the world would end—not with a bang, but a whimper.

Adam finished his Bloody Mary and set it on the flagstone beside the deck divan, where he was lying with his legs stretched out.

Always, Adam had thought he would love a garden, and it was some-how typical that Billy would hate it; typical that. Adam had read books on gardening without any hope of having a garden of his own; typical that Billy had said last night: "You want to have drinks out *there?* Hell, Addie, there are bugs and soot, and it's a pain in the ass, Addie!"

It had been a concession to Adam that Billy had finally agreed to night-caps in the garden; a "going-away gift," as Billy had put it; and it was also typical that it was Billy who was going away; Billy giving Adam the gift because Adam was not going away.... Trust Billy to live like *this* in New York City, Adam thought. Three-and-a-half rooms, the garden, and an address off Fifth in the Nineties—all for a piddling $140 a month. By Billy's standards, anyway, it was a piddling drop-in-the-bucket rent; by city stan-dards the apartment was a find. And by Adam's standards?... A question mark.... "The way it looks now," the lawyer had told Adam, "it most prob-ably will be a sizeable sum, but it's going to take time, you know. Probate court works slowly, and there are taxes to figure out, the usual red tape.... Don't make any big changes in your life just yet, that's my advice."

Adam smiled, leaned his head back and felt the sun's warmth. He could wait.... Last night when he was telling Billy about his plans, he had prac-ticed great patience and restraint. After all, Billy did not know the true story. Billy thought Adam was already part-owner of The Mart, already something of a success. That was another reason none of it seemed real to Adam yet; he had had to maintain the pose.

Inside, Billy was telephoning.

"...thought I'd buzz you before I took off," Adam could hear him say. "Idlewild at two-fifty, yes... It's premature because of Father, but I expect I'll keep to the same itinerary after Switzerland.... No, I'm not going *near* Rome this year. Tired of it; you know how it is."

Adam dropped his cigarette on the flagstone, letting his leg swing down and rub it out. He had always dreamed of going to Europe. Now that it was going to be possible, Adam supposed he should dream of being tired of Rome one day. . That was Billy's style, all right. Tired of this, tired of that; his money made him tired, was all. Last night Adam had sampled one of Billy's French cigarettes. Billy was tired of the bland American kind, he had told Adam. The cigarette had nearly turned Adam's stomach with its harshness. Adam had remarked favorably on it, and smoked it down to the end. He felt that Billy was rather pleased with Adam's entire demeanor as they drank their nightcaps. Much more about Adam than his obvious loss of weight surprised Billy, Adam felt. Without any of Billy's advantages, Adam Blessing was a far cry from "Fatty Addie" of Auburn, New York. Wasn't that what Billy thought?

As Adam sat up to light a cigarette, he glanced at his watch again. It seemed that these hours before Billy's departure were interminable. As Adam smoked, he became aware of sudden noise. In the garden adjoining Billy's, he saw half a dozen young boys romping around, some on swings, some in sandpiles; one yanking at the fence separating the gardens. With them were a man and woman, standing by an iron slide, observing them.

"I forgot to tell you about *that!*" said Billy's voice behind Adam. Billy crossed the garden carrying a fresh pitcher of Bloody Marys. He poured Adam's glass full, and set the pitcher on the marble-top table. "*That,*" he said in an annoyed tone, "is King School. Oh, don't worry; it's a day school for one thing. And it closes for the summer the second week in June."

Billy was fastening his cuff links to his shirt, the same ones with the simple, soft-printed B embellishing their faces. They had come from Olga Tritt, Billy had told him last night; they were 22 karat, worth, Billy guessed, about $150. Charity Cadwallader had given them to Billy. He had told Adam that while they were having their nightcaps, Billy with his Sulka tie loosened and his collar unbuttoned, Adam with his tie knotted neatly and his coat on. Ostensibly, Adam could have been the apartment's occupant, and Billy the outsider, Adam was thinking that as he listened to Billy's bragging–as he watched Billy's appearance grow sloppier while they drank. Yet at a later point in the evening, Adam had realized his own speech was a trifle thick; he knew he was much higher than Billy was. When Billy suggested they "call it a night," he was polite enough to say "we've" had enough. It was the first thing Adam had remembered when he woke up in Billy's bedroom. As Adam recalled Billy's condescending way of ending their evening, he vowed that even if he had to sit home by himself and drink night after night, he would acquire a greater tolerance for liquor. *That* was something he had neglected. Billy Bollin had been holding cocktails and highballs in his hand since he was seventeen. He needed no practice.

Now as Adam regarded Billy standing there in the garden, he felt a certain sense of scorn, striped with a heady feeling of superiority. Acquiring a tolerance for liquor was perhaps just a worm's step in the direction Adam wanted to go. He would go past Billy, in that way and in every way. He envied Billy's herring-bone-pattern silk tweed suit, silver gray with the black slub and the long roll to the lapels, but he decided that he would never imitate Billy's taste in anything. Adam would be ultraconservative, just as Billy's father was. If Charity Cadwallader ever gave Adam a gift, Adam would not mention the shop it had come from, the karats, and certainly not the cost. That thought of Adam's was followed by a sudden, sharp headache.

"Is there any aspirin in your medicine cabinet, Billy?"

Billy said, "I have a prescription for something much better. Fix you up in no time, Addie. It's in a blue jar on the right."

That too, Adam mused as he crossed the garden, was somehow like Billy, to have a special headache pill, unavailable without a prescription.

In the living room, Adam stepped over Billy's luggage. All of it was plastered with customs' stamps and stickers from those hotels listed in guidebooks under "Luxury Class." Adam decided that when he *did* go to Europe, as soon as the money came through, he would stay in all the best places, and he would not allow anyone to put stickers on his baggage. He would swing to the opposite pole; be unostentatious about everything.

Last night with a bravado afforded by about seven-and-a-half drinks, Adam had asked Billy about Charity Cadwallader.

"Charity?" Billy had said in an off-hand way. "We're just friends now."

Adam had said that he thought she was quite pretty and that she had seemed very interesting. He did not know why he was unable to use the word "beautiful," instead of the bland understatement. The word interesting was not appropriate either, since she had hardly spoken to him, but he wanted to avoid saying something as dull as "nice."

Billy had jiggled his glass of bourbon thoughtfully for a moment, watching the ice cubes swish around. Then he had said, "I take it you're not serious with this Schackle-what's-her-name?"

"Not at all."

"Nor any girl in particular, ah?"

"I don't know any."

There was another brief pause, and then finally Billy said it right out. "Charity's family is very–well–prominent, Addie…. I guess one would have to know Charity about five years before even so much as walking her to the corner for a soda. In their view, anyway."

"She's free, white and twenty-one," Adam had said foolishly, sounding angry when he wanted most to sound simply matter-of-fact.

Billy had looked at him with a very wise tip to his lips: "Addie, you know that has nothing to do with it! You know full well what I'm telling you."

Adam immediately protested that he had meant nothing by his questions about Charity; the last thing in the world, he had declared staunchly, that he had on his mind was asking her out. But he knew he sounded completely unconvincing. It was shortly after that point in the evening when he began to show his drinks.

The phone rang while Adam was in the bathroom getting something for his headache, and once again Adam could hear Billy bubbling into the mouthpiece… about leaving Idlewild at two-fifty… about not going *near* Rome this time… then about Adam. Adam leaned against the door, which was ajar, and listened.

"Actually, I've known him all my life," Billy was saying, "We grew up back in Auburn. Haven't seen him in years, then we ran into each other a day or so ago. He's a nice enough fellow. He was an orphan. Used to cut our lawn… No, nothing like *that*. He has *some* polish…. Anyway, he's certainly reliable."

Certainly capable of watering the plants and forwarding the mail, Adam thought bitterly, even though he couldn't take Charity Cadwallader to the corner for a soda.

Adam swallowed two of the pills and walked back to the garden after Billy finished with the phone call. Billy was pouring yet another Bloody Mary, and Adam was already feeling his. Adam sat down beside Billy, wishing suddenly that he knew some friends he could ask by for drinks after Billy went. Crazily he realized that the one person he would have liked to ask by for a drink in an apartment like this, was Billy Bollin himself.

"Look over there," Billy was saying now. He pointed to the small boy whom Adam had noticed earlier, the one yanking at the fence separating the gardens. The youngster wore glasses which were incredibly thick, and he was shouting something. Billy held his finger to his lips in a shushing ges-ture.

"*Regardez* Timmy Schneider everybody!" the youngster was calling. "*Regardez* Timmy Schneider!"

Billy snickered. "He's always yelling that. The whole bunch of them are psychos."

Adam said, "What do you mean?"

Billy wiggled his finger in circles by his ear. "Nuts. *You* know. Crazy."

"Is it a hospital?"

"No, it's King School. It's a school for difficult children. They're all bats."

Adam looked across and through the fence at the children. They seemed to range in age from eight to thirteen. The iron slide, the swings, the sand-piles reminded him of the play yard at the Home.

"They look all right," he said.

Billy said, "Oh, they're not morons or anything like that. But they all have something crazy about them."

"It looks like the Home."

"Addie-boy, it's a far cry from the Cayuga County Orphans' Home. Those kids were born with silver spoons in their mouths, never mind the bats in the belfry. That one I pointed out–the one with the goggles, for instance. Does the name Schneider mean anything to you?"

"No." Adam felt suddenly tired. Perhaps it was thinking of the Home again, being able to visualize it so well after seeing the back yard of King School.

"Well, Luther Van den Perre Schneider is the kid's old man. That little fellow with the goggles, Addie-boy, is heir to millions. Sole heir, I might add. And he's cracked."

Adam had a dizzy sensation all through him. He hoped Billy would not notice anything was wrong. He managed to say, "How do you know all this?"

"My maid gets it from their cook. This will hand you a laugh," said Billy, tapping Adam's wrist. "My maid told me they punish those kids by making them sit out in the hall until they can be good. My maid says the halls are filled with kids sitting there masturbating." Billy hooted over his own story. "My maid didn't put it that way exactly. She said the kids sat in the hall 'touching their privates.'"

Adam felt unbelievably dopey. He tried to laugh at Billy's joke, but he could barely grin. He felt his eyes want to close, and he forced them to remain open.

"Luther Schneider owns Waverly Foods," Billy said.

Those were the last words Billy Bollin spoke to Adam Blessing for over a year.

5

"Marshall Bollin chose me as the orphan he would be nice to, in a random way, I suppose. He probably took my name from the top of the list, since the names were arranged alphabetically and I was the very first. Actually I saw very little of him. On those days I was asked to the Bollins', Billy entertained me. I cannot help thinking my whole life would have been different if Marshall Bollin had not had a son. Then he might even have adopted me. I used to dream that something awful had happened to Billy, and that Mr. Bollin came to the Home and asked me to be his son.

FROM ADAM BLESSING'S JOURNAL

Adam was dreaming. Mrs. Auerbach was hanging by the rope in the storeroom. He took a knife from his pocket to cut her down. When he looked up at her, she was scaling a fence. He followed her. Then he hung to the fence. Below him was Billy Bollin.

"*Regardez* Adam Blessing!" Adam shouted.

Billy made circles around his ear with his finger. "You're cracked, Addie," he said.... Adam thought: This is only a dream, and promptly woke up.

He was stretched out on the deck divan in Billy's garden. He was shoeless, and his tie was loosened. It was not yet full evening, but the sun was down, and the chill of a dusk in early May made him shiver. His headache was even worse than his instant anxiety at what had happened. As he got up and crossed the flagstone, he had to hold his head with both hands to ease the pain.

He found the light switch in the living room. There in the room's center was a piece of white typing paper on the rug, a large bottle of Remy Martin holding it down. As carefully as he could manage, jarring his head as little as possible, Adam bent over and picked it up.

Addie, you took the wrong pills, buddy! You took the ones in the white bottle. They're for sleeping.

Pleasant dreams.

Please pass on the enclosed itineraries to friends who call. It'll be effective as of June third, if father is all right. I hope you straighten out everything at The Mart. If you need any special legal assistance, my lawyer's name is on my phone pad. I wouldn't trust any lawyer recommended by the YMCA, but that's your business.

So long, B. B.

Attached with staples were several mimeographed sheets with the heading: TENTATIVE ITINERARY OF WILLIAM COVINGTON BOLLIN THROUGH SEPTEMBER.

Adam sank into the soft folds of the living-room couch, dropping Billy's note and the itineraries on the pillow beside him. He was still quite groggy. His mind seemed unable to focus on anything but thoughts that strayed into senseless daydreams. He imagined his lawyer phoning to tell him the will was invalid; then imagined himself calling Billy's lawyer; imagined Billy's lawyer saying snidely: "But I thought you were part-owner of the business! You mean you were just a clerk?"... Then his thoughts concentrated on a plan whereby Billy's itineraries would become misplaced, so that none of his friends would be able to communicate with him. He imagined Billy's face, as day by day there was no mail for him. Billy was always so keen on the number of friends he had.... He started a new daydream about Billy's sleeping pills having killed Adam, and Billy being tried for his murder. The prosecuting attorney was saying to Billy: *Isn't it a fact, Mr. Bollin, that you were always bullying the deceased when you were growing up with him back in Auburn, New York?* Before Billy could offer his defense, the phone rang. He leaped up.

"Hello!" said a girl's voice. "I'm calling Adam Blessing. Is he there?"

"I'm Adam Blessing." For one self-deluded half-second, a fierce hope sprang up in Adam, but it was only Dorothy Schackleford calling.

Adam sank onto a white-and-gold Empire chair, sighing.

"Well, *you* sound enthusiastic. You'd think I was the local funeral director."

"Very funny," said Adam.

"Oh, gosh, Adam—I'm sorry. I keep forgetting Mrs. Auerbach."

Adam said, "Oh well, it doesn't matter.... It's over now.„

"I got your number from the Y, Adam. Did you move already? Didn't you go to work today?"

Adam told her about Billy's offer, and as he did, he listened to her squeals of delight with a certain uneasiness. There was just enough about Dorothy Schackleford which was like Adam, to make him annoyed by her.

"Off Fifth!" she was exclaiming. "Ver-ree-rit-zee!" whistling for emphasis.

Her rhapsodic reaction made Adam tighten. "It's not so grand," he said, "and furthermore I can afford the same now." He stared across the room at a forgotten dirty breakfast plate which Billy had left under a velvet-covered chair. An Etrusan chair, Billy had called it, or what was it? Etriscan? Etruscan?... Tomorrow he would go to the library and take out a book on furniture.

"...so I'm going to move in with these girls," Dorothy Schackleford was chattering on. "You can't live with your family all your life, can you, Adam?"

Adam said he guessed not.

"Nothing gets a rise out of you, Adam... I'm sorry. I know you still must feel just awful about Mrs. Auerbach!"

Adam felt like telling her that he did not feel anything about Mrs. Auerbach. He had tried, but it was hopeless.

"I have the perfect housewarming gift for you, Adam," Dorothy was continuing. "A Pan-Trans ticket agent got me two forks and two spoons from the Excelsior in Rome. I'll give you a pair."

"Thank you," Adam said.

"You really are taking it badly, aren't you, Adam?"

"No, I'm not," said Adam. "I'm just–tired."

"Your voice is funny."

"Tired." Adam repeated.

"I was wondering Adam... I know tomorrow's a weekday and all, but, at this place I'm moving into, we're having a little impromptu get-together tonight. Have you eaten?" Before he could answer, she forged ahead. "Oh, it's nothing much–just spaghetti and a tossed salad, and we'll be sitting around drinking wine and all, but I thought maybe you'd–" and her voice trailed off.

"I don't think so, thanks."

"I suppose the people wouldn't interest *you*. I mean, *any more.*"

"Don't be silly. It isn't that."

"We haven't even got all our furniture either."

"That wouldn't bother me, Dorothy."

"Adam... I agree with you about imitation fireplaces now."

"What?"

"That time you criticized my girlfriend for having an imitation fireplace, remember? Well, I know I was awfully mad, but you were right, Adam."

Adam said, "What do I know about furniture? I was just drunk that night."

"These girls I'm moving in with aren't like that, Adam, honest! They've all been abroad. I mean, they all work for the airlines. I guess they're not big intellectuals or anything but–"

"Sometime I'd like to meet them," Adam lied.

"I just thought tonight would be nice."

"Dorothy," said Adam, and in the next breath Adam told her he would be there, shortly after seven.

After he hung up, he realized that the few times he had been out with Dorothy, *she* had asked *him*. He had always begun with a refusal and ended up accepting. Each time, too, he had vowed it would be the last time, but against a girl of Dorothy Schackleford's ilk Adam had no more chance of keeping that vow than the Excelsior had of keeping its silverware.

Until his headache subsided, Adam read for a while. It was a guide to Rome he had found in Billy's bookcase. He read an elaborate description of the gardens in the Pincio there, and he began to feel better. He thought that tomorrow he would perhaps arrange for a small memorial service for Mrs. Auerbach. He supposed very few people would even attend, but some of the merchants on Fifty-seventh might send representatives as a token gesture, and he might look up a few of her neighbors that would come, if only out of curiosity. Mrs. Auerbach would probably have hated such an idea, but Adam felt he ought to do something.

As he dressed for the evening, Adam was unable to resist wearing a pair of Billy's cuff links. They were in the shape of poodles, with ruby eyes, and Adam was amused and pleased by them. He also chose one of Billy's Countess Mara ties to wear, and these additions to his wardrobe gave him a lift. On an impulse, he also pocketed a package of Gauloises, Billy's French cigarettes.

At Ninety-sixth and Madison, Adam paused at a newsstand to buy a copy of *Art News*. The inspiration for this choice he could trace back to his conversation with Billy last night in the garden. Billy had said he hoped to visit The Prado in Madrid.

"You know," Billy had said, "they have the best Bosch in the world."

Adam had thought he meant the soup, borscht; he had thought the Prado was a restaurant. He had made some stupid comment about thinking Russia was more famous for it, adding that he had tasted it several times in the Russian Tea Room, right here in New York. Billy had choked with guffaws, apologizing as he choked, and ended by explaining in a very supercilious way that Hieronymus Bosch was a fifteenth-century painter; that The Prado was one of the most famous museums in the world.

"It's not your fault, Addie," Billy had said, still trying to stop laughing. "I wouldn't expect you to know about things like that."

Adam had smarted under the ridicule. Before he had fallen into bed last night, he had drunkenly scribbled, "Learn more about ART," across a back page of his Journal. Above it, in a sober script, there was a sentence which he had copied from *Of Human Bondage*, after he had read it two years ago:

"Money is like a sixth sense, without which you cannot make use of the other five...."

On the bus, and then on the subway, Adam tried to concentrate on the magazine. Instead he found himself wondering about Charity Cadwallader. With the fatuous license of the daydreamer, he found himself honey-mooning with her in Rome. He saw himself walking into the Pincio with her, seeing it all as it had been described in the travel guide. He sat across from her in the Casino Valadier, while they sipped sherry, with the swal-lows darting about the balcony terrace, and the superb view of Rome in the distance. He heard himself suggesting a walk along the edge of the Piaz-zale del Pincio, and he felt her hand tighten in his as they stood looking up at a summer sky, as pink as flamingo feathers.

The subway jerked to a shaky stop at One Hundred Eighty-first Street, just as Adam was kissing Charity by the Fountain of Moses.

As he made his way through the dank underground station, he decided a honeymoon in Rome would probably only bore a Charity Cadwallader.

"Everyone's going to Russia these days," Billy had said last night, "or the Orient!... Europe's been had! I suppose this will be my last trip there."

He tried to imagine himself somewhere in the Orient on his honeymoon with Charity, but even in dreams he was a captive of his limited experience. The Orient looked oddly like the pictures Adam had seen of Europe, and when he tried to fill in for himself, everything looked like upstate New York. He could see Charity Cadwallader yawning in his mind's eye, as he went through the subway stile.

When he arrived at Dorothy Schackleford's, Dorothy was already a lit-tle high. Her lipstick was worn away and there was a purple wine mark along her lower lip. She was wearing toreador pants and a Venetian gon-dolier's shirt; she was barefoot and her toenails were painted scarlet.

"Adam!" she said, gripping his hand in a hearty shake, "*Alors,* Adam! *Entrez! Mucho* welcome, *Adamo!*"

There were sling chairs and burlap curtains, and Chianti bottles with can-dles stuck in them; bare floors, and few people. Everyone was playing Cha-rades; everyone was assigned to a team. Dorothy handed him a paper cup of sweet port, and Adam sat on a pillow on the floor, until the round of Charades was over.

On the glass-top coffee table beside him, there was the ashtray from the Stork Club, which Adam had given Dorothy. There was one from Maxim's in Paris, too, and the matchbooks on display were from places in Germany, Switzerland, Italy and France... For some reason, a girl opposite Adam was answering *"Mais oui!"* to everything; and beside her, another girl was wearing a Japanese kimono. Adam and a chubby, bespectacled young man with a bald head, were the only males present.

After Charades, someone put on "Gypsy." The fat man danced with the girl who said *"Mais oui,"* and Dorothy turned to Adam and smiled. *"Alors,"* she said, *"wie gehts?"*

"Fine," said Adam.

Dorothy pointed to the girl in the Japanese kimono. "Remember her, Adam?"

"No."

"That's Shirley Spriggs. We ran into her one night at the Blue Mill. Remember that night we went to the Village for steaks?"

"I guess so," said Adam.

"Poor Shirl," Dorothy said, without elaborating. *"Beaucoup* troubles."

Adam could think of no response. He noticed as Dorothy sat with her bare legs crossed, that the soles of her feet were black with dust. Wine was spilled down the Venetian gondolier's shirt, and the nailpolish on her right hand was chipped. He remembered suddenly that Charity Cadwallader had worn no nailpolish; that her hands were long and soft-looking, clean and quiet.

"Hey, did you meet Norman yet?" Dorothy pointed at the other male present. He and his partner were busy with the Charleston.

"Norman's in tickets at World-Wide," said Dorothy. "I met him in Madrid two summers ago when I got my three weeks off. Course only one week was with pay, but I took the other two. He really has a fabulous sense of humor. *Très* funny, is Norman."

Adam said, "He's good for a fat boy."

"I don't think that's very nice, Adam."

"I didn't mean anything by it."

"Norman's sensitive about his weight. He's tried everything."

"Look, I was fat once. I was very clumsy. I just meant–"

"His is glandular," Dorothy Schackleford persisted. "He couldn't do anything about it if he wanted to."

"I'm sorry."

"Sometimes you're really not very nice, Adam. You think you're better than most people just because you read up on things."

"That's not true," Adam began, but before he was able to finish, Shirley Spriggs came across in her kimono, and threw her arms around Adam as though they had always known one another as fast friends.

"You be nice to Shirl while I fix my face," Dorothy told Adam.

After she left, Adam asked Shirley Spriggs to dance. Immediately, he regretted it. The invitation was declined, but it had succeeded in launching her on a long explanation of why she was not going to dance for two years. It was a tribute to someone who was dead.

"It was Flight 791 out of Shannon," she said, "and it could just as well have been me, Adam. I knew Ginger Klein like I knew my own mother, only of course she was my age, and she was engaged and everything to this dentist. She had a half-a-karat diamond he gave her right on her wedding finger when the plane went down, and a wallet she bought him in Florence and everything—all lost in the ocean, and it was going to be her seventy-sixth trip too, and after that she was going to marry; well, when I think of it—" and she was unable to continue for a few moments. Adam lent her his handkerchief, and he realized she was rather high as well; quite drunk, in fact. Her next words were thick and teary: "It was one of those fweak—freak things, plane just blew up; we face it every trip but never think—" she could not finish.

Dorothy Schackleford flew across the room to guide Shirley Spriggs into the bathroom.

"Gingy wouldn't want you to break down like this, Shirl," she said. "You know how Gingy was."

Adam lighted a Gauloise and some seconds later the boy named Norman wandered over with the girl who said *"Mais oui."* Her name was Rose Marie Scoppettone, which meant "big gun" in Italian, she said; and then she said: "What smells like manure?"

"My cigarette," said Adam. "It's a Gauloise." As he looked about him at the collection of foreign matchbooks and ashtrays, he wished suddenly that he had bought his own pack of Chesterfields. Birds of a feather, he thought tiredly.

Norman said, "Oh, I thought it might be a dung-hill," at which all the girls giggled, inspiring him to repeat the quip three more times.

Adam danced with a girl named Eloise Siden, who booked New York-Caracas, and smelled of garlic. She danced Adam off into a corner.

"Shirley's a mess," she said in a confidential tone, "Gingy Klein was her best friend. They were like sisters. Gingy was going to live with us. We got Dotty instead."

"Good," said Adam. "I mean, I'm glad you could get someone."

"You know, Dotty's got a case on you, mister."

"Me? She hardly knows me, Shirley."

"I'm Eloise, remember?"

"I'm sorry."

"I don't mind telling you she could be very serious about you, Adam."

"You must be mistaken, really."

"Listen, mister, I know! Dotty's a great girl too. A guy would be fortu-nate."

They were very nearly standing still as they moved to the music. Adam edged into a corner of the room.

Eloise Siden said, "You don't have a special girl or anything do you?"

"No," said Adam. "But–"

"Don't But with me, mister," she said out of the corner of her mouth, "I'm giving you the straight poop and I expect the same from you. I'm from Texas, and we don't fool around much down there."

"Well," said Adam, "I just don't know Dorothy well. I don't know her well at all."

"You don't think you're too good for her or anything like that, do you?" Adam felt his face get red. "No," he said.

"I thought you might have that idea. I thought to myself, 'Kid, if that's what that fellow has up his nose, just toddle on over there and give him the word.' Okay," she said, squeezing his shoulder, "no hard feelings. I just want it down in the record, Adam."

Norman danced up beside them and said, "What brand cigarettes you smokin' pard'ner," grinning widely at Eloise Siden as he said it–"dung-hills?"

There was another round of guffaws; then the music was over and the girl whose name meant "big gun" in Italian was shuffling through the records for another L.P.

"I just hope Shirl's O.K.," said Eloise. "Boy, I mean, she was thrown for a looper by that plane crash."

"Why don't you go see?" said Adam.

"You know, that's a thought. A gooder!"

"Yes, go see."

"I'll be back di-rectly. Don't go away, friend!" She gave his shoulder anoth-er healthy squeeze, and winked meaningfully. "You and Dot's got to get to know one another better, right quick!"

The moment she turned, Adam made his way rapidly down the hall and out the door. He ran down the two flights of stairs, out into the street. Then he ran all the way to the One Hundred Eighty-first subway station.

Standing inside on the platform, while he waited for the D train, he mopped the perspiration off his face. He had left behind his copy of *Art News*. Momentarily, he studied the graffiti on the posters. He came to one which was the blow-up of that week's *Our Time* magazine—the picture of a man. Someone had drawn spectacles and a mustache on his face; someone else had scribbled across the face in red crayon: *His stuff stinks! Don't eat it!...* As the D train approached, Adam glanced down at the printing under the man's picture. It said:

> LUTHER VAN DEN PERRE SCHNEIDER
> WAVERLY FOODS: AN EMPIRE

At one Hundred Twenty-fifth Street, where Adam changed to a local, he bought a copy of *Our Time* from the vendor.

6

"...and yet despite his robust appearance and his indefatigable approach to the management of Waverly Foods at all levels, 'Lute' Schneider is a somewhat solitary figure in his personal life. On one of the rare occasions when he granted permission for an interview, the reporter came away knowing far more about Schneider's silver collection than about his family, friends, or the complicated manipulations of his empire. Above all else, he seemed most enthusiastic about two possessions: a very rare, old English silver and tigerwear jug, and a Sheffield plate epergne on a revolving base; circa 1770.

Married seventeen years to society beauty Win Griswold, they have a son Timothy, age 9. Their town house in the East Nineties is..."

The sharp sound of the outside buzzer interrupted Adam's reading. His watch said eleven-thirty. The phone had rung four or five times since he had come back to the apartment that evening, but he had not bothered to answer it. He was convinced it was Dorothy Schackleford, calling to see why he had run off.

On the table beside Adam was a bottle of Clos de Vougeot, which he had taken from Billy's wine closet. Adam had already drunk a little more than half. As the ringing of the buzzer became more insistent, Adam crossed the living room determined to get rid of Dorothy Schackleford as quickly as he could. Pressing the release button, Adam was angry. He had been enjoying himself for the first time since Mrs. Auerbach's death. Sipping the wine and reading about Luther Schneider, the cool breeze from the garden wafting in on him, he had forgotten for a while about everything. A Gauloise hung from his lips. It was strange, he had a taste for them now.

He heard the noise of high heels on the black-and-white marble outside; then two bleeping rings of his doorbell. Before he opened the door, he loosened Billy's Countess Mara tie, and mussed up his hair, hoping the dishevelment would add credence to his story, that he was suddenly taken ill. A migraine, he would say, remembering how suddenly Mrs. Auerbach's migraines used to occur. So sure that it would be Dorothy Schackleford, Adam did not recognize his caller immediately.

"It's *you,*" she said. "I thought it would be you."

Charity Cadwallader was not exactly smiling, but regarding him instead with a sort of amused curiosity. She was taller than Adam had remembered, or her heels were higher this time. Adam could not be sure whether she was slightly taller than he was. He was so stunned by her appearance there that his mind could fasten only on the insignificant particulars: she was wearing a different watch this time, a larger one, silver and shell-shaped; her black hair was pulled back in a chignon; and now he noticed the color of her eyes, green–like a cat's. Adam's fingers rushed to straighten his tie, smooth back his hair.

She was already inside the apartment. "I rang," she said, "two times. Don't you answer phones?"

"I thought it was someone else."

"I'm sorry, Addie, but Billy *promised* he'd drop off my tennis racket before he left. I have a tennis date tomorrow."

"I haven't seen it here." He hated her calling him "Addie" as Billy always did.

"It's here, all right." She glanced in the living room. "Billy got off all right?"

"Yes."

"Earlier I saw the lights from the street. I didn't know for sure who was staying here. Billy mentioned someone would be living here."

"Would you like a drink?"

"I don't like liquor, but Billy keeps celery tonic around. On the rocks, please."

While he was breaking ice, she walked back and forth. "I hope Billy's father's all right. He's very close to him, isn't he?"

"I guess so."

"Guess?... Billy always talks about him. Does he look like Billy?"

"Mr. Bollin was always ill. He's sort of frail. He's a little man."

"Funny, I pictured him as a big, heavy sort."

"He's very kind, too."

"And Billy isn't."

"I didn't say that."

Adam handed her a glass of celery tonic. "Do you live in the neighborhood, Charity?"

"Off Park, next block.... Billy told me about your partner's death. I'm sorry."

"Yes," Adam said. "It was sudden. I'll have a lot more responsibility now."

Charity Cadwallader did not really sit down, but perched on the edge of the conch-shaped couch, as though she were having the drink on the run, with little enthusiasm.

She said, "Billy and you grew up together, hmmm?"

"I was an orphan. Some of the 'better-off' families in Auburn picked out an orphan to invite to dinner now and then. Mr. Bollin picked me."

"What was Billy like?"

"Mean," said Adam.

She laughed at that. "I'll bet!"

"Did he ever tell you that he used to keep snakes? He had a regular herpetorium in his cellar. It was a reptile house as fancy as any zoo's."

"He said he used to like snakes. Tell me about it."

"He had this cobra," said Adam. "He called him 'Poopsy.' Poopsy ate six-foot black racers. Billy'd put one in the cage with Poopsy, and Poopsy's head would peer around a corner of the water tank, and then there'd be a motion like lightning. The black snake would make one desperate attempt for his life. He'd try to coil around Poopsy's throat, but before you knew it–you couldn't even see it, it was so fast–this black head would be caught in Poopsy's jaws, and Poopsy'd draw this fighting black snake inside him."

Charity Cadwallader had no particular expression on her face, merely listened.

"Poopsy'd pause for breath now and then in the process of eating him," Adam said, "but he'd get him down, inch by inch.... I used to stand there shaking, wet clear through my clothes from perspiration."

"I've never much liked snakes either," she said, "What else?"

"Billy used to tease me a lot. One day he was behaving very differently toward me. He was going to move soon, and he said since we wouldn't be seeing each other much, we ought to try to get along better... Another thing about Poopsy, he wouldn't eat little snakes, only big ones. There were never enough big ones available, so Billy had to produce one artificially. He had a black-snake cage. Up in the top of this cage-tree, there'd be a whole bunch of little ones hanging. They were all twisted together like rain worms, all knotted up. Billy'd look for the biggest in the bunch, and then he'd disentangle them until he got it. I only saw him get bitten twice doing that. He was good at it."

Charity said, "I can imagine."

"He'd pull this snake out of the bunch, Charity, and then he'd hold him, squirming and wiggling by the tail." Adam looked into her eyes, wondering why she seemed completely bland about his story, not like most women when snakes were discussed. He said, "Then like the lash of a whip, Billy would whirl the thing through the air and there'd be a snap!"

"The snake would have a broken neck, is that it?"

"That's right."

"Then?"

"Then," Adam said, "Billy would stuff frogs down the dead snakes throat, to make him look bigger, so Poopsy would eat him."

"Very clever."

"Yes... clever." Adam wondered why he wished she had been afraid at the story, and not so cool and unconcerned.

"You were telling me about one day in particular."

"Not very interesting. You have to be afraid of snakes to know how I felt."

"Tell me."

"Billy said we were going to turn over a new leaf. He said he wanted me to help him feed Poopsy. More moral support than anything else. Usually the Bollin's chauffeur went along with Billy for the feeding, but it was the chauffeur's day off. I agreed to go along. Billy told me to turn my back, if I wanted to while he broke the black snake's neck."

"And you wanted to."

"Sure! Well, I told you! I was afraid of snakes."

"Go on."

"After I turned around, the next thing I knew, that snake was around my neck, and down my shirt, and I began to run up the stairs, trying to pull my shirt off, but mostly going crazy! I was really afraid of snakes."

"Yes," she agreed.

"You can't imagine what that's like unless you're afraid of them too."

"And then?"

"It turned out it was only a garter snake. It didn't bite me or anything.... But I didn't get over it for days. I remember I stayed for dinner at the Bollins' that night, but I couldn't eat. Billy's father knew something was wrong. He knew Billy pretty well. I wouldn't tell him what happened, but he knew, and I remember that before we went into the dining room that night, Mr. Bollin put his arm around my shoulder and said: 'Adam, I'd be very proud if you were my boy.'"

Charity did not say anything for a few seconds; then she said, "And you always wished you were."

"No... I envied certain advantages Billy had."

"Money."

"Yes. Money."

"People with money fascinate you, don't they, Addie?"

"No. They don't *fascinate* me."

"But you like to read about people like Luther Schneider?"

Adam blushed, picked up the copy of *Our Time* from his chair, and put it beside the wine bottle on the table. "I could have been reading any article in there."

"But your face is so red." There was a pause. She did not smile. Then she changed the subject abruptly. "I can't imagine you fat."

"I was... very. I ate cake all the time. I ate it when I was terribly happy, and when I was very sad, and in between because I felt neither way. I had to work like the devil to get down to a normal weight. But I did it."

"Congratulations."

"Sarcasm?"

"No. I like people who are determined.... Now that you've come into a little money, I suppose you'll catapult it to millions, is that what you want to do with your new inheritance?"

"Sure," said Adam, "I'm on my way to becoming another Luther Schneider, or a Billy Bollin. How about that?"

"Billy's in his twenties and has an ulcer, and Luther Schneider has a son who's deranged and a wife who drinks. What will you come down with?"

You, Adam wanted to say.

He said: "Money will do things *for* me, not *to* me.... Besides, money didn't make Luther Schneider's boy crazy, and I doubt that it made his wife drink. He enjoys his money, what's more. He collects fine silver, raises orchids–before the war he even trained horses that ran at Ouilly, in France. That doesn't sound like a miserable existence!"

"It sounds as though you read the article in *Our Time* very, very thoroughly."

"You have me," Adam said.

Charity Cadwallader laughed for the first time. "Promises. Promises."

She had three more celery tonics before she called her home and left the message. The gist of it was that if her parents wanted to know where she was, she was staying with a girlfriend. Then she called the girlfriend, waking her up, making her promise to cover for her if anything should happen. Adam could hear both conversations from the garden.

When she rejoined him, she took the brandy snifter from his hand. "Don't drink any more, Addie. Wine and brandy don't mix."

"Adam."

"All right–Adam."

She pulled him to his feet, and he felt her arms reach up around his neck, the same gentle way she had kissed him when she had first crossed the living room, a few hours earlier. He kissed her, slowly, thinking of nothing else, and she seemed to enjoy it with a certain calm. When he had first kissed her that night, he had blurted out a long speech about feeling a great warmth for her the first time he ever saw her, but she seemed uninterested in any declarations or clarifications, so he dropped it. They had talked about Billy, and she had said once quite emphatically that she hated Billy, but she would not elaborate.

After the kiss in the garden, she said, "You don't really want to finish your brandy, do you? It'll make you drunk, Adam."

They went inside, and it embarrassed Adam a little that she wanted him to take a shower with her first. In the shower, Adam realized that he was quite drunk already.

When he woke up in the morning he thought she was gone. Instead, she was in the kitchen making coffee, washing last night's glasses. He hurried into his pajamas and went out there, and she greeted him with a half smile. "Don't kiss me," she said when he came close to her. "I haven't brushed my teeth yet."

"I don't care."

"I do."

He leaned against the wall and watched her for a bit. Then he said. "Look, I'm sorry. I was just too drunk."

"It doesn't make any difference."

"These last few days have been upsetting, too."

"It happens all the time. Don't think about it."

"It doesn't happen to me," Adam lied.

"Well, it did last night," she said pleasantly. "Let's forget it. There's orange juice in the pitcher there. If there'd been fresh oranges I would have squeezed some. I'm afraid it's frozen."

"Are there any eggs?"

"None. Sorry."

"I'll slip on something and get some. Look, Charity, wouldn't you like a big breakfast?"

"All right."

"I won't be long," he said.

She said, "I'll have my shower while you're gone."

As Adam was leaving, the shower was running. He would buy sausages and rolls, he decided, and he would find some place where he could buy flowers. He took all the money he had with him, which was fifty-two dollars, the last of his cash. He knew why he took so much when he passed the jewelry store on Madison Avenue, after he left the grocery and the florist. He paid thirty-two dollars for a pearl teardrop on a tiny gold chain. When he returned, she was gone. The note was on the kitchen table.

Dear Adam,
    I just remembered my tennis date–at one o'clock. It's past noon now. I make eggs pretty well, and I would have liked making some for you. *C'est la vie.* Charity.

That was it.

He felt like weeping or punching something. Instead he left all his purchases, including the small bunch of violets and the jeweler's box, on the Etruscan chair in the living room, and he flopped on the unmade bed. He lighted a Gauloise, smoked it halfway down, then still in his clothes, hugged the pillow that smelled faintly of her perfume, and fell into a deep sleep. He dreamed of her in a fit of fifty or more snapshot glimpses, like the dream of someone drugged. When he woke up, he was perspiring in his clothes, the phone was ringing; it was after three in the afternoon.

"Hello, Adam?" said Dorothy Schackleford. "Are you all right?"

He was out of breath from his dash for the phone. "I'm sorry I had to leave last night," he managed. "I had a migraine."

"We wondered what happened. Norman went looking for you and everything."

The robe of Billy's which Charity had been wearing was on the couch. He walked across and picked it up, carrying the telephone in his hand. He sat down and put the robe near his face, to smell it. Then, thinking of Billy's having worn it, he flung it to the floor.

"I'm sorry," he said.

"I thought you might be mad at *me.*"

"It was a headache," he said. He suddenly remembered that Charity Cadwallader had cried last night; it was so vague he could not be positive, but he remembered himself saying not to cry. It was all blacked out then.

"I wouldn't have left you, Adam, but Shirl was real upset. You see, she and Gingy Klein were–"

"I know all that!"

"Don't bite my head off, Adam. I'm just trying to explain!"

"Never mind."

"You didn't go to work today either, did you?"

"No!" Adam said angrily.

"You're not very pleasant, Adam."

"I'm in a rush," said Adam, "I'm on my way out." He thought: the tennis racket: he had not even seen this tennis racket Charity had come for. He wondered if there was one, or if she had made it up.

"I thought you felt ill!"

"I'm going to the doctor!"

"Well, thanks a lot Adam, for being so nice. I have to get back to work now, but thanks a lot. I couldn't have spent my coffee-break in a nicer way."

"I'm sorry," he said.

"I'll never call you again, Adam."

Adam heard the click, then the dial tone.

While he was having some of the coffee Charity had made that morning, he remembered she had mentioned a luncheon she was going to at the Colony tomorrow. He took the coffee out into the garden, along with the Manhattan telephone directory. He smoked another Gauloise and balanced the directory on his lap.... Just as he had thought, there were no listings for any Cadwalladers in the Nineties, nor on Park Avenue, nor on Madison Avenue. He sat trying to think what she could have meant when she told him that she lived just around the corner... or had she said 'in the next block'? He smoked the last of the Gauloises and finished the coffee. In the adjacent yard the children were being let out to play, and momentarily he looked for the small boy with the thick glasses, the son of Luther Schneider. He could not seem to pick him out from the others. While he was watching the yard of the King School, his phone rang a second time. Adam Blessing nearly turned his ankle racing for it. It was the Bennan-Olicker Cremation Company. They wanted instructions for Mrs. Auerbach's remains.

7

GOOD THINGS TO KNOW:

1. Rare, fancy restaurant: Ficklin's, East 59th Street. No sign out front. Dinners about $8 apiece. No liquor, but wine. No menu so don't make a fool of yourself by asking for one. Intimate, candlelit. Must have reservations.
(Source: "A Sophisticated Guide to New York.")

2. "The only red wines that may profitably be chilled are Beaujolais and Swiss Dole."–from Gourmet Cookbook.

FROM ADAM BLESSING'S JOURNAL

At noon on Thursday, Adam sold "The Lucy Baker Album" for $1500. He deposited $500 in his checking account, and $500 in the cash register of The Mart. $300 he put in his wallet. With the remainder he arranged for a small memorial service for Mrs. Auerbach, at Unitarian church. The serv-ice was to be held that Saturday evening, and Adam spent the rest of Thursday notifying the merchants on Fifty-seventh, and tracking down a few former tenants from Mrs. Auerbach's building. He also bought himself a chalk-striped black wool worsted suit for the occasion. Mr. Geismar, Adam's lawyer, advised Adam to go more slowly, since Adam was still not Mrs. Auerbach's legal heir, but Adam felt Geismar was something of an old maid in his cautious attitudes.

At Wadley & Smythe, Adam paid for twenty dollars' worth of long-stem red roses. He remembered that Charity had said she was going to a lunch-eon at the Colony that noon. The flowers were to be delivered to her table. Adam enclosed the tiny pearl teardrop on the gold chain, and after consid-erable deliberation about what to write on the accompanying card, chose simply to say: "Always, Adam."

Before he closed The Mart that evening, he took care of several other things. He placed an advertisement in the *Times* for a helper, and he peti-tioned for membership in The Diners' Club. He ordered new stationery, with his own name printed on it, and the single word "owner" under his name. He made a draft of a letter to be sent to dealers, advising them of the availability of several albums Mrs. Auerbach had been loath to sell, and he cleared the premises of old rum bottles, and sundry trash can "souvenirs" Mrs. Auerbach had collected over the years.

It was after seven when Adam arrived at his apartment. Before he fixed himself a highball, he called the Colony to check whether the flowers had been presented to Charity. He was assured they had been, and as he sat out in the garden sipping some of Billy's Scotch, his sense of well-being was at its peak. Yesterday had been sloppy, all right–he had gotten off to a bad start–but that was over. Things were going along rather well now, he decided, and he felt some secret delight in the thought that he was doing everything with a certain flair.

Since he did not know Charity Cadwallader's phone number nor even her address, he was not sure when he would see her again. He felt certain it would be soon. He reasoned that it was Charity who had made all the moves. Why he had not seen that before, he would never know. He had been incredibly stupid about the whole business. He was naïve about women. He had never been able to figure them out, nor had he ever had much interest in the matter; but it was different now. He sipped Billy's Scotch and imagined his second meeting with Charity. They would dine at an expensive restaurant. He would remind the waiter to chill the Beaujolais. If he took her to that restaurant he had read about, which did not present a menu, he would not have to worry about stumbling over French or Italian. Everything would be served them. Over candlelight he would tell her about his business. He had so many ideas, good ones. Just this afternoon he had thought of an idea for a tie-in with a nonprofit organization like the Heart Fund. The organization could buy dollar autographs of famous people. Adam would have cards printed up which would say: *This autograph is a token gift. It symbolizes a $20 contribution to the Heart Fund made by (name of donor) in your name. Because you are the kind of person who would rather give than receive, this is your kind of gift....* It was an idea that had everything–snob appeal, an attraction for a person's vanity, conscience, and benevolence. Adam could see endless possibilities in the idea. He had thought of a wonderful slogan to promote it: FOR THE PERSON WHO HAS EVERYTHING, INCLUDING A HEART.... He imagined Charity listening with a certain warm respect for him, as he told her about his idea. He imagined her writing to Billy, telling Billy what a fine person Adam was, not only kind and imaginative, but having a good business head as well. He was so delighted with this fantasy that he promptly made himself another drink, using two fingers of Scotch instead of one this time.

At nine o'clock, Adam was a little high. He had used up practically every background in his imagination, and in every candlelit restaurant, on every tree-lined walk, in all the various and fabulous places he had visited as he sat in Billy's deck divan, Charity had watched him with admiring eyes. He had been brilliant and dynamic; he had even been a bit amusing, which was rare for Adam. Charity wrote so many enthusiastic letters to Billy, that by nine, Billy was writing back, "Are you in love with Adam, or something?"... and Adam was laughing aloud. Let the neighbors think he was some kind of nut, he thought. He had never had a better time. His spirits were so buoyed by his daydreams that Adam had an uncontrollable desire to con-tact Charity that very night.

He went through everything of Billy's looking for her address. When this failed to produce any information, he decided on a direct course of action. She had told Adam she lived nearby. He parted his hair carefully be-fore the hall mirror, slipped his suit coat on, and left the apartment whistling. "Another thing about Adam," Charity was writing Billy as Adam walked into the night; "he's so forceful."

At every apartment building where there was a doorman, Adam simply said: "What number apartment is the Cadwalladers', please? I'm expected." He was continually told there were no Cadwalladers In the building.

Where there were no doormen, Adam read the nameplates on the bells.

He walked up and down Ninety-third Street and Ninety-second, and the block between on Park. When he came to Ninety-first Street, he started at Fifth and decided to work toward Madison. It was in this block that he came across them.

It was the boy he saw first. It was the piercing glint of the boy's thick glasses, caught in the streetlamp's light–the owlish look of the youngster. Adam saw him, and, once it registered that it was the same boy he had seen hanging on the garden fence of King School, he noticed the man and woman with him.

The woman wore dark glasses, though it was now past nine-thirty at night. Her hair was pulled back in an untidy bun, so that wisps of it strayed in the evening breeze, as though she had been hurrying and had not had time to secure it. It looked blond, or red–Adam could not be sure. A mink stole hung off her shoulders, again giving the appearance of slight dishevel-ment. She was a small woman, unusually thin. It seemed to Adam that she was frowning, though her face was half in the shadow. She held Timothy Schneider by the hand in a way which was not "holding hands," but more pulling him along, as though he were a heavy cart that held her back. The boy was looking behind himself at the man, holding his other hand out for the man to take. The man was a few paces away, and when he tried to take the boy's hand, the woman gave the boy another yank forward.

Adam was close to them then. It was then that he got his first glimpse of
the man. Luther Schneider did not look at all as Adam had thought he
would. He resembled the portrait on the cover of *Our Time* only vaguely.
The features were the same, but there was something in his expression
which Adam was surprised by. Adam could not remember ever having
seen the single emotion of disappointment written on the face of a stranger,
but he saw it on Luther Schneider's. It gave Adam a bewildering sensation,
which manifested itself in an urge to break the woman's hold on the boy
with his own hand.

If any of the threesome noticed Adam, they gave no sign. As they passed,
the woman was still edging ahead, pulling the boy. Adam heard her say: "...
keep him up this late, not mine! Do you hear me making excuses for him? I
gave that up long ago. Tiresome excuses!" Then she said something else
Adam could not entirely hear, about never learning discipline.

Adam saw Luther Schneider sigh. It was a sigh of "giving up." Schneider
was so tall as to make the woman look nearly comical by comparison, but
there was nothing comical about the scene. He sighed, and then his shoulders seemed to relax in a slump. He fell back a few more paces, so the
woman and boy were well ahead of him. Adam could hear the boy's high,
nervous whine, as he was pulled along; then a shrill retort from the woman.
Silence then, save for the groan of a bus starting on Fifth Avenue, and the
clatter of the woman's heels.

Adam lighted a Gauloise and leaned against a chestnut tree near the curb.
Mid-way in the block, by a street lamp, the woman turned in at a red brick
house with a small spiral staircase leading up to it. With some difficulty, she
yanked the boy with her. He caught the iron rail with his hand, letting his
feet swing, to make it harder for her, but she jerked him away from it. A
yellow door flashed open and shut. After a minute Luther Schneider
turned in at the same house.

Adam tossed his Gauloise in the gutter. His search for Charity Cadwallader seemed suddenly pointless. The disappointment he had seen in the
face of Luther Schneider was somehow contagious, for he suddenly felt a
keen sense of disappointment himself. But at what? He walked toward
Madison Avenue. He thought about the woman, and about the fact that he
had never speculated at all as to what his own mother had been like. He
had that one memory of her, but he had never built on it. His childhood
fantasies of being like other boys never actually sketched a mother; only a
father. He could not even recall anything very specific about Marshall Bollin's wife. She was simply Billy's mother, and he could not remember one

conversation he had ever had with her, though there must have been many. Nearly all the employees and counselors of the Home were women, yet Adam had forgotten half their names. Those whose names he did remember, he did not remember pleasantly.

At Madison and Ninety-third Street, Adam turned in at a bar. He ordered a double Scotch and sat far down at the end, away from the small congregation of people toward the front. Most of them had come into the bar alone, but they were talking back and forth the way they did in neighborhood bars. Let them, Adam thought; he even felt sorry for them. A bald, middle-aged man was saying very unfunny things at which they were all laughing uproariously. Adam put a quarter in the jukebox, forcing the bartender to turn down the sound on the television. The music helped drown out the laughter and the unfunny things the bald-headed man was saying. Adam had another double Scotch. The last thing Adam remembered clearly was taking off Billy's poodle cuff links and putting them down on the bar.

8

Geneva, Switzerland (WP) The four-year-old son of wealthy Doctor Thomas Zumbach was kidnapped from his home here last night. A note demanding a ransom of $100,000 was tied to the cord of the window shade in Thomas Zumbach, Jr.'s room. The Zumbachs' home is in Klatz, a small village on the outskirts of Geneva. Dr. and Mrs. Zumbach begged for police and public cooperation in being allowed to make a rendezvous with the kidnapper, in order to pay the ransom, and secure the safe return of their child.

Adam missed the poodle cufflinks as he was dressing Friday morning. On the Madison Avenue bus, with a blinding hangover, he tried to forget about it. When he read the story of the kidnapping in the *Times,* his eye caught the word "Klatz," and he was reminded of his carelessness all over again. That morning he had received an airmail postcard from Billy. Billy was staying in Klatz, commuting to the hospital in Geneva where his father was a patient.

Adam told himself the first thing he would do at the day's end would be to return to the bar where he had gotten so drunk last night. If the cuff links were not there, he would simply have to replace them, regardless of cost. He had no idea why he had taken them off in the first place. There were some dim recollections of talking to people in the bar, but they were too vague to explain anything. This morning, scrawled across a page in his Journal, he had found this notation: "Buy the Madison Avenue Inn and fire bartender!!!" He had scratched it out after he read it, and written under it: "Watch drinking!"

It was a steaming New York day, too hot and humid for mid-May. That fact, coupled with Adam's headache and stomach upset, made his work go rapidly and smoothly. Adam found that he was much better at business when he did not feel well, particularly if half of his difficulty was his own fault. By noon he had paid the piper more than his due. He had interviewed seven young men, and hired one to start as his helper in a week. He had concluded the lengthy correspondence on the Poe manuscript, and sent out four copies of the letter he had drafted yesterday, on the availability of the autograph albums. He had sorted the mail, made arrangements for a rare-coin concession to be added to The Mart, and talked at length with Geismar on the telephone. Geismar reiterated that he could not advance Adam anything against the inheritance, and Adam did not bother to enlighten him about the sale of "The Lucy Baker Album," the proceeds of which he could live on for some time.

Adam padlocked the door of The Mart at twelve-thirty. While he waited at the bar of the Villa D'Este, for a table, he called Dorothy Schackleford at her office. She was delighted with Adam's invitation for dinner, after Mrs. Auerbach's memorial service tomorrow night.

On the second Martini, Adam felt fine again. He ordered *suprême de volaille* for lunch, pointing to it so that he did not have to attempt pronunciation of the French. When the waiter repeated the order, Adam made a phonetic spelling of it in his notebook, and when it was served him, he wrote under the spelling, "breast of chicken." For dessert, Adam had Cherries Jubilee, coffee and a brandy. Over the brandy, he thought again of Charity Cadwallader. He liked to remember her saying how she hated Billy. Now that he had Billy's address in Switzerland, he might even drop him a line and hint at her feelings about him. He would not do it in a brash way. He might simply say: "The other night when Charity and I were having drinks, I tried to point out that she was all wrong about you. Women are so stubborn! They often fail to see the real worth in a man."... Something like that.

He ordered another brandy. What if he did write Billy a letter like that, and his letter crossed with one of Charity's? What if Charity wrote Billy that she hated *Adam*? You couldn't trust women... Why hadn't she called to thank him for the roses and the pearl teardrop?... The more Adam thought about the matter, the more determined he felt to find out Charity's address immediately. He had to know where he stood. If she was going to make a fool of him in Billy's eyes, he had to plan a counterattack! He had a third brandy, smarting a bit when the waiter presented the check along with it.

On his way back to Fifty-seventh Street, he felt himself weaving slightly. The Madison Avenue bus passed him. For a fast second he thought he saw Charity looking out the window of the bus, looking and then laughing at him. He felt his face hot and red with embarrassment, and he made a great effort to walk in a straight line. He could not be sure whether or not people were laughing at him. When he tried to walk faster, he weaved more. He felt sorry for himself. He had not had dinner last night, and this morning his only breakfast had been a glass of juice. No wonder the drinks had hit him. What did the people who were laughing at him know about his troubles? He could be physically ill, bereaved—anything; they would still laugh! He had always wanted to protect Mrs. Auerbach from their laughter, but now they were laughing at him. Who wanted to protect him? When he arrived at The Mart there were tears in his eyes.

At seven-thirty that night, Adam woke up on the couch back in the storeroom. He splashed water on his eyes, combed his hair, and locked up. In the street he bought an evening paper, and read more details on the kidnapping as he rode the Madison Avenue bus. There was a picture of the little boy. He had long curls and a round collar with a big black bow. His father, the newspaper reported, would pay *any* price for his safe return; it was his only child.

At Madison and Ninety-third, Adam got off the bus, and walked into the Madison Avenue Inn. There was a ballgame on the television, and only one man at the bar. The bartender was sitting on a stool, looking up at the television set. He did not look at Adam right away, but when he did, he spoke before Adam could.

"Well, well, well, Mr. Bollin," he said. "How are you this evening!"

It had been a long time since Adam had posed as Billy in a bar. He must have been *very* drunk last night, he thought, and he was glad that the bartender had given him that cue.

"I'm fine," he said. Then he explained that he had lost his cuff links, that he had remembered removing them there and putting them down on the bar.

The bartender said, "Oh, I remember too, Mr. Bollin."

"Well, may I have them back?" said Adam. "I hope they're here."

"They're here." The bartender was not smiling any more. His large hands were placed squarely on his hips. He was rocking back and forth on his heels, eyeing Adam coolly.

"I intend to have a drink," said Adam, "and I'd also like to have my cuff links back."

"I don't intend to serve you a drink, buddy!"

"I'm sorry if I was—out of hand last night... was I out of control or something?" The man at the end of the bar was not watching the ballgame now. He was looking at Adam. Adam decided to be as courteous as possible; it was the only way in such an embarrassing situation.

The bartender said, "I don't serve a fellow who's had too much to drink, buddy. I don't care what they offer me."

Adam tried to smile, but his mouth felt dry and tight. "I guess I offered you the cuff links... is that it?"

"That was *one* of your offers."

"I'm very sorry," said Adam. "I hadn't eaten, you see. My drinks hit me rather hard."

"A fellow with hundred dollar bills in his wallet ought to be able to buy himself a meal," the bartender said. He leaned on his elbows on the bar, watching Adam as though Adam were not all there.

Adam said, "I didn't have time to go to the bank yesterday. I had a very busy day. That's why I didn't get a chance to eat, you see. I didn't mean to be ostentatious."

The bartender said nothing, simply looked at him suspiciously.

Adam felt slightly irritated then. "If I bothered you, I'm sorry," he said. "I'll leave as soon as you give me my cuff links."

"I don't mind a guy who's had too much to drink," the bartender said. "I don't serve him, but he doesn't get my goat. You get my goat! Trying to throw big bills around is your business, buddy. The cuff links are another matter."

"Do I have to get a policeman?" said Adam.

The man at the end of the bar had moved down two stools. Adam began to be afraid.

"I wouldn't get a policeman if I were you, Mr. Bollin. That's your name, isn't it?"

"Yes, it is. And my initials are on my cuff links."

"Oh, I know that all right, buddy. I know something else too. I'm the one who ought to call the policeman. I just don't like any trouble, so I'm not going to call the policeman. You see, buddy," he said, leaning so close to Adam that Adam could smell onions on his breath, "this is what you might call a neighborhood bar! People in the neighborhood get to be pretty good friends, get to know each other, buddy. For instance, I know Mr. Bollin, and you ain't him!"

Adam was speechless. The man three stools away was staring at him, as was the bartender. The ballgame in the background was forgotten.

The bartender said, "Mr. Bollin has gone to Europe. He was in just last Saturday night. His old man is sick in Switzerland. You come in here last night and tell me you're Mr. Bollin, and you tell me you live where he lives. I'm not going to call any policeman, buddy, but you ain't getting Mr. Bollin's cuff links back. I'll just put them in a safe place for him, see, buddy? And if I were you, I'd pick some other guy to be. Some guy I don't know, buddy!"

Adam said, "Look, I'm a friend of Billy's, I–"

"I don't give a damn what you are, I don't like the looks of you! I met lots of Mr. Bollin's friends, and there's not a one like you! Not a one pretending he's someone he ain't either! Don't pull none of that stuff in *this* neighborhood! We all know our customers!"

The man at the bar said, "You need any help with him, Eddie?"

Adam did not wait to hear the bartender's answer.

He turned and left the bar. He was perspiring through his suit.

The incident had its good results. Adam learned this as he munched a hamburger in The Soup Bowl three blocks away. Still shaken by the experience, so that his hands could hardly raise the coffee cup to his mouth, he had kept his head turned from the other people at the counter. His eyes focused on a florist shop at the corner of Ninety-sixth and Madison. He kept remembering how difficult it had been to find a florist in the neighborhood, that morning he had gone for eggs while Charity was at the apartment. He had finally found the one across the street from The Soup Bowl, the one he was looking at now. He had bought the bunch of violets there, and it occurred to him that Billy probably bought flowers at that florist's. He remembered the bartender saying that everyone in the neighborhood knew their customers.

Adam finished his hamburger and coffee, and headed across the street. He straightened his tie, and smoothed his hair back before going into the florist's; then he asked for the owner. He introduced himself and explained that he was a friend of Mr. Bollin's. The florist's face broke into a wide grin, and he put his hand out to shake Adam's.

"I got a letter from Mr. Bollin only this morning," said Adam. He went on to say that Billy was staying in the same village where that dreadful kidnapping had occurred, and that Billy was visiting his father, who was ill in a Geneva hospital. The florist was gracious and smiling. He did not know Mr. Bollin's father was not well; he was so sorry to hear it; he would miss Mr. Bollin.

"Mr. Bollin wanted me to send flowers to a Miss Charity Cadwallader," Adam continued. "He wanted them to go out tonight. I'm afraid I left his letter at my office. I haven't any idea of the address."

Instantly the florist said, "Twenty-nine East Ninety-fourth. We do a lot of business with the Cadwalladers, too."

Adam suppressed a smile of victory. He ordered two dozen red and purple mixed anemones. On a card, he wrote: "If you don't call me at home tonight or at The Mart tomorrow morning, I'll call in person tomorrow night. Adam." He sealed the envelope while the florist assured him that delivery would be made that evening, before ten-thirty.

9

DANGER SIGNS IN HANDWRITING
1. The circle i dot: this person resorts to attention-getting devices.
2. A break in the lower section of the letters a & o: dishonesty.
3. t bar slants downward: arrogance and cruelty.
　　　　　　　　　　　　　FROM ADAM BLESSINGS JOURNAL

On Saturday Adam did not open The Mart. The night before, near midnight, Charity Cadwallader called him. She agreed to meet Adam for cocktails and dinner. The call so elated Adam that he broke open a bottle of
Billy's Nuits Saint-Georges. He sat drinking the wine until four in the
morning. His mind seemed to swell with new ideas. He invented a game for
adults that would teach them the calorie count in all foods. The winning of
the game would depend partly on their knowledge of calories, partly on
their knowledge of other nutritional information, and partly on chance.
Adam believed it would sweep the country much as Monopoly had in the
years after the depression, when money was foremost in people's mind.
Health was the new concern. Adam called his game DO OR DIET. It was
a penalty to DIET, a point to DO. He designed a simple board on which
the game would be played. He planned to find a small manufacturer who
would make up a lot of 100.

Another idea Adam got was for a way to promote the sale of autographs.
He would place an unidentified autograph in The Mart's display windows
on Fifty-seventh, with an analysis of the handwriting underneath. He
would give several clues about the identity of the person, and offer a free
handwriting analysis to anyone who could guess who it was. He might
even offer a free handwriting analysis to anyone who made a purchase in
The Mart.... One day, he would write an entire book on the psychology of
handwriting.

The more wine he drank, the faster the ideas came. He had the money
now to back his ideas, and there was something else. He had a new force-
fulness, he felt. There was nothing he could not do now. He fell asleep in
his clothes on Billy's couch and dreamed that he tracked down the kidnapper of the Zumbach boy, by analyzing the handwriting on the ransom
note. Dr. Zumbach turned over the ransom money to him. Dr. Zumbach
looked like the bartender in the Madison Avenue Inn. He apologized to

Adam for not believing Adam was Billy Bollin.

It was not just his hangover that kept Adam from going to The Mart. He had overslept for one thing, but his real reason for staying home was that he wanted to clean the apartment. Charity was coming there that night for cocktails, before they dined out. Adam spent the entire afternoon cleaning, pausing only once at three-thirty, for a sandwich and a cold beer in the gar-den. It was then that he caught his third glimpse of Timothy Schneider.

He noticed the boy hanging on the fence, the same way he had first seen him. The boy was calling out the same thing: "*Regardez* Timmy Schneider," over and over. No one seemed to be paying any attention to him, but when a smaller boy wandered by, Timothy Schneider stuck out his foot and kicked him. The smaller boy screamed, and suddenly a man in a tweed suit yanked Timothy from the fence.

Adam heard the man say: "You feel hostile today, don't you, Tim?"

"I didn't hit him on purpose," the boy answered.

The man had him by the arm. "Oh yes, you did. Don't lie, Tim."

"I didn't see him!"

"Don't use that old excuse, Tim."

"I didn't see him! I didn't! I can't see everything!"

Adam set his bottle of beer down on the flagstone and leaned forward to watch the scene more closely. The Schneider boy was trying to pound the man's stomach with his fist. He kept repeating that he had not seen the boy he kicked. Finally, the man reached down and took the boy's thick glasses from his face. He held them in his hand.

The boy blinked and squinted, feeling the air around him with his fingers like a blind person.

"You only hit people when you can't see them, Tim," said the man. "So when you don't feel like hitting me any more, I'll return your glasses. You wouldn't hit me if you could see me, would you?"

The boy began to whimper. He reached for the fence and held on to it.

"You don't feel like hitting me now, do you?" the man said.

The boy shook his head from side to side, hanging to the fence with both hands.

The man said: "We all know you have bad eyesight, Tim, but don't use it as an excuse to be belligerent."

"I'm not belligerent!"

"You saw Robin. You kicked him deliberately."

The boy said nothing. He hung to the fence whimpering. The man in the tweeds walked over to him and put his arm around his shoulders. He gave

the boy back his glasses. He said, "Will you apologize to Robin now?"
The boy nodded. He put his glasses on. Then he began to laugh.
"Laughing is good for you," the man said.
The boy shouted out *"Regardez* Timmy Schneider, Robin!" and he skipped wildly across the yard to shake the smaller boy's hand.

Adam finished his beer, thinking what a waste it was for a millionaire to have a son who was balmy. He remembered the disappointment in Luther Schneider's face. Adam wished he could think of an idea that Waverly Foods could use. Adam would call on Luther Schneider personally and present the idea. He imagined the scene, imagined Luther Schneider leaning back in a large leather swivel chair, a reflective expression on his face, his eyes watching Adam with growing interest.

"You say you got this idea yourself?" he would say.

Adam would nod modestly. He would have on a dark suit, with a fresh white shirt, and a quiet tie; his hair combed neatly, carefully parted, a half inch of clean white handkerchief showing from his pocket.

"Tell me about yourself," Luther Schneider would invite.

Adam's daydream was interrupted by the shrill sound of the ringing telephone. It was Geismar. Geismar wanted to know what Adam thought he was doing not keeping The Mart open. He was angry with Adam, and he made an unnecessary remark about Adam having retired a little prematurely. The call angered Adam, and when it was over, he made his first drink of the day—two fingers of whisky, neat.

By the time Charity arrived, Adam felt as good as he had late last night. He was inpatient at the fact Charity wanted to discuss the kidnapping in Switzerland. Adam did not feel like talking about dreary situations or people he did not know. He wanted to talk about his new ideas.

In addition, it irritated him that Charity would not have a drink. It took away any festiveness. Adam himself was drinking double shots.

She sat across from him on Billy's conch-shaped couch. Several times Adam tried looking deeply into her very green eyes, but each time she lowered her lashes. She did not make the gesture shyly; she simply seemed disinterested in any sort of personal contact with Adam. Last night on the telephone she had said something about "settling everything for once and for all." After three strong whiskies, Adam interrupted her speculations about whether one or two people had kidnapped the Zumbach child.

"I want to ask you something," he said.

"Go right ahead." She sounded almost defiant; Adam could not figure her out.

"What did you mean about settling things? You said that last night."

"I wanted to thank you for the flowers and for the necklace," she said, "and I'm sorry you went to so much trouble."

"Why are you sorry?" Adam realized he was speaking in a loud voice. He interrupted her answer to apologize for it.

She said then, "... as I was saying, it's just been a mistake. I wanted to tell you that. And I know it was my fault."

Adam said, "I suppose Billy was such a good lover!" He got up and stomped into the kitchen, tipping the neck of the whisky bottle into his drink. Women were animals! He called out: "You said you hated Billy! Why did you hate him if he was such a great lover!"

She was behind him, on her feet with her bag and gloves in her hand. "Who mentioned Billy?" she said. "I didn't! I didn't say anything about anybody being a good lover, *or* a bad lover. You're drinking too much!"

"Does somebody only get one chance with you?" said Adam. He had a passing thought then that he did not even want another chance with her, not that way.

She walked over and touched the sleeve of his jacket. "Adam," she said, "it wasn't *that.* Believe me!"

"Oh, yes it was!" said Adam. "Billy's good and I'm rotten!"

"Let's forget about it, Adam. Let's go out and have a good dinner. Remember, we were going to dinner?"

"Where does Billy take you to dinner?" said Adam. "I might take you to the wrong place."

There was a soft look in Charity Cadwallader's eyes. They were so very green. Adam thought how he would like to just sit and look into her eyes, and have her look back at him–the way she had that first night at the Roosevelt. Everything was so complicated suddenly. She reached out and took the glass of whisky from his hand. "Come on, Adam," she said. "I'm hungry."

"Did you write Billy about me?" said Adam.

"Why do you care so much about Billy, Adam? Let's forget Billy for tonight. We'll just have a nice dinner somewhere."

"I hope you told him you came here and offered yourself," Adam said, "I hope you made *that* clear!"

She turned away from him abruptly and started toward the door. Adam caught her arm, holding it tightly. He felt himself choke up. He managed: "We're having dinner, aren't we?"

Charity looked closely at him; an unpleasant look. "You're not a very nice person, are you?" she said.

Adam felt tears start to sting his eyes. Even to himself his voice sounded infantile. "You said you'd have dinner with me–" self-pitying, mulish. He wished she would go; he wished she had never come at all. "Please!" he begged.

"Let go of my arm, Adam!"

"But you said–" Adam's voice broke. Tears began to run down his cheek. He let go of her arm. "Please–" and it was a sob. "It's so important," he whimpered.

"If we have dinner, Adam," she snapped at him, "I want to leave right now."

"My eyes," Adam whined, "they're all–"

"Splash cold water on your face!" said Charity Cadwallader.

They sat in one of the high-ceilinged back rooms of Luchow's. Adam was amazed at how he had managed to pull himself together, in the short while it had taken them to cab there. Over a dark beer he told Charity he had been under considerable strain these past few days. He discussed his difficulties at The Mart with remarkable clarity, considering the fact that half of what he discussed was a lie. Leaning back in the wooden chair, smoking a Gauloise, he was himself again. He complimented Charity on her ability to use words of more than two syllables, adding that he had never found this "indigenous" to young women. Adam had no idea whether or not Charity did use words of more than two syllables, but he knew that nearly everyone liked to hear it, and almost no one thought they did not speak well. It was delightful the way he was taking hold. He was able to remember all the words from his own vocabulary list, which he had painstakingly copied into his Journal each week. He spoke with a delicious fluency, and he felt utterly controlled. Some of his German from his adult education classes came back to him. He was able to say *Bitte* to the waiter, and to point out to Charity that Koenigsberger Klops were meat balls. Even the fact that Charity told him she already knew that, did not irritate Adam. He was invulnerable. Despite her objections, he had a second beer before ordering.

During the second beer, Adam got a marvelous idea. Why didn't restaurants instead of having menus and dozens of waiters, work out a master electronic selector? It could operate the way a jukebox did. One could sit at the table, punch "Sauerbraten" or "Alpenragout" and have it recorded mechanically in the kitchen, at the same time the price was tabulated automatically on a check. Waiters would only be needed to serve the food.

Charity seemed impressed. At least she was quiet and did not try to change the subject; she smiled and enthused, and Adam had a third beer while he waited for the wine list. He began to tell her all his ideas.

In the midst of his description of DO OR DIET, the waiter brought the wine list. It annoyed Adam. Waiters were always fast when you wanted them to be slow, and slow when you were in a hurry. Adam chose a Beaujolais, with instructions to chill it. He added an aside to Charity that Beaujolais and Swiss Dole were the only red wines that could be profitably chilled.... Adam was continuing with his explanation of the game he had invented when he realized the waiter was lingering.

"Well?" said Adam.

"The lady is having Savannah Shad and you're having the duck?"

Adam nodded.

The waiter pointed out that a cold Moselle might be preferable.

Adam's heart began pounding.

"I think he's right, Adam," said Charity.

Then suddenly Adam regained his composure. Still, Adam was invulnerable; still he had hold. He very graciously instructed the waiter to bring whatever wine the waiter thought best. He used the word "indubitably;" indubitably the waiter knew wines better than Adam did. Charity was smiling and the waiter was smiling, and Adam began to smile too. He handed the wine list back with a flourish.

During dinner, Charity only played with her glass of wine. Adam no longer minded that she did not drink. It meant more for him, and he had the whole bottle, save for the tiny amount in her glass. He felt wildly happy and expansive. He said that tomorrow he was going to offer the Howard Johnson chain his idea for an electronic menu. He said he even knew a way to help finance the project, and the idea for this came as he talked. He would call on Luther Schneider, the head of Waverly Foods. A deal could be worked whereby Schneider would pay for the installation of the machine, if Howard Johnson's allowed Waverly to print across the machine's top that Waverly Foods were served. It would mean business for both he told Charity, and as he told her this he realized he had not even finished his duck, and the bottle of wine was empty. He called for another beer then changed the order to another bottle of Moselle.

Charity was frowning slightly. Adam reassured her. It was one of those nights when his liquor simply did not affect him.

"But let's talk about you!" he said. He leaned back, no longer interested in eating the rest of the duck. "What are your summer plans?"

"I'm going to Europe," she said. "Very soon."

It was a surprise to Adam, but on this fantastic evening nothing daunted him.

"I'll go along," he said. "Where will we go? Rome is a bore, so let's not go there."

She laughed. He did not like that laugh. He asked her what she was laughing at, and she said she was not laughing at anything. "I mean it," he said. He did, too. He would sell the *Stammbuch* tomorrow. He would let his helper run "The Mart" for the summer. It was his *Stammbuch;* it was his business, for that matter; he could do with The Mart what he pleased.

"Have you ever been to Europe, Adam?"

"Not because I couldn't afford to go," he said.

The waiter opened the second bottle of Moselle. Adam asked him if he had chilled it. The waiter smiled and nodded. Adam said to Charity: "Beaujolais and Swiss Dole are the only red wines that can be profitably chilled."

"Don't you want some coffee, Adam?"

Adam said, "Certainly! *After* dinner!"

A party at the table opposite them were smiling. Adam smiled back, giving a smart little salute with his right band.

Adam said, "In Europe we'll look Billy up! Won't *he* be surprised!"

"I dare say," said Charity. Then she said, "Adam, it's very late and I'm tired."

"Be glad you're a rich girl," said Adam. "You don't have to go to work tomorrow."

"Tomorrow's Sunday, Adam."

"All the more reason for celebrating," said Adam. "It's Saturday night."

As he said the words "Saturday night," something seemed to want to occur to Adam, but nothing did. He reached for the neck of the wine bottle and poured himself another glass. Some of the wine splashed onto the tablecloth.

Adam said, "It's the waiter's job to pour the wine. This fellow's not working very hard, is he?"

Suddenly Adam realized that Charity was calling the waiter.

"Look," Adam said, "I didn't mean to criticize him. I'm perfectly able to pour the wine. Let him alone. Let's talk about our trip! We might even start off at Klatz, hmmm?"

Charity persisted in calling the waiter. Adam was pleased that she was looking out for him, trying to please him. He said, "It's very nice of you, but maybe the fellow's had a hard day. Sunday's busy in Luchow's, and tomorrow's another new week. Let him be, Charity."

Adam sipped his wine. He liked the idea of starting off their European jaunt in Klatz. They could drive to Geneva and visit Marshall Bollin. Adam made a mental note to learn to drive a car before they sailed.

When the waiter finally appeared, he presented Charity with the check.

Adam said, "Good God, this fellow really is falling down on the job!" He reached across and took the check from the table.

Charity said, "Pay it, Adam. And then let's go!"

Adam couldn't blame her. A bad waiter could ruin everything. Adam hated to leave a half-full bottle of wine, but Charity was right. He should pay up and leave, and not bother to tip either. It did not have to mean the evening was over. They were very near Greenwich Village. They could go to some nice bar and have a brandy.

"I'll take care of everything," he smiled at Charity. "Don't let him upset you."

The waiter's handwriting was sloppy, and Adam had difficulty reading it. The *t* bars slanted downward and there were breaks in the lower sections of his *o*'s.

Adam said, "He's not only lazy, he's dishonest. You should see this writing, Charity."

"Never mind it, Adam, please. Let's go!"

"You're absolutely right," Adam said. Again the people at the opposite table smiled, and again Adam smiled back and gave another salute. They seemed to like him immensely. If the waiter had not been so irresponsible, Adam might well have asked them to join Charity and himself in a round of drinks.

When Adam reached for his wallet, it was gone. He searched all his pockets, twice. He said, "That does it!"

"Don't shout, Adam!"

"I don't mind a lazy waiter," said Adam, "but I'll not tolerate a thief!"

"Adam, please!"

Adam said, "He stole my wallet, Charity! I can't stand for that!"

"He didn't steal your wallet. You must have it."

"I don't! That's all there is to it!"

Charity looked angry. Again, Adam could not blame her. She said, "Wait a minute," and left the table. By rights, Adam knew he should go with her while she complained to the management, but he had a rather dizzy sensation. The wine was probably inferior, he decided. Bad whisky could do the same thing. He sampled a bit more of the wine. He felt so dizzy that he had to steady one hand with the other as he raised the glass to his lips. Some of the wine spilled onto his shirt. He saw the people at the next table watching him.

"Bad wine!" he called. "Poison! And my wallet stolen in the deal."

"Poor thing!" one of the women said to the man beside her. It was nice of the woman to sympathize. They were all nice people.

"Thank you," Adam cried out. "It's a good thing to know people care!"

He had more of the wine, holding it in his right hand, which was steadied by his right elbow leaning on the table. With his left hand he propped up his right arm, pushing the glass toward his mouth. Then the glass fell out of his hand, and the wine spilled all over his shirt, his suit, and the tablecloth. Another waiter—not his own—came hustling across the room.

"Ask my waiter to bring me another glass!" said Adam.

"If you'll come with me you can talk to your waiter," said the other waiter.

Adam shook his head from side to side with amazement. What kind of a place was it where the customers went to the waiters!

"Come on, sir!" the other waiter said. He had Adam's arm and he was actually trying to pull Adam to his feet. Adam felt very sad for the people at the next table. They would be treated the same way, no doubt, and they were nice people. Adam stood up, leaning against the other waiter.

"What kind of a place is this?" he said to the whole room. "You don't deserve this! Hang on to your wallets!"

The nice woman at the next table looked very sad. Adam wanted to comfort her. He tried to walk across to her, but the waiter pulled him back. Adam called to her: "Don't stay here! Look what's happening to me!"

Tears were suddenly streaming down his cheeks. They were all such nice people, all duped too. "Look at the handwriting," Adam said. He wanted to explain it, to tell them all to notice their waiters' handwritings, but he felt too tired now, and the waiter was stronger; the waiter was propelling him out of the room.

His own waiter was waiting at the EXIT with a man in a dark suit. The manager?... Adam pointed his finger at the man. "My wallet! I can't pay until the waiter gives it back."

"The lady has settled already, sir," said the man. "Good night, sir."

"The lady?" Adam said. What lady? The one at the next table who had smiled? Adam wanted to thank her, but the man in the dark suit had already opened the door, and Adam walked into the fresh air like a newly-freed prisoner.

"Here's the cab money she left for him," a voice said behind him.

Adam stood in the clean cool night. He saw his waiter out in the street trying to hail a taxi. He was making a get-away, Adam decided, and he had Adam's wallet with him. Adam began to cry again. Didn't anyone care that there were thieves loose in the world? He asked some of the people who passed him there on Fourteenth Street, but they only laughed and the more they laughed, the more Adam wept.

10

Klatz, Switzerland

Dear Addie,

Father died last night. It came as a shock since he was doing so nicely when I left him yesterday afternoon. It was his desire to be buried wherever he died (you know how father hated fuss) so I am arranging a service for him in Geneva. Mother is flying here for it. There is no more to say on the subject, I guess. Please skip the usual sympathy note, since like father I agree that these things should pass with a minimum of ceremony.

What I am really writing to you about is Charity Cadwallader. You may have gathered that at one time Charity and I were rather close. I had intended to break off our relationship at the end of the summer, even before I left for Europe. Father's illness necessitated a sudden, and perhaps premature, break-up. I am fond of Charity, God knows, but we are two people who simply cannot "work things out." The suddenness of our very necessary split may prompt Charity to do something she would be sorry for later. I think she is quite hurt by the whole thing; even slightly antagonistic toward me. I do not expect you to understand this fully, since it is a most delicate and complicated involvement between two difficult people. However, I want to suggest that Charity might bring you into the matter as a way of getting even with me. She knows of our relationship as children, and she may misinterpret it to think I would be enraged were she to see you. Nothing could be more untrue. She can see whomever she pleases. However, it is only fair to warn you that her reasons for seeing you might have more to do with me than with you.... Don't take this the wrong way, Addie. If I were in your situation, I would want to know the facts. Thus, my openness.

Charity has been seeing a psychoanalyst for years! I would not call her a bona fide neurotic, but neither is she a normal carefree young lady. She is a far cry from the girl you were with the night we all met, for example. She has none of that sim plicity, nor any of that "above-board" honesty. In addition, she comes from a very good family, probably an overly-permissive family, which makes her a bit spoiled. But her family can trace their ancestry back to the Mayflower (no kidding either, Addie) and I hope you know what that means in terms of anyone they would accept as a proper young man for Charity.... I don't care about such things, but again—were I in your shoes, I would like to know the facts.

God knows I would be the last person to try and run down "Chary," but she is not what she seems to be. She is a very "mixed-up kid" who cannot use any more complications in her life. It is for this reason also that I ask you to consider all this. One of the many things I've always admired about you, Addie, is the fact you do not try to push in where you do not fit. Don't take that the wrong way. I mean it as a friend of long standing. I think very highly of you, or I would not have left you in my apartment where you have access to all my things.

I'll be here at least another ten days. The big news from here is the kidnapping, of course, but with father's illness and now his death, I have little time to be interested in anything else.

Yours,

Billy.

P.S. I am in need of my poodle-shaped cuff links. Be sure and insure them as they are very expensive.

Adam had no clothes on when he woke up Sunday noon. The thin Airmail Special was wadded up in his hand like a dirty tissue, so he did not pay it any attention right away. It had been pushed under his door last night. He had read it when he returned to Billy's apartment, but he did not remember it. He did not remember anything—not immediately. He lay on his stomach, his face in the pillow, his hands and wrists under the pillow. Columns of sunlight striped his back and his buttocks, and he could tell by the smell of everything that it was a very hot May day, no breeze and muggy.

It took him several long seconds to discover where he was and what day it was; then a few more such seconds to realize how he felt. Gradually, painfully, his memory began the play-back of last night. As far as it went, it was a faithful reproduction, but it ended with the waiter bringing a second bottle of wine. The rest was sketchy. His wallet had been stolen. Charity had complained to the management. A woman at the next table had paid the bill. He was not certain about any of it. He could not even remember taking Charity home, nor could he recall his arrival at Billy's. Here he was at any rate, so he must have seen her home, too; he had no recollection of an argument either. So far, so good.

A dream. Billy's father had died. Billy had told him to leave Charity alone. Or had Billy called him? A ringing phone seemed to stick in his memory; ringing, ringing, and he had not been able to pull himself from bed and answer it. . Was that right? He lay there thinking about it until his thirst became unbearable.

When he sat up, he saw his clothes strewn about the bedroom. Beside the night table, on one of the Etruscan chairs, was his wallet. He took that in at the same time he felt the wad of thin airmail paper balled up in his fist.

His wallet had not been stolen after all, but he *distinctly* remembered... never mind. The letter next. Geneva postmark.

For twenty-five minutes he was sick in the bathroom. In between bouts of nausea, Adam sat on the top of the toilet cover, holding his head with his hands, his elbows propped on his knees. He could feel nothing about Marshall Bollin's death, only rage at Billy. In his mind he composed several letters to Billy. I'll-do-as-I-please letters and Who-do-you-think-you-are! letters. One of them said: "Of course I won't write you a sympathy note concerning your father. What a break for him to have you eternally out of his sight! I would rather write him a note of congratulations!"... Another said that Charity Cadwallader, for all her "alleged" fabulous ancestry, had come to Adam offering her wares in the venerable tradition of any common whore.... After his sickness subsided, Adam got up and made himself an Alka-Seltzer. While he watched the bubbles, waiting for the tablets to dissolve, he composed another letter. Short, subtle, designed to infuriate Billy. In it he said he felt he could handle Charity; in fact, they would probably travel through Europe together this summer.

He did not even bother to dress. He sat naked at Billy's tambour desk, scratching the words across a piece of Billy's stationery, using Billy's quill pen. The phone interrupted him; a girl's voice. He did not recognize it.

"Yes, this is Adam. Who's this?"

"Eloise Siden, remember?"

"Eloise Siden... I think I remember."

"Dot's roomie."

Then he did remember. The girl from Texas who booked New York to Caracas and smelled of garlic. "Oh, how are you?" said Adam.

"I'm fine, bub, but I can't say the same for Dot, thanks to you! Who in blue blazes do you think you are, bub! I suppose it's your idea of fun to stand someone up! First you get her to do your dirty work and show up at the confounded funeral service and then you hightail it off someplace else and don't even–"

God! Adam held the telephone arm away from his ear. He had completely forgotten the service for Mrs. Auerbach last night; forgotten his date for dinner afterward with Dorothy Schackleford!

"Listen!" he tried to interrupt Eloise Siden's bombardment, but he was glad that he could not, for he did not know what he would have said anyway. He was lower than a rat, said Eloise Siden, too low for worms to crawl under him. Eloise and Shirley Spriggs and Rose Marie Scoppettone and Norman had been up until all hours trying to quiet Dorothy down.

"Dotty said you must have been in an accident," Eloise Siden continued, "and she kept making us phone your place, but I knew the straight poop, bub! You never fooled me for a minute! Norman either! He'd like to plant one on your kisser good!"

Again, Adam held the telephone arm away. Shirley Spriggs, the girl in the Japanese kimona who had vowed not to dance for two years; and Rose Marie, whose last name meant "big gun" in Italian; who answered *"Mais oui."* Norman, fat bald slob Norman.... Adam could picture the whole affair.... Tomorrow he would call Dorothy Schackleford at her office. He would think of *some* explanation. He would take her to dinner at Ficklin's, the fancy restaurant without menus; he might even get theater tickets. It would be easy enough to straighten out the whole business where Dorothy Shackleford was concerned, but what about Geismar? Lately Geismar was sarcastic and suspicious, as though he were sitting in judgment. Adam knew Geismar had attended Mrs. Auerbach's service; Geismar was a goody-goody if Adam had ever seen one. Adam would have to invent an air-tight excuse for *that* one! He brought the phone back to his ear. Eloise Siden was calling him a two-faced turd. Adam hung up on her.

He finished the letter to Billy, addressed it and sealed the envelope. Tomorrow he would sell Goethe's son's *Stammbuch.* With part of the money he would replace what he had spent from the sale of "The Lucy Baker album." That would satisfy Geismar that Adam was doing nothing crooked. The *Stammbuch* was Adam's, after all; he did not have to wait for the will to be probated to sell something that was already his. With the rest of the money, Adam would go to Europe with Charity. He would still have enough left over to live on for years!... When he returned from Europe, he would re-open The Mart. He would remodel it, hire several helpers, and expand the business. He would marry Charity and invite Billy to be best man. He would name his first son after Billy. Oh, he would show Billy some tricks! Adam's spirits began to soar! His headache went and he began to feel marvellous. He would ask Billy to be his son's godfather. Adam laughed aloud. He even felt a certain affection for Billy at that moment. Life would become a game he would play with Billy. It was a fascinating idea. Perhaps Adam would one day write a novel about it–call it *The Eternal Contest.* It would be a best seller and Adam would dedicate it to Billy. Adam was so pleased with his reflections that he walked to the kitchen and made himself a Bloody Mary. Since he did not know Charity's telephone number, and it was not listed, the only choice Adam had was to call on her. He would do just that after his drink. He would shower and shave and dress in his new chalk-striped black wool worsted suit. If the florist was open on Sunday, he would buy a bouquet for Charity's mother. He drank the Bloody Mary, hoping that both Mr. and Mrs. Cadwallader would be at home. After all, he smiled to himself, he had to meet his future in-laws sometime, didn't he?

11

*...and that in any event, Charity is leaving for Europe very soon. It behooves you
to bear in mind that up until now, we have tolerated you in a manner which is
completely out of proportion to the embarrassment and general harassment to
which you have subjected us.*

*This past week has been one importunity after another. Your sober apologetics
have been every bit as vulgar and distasteful as your inebriated demonstrations,
and your primitive persistence is alarming. As I have pointed out to you more than
once, Mr. Cadwallader is a cardiac. Not for that reason alone am I warning you
now that any attempt at future contact with this family, will result in Police action. None of us wants to see you or hear from you nor receive anything in the
way of gifts, notes, letters or the like. I hope I make myself very clear, for there is
no exception to the rule. One move on your part will mean my reporting you
instantly!*

> *Sincerely,*
> VERA CAMERON CADWALLADER

It was Mrs. Cadwallader's letter that drove Adam to the Gracie Branch
Post Office that Monday morning in June. He knew now that she really
meant it. As he filled out the regulation change-of-address slip, he felt sad
and sorry that he was forced to do something so under-handed. He wrote
down Charity's name and address in the proper space, and then in the
"changed to" space, he wrote Charity's name again, and "c/o William
Bollin," with Billy's address following. In about two days, Adam would
find Charity's mail in his box. Carefully, he signed Charity's name as she
wrote it, the tightly-knotted *a*'s and all. The *a*'s meant that Charity was
extremely secretive. That was another reason Adam had to go to such
lengths.

Even though Adam had presented Charity with Billy's letter about her,
Charity did not seem to realize that Billy was really against her! Once during Adam's calls on the Cadwalladers last week, Charity had even shouted that she loved Billy. Adam had been even more disheartened when Mrs.
Cadwallader put in that Billy was a fine person, far more decent than
Adam was. Either both of them were gullible beyond belief, or there was
something Adam did not know. Adam had mulled it over in his mind
throughout the long week end. Perhaps his own behavior had not been

exactly exemplary; nonetheless it should be perfectly plain to the Cadwalladers that Adam thought more highly of Charity than did Billy. Adam had even tried to reason with Charity's mother, explaining to her that he would certainly never write in a letter that Charity was neurotic! In addition, Adam had pointed out that the Cadwalladers knew nothing at all about his character, and the fact that they were so against him from the start meant that Billy had been busy sabotaging Adam in some way.

Something was wrong somewhere; Adam knew it! An entire family simply did not turn on a young man without reason. He could appreciate the fact that they disapproved of Adam's appearances when he was not wholly sober–they were not drinking people; but Adam had never made "demonstrations" as Mrs. Cadwallader said he had. He had simply tried to reason with them. Only once had he leaned against the doorbell of their apartment after they had asked him to leave; and that time he had simply wanted to reassure Mr. Cadwallader that he was not interested in Charity because of her money. He had just wanted to say that, then leave, but they had made such an issue of it, even threatening to buzz the elevator and get help from the elevator man. It was shabby treatment all around. Maybe he was not Billy Bollin, he told them, but he was a human being with feelings just the same.

It surprised Adam that *Mrs.* Cadwallader had written the letter. She had seemed so nice in the beginning, trying to be polite, telling Adam he was a nice young man, but Charity simply was not interested in him. Adam explained that Charity had not even given him a chance, and a chance was all he wanted. Mrs. Cadwallader had acted as though she was sympathetic to him, but she told Adam there was nothing *she* could do. She could persuade Charity to see him, Adam pointed out. This she refused to do, and Adam was sure Billy was behind it....

Charity herself Adam would never figure out. She told Adam that he had embarrassed her at Luchow's, but when Adam asked her how, she said there was no point in going into it. Adam tried to exact the evening's events from her, but she would not even show him the courtesy of sitting down with him and discussing it. What angered Adam most of all, and hurt him most deeply, was that Charity would not even make an appearance the last few times. Mr. Cadwallader said she was afraid of Adam, and Adam actually wept at that, right in front of Charity's Parents. Billy again–he knew it! Anyone who knew Adam knew he would never lift a hand to a girl, never! Nor to any person! What did they think he was! He wept, and Mrs. Cadwallader added insult to injury by saying that Adam needed "help." Adam knew the kind of help she meant!

Of course he had apologized in a long letter. He had sent roses twice. When he attempted to send Mrs. Cadwallader a plant, toward the week's end, the florist told him in a thoroughly unpleasant manner, that the Cadwalladers were not accepting any more flowers from Adam.

Adam handed the change-of-address slip to the postal clerk.

"My sister asked me to drop this off," he said. "My sister's getting married to Mr. Bollin."

"Good for her!" said the clerk with a broad smile. Adam smiled back. The clerk was a nice fellow. There were some nice people left in the world after all.

On the way out of the post office, Adam rumpled the hair of a small boy in a playful gesture. He hoped the postal clerk noticed him doing it. There would be no reason for the clerk to be suspicious of him, but Adam liked to put in little touches. The clerk would think: pleasant young fellow, happy over his sister's marriage . He would file the change-of-address slip automatically.

When Adam did begin receiving Charity's mail, he was sure there would be a letter from Billy among the others, confirming Adam's suspicions that Billy was writing lies about Adam. Adam only wanted one scrap of evidence. When he got it, he would simply file another postal slip, re-routing Charity's mail back. If he was confronted with the same clerk, he would simply say that his sister was not marrying Mr. Bollin after all. He might even embellish the story a bit and say his sister had run off with a chap named Adam Blessing on the eve of her wedding.... Adam smiled and walked out into a cool spring's end day.

The Mart had been closed all last week. Geismar was furious with Adam, but Adam no longer cared what Geismar thought. Ever since their fight over his not having shown up for Mrs. Auerbach's service, Adam had made it clear that Geismar worked for him, and that he was not Adam's priest. Geismar called Adam "cold-blooded" and expressed some doubt at Adam's intentions to operate The Mart as Mrs. Auerbach had hoped he would. Adam told him that was none of his business.

Geismar would see what Adam would do with The Mart! Meanwhile, Adam had to concentrate on the present. He still had not located a buyer for the *Stammbuch.* He had filed for a passport, and he was already making inquiries with the steamship lines and airlines in an attempt to learn if Charity was booked yet. A surprise party, he explained, and while they were perfectly willing to try and help him, so far he had no information as to when she would go, or how.

Again, a letter to Charity from Billy might disclose details. Adam was only sorry he would never be able to tell Charity how he had found out any of the information that would be revealed, once he got his hands on a letter Billy wrote her. Charity would always believe that one of Billy's letters had been lost en route. Perhaps by the time she did discover it, she would not care a bit. In between then and now, Adam would convince her somehow that Billy was a very shallow person; that she had been totally wrong about Adam as well. He would follow her to the Orient, if necessary; in a thousand ways he would demonstrate to Charity Cadwallader that he, Adam, was the person she deserved. At some point afterwards, years away–the three of them might all be fast friends. Maybe then Adam would tell both of them about this very day and the trick at the post office. Adam imagined Billy's face, registering amazement at first, incredulity, then the break-through of laughter, the laughter of bygones-be-bygones. He could almost see Billy's head tossed back as he laughed, the shock of red hair bobbing, laughing and telling him he never would have guessed, and Charity laughing with them, the three like a happy family

On Tuesday Adam had another fight with Geismar.

Geismar said he rather imagined the State of New York would get everything Mrs. Auerbach had, if Adam did not knuckle down to business. They were going to need character witnesses and affidavits proving Adam's devotion to both Mrs. Auerbach and the business, said Geismar, and already too many merchants on the block with

The Mart were aware it was not open lately. Adam explained that his helper would report at the week's end; meanwhile Adam made arrangements to go to Washington, D.C. A dealer had expressed interest in the *Stammbuch*. Adam felt he could get the price he wanted for it, upwards of $30,000.

At four-forty-five Wednesday, Adam returned from his trip. After he got out of the cab and paid the driver, while he waited for his change, he saw King School letting out. He spotted Timothy Schneider immediately. The child was walking by himself, carrying a large briefcase, which he half-dragged along the sidewalk. A red sweater was tied about his waist, and he was dawdling as he walked, touching car fenders and walking with one leg in the gutter, one out. The sun made his glasses look like huge reflectors. On an impulse as he passed the boy, Adam said, "*Regardez* Timmy

Schneider." He smiled at the boy when he said it, but the boy just stared after him, with his finger in his mouth, frowning. As Adam turned in, he looked back and saw the boy still staring, hanging to a parking-sign pole, the briefcase twirling in his hand. Adam had one second's thought about whether or not the boy should be loose like that, but he abandoned it when he opened his mailbox with his key. The letter from Billy was there. Mr. William Bollin to Miss Charity Cadwallader. Charity's address was inked out and Billy's New York address written to the side.

Adam dropped the rest of his mail into his coat pocket. He noticed a Special Delivery among some bills, and he hoped it was from the man in Washington making the sale definite. He recognized Geismar's handwriting on one envelope, and he saw a bill from the florist on the corner. There was also a bill from Saks, addressed to Charity and forwarded. Adam let himself in the apartment. He felt no compulsion to drop everything and rip open Billy's letter; quite the contrary. He wanted to enjoy it fully, savor it comfortably, out in the garden in the cool air. After he made himself a double Scotch on the rocks, he took the letter with him there. He took a swallow of the Scotch and began it:

My dearest Chary,

Father was buried and there was a very simple ceremony. I'm sorry I have not had much chance to write since our talk on the phone. Believe me, I was not angry (as you thought) because you called. It was what you told me about Addie, and you going to call on him. I know you were very guilty because of it, and in your usual depression. I know you thought it would hurt me or make me jealous (laughable in view of the fact it was Addie), and I know you realize now that you were wrong... That Chary, you were just involved in another of your neurotic schemes which never have brought you any happiness.

I was angry on two counts. I was angry because I love you in my way, and I hate to see you hurt yourself. Also, I was angry that you ever brought Addie into the matter. It was my own fault for introducing you to him in the first place. Naturally you thought he was my friend, particularly when I let him stay in my place. The truth, of course, is that Addie is someone I pity. That night we joined him and that girl I thought it might make Addie feel important. I hadn't seen him in years, and I didn't want to simply say hello and goodbye. Father's illness made it imperative for me to have someone to stay in my place immediately. Addie seemed logical enough. He's harmless and all that.... Normally, though, I doubt that I'd even invite Addie for a drink at my place. Not that's he an unbearable person... just that he's always been rather silly. He was a terrible pest in his younger years, with one of these asinine "crushes" on my father. Poor father used to be so embarrassed by him, he would retreat at the sound of his voice, stay locked in his study until Addie had finally gone. I haven't kept track of Addie, but I suspect he's something of a phony, pretends to be more than he is and all that. For example, he told me he was part-owner of that business. Later when he drank with me, the eve of my departure, he told me he had hired some lawyer the YMCA recommended to help probate his partner's will. It just doesn't add up that a partner would not have a lawyer of his own, if for no other reason than to legalize the partnership. Also, consulting the YMCA for a lawyer isn't done by anyone very familiar with business and its ensuing responsibilities. It sounds fishy to me. I don't care, because who the hell is Addie to me! I just want to set you straight.

You say he's wearing my cuff links and my ties, also helping himself to my liquor. Let him. (Except for the cuff links. I know you hate them, but father gave them to me. I've already written him asking to have them returned. DON'T WORRY–I DIDN'T MENTION ANYTHING ABOUT OUR CONVERSATION, OR EVEN THAT I KNEW YOU'D BEEN TO SEE HIM.) Nothing in my place is of great value that he could wear or drink. He's the petty-thief type, not a real threat to anyone or anything–so I'm not worried about that.

Enough about Addie. Just steer clear of him is my advice. He won't bother you; he's too much of a vegetable. About your plans to arrive here on Sunday the 17th. Chary, I can't promise you anything, much less that I'll even be here. This is to say that I don't want you to come. It will do neither of us any good. Believe me, Chary, it's better to leave things as they are. You know our problems. You know how miserable we make one another. I can't face it any more, and I know now nothing will ever improve between us. Chary, I hate to rub things in, but your conduct with Addie–that whole thing, is just more of the same, and for me, the last straw. Addie, of all people, too! Rather a goat! It's your own business if you want to visit Europe, but count me out. If we happen to be in the same place at the same time, I suppose we're able to contain ourselves long enough to enjoy a drink together, but beyond that, Chary–no! With father's death I have increased responsibility and a great deal of business to attend to over here. Of all times, this is not the time for another lesson in how impossible it is for us to be with one another.

Weather fine, and mother under control. Hope you will finally learn that your impulsiveness only ends up in your misery. Don't come here, Chary. I don't want you to. It's done.

Billy.

Adam had begun crying at the point in the letter where Billy said he was a silly person. Now as he put the letter in the pocket of his shirt, his face was wet with tears. He wiped it with one of Billy's monogrammed hand-kerchiefs, which he took from his trousers, and he sat there letting more tears come, and wiping them away. He thought of how ironical it all was—of how only a few days before he had actually been looking forward to being friends with Billy, having him to his home—Charity's and his; and of the three of them laughing and reminiscing.

The fact that Charity had betrayed him did not sadden him as much as the way Billy wrote to her about him. Women were never to be counted on, but where were you when you could not count on a man you had grown up with? Adam went inside and reread the letter. He lay down on the bed and buried his face in the pillow. Now that he was free to sob as loudly and as much as he wanted, he found he could not. Perhaps he was sobbed out; he had been weeping more and more lately, the way he used to when he was much younger. It all went back to Billy. Adam rolled over on his back and lay wondering about this mysterious relationship between Charity and Billy. It sounded so intense to Adam. He could not imagine what it all involved. They were both play-acting, he decided; rich people who had nothing to do with their time but think about themselves. The more Adam pondered it, the more dejected he became, until finally he was in a very deep depression. He wondered if Charity had told Billy every-thing about that night, including the fact that Adam had been too drunk. He felt a sudden urge to simply get up, pack, and go back to the YMCA. Never think of either of them again... but in the next moment he saw him-self bringing about a reconciliation between Charity and Billy, saw himself as the wise friend, listening thoughtfully to one and then the other, plan-ning a dramatic and unexpected meeting of the pair. Charity and Billy would be face-to-face, alone.... All due to Adam, everything ironed out between them because of Adam's advice to each. Then the three of them would be great friends, with Charity and Billy always saying how it was Adam who had accomplished the whole thing; how it was dear Adam... dear Adam... Adam was in tears again. He got up and made himself a sec-ond drink, three fingers of Scotch, neat.

On the fourth drink, he remembered the rest of his mail. A florist bill for $132. A postcard from Dorothy Schackleford. It was mailed from Mystic, Connecticut. "Here for the day," it said. "Driving back tonight. Norman and me. We ate at this restaurant. $6 for a lobster but worth it. Am not mad at you any longer. Forgive and forget, my motto! Love, Dotty." In the envelope from Geismar there was simply a bill for $50, with a notation on a typewriter: "for services rendered." Under it Geismar had written: "Under the circumstances this is just for minimum expenses." Geismar had quit, was that it? Adam shrugged. Let him, he thought. He poured another shot of Scotch and opened the Special Delivery.

Dear Mr. Blessing:

I will be here at the Commodore Hotel for three days more before I move into a new apartment. You may contact me here. Mr. Geismar informs me you are in Washington, but are expected back any day. I will appreciate your getting in touch with me immediately. I just read of my sister's death in a Denver paper three days ago.

Foremost in my mind is the return of the *Stammbuck* of Goethe's son, which my sister had always promised to my own boy. We are not interested in selling it, so if you are involved in any such negotiations, please cancel them.

In going over things today at The Mart, I notice an book called "The Lucy Baker Album" was sold for $1500, since my sister's death. You must have the bankbooks with this amount deposited, and I would appreciate having them–any that you are holding. The business and the inventory will be put on auction in August, but I will not need any assistance in this matter or in any concerning the business, as I have arranged for that elsewhere.

My sister and I stopped corresponding about a year ago, but up until then we corresponded several times a year. I do not remember her ever mentioning you, Mr. Blessing. However, I am sure you are reliable and I can count on you without having to put undue pressure on you. I am quite concerned about the *Stammbuch* and the Lucy Baker money. Please call at once.

> Sincerely,
> Ida Gottlieb Vickerstaff

Adam was drunk when Geismar called an hour later.

"There was always a chance an unknown relative would show up,

Adam. She's a reasonable person. If you've spent some of the Lucy Baker money, she'll let you pay her back gradually."

Adam managed to say, "But the *Stammbuch* is mine! It's my *Stammbuch!*"

"Look, Adam," said Geismar. "The bubble's a bust. That's all."

"Bubble," Adam repeated to himself. He seemed to see many bubbles then, bubbles that danced in the pink glass of Chiaretto del Garda which Adam held in his hand. Each bubble had a face–Billy's. Adam set the glass on the table by the telephone and tried to bust the bubbles with his fingers. It only made Billy's faces laugh and fizz.

"Good night Adam," the telephone said.

Adam put the phone's arm in the pocket of his trousers. He picked up the neck of the wine bottle and poured more wine over the bubbles, until the bubbles spilled over and dribbled along the table and died on the rug.

"Good night, Billy," said Adam. He lay down on the rug with his cheek caressing the dampness. It was cool. He passed out, smiling.

EPILOGUE

From *New York World*—

TIMMY IS SAFE!

June 13 (W.P.)–Nine-year-old Timmy Schneider is safe. He is confused and sleepy, and he does not have his eyeglasses, without which he sees very little, but he is safe.

Kidnapped from somewhere between King School and the Schneider home, on an afternoon three days ago, young Timmy was not able to enlighten authorities on his experience, other than to say this: "A man bumped into me and my glasses fell off. There was a crunch and the man said they were broken. He said he knew me and had come to take me home, but first be said we would get them fixed. I told him I had a pair at home if he would take me there, but he said my father was waiting for me, and we would fix my glasses on the way. He called me Timmy and asked me where my big briefcase was, and he teased me about it. We laughed a lot. We took a bus a long way, I think, crosstown, uptown, I'm not sure. He took me to an apartment and a dark room. There were no sheets on the bed, and no furniture but a bed. I slept a lot. He gave me aspirin and it made me sleepy. I think I spent a few nights there. I woke up here, that's all I remember."

"Here" was the lobby of King School. Timmy was found there this morning at ten-thirty, by painters who are redecorating. The school closed for the summer the day after Timmy was abducted. Timmy was found curled up in the vestibule. He had no recollection of how he got there, but the painters say he was not there at seven-thirty when they reported. King School is a private school for "special" children.

Between the time Timmy was kidnapped and returned, Luther Van den Perre Schneider paid a ransom estimated to be $100,000. How it was paid, where it was paid–these details are known only by Schneider and the kidnapper. Throughout the ordeal it was Schneider's wish to keep authorities out of the affair. Schneider expressed "complete confidence" in the kidnapper of his child, saying he believed that once the money was turned over, his boy would be returned safely. Schneider's five words, "I have faith in him," will perhaps go down in criminal history as one of the ironies of the human spirit. There seemed to be almost a mystical character to Schneider's conviction that the kidnapper would abide by the pact he had set up with the boy's father. In the ransom note the kidnapper had said: "I need the

money as you need the boy. You do this for me, and I will not fail you, sir."
The whole atmosphere of this case was that of a "gentleman's agreement."
Once Schneider appeared at King School to claim his boy, he refused to
discuss any details. He seemed angry that reporters had questioned his son,
and he stopped the boy from describing the man who had held him captive.
Timmy Schneider had gotten only so far in his description, only far enough
to identify his captor as a "thin" person. Schneider interrupted his son, and
explained to reporters that Timmy, without his glasses, saw only shadows.
"He can tell you nothing!" Schneider snapped. "And I won't discuss this
matter ever."

"Gentleman's agreement" or no, there was some speculation at whether
or not the kidnapper had threatened Schneider with further violence to
Timmy, if Schneider gave him away in any detail. Police were nearly enraged at the wealthy manufacturer, president of Waverly Foods, for his
total lack of cooperation with them. Schneider's wife, the former Win Griswold, one-time society beauty, was the one to report the kidnapping, and
to give the few details police had. She subsequently broke down, and was
unavailable to anyone but members of the family. Schneider explained she
had been very ill this past year.

This was the second major kidnapping in two months. The first was that
of Dr. Thomas Zumbach's son in Klatz, Switzerland. Thomas Zumbach, Jr.,
age 4, was found choked to death in a woods between Geneva and Klatz,
shortly after Zumbach had made arrangements to pay the ransom. The kidnapper was apparently frightened by police who had trailed Zumbach to a
rendezvous spot. The kidnapper did not show up, and the boy was found
nearby. Police working on the Schneider case felt the facts of the Zumbach
case influenced Schneider to work independently of them.

A doctor who examined Timmy said the boy had been fed pills of some
sort, undoubtedly tranquillizers or sedatives. The nearly-empty bedroom
the boy described, and the mattress without sheets, led authorities to believe the kidnapper had perhaps rented a place especially for this purpose.
Police were checking with apartment-house superintendents.

PART TWO

12

...and I often think of Timmy, too, and see him asleep on Billy's mattress, after-noons when I would sit there in the dark and watch him. I suppose one of my smartest moves was to strip Billy's bedroom of rugs, furniture and blankets dur-ing those few days when Tim was my guest, but I wish I had been able to make him more comfortable. It does not seem that a year has passed. Too much of it was spent in Bidart! Ah well–"

FROM ADAM BLESSING'S JOURNAL

He was huskier now, not quite "plump." He saw his reflection in the win-dow of the small cafe, as he nursed an aperitif before lunch, at an outside table. His hair was no longer parted and cut short, but thick now, combed straight back with an almost pompadour effect, and longer than he wore it back home. He had grown a beard, too. In Europe no one looked twice at a man with a beard. Adam liked his–it gave him a certain dignity. To his sur-prise and delight, it had grown in darker than his hair, and the contrast was interesting. White-blond hair, nearly black beard, and his face was tanned from a spring of warm sun, spent in southern France. His jowls were a bit flabby, and his cheeks had filled out more than he liked, but he could blame that on the wretched starches the hospital had served continually. He was glad to be away from there; glad to be back in Paris. His breakdown had occurred in late January. One morning he had awakened in his room at the Quai Voltaire, to discover he had forgotten how to tie his shoes. A psy-chiatrist told him of the "rest" villa for overwrought businessmen, in south-ern France. It was located in a sleepy Basque village called Bidart. A total of five months Adam had spent there.

He ordered another Cassegrain. The restaurant was famous for this aper-itif–a glass of Montrachet colored by a drop of black currant liquor from Dijon. In the months before his breakdown, he had come here often. He needed the stronger stuff in those days; no aperitifs about it. Now it was moderation in all things. Adam smiled, remembering Dr. Melnik's advice: "Moderation in everything, Adam; moderation in moderation, too."

A feeling of bitterness followed the smile. He had almost begun to trust Melnik; he had nearly believed they were friends. During the months

Adam had been there for recuperation, Melnik had become fascinated with
Adam's handwriting analyses. For his own amusement, Adam had done
analyses of his fellow patients. Most everyone had looked upon it as a form
of "fortune-telling," more than character reading; few had taken it seriously. It was considered great "fun." Melnik knew better. He had studied
graphology in Zurich, and he congratulated Adam on his remarkable intu-
itiveness. When Adam was practically recovered, Melnik often invited
him to his quarters for dinner. Together they would discuss this one and
that one, and Melnik would listen to what Adam had to say, as though
Adam were a colleague. It had inspired him to work harder at his system,
to improvise and add to his theories with a seriousness he had never had
before. He felt useful and important, and before long many patients were
good-naturedly calling Adam, Dr. Blessing.

A month or so before he was ready to leave, Adam went to Melnik with
an offer. He would stay on as staff. He did not care about a title nor a salary.
It was a place for him. He would even do menial work as well. Melnik
refused the offer.

"Many patients," said Melnik, "think they want to stay on here after
they're well. They offer to empty bed-pans for the privilege. But the most
important part of getting well, Adam, is leaving."

Adam had been hurt at being classed with all the others.

"Then you were just flattering me, after all. The same as you would praise
someone's idiotic finger-painting!"

Melnik had frowned: "If you start thinking that way again, you'll get sick
again."

So Adam had been cast out again. Again, he was on his own.

The waiter served him sweetbreads with truffles, and Adam resisted a
temptation to wash it down with a bottle of fine wine. He had discovered
that if he read along with his meals, he did not miss the wine nearly as
much. He unfolded a copy of the Paris *Tribune,* and spread it out beside his
plate. As he read the theater ads, he thought of his newest idea, which he
had dreamed up on the train from Biarritz. Since Adam had been in Europe,
the theater had become his main sober distraction. On the train from Biarritz, he had been looking forward to the theater again, after so long an exile.
He had pictured himself standing in the familiar line for tickets. Then, it had
come to him—his idea. There ought to be an electronic ticket machine which
could be installed in hotels, restaurants, department stores—in places all
over the country. One could buy tickets to the various hits by consulting

the availabilities which would be registered on the machines. Halfway to
Paris he had taken his pocket dictionary out and begun composing a letter.
In it, he informed a likely manufacturer that he himself would invest a con-
siderable sum in the project.... The letter, unfinished, was still in Adam's bag
at the hotel. Maybe, Adam mused, he would really get busy on *this* idea.
Melnik had told him it was essential that he get busy.

Adam read on in the *Tribune*, half of his mind mulling over the possibility that Melnik might be actually jealous of him. After all, Melnik worked
hard for very little money, and it was no secret to Melnik that Adam had
plenty. Adam had told him the same story he told everyone else: that he
had inherited money and realized handsome gains from wise investments.

Adam had not yet made any investments. Part of the reason was that he
did not trust a broker, and he was never without fear that such a transac-
tion might cast suspicion on him. He had no knowledge whether large investments were reported to the police; it seemed anything was likely so
long as the authorities were searching for him. Adam was convinced by
now that Schneider had kept his word; he had not marked the ransom
money. Adam hoped to invest the money some way, to perhaps interest a
manufacturer in one of his own ideas, to ultimately double the amount
remaining. It was his dream to repay Schneider. He had paid back Mrs.
Auerbach's sister for the Lucy Baker money gradually, so as not to be suspect. The day after he had returned Timmy, Adam had taken a job in
Macy's, and stuck it out three months. He had told Dorothy Schackleford
the *Stammbuch* was his, and he was working at the Macy's job until he
could arrange for the *Stammbuch's* sale. Each pay day he gave Mrs. Auerbach's sister $60, so that at the end of three months, moved by his earnest
endeavors to make up the money, she dropped the remainder of the debt.
He was free then to go to Europe; certain, by then, the money was
unmarked; out-of-debt, and clear.... Adam never liked to think of his money
as "the ransom money." It was "the loan" in his mind. He felt a nearly ethe-
real tie with Luther Schneider, every bit as strong as a blood tie. During
their one telephone conversation, when Adam had arranged for Schneider
to leave the money in King School's outside trash cans, Schneider had said:
"I keep my promises. I know you keep yours, too. I believe in you. Remember that." No one had ever said such a very touching, kind thing to Adam
Blessing. He would make it up to Luther Schneider someday, somehow.

Last Christmas from Biarritz, Adam had sent a model of a tiny Basque
fishing boat to Timmy Schneider. He had so much wanted to sign his name
to a card and enclose it. Perhaps Luther Schneider would never guess who

"Adam Blessing" was–Schneider had so many business involvements all over the world; it could be just someone he had forgotten. Yet what if he did suspect who Adam Blessing was? Adam liked the idea of Schneider knowing his name, knowing that at Christmas he had remembered Timmy. He wanted, in some way, to tell Schneider that he was not just a crook, not just someone who did not care... In the end, he chose not to include a card. He would remain anonymous until he could come face-to-face with Luther Schneider, hand him a check for the full amount of "the loan," thank him, and then perhaps invite Schneider to have a drink with him. He would honestly like to know Schneider better. He would like to tell Schneider how he had managed to double the money; win his respect and admiration. . Last Christmas Adam had been so very lonely... He had thought of Luther Schneider often.

Midway through the sweetbreads, Adam decided to buy a gift for Schneider after lunch. Adam was not a stranger to the man's tastes and habits. Those three months in New York last summer, Adam had visited many back-number magazine stores. There was the portrait in *Town and County* on Schneider; the piece in *Fortune,* and the cover story in *Our Time.* In addition, all the newspapers had been filled with stories on Schneider and his family, during the kidnapping period. Adam had pored through them.

While Adam was "resting" in Bidart, he had read a few books on silver. Luther Schneider was an avid silver collector. Adam would find him something special–a Sheffield-plate egg stand, perhaps, or one of those rare, helmet-shaped silver cream jugs. It would be something interesting for Adam to do with his afternoon. He was tired of going to the movies, and tired of listening to his French and Italian language records back in his hotel room, tired, as well, of his immense loneliness. It had been the latter that had gotten him into so much trouble before his breakdown. He had done remarkably well about his drinking during the three months in New York last summer. Loneliness had never really plagued Adam until his arrival in Europe; then he had needed to drink to forget it. No more of that. In Bidart he had made up his mind that upon his return to Paris he would get things under control; start doing constructive things about his ideas. He liked the idea of buying Schneider the gift, as a sort of symbolic token of a turning-point. From now on he would work to repay Schneider. Adam was pleased with the thought. Euphoria began to creep in. Still–he did not order the wine his meal so dearly lacked. Indeed, a turning-point. He smiled and turned the page of his newspaper, and then he came upon the short notice in the *Tribune's* "Americans in Paris" column.

It was a single-line entry: "Mrs. Vera Cameron Cadwallader of New York City is staying at the Hotel Continental."

At six-thirty that evening Vera Cameron Cadwallader was waiting for him in the Continental's Cour d'Honneur. She was sitting at a table under one of the red-and-white striped umbrellas. In the note which Adam had dropped off at the hotel that afternoon, he had simply said that he was a friend of Charity's; that he would very much enjoy having a cocktail with her. He put an undecipherable signature at the end, and arrived a few minutes later than the appointed time, for fear she would see him and refuse to join him.

Adam sat down. "You don't remember me?"

She seemed anxious to please, but suspicious. She did not remember him at all; the beard, the extra weight–Adam supposed she was thinking that Charity did not know anyone who wore a beard. She smiled. "I'm sorry. Your name–I can't think of it, and on your note I couldn't make it out."

"First of all, I've changed a great deal," said Adam, "not just in appearance, Mrs. Cadwallader. I want you to understand that before I go on any further. I'm a different–"

"Blessing," she said then. "You're that Adam Blessing."

"Not *that* Adam Blessing, Mrs. Cadwallader, I assure you. You were so very right when you made the remark that I needed help, remember?"

She was looking down at her white gloves, playing with the fingers nervously. "I don't remember."

"Please just give me a few minutes to talk with you."

"Of course," she said. She did not look across at him. She sipped her aperitif, still occupied with the gloves.

"I was an awful fool, but that's all changed now. I was in the midst of a nervous breakdown."

"I'm sorry," she said.

"I make you nervous, don't I? I don't want to. I have great admiration for you."

"How long," she said looking at him then, "are you going to be in Paris?"

Adam knew she meant to keep the conversation as impersonal as possible.

"I live here now," he said.

"How nice for you."

"And Charity? How's Charity?" He did not mean to say her name so soon after the conversation had begun, but Mrs. Cadwallader's nervousness was contagious.

"Very happy," she said.

"I heard they were abroad. I thought you might all be traveling together." It was a shot in the dark. He had no idea where Billy and Charity were.

"No, they're in Rome," she said.

"I thought Billy was bored with Rome. I thought he hated Rome!" He told himself to go easy; the old tone was back in his voice, the breathless feeling. He saw Mrs. Cadwallader look more closely at him, and he laughed. "It's a joke Billy and I had," he said. "I used to kid with Billy about Rome."

"What about Rome?"

"Just a joke Billy and I had," said Adam.

"I don't understand."

"Oh, well, it's not important. I–I don't even know how it came up." There was silence. Adam wanted to signal for the waiter, but he was afraid that it would simply give her an excuse to say she could not join him in the drink, an excuse to pay for her own drink and leave. Adam said, "It's lovely here, isn't it?"

"Yes, lovely."

"I was very happy when I read of their marriage last summer." He coughed, to camouflage his shortness of breath. "It must have been very romantic, eloping that way, spur of the moment and all."

"Yes."

"I read about it in the newspaper," said Adam. "I read about it just a week before I left for Europe. I'd hoped to run into them, but we were never in the same places, it seems." In Venice, though, I came close, Adam thought grimly; missed them there by two days.

"Are you working over here, Mr. Blessing?"

"I'm hunting down some rare silver pieces for a New York collector," said Adam. "It's very interesting... I suppose Billy is working for his father's firm. I mean, he took it over, didn't he?"

"Yes."

"Yes, I thought so. I thought it would be something like that." Adam's voice was husky, his throat very dry. Out of the corner of his eyes, he could see the waiter, but he did not chance signaling him. Mrs. Cadwallader had nearly finished her aperitif.

"How's Mr. Cadwallader?" said Adam.

"He passed on at Christmas time."

"I'm sorry."

"Mr. Blessing, I have a dinner engagement and–"

"I know I said the wrong thing. I should have kept up on things more," said Adam, "but it's hard over here. I'm sorry about Mr. Cadwallader's death. I know it must be hard. I don't mean to keep saying the word "hard." I guess sometimes life just seems that way. I wish you wouldn't leave just yet, Mrs. Cadwallader. I thought we might have one drink together." The words rushed out of him, and Mrs. Cadwallader seemed to be looking at him as though he were very strange.

Adam said, "Please... I mean–I was in love with Charity." That, he had never intended to say either.

Mrs. Cadwallader stiffened and took her gloves from the table, placing them in her lap. "I have a dinner engagement," she repeated. "Young man, you hardly knew Charity. It's something you made more of than the situation warranted. Now, I'm very sorry, but there's nothing I can do."

The old symptoms were returning. The feeling of wanting to cry.

Adam said, "Their marriage was my fault."

"You don't know what you're talking about Mr. Blessing." She tried to catch the waiter's eye with a raised finger, but the waiter hurried off in another direction. She opened her purse.

Adam said, "Billy didn't even want her to join him. She went without even knowing that, Mrs. Cadwallader. I was busy trying to get enough money together to go after her and bring her back, but I didn't have time."

"Mr. Blessing, Charity and Billy are very happy." She was taking out bills from a large foreign billfold.

"Doesn't it mean anything to you that Billy never intended her to join him? He wanted to call off the whole thing, Mrs. Cadwallader. I can't tell you how I know that but–"

She interrupted him. "I'm sorry, Mr. Blessing," placing the francs on the table, rising, "I must go now."

Adam rose and went alongside her. "It's my fault, the whole thing," he said, "and you don't know what I've been through. I wish you knew! Even after their marriage, I was ready to help Charity, take her back home. I tried to find them. Sometimes I just went from city to city looking for them and–"

Mrs. Cadwallader stopped at the exit of the Cour d'Honneur. "Mr. Blessing," she said, "I want you to leave my company. I will report you if you don't. You are a very ill person, in my opinion."

"Not any more, Mrs. Cadwallader! Believe me, I *had* my breakdown! I was in southern France, in a town called Bidart at a hospital. You can call Dr. Melnik there! Ask him!"

She was walking away from him.

"Dr. Andre Melnik!" Adam called after her. "Write him, Mrs. Cadwal-lader!"

People were staring at Adam. He knew his face was very red, perspiring. He tried to get his breath. He saw Mrs. Cadwallader stop a uniformed employee of the hotel, speak with him momentarily, turn and point Adam out.

Adam hurried through the archway, along the stone sidewalk to the Rue de Castiglione. Once in the street, he lighted a Gauloise and leaned against a pillar until he could stop shaking. Over and over as he stood there, he tried to convince himself that this is where it should end. That part of his life was all over, wasn't it? He was well now; and if it had seemed for those few moments in the Cour d'Honneur, to be starting up again, well, then—let it end again.

But like all the other endings, it was a beginning. Adam realized this. He drew a deep breath, let it out, gave in. There you have it—he was glad, too. He looked forward to what he knew was ahead of him. A little chill of excitement ran through him. Packing again, it would mean, and consulting the train schedules; then the embarkation, with its sweet, nervous antici-pation; and the journey itself, too tense to read or sleep or think of anything all through it but the journey's end... the inevitable round of hotels, the inquiries, the coming closer and closer.... This time though he was ahead of the game, he knew positively that Billy was in Rome.

"What is it you really want from him? Or her?" Melnik used to ask.

And it used to stump Adam. He could never answer Melnik, and soon there was no need any longer for Melnik to ask. Now, the answer was so simple Adam began grin as he thought about it. He did not want anything *from* them—of course, that was a silly way of putting it, and damn Melnik for that! Adam simply wanted to be with them, to help them, too. Why had he never thought to put it that way to Melnik?

Adam tossed the Gauloise to the gutter with a flick of his finger, and with a new, but very familiar spring to his step, he started off.

13

The Bartender
Madison A venue Inn,
Madison and 93rd
New York, New York U.S.A.

You don't remember me, probably, but once you put me out. I'm Billy Bollin's friend.
I bear you no ill will and send this as a token of my good wishes. Adam B.
POSTCARD FROM PARIS MAILED IN JANUARY

Adam checked first with the Grand, then the Excelsior when he arrived
in Rome, and on his third try–the Mediterraneo–he located them. They
were not in. Adam left a note for them saying he would be by at six o'clock.
Then he set out to find himself a place to stay. Because it was June and the
height of the tourist season, it was not easy, but shortly after two in the
afternoon, he found a room at the Delle Nazioni. He spent a few hours loaf-
ing about in his room, waiting for the stores to open. The last time he had
been in Rome, sometime in early October, he had not understood about the
stores staying closed between one and three or four in the afternoon. It
was an unhappy memory, and an unhappy period. He had gone to Rome
on the chance he might find them yet, though he knew Billy disliked Rome.
He had gone everywhere that fall on chance, and each failure brought on
a brief bout of drinking, which invariably delayed his departure. In Rome
he had suffered through one of his most extended binges, starting at breakfast usually, so that by lunchtime he was already drunk enough to be
laughed at. He remembered one afternoon on the Via Francesco Crispi,
pulling on the iron gate that locked a small handicraft shop, begging to be
let in at the top of his lungs. Somehow he had thought the shopowners
were against him in particular, that they had been warned (perhaps by the
proprietor of the cafe where he had lunched) that he was coming in their
direction. A nasty scene ensued, with police dragging him away, passers-by
gaping and snickering at him. He had left Rome the very next day, vowing
he would never return to face such humiliation again.

Adam realized now that all of the trouble last fall and winter had been
his own fault. A breakdown, Melnik had termed it. Adam had wished he
could tell Melnik the reasons for it, the tension he had suffered through,

the fear that any moment the authorities would find him out. A lot of businessmen, said Melnik, can't take the pressure any longer, crack under it.... Stop reading the stock quotations, said Melnik... rest awhile and work on "the other thing"... Billy was the other thing. A business rival, Adam had explained, married the woman I wanted to marry, without even loving her.... Melnik's advice was to accept the fact of the marriage. What was the word Melnik used? Scotomise ... Don't scotomise it... Well, Adam did not intend to scotomise it. He simply intended to be sure everything was all right with them. It was Adam's fault Charity had never received the letter Billy wrote her, telling her not to join him in Switzerland. That much he owed them, anyway–to be sure that everything was all right.

Around four o'clock, Adam walked in the oppressive summer heat to the Via Condotti. At number 84, he bought a handsome foulard and damask tie-silk dressing gown. explaining that he wished it gift-wrapped. A wedding gift for Billy, if they were still determined to carry on with their marriage. Otherwise Adam would keep it for himself. From the Via Condotti, Adam went to Via Frattina. At Myricae he bought a brocade evening bag for Charity. There were bright threads of green in the pattern to match her eyes, and Adam smiled to think of her pleasure as he presented her with it. "You surely didn't think I'd be sour grapes," he'd say. . And if things were not going smoothly between Charity and Billy! . . "A little remembrance to make you feel better, Chary."... While the woman was wrapping the bag, Adam's eyes fell on a small Tyrolean carved angel. In a burst of good feeling he made arrangements to have it sent to Mrs. Cadwallader in Paris. He enclosed a card: "I do not look back on our brief meeting with any bitterness. Best of luck in all things, Adam Blessing." Adam spent the rest of his afternoon back in his room, recording the big day in his Journal. It was odd that as much as he had looked forward to this time, now that it was here, he was not sure what he wanted to say about it. He described his purchases, made a note of his expenditures, and then wrote rather banal things like "What will we all say to one another?" and "Even the weather looks promising, seems to be cooling off."

At twenty minutes to six, Adam left the Delle Nazioni, packages under his arm, his heart pounding under his jacket. A peddler near the taxi-stand was selling some blue and yellow flowers. Adam decided that tomorrow he would drop a postcard to that florist on Madison and 96th. Say something short and nice, like: "Visiting here with Charity Cadwallader and Billy Bollin. Did you know they were married? Best wishes, Mr. Blessing." Before Adam got into the taxi, he paid for a bunch of the flowers, but refused to take them when the peddler held them out. "Give them to your wife!" Adam smiled. The peddler shook his head, not understanding. *"Moglie! Moglie!"* Adam said, pleased that he had remembered the Italian for "wife." The peddler nodded and said, *"Si, Moglie!"* trying to give the flowers to Adam again. Adam pointed at the peddler. *"Your moglie!"...* The peddler made a face at Adam. He looked angry, and as Adam got into the taxi, he believed the peddler was cursing him. Adam could not understand it, and as he rode to the Mediterraneo, his feelings were hurt; there was a slight edge off the evening; a blemish, ever so small.

"Addie?" a voice behind him said.

Adam whirled around in the Mediterraneo's lobby and shouted, "Billy! Billy! My God, Billy!"

"All right," Billy said. "Let's calm down, Addie."

Billy was not smiling, and slowly Adam's broad grin faded from his face.

Billy was saying that they could have a drink at the bar, and he was walking ahead, with Adam following, a bit dazed by Billy's abruptness. In appearance, Billy was the same; still dressed as neatly and elegantly as ever. His back was to Adam, but already Adam had begun to admire the silver-blue nubby-silk dinner jacket Billy was wearing, with the dark evening pants and black pumps. Billy pointed to a small table in a corner.

"Sit down," said Billy. "Scotch?"

Adam had intended to sip a sherry, go very easy, but he was so bewildered by Billy's cool greeting, he agreed to the whisky.

Billy spoke Italian to a waiter standing nearby, then he sat down at the table opposite Adam.

"It's good to see you," said Adam. "I'm sorry I'm not dressed."

Billy was looking him over carefully, wordlessly. "What's the beard for, Addie?"

"It's not a disguise or anything," Adam forced a chuckle. "You know... in Europe and all."

"Taken on a little weight, haven't you, Addie?"

"It's this suit," said Adam. Billy made him nervous, staring hard at him that way. Adam added, "Oh, I suppose you mean my face is fuller. I guess it is."

"Everything is, Addie," said Billy.

"You look the same, Billy."

"I am the same."

"Well, good! I couldn't be more pleased!"

There were several moments of awkward silence then, broken by the waiter's arrival with Adam's Scotch. After the waiter left the table, Billy leaned forward, his elbows resting on the table top. "Now, let's get everything straight right now, Addie, all right?"

A chill ran through Adam. "Yes. How are you? How is everything going?"

"The first thing we'll get straight, Addie, is that how *I* am, and how things are going with *me,* is none of *your* goddam business!"

Adam gulped while he lived through another chill. Billy said, "I wrote you the week before I left Switzerland and told you to get out of my apartment. Let's start there. You stayed on until the end of August."

"I didn't take you seriously, was all, Billy. I get mad and say mean things, too... I just—didn't take you seriously."

"What did you take seriously, Addie?"

"Look, Billy, you never wrote after that, did you? Not a word! Not one word! I had to read about your marriage in the newspapers! How did you think I felt?"

"I didn't write after that because I thought you knew enough to get the hell out when someone tells you to!"

Adam took a gulp of his whisky. "You're not using a very nice tone of voice, Billy. We all make mistakes!"

"Mistakes!" Billy rolled his eyes back in his head and hit his palm with his fist. "You were harassing the Cadwalladers to a point where they were threatening to call the police! Do you think you were welcome in my place after that!"

Another gulp of whisky... Adam said, "Yesterday I had drinks with Mrs. Cadwallader—no it was the day before. Anyway, I'm telling you the truth. We had drinks and today I bought her a gift right here on the Via Frattina, Billy!"

"I know all about the day before yesterday, and if I were you, Addie, I'd cancel the gift."

"She told me you were in Rome. What would she have told me that for, if she didn't like me?"

"We all make mistakes, as you say, Addie. Mrs. Cadwallader called us to warn us you were around."

"I'll have another drink," Adam said, draining his glass.

"Not with me, mister!"

"What's the point in asking me for *one* drink?" Adam said.

"Addie, goddam it, *I* didn't ask you!"

"No," Adam said, "you didn't." His eyes were a blur of tears. He hoped Billy could not see them in the dim light. If he could change the subject, it would be O.K.... he could get hold... he had not really lost hold yet. "I like your dinner jacket very much," he said. "Did you have it made here?" He did not trust himself to raise his head and look into Billy's eyes, fearing tears would roll from his own. He said, "Since my money–since I came into it, I've not gone in for flashy things myself. I've always been more conservative."

"That's another thing," said Billy, "this money you've come into! Christ, Addie, why kid yourself! You must have about a thousand dollars of that money left!"

"The Mart was worth more than that, Billy. You never thought I could become involved in a big business, did you? Well, I was."

"I suppose you're going to tell me you sold out?" Billy was holding his glass, rubbing the sweat off the sides of it with his finger, eyeing Adam suspiciously.

"Yes, I sold out. What did you think?"

"I *know,*" said Billy. "I don't have to think, Addie. I met an old friend of yours a month or so ago. Dorothy Schackleford, remember her, Addie?"

"She wasn't a particular friend. She doesn't know my business!"

"She was a better friend than you deserved, mister. She told me the only thing you got from that whole deal was that album that belonged to Goethe's son, the one you showed off that night we all met for the first time." Billy sipped his Scotch, finishing it, signaling for the waiter as he said, "She told me you got about $50,000–period, which wasn't bad pickings for a clerk!"

Adam laughed. "I don't care if you do know I was a clerk! You think I care?"

"Enough to *lie!* What'd you lie for? Christ, Addie, you're such a goddam small-time snob!"

"Dorothy Schackleford doesn't know anything about me or my money!"

"Keep your voice down, Addie."

"Let people stare! Do you think I'm not used to it?"

"I just bet you're very used to it!"

"You're not my friend," Adam said, and now the tears were starting, down his cheeks. He took out his handkerchief and brushed them away. Billy watched him with a look of disgust. The waiter came, and Adam said, "Another for me!"

The waiter looked questioningly at Billy, but Billy shook his head. "I'm leaving," he said to Adam.

"I have something for you. For you and Charity." Adam took the packages from under the small table. "Look, I have something."

"We don't want your gifts, Addie. Thanks just the same."

"But I bought them for you! They're wedding presents."

"It's a little late for that, Addie."

"Why? Something's wrong, isn't it? Things aren't going well, are they?" Billy stood up. He tossed some large paper bills on the table. "Dorothy Schackleford's working here in Rome, in case you're interested, Addie. You could probably benefit by looking her up. She works for the Fellow's Rome Foundation. Some kind of *missionary* work... Good-by, Addie." He started out the door, but Adam jumped up and ran after him. "Your presents!" he said; "if you don't want yours, at least take Charity's!"

"She doesn't want hers either, Addie!"

Billy had stopped, just outside the entranceway of the bar. He was fairly gritting his teeth, his eyes narrowed, his words very nearly forced out of the sides of his mouth, softly, slowly: "You've turned into some kind of nut, mister! I don't know what kind and I don't give a goddam, but stay out of my way, I warn you!"

"Hit me," Adam said, "go ahead and hit me, if you want to!"

"Beggar!" Billy said, "You beggar!" And he left Adam standing there, holding the gifts, trembling....

14

Safety Deposit-South Orange, N.J.	
(Savings and Trust)	$10,000
In $20 bills, black suitcase, (802)	$16,040
In $50 bills, cowhide suitcase (400)	$20,000
In Traveller's Checks (Am. Express)	$10,000
Spent since September:	$19,560
	$75,600

FROM ADAM BLESSING'S JOURNAL

"You have been so very kind," said Adam to his new friend.

"Nonsense," Ernesto Leogrande said. "I am bored with the way my people treat the American tourists."

Adam had been quite drunk when Leogrande had come up to him in the bar opposite the Mediterraneo. Leogrande had prevented the waiter from overcharging Adam by a thousand lire, after which he helped Adam leave, supporting Adam by crossing one of Adam's arms over his shoulder. At another bar, he had gotten a coffee for Adam, and sat with him while Adam sipped it slowly and pulled himself together. He had brought Adam to this small *trattoria* on the Portico di Ottavia.

Adam said, "It's not the money, Ernesto. I hope you believe that. I was just treated rather cruelly by a life-long friend, then for a perfect stranger to help me—well, I appreciate it."

"Si,si—" Leogrande brushed aside Adam's gratitude, and took another stab at his veal. He was a large, hook-nosed Italian with a sunburned face and straight, dark eyebrows, black wavy hair and a wide white smile. He wore a light blue shirt open at the neck, a brown-andblack checkered sport coat, and light blue slacks. While he ate and drank, he smoked a cigarette that rested in the plastic ashtray beside his plate, and around his neck on a silver chain he wore a religious medal. His English was good. He was from Civitavecchia, he told Adam. His family ran *a pensione* there, and all spoke English. He was in Rome on a holiday.

Adam said, "I insist on taking you to dinner, Ernesto."

"No. no, forget that! You are my guest. Besides, hang on to your money. Rome is expensive. Save enough to come to Civitavecchia. We have a good beach. You like to swim?"

"I never learned," Adam said. "I was fat as a boy. I was afraid I would sink."

Ernesto threw his head back and laughed as though Adam was a great comedian, and Adam joined in, warmed by his friend's congeniality.

"Don't worry about my money," said Adam. "I have enough."

"But be careful in Rome, Adam. All the hands are open."

"I insist on taking you to dinner," Adam said again. "Really, Ernesto, I have enough money and more!"

Leogrande changed the subject. He told Adam that this section where they were dining was the old Ghetto.

"Some say the persecution of the Jews was bad with Hitler," said Ernesto, "but here in the Middle Ages, much worse." He told Adam that it used to be during Carnivale that the Romans rounded up the Jews and made them run race, down the whole length of the Corso, naked. "Cruelty," he said, "such terrible cruelty! What's the matter with mankind anyway, Adam?"

Adam had never talked very confidentially with anyone but Mrs. Auerbach. He found himself able to open up with Ernesto, and he told him quite a lot about Billy and Charity. "You mentioned cruelty awhile ago," he told him. "How do you think I felt when after all this time I was brushed off like a fly by Billy? I didn't even see Chary. I call her that. Pet name."

"A sad tale," said Ernesto. "Tonight we eat and drink and forget, Adam! How about that?"

The idea appealed to Adam immensely. He would be all right with Ernesto, no matter how much he drank. The trouble in the past was that he had been alone, with no one to talk to. He felt as though he could tell Ernesto anything, almost anything. The pair ordered another litre of Frascati, and clinked their glasses together in a toast to the Alban Hills, where the wine came from, Ernesto said. Ernesto was a great talker. The *trattoria* was within sight of the theater of Marcellus, and looming over the whole area was the huge, gloomy Palazzo Cenci. Ernesto told Adam about the Cenci family and the hideous crimes that stained the family name. Adam listened while he imagined himself dining at this spot with Billy and Charity, expounding as Ernesto did on the history of the area, ordering more Frascati, proposing the toast to the Alban Hills—all of it, while Billy and Charity admired his intimacy with this unfamiliar part of Rome, complimented him, perhaps, on his remarkable acclimation to Europe.

"... and I mean every crime imaginable," Ernesto was saying, "that was the Cenci family for you. Rape, murder, incest, torture—and plain old-fashioned robbery! No excuse for it—man's inhumanity to man!" He poured more wine in both their glasses. "But I do all the talking, Adam. You talk."

"What did you think of the Zumbach kidnapping?" said Adam.

"Detestable!"

"Yes. I thought so, too. At least the other one–the one in our country was not so bad."

Ernesto said. "I remember hearing of your Lindbergh child."

"Oh, this Schneider case was different. The child was returned safely."

"And his kidnappers?"

"There was only one, I think."

"Usually there are two, no?"

"I think only one in the Schneider case. A civilized sort, you know what I mean, Ernesto? He never harmed a hair on the child's head."

"Ah, well... crime is crime." Ernesto picked up the check and began adding it up.

"Please," said Adam, "I would like to pay for this. I have plenty of money on me."

Ernesto, with a wave of his hand, brushed aside Adam's offer. "On me," he said, "and in Civitavecchia, you stay at our place."

"I'll pay," said Adam.

Ernesto smiled. "Of course... there, I am in business."

"I'll come as soon as I can," said Adam. "I may even bring friends with me, my friends I told you about."

"You have forgiven them already?"

"Well–" Adam hesitated. Ernesto leaned across the table and gave Adam a friendly push with his long arm. He said, "Ah, you, you are a softie! I like you, my friend. I consider you my friend."

Adam's whole being was swollen with sudden joy.

After Ernesto paid the bill, the pair decided to have still another drink. Strega, Ernesto suggested, just the thing. Adam was a little drunk, but it was a pleasant sort of intoxication, warm and easy, not sloppy, and the only urgency, Adam's growing desire to tell Ernesto more about himself. They had a Strega after the first, and one after the second, and Adam told Ernesto how Mrs. Auerbach had left him everything, and how her sister had come along and taken it all away from him.

"But how do you have anything?" Ernesto said.

"She left me one piece of stock worth plenty of money," said Adam, and he felt bad that he had lied to his friend at their very first meeting. He want-ed to undo the lie and tell Ernesto the truth, and he was very nearly on the verge of doing just that, when suddenly Ernesto said, "Well, how about it, Adam, we find some girls now!"

"Girls?" Adam blinked, dumfounded. He had expected to stay on drinking with Ernesto, the two of them together in a great camaraderie.

"Girls!" Ernesto said again, "we're forgetting every thing tonight, aren't we?"

"1 thought we would be by ourselves," Adam said "talk more, and have more Strega."

"Three is all the Stregas we need. Too sweet. There's wine where the girls are, Adam! C'mon!" He was getting up, shoving his chair back, taking a long toothpick from his jacket and digging at his mouth with it. "It's not far away either. We can walk."

"Are you sure we want to?" Adam said. He remained sitting at the table.

Ernesto looked down at him, taking the toothpick from his mouth a moment, his face thoughtful. "Hey, there's not anything wrong with you, is there?"

"What do you mean?"

"You like girls, Adam, don't you?"

Adam's face felt hot, and he became angry. "Of course! What do you think I've been telling you about my Chary! What's the matter with you anyway! I've bee: following her all over Europe!" Adam was disappointed in Ernesto for having such a thought. He had imagined Ernesto knew him like a brother, instantly.

Ernesto laughed, came around and clapped Adam on the back. "All right then! Let's go! It's the only way to forget your Chary, my friend. I know a girl who can make a man forget his last name!"

Adam got up. He said, "But I may be too drunk."

"This girl," Ernesto laughed, "can take care of that too! "

To get there, Adam and Ernesto had to make their way through twisting streets, where the houses huddled together, their shutters closed against the heat, giving the appearance that no one lived in them; there were no lights, and only vague signs of life–a cat prowling in an ashcan, an old man on a front stoop asleep with his head in his arms, a couple pressed against the side of a building making love, and in an alleyway a few doors from their destination, a drunk urinating.

Adam smiled back at Ernesto uncertainly, and then he found himself standing in a kitchen of an old house with his friend. In the sink as they entered, a candle stuck into a wine bottle, was the only light. Ernesto called:

"*Signora! Subito! Ai! Signora!*"

A thin old woman came rushing out, shushing him. She wore a bright green satin dress, and a matching ribbon in her gray hair, rouge and eye make-up, shiny black high-heels, with no stockings and ugly blue veins on pale white legs. Ernesto spoke to her in rapid Italian, only some of which Adam caught. An American, Ernesto said, a nice girl for him, young but not too young, and other things Adam could not understand. Then there was some dickering about money, ending with Ernesto's emphatic: "Ten thousand lire!" The thin woman frowned and Ernesto pinched her cheeks, which made her laugh and agree.

"They don't know any English," said Ernesto to his companion, "so you are in a sinking ship together, ah?" He laughed, and punched Adam's arm playfully. "But before the ship goes down, you–" he made an obscene gesture. Then he left through the beaded curtains with a blond girl, who appeared suddenly and the thin woman pushed a brunette in Adam's direction. She was smoking a cigarette, the hot ash dangerously close to her lips, her hands folded across an immense bosom. She shrugged and walked toward Adam, indicating with her thumb that he should follow her. He held out the lire to her, and with another jerk of her thumb, she indicated that he should give it to the thin woman. Then Adam followed her down a dark and narrow hall, into a very small room, with a bed in it, a screen hiding what seemed to be another sink, a white bowl on a table beside the bed, and a hassock with fringes on its side. The girl took her clothes off without a word. Adam removed his shirt, and stood helplessly by the bed. The naked girl came across the carpet scratching her arms, lighting another cigarette. Adam sat on the bed and removed his shoes. From behind the bed table, the girl took out a bottle of wine. She offered some to Adam in a dirty glass. He wanted to decline, but he wanted a drink just as badly.

She spoke to him in Italian. "Is that all?" meaning, was that all he was going to take off.

Adam shrugged, and she shrugged. She said, "Ready?"

Adam sighed. He started to undo his pants. The girl walked over and began to help him. "You don't want to take them off?"

"No."

She bent and tried to kiss him. She smelled of something like rotten peach pits, and Adam could not bear it. He turned away. The girl asked him a question he could not understand. She repeated it, and he understood the sentence after: "Is that what you want?"

"Drunk," said Adam, and in Italian: "Intoxicated."

In English the girl said, "I take care. I know."

She pushed Adam back in a gentle way which surprised him, and he realized as his head hit the pillow and he shut his eyes, that he was dizzy, that his drinks had caught up with him at last. It did not matter at all, for he found out that nothing was expected of him, and afterwards, he slept.

15

Dear Billy and Chary,

How is everything? I hope you are enjoying your stay in Roma as I am. After I left Billy last night at the Mediterraneo, I went across the street and had some drinks. I made the acquaintance of a very nice chap from Civitavecchia–a real Italian! We went on the town together, and believe me, it was great fun! We hope to do it again very soon.

I left your wedding presents with the desk clerk. You don't have to thank me. I realize they are long overdue, but then we sort of lost track of one another, didn't we? Bygones be bygones–here we are in The Eternal City! How about having dinner with me one night this week? There's a fascinating *trattoria* on Portico di Ottavia, where I would like you to be my guests. Please call me here at the hotel any day between noon and two. I'll wait for your call.

Believe me I hope your marriage is a great success! Billy mentioned Dorothy Schackleford the other night, saying she had a job here. I would like her address, if it is not any trouble. How on earth did you get together with her, not that I have anything against her–just curious.

If I seemed slightly nervous the other night, please understand that I was under some strain. I have been traveling incessantly this past year. I kept thinking I'd run into you, but no such luck. Anyway, as I said, here we are reunited. Let's make the most of it. I'll be waiting to hear from you.

Always,
Adam.

Adam had written the note to Billy and Charity three days ado, the morning he returned from his night with Ernesto. Before he had parted from his new friend, he had loaned him a little less than twenty-five dollars. Ernesto explained that the blond had helped herself to his wallet, that after he got some sleep he would go back to the house and demand the return of his money.

"You have to watch their kind," said Ernesto, "and to think they would try it with me, a good customer!"

"I have a funny feeling, Ernesto, that I talked to the girl I was with, told her some things I don't want anyone to know."

Ernesto had laughed, "She speaks no English, Adam! Forget it!"

"It may have been a dream anyway."

"A dream, of course. You were fast asleep when I pounded on your door. She must have been good."

The conversation had taken place at dawn on the Via Monte Cenci. They shook hands, Ernesto explaining that he stayed within walking distance, that Adam would find a taxi-stand three blocks over. Ernesto said he would come to Adam's hotel the next night, when he got his money back. He would repay Adam then.

"I wish you would just keep it, Ernesto, a gift from me."

"Nah! Nah!" And with a wave of his hand, "Tomorrow, Adam," he was gone.

Now he sat opposite Adam, in Adam's small room at the Delle Nazioni. He smoked a cigar and wore the same brown-and-black checkered sport coat, and blue slacks. His shirt was different, a gaudy yellow one with Aloha written across it countless times in blue, and white flowers splashed in between. Adam would have liked to give him one of his shirts, but he was familiar with Ernesto's stubborn pride.

"So you thought I would not show up, ah?" Ernesto laughed.

"I'm glad you're here. Not for the money." When Ernesto had entered the room, the first thing he had done was to slap the fifteen thousand lire onto the bureau top.

"What have you done since Wednesday, Adam?"

"Nothing, really."

"You have no business?"

"Oh, I have investments, you see, Ernesto."

"Good! I like to have my friends free from care!" Ernesto walked around Adam's room puffing on his cigar, admiring a tie of Adam's ("You can have it", said Adam—Ernesto would not hear of it) and Adam's military brushes, and his cowhide luggage. Adam watched him, wishing he could have the courage to unburden himself to Ernesto. Adam could still not get it out of his mind that he had told the brunette—everything. Still it was all mixed up with a dream of meeting the Cenci family, and running naked down the length of the Corso, while Billy laughed and threw poodle-shaped cuff links with ruby eyes, at his body.

Over a bottle of Maccarese Adam sent for, they talked. Ernesto told Adam of his father's illness, which he had heard of just two days ago. "Serious," said Ernesto, "and perhaps it will mean I will take a job for a while here in Rome." He explained that his sisters could help his mother run their place in Civitavecchia; that it would be better if he found something to pay well. Guide work, he thought; he had once worked as a guide at the Colosseum, another time as one in the Palazzo Pitti in Florence.

"But Ernesto," Adam interrupted, "let me help you. Let me lend you money for your father."

Ernesto looked embarrassed. He changed the subject immediately. Did Adam like the brunette the other night?

"I'm sorry," he said, not waiting for Adam's answer; "she was probably a pig. I hear she takes everything off. Even among whores that is thought indecent. A good whore, Adam, always keeps her stockings on. There is an expression we have here. We say that a whore who takes her stockings off is not in business. You see? She enjoys taking her clothes off. A whore is not supposed to enjoy her work. Only a pig-whore." He bit the end off another cigar, which he took from his shirt pocket. "The occupation spoiled her, Adam. She knew all the soldier, always joking and laughing with the Germans. Then with the Americans."

Adam's heart missed a beat. "But she doesn't know English?"

"Who knows what a pig knows, Adam?"

"But you said she didn't."

"She probably doesn't."

"Ernesto," said Adam, "The other night she said something in English to me. I remember. She said it very plainly: 'I'll take care of you.' I believe that was it."

Ernesto grunted. "You should have shoved her face in the wall, the pig. I hope you told her you would take care of things, not her! They do anything to save their backs, their kind."

Adam was perspiring, his heart hammering. "You don't understand, Ernesto. I think I told her something. I don't know if I dreamed it, or if I told her—but she could get me in trouble, Ernesto, if I did say it—if she speaks English!"

"You, Adam? You're making a joke on me. What could you have done so bad! Forget it!"

"Ernesto, I'm telling you, it could get me in trouble."

Ernesto took his cigar out of his mouth, leaned forward in the leather chair and said, "My friend, you are serious, aren't you?"

"Yes. It's—well, a long story. It's—but I don't like to tell it." Adam was thinking that it was not that he did not trust Ernesto; it was that he was afraid Ernesto would dislike him. "Crime is crime," Ernesto had said the other night.

Ernesto stopped Adam from continuing. "You are in trouble.‑

"Not yet. It's not really bad." He was remembering that the other night when he told Ernesto how the Schneider boy had been returned without a scratch, Ernesto seemed unsympathetic. Crime is crime... Adam said, "It just might look bad. I wouldn't want someone like that girl to know it."

"Are you sure she does?"

"No, no! That's just it. I'm in the dark! Ernesto, I'll tell you about it. You see–"

But Ernesto held his large hand up. "Stop, Adam! Don't trust anyone! I don't want to know, do you see? If you are guilty of something, I don't want to know. Then you would never think I gave you away."

"I'd never think that," said Adam.

"Good! But don't tell me. Trust no one, Adam, particularly not someone you know less than a week."

Adam smiled. "You are wonderful, Ernesto."

"Nah! Listen, my friend, I'll go and visit that place tonight. I'll find out if you said anything or not. Believe nee, I'll not listen to whatever it is, if you did say it. I'll stop her from repeating it, but I'll find out... If you said some‑thing, well–that can be fixed. A pair of stockings, a pretty dress–those pigs don't know enough to be vicious. Besides, you probably exaggerate your wrong. I know you."

Adam said, "I don't exaggerate it.... I could tell you this much–"

"*Basta!*" Ernesto stopped him. "I don't want to hear."

They finished the bottle of Maccarese. Ernesto said he must hunt a job. Adam was able to convince him to borrow at least a hundred dollars, half to buy clothes he would need for a job (he had brought only a few shirts for his holiday in Rome) and half to send immediately to his father.

Adam planned to spend the afternoon searching for another gift for Luther Schneider. He changed his clothes and took a shower, then headed for the Via dei Coronari, where there were antique shops specializing in silver. At the Via Veneto, he could not resist stopping for a cold beer. Over the drink he lost interest in his afternoon's plan. Why should he buy Schneider any more gifts? Schneider had really not had faith in him; he had simply feared for Timmy's life. The money Schneider had paid Adam was nothing to a man that rich, no more than the sixty thousand lire Adam had handed to Ernesto. Why had Adam not seen that before? It would be ri‑diculous to buy another gift for Schneider. Adam chuckled to himself. Ernesto had been right last night when he had called Adam a softie. Look at the way Billy and Chary were treating him, and after Adam had taken such pain, to pick out presents they would enjoy. Adam wished he had told Ernesto about that! Ernesto would have had something to say about that sort of shabby treatment. Adam smiled as he finished his beer. He could see Ernesto's dark eyes flashing with anger, see him grabbing Billy by the fancy narrow shawl lapels of his dinner jacket, hear Ernesto shouting, "Adam is my friend, do you understand! Apologize to my friend!" . . Adam ordered a Martini when he finished his beer. "What do you mean making a friend of mine wait around day after day for your phone call!" Ernesto would demand... "and don't call him Addie any more!" said Ernesto over Adam's third Martini, and gently, Adam put his hand on Ernesto's arm to restrain him. A look of gratitude came in Billy's eyes. "Thank you, Adam. Thanks a lot."...

It was anger that made Billy's eyes so hard.

"How the hell much longer are you going to keep this up!"

Instinct, impulse—whatever it was that had led Adam toward the vicinity of the Via Nazionale, onto the Via Cavour, to the Mediterraneo, it was opportunely timed. Adam stepped over Billy's luggage, walking right past Billy as he stood holding open the door to his room. "Where are you going?" Adam said. "Were you going without telling me, Billy?"

"You know, Addie, you're sick! I mean, you're very sick" Billy let the door swing shut, and he crossed to one of the twin beds and an open suitcase into which he was putting shirts and balls of socks. "Why don't you go see a doctor, Addie?"

"You're not wearing your present," Adam said. Billy was wearing a green robe with a faint charcoal gray stripe in it, some sort of cotton fabric, with a shirt under it, and light gray pants.

"Okay, Addie, let's stop talking about the presents. They're right where you left them, at the downstairs desk. I'd pick them up on my way out, if I were you, exchange them. And incidentally, Addie," he said, turning and facing Adam with the same hard look to his eyes, "When I was in New York this spring, I found out you were going around saying you were me. I got my cuff links back too. What's with you, Addie? Do you need a head-shrinker or something?"

Adam said, "Why do you live in the past so, Billy? Here we are in Rome together. Can't we be friendly?"

"You've been drinking, too," said Billy. "You never could drink, could you?" He slipped his robe off then, and began folding it. "Why don't you lay off the stuff? See your friend Dorothy Schackleford. I tell you she's with some group who helps people."

"Ever since we were children you've wanted to insult me and hurt my feelings, haven't you, Billy?"

"Rubbish!" Billy dropped the folded robe on the shirts in his suitcase. "Here, I'll write down her address. I've got it somewhere here in my book." He was fumbling through the pages of a small, green leather address book, with fleurs-de-lys stamped on it. From Florence, Adam thought; Adam had bought a cigarette case, the stamping identical... so they had been to Florence, too, and he had missed them there as well. Or had they been running from him? Were they running from him now, again? And where was Chary? Why hadn't he seen Chary yet?

"Here it is," said Billy. "I'll jot it down for you... You know, Adam, you have a tendency to exaggerate almost everything. For example this crap about our being childhood friends. Now you know damn well who I hung around with–Dick Nolan and Pete MacGuire... Now hell, Addie, why aren't you just more realistic? We only saw each other two or three times a month when we were kids! Here–" he handed Adam a card with an address scribbled on it. "We ran into Dorothy one afternoon on the Via Veneto. She asked about you."

Billy closed the lid of the suitcase, and snapped the silver locks. "That does it," he said. "Well, Addie–" holding out his hand, "This is it."

"And Chary? Where's Chary?"

"She's not here, obviously!"

"Then there is trouble!" Adam smiled. He sat down on the bed. "I knew it wouldn't be long before it all came out.,,

"There isn't any trouble Addie, and you have to get out now."

"Without seeing Chary?" Adam's eyes began to fill.

"And cut out the Chary, Addie! Since when do *you* call her Chary!"

"It's too bad you're leaving before you meet my new business partner," said Adam. "His name is Ernesto. We're opening a beach club in Civitavecchia." As he said it, Adam decided it was a very good idea. He and Ernesto could expand his family's *pensione.*

Billy was running around checking drawers and closets for anything he might have forgotten. Adam said, "We're opening a very interesting club, the club–" he searched for some name, thought of Ernesto's shirt with Aloha splashed across it, and after a few more bullet associations, said: "The State Fifty, is what we're calling it. We're sort of using a Hawaiian theme. We might even call it The Fiftieth Star. We don't have it all figured out yet," said Adam, following Billy around back and forth as he talked. "We have long discussions about it. What do *you* think we ought to call it, Billy?"

Billy slammed the door of the bathroom cabinet, colliding with Adam in the entranceway. "Get the hell out of here, will you, Addie, or do I have to call the manager!"

Adam was stunned. He had felt that everything had been going all right, and now Billy had suddenly turned on him, without any explanation.

"Billy," said Adam, "it's a wonder you have any friends."

Billy looked as though he were actually going to punch Adam in the nose then, but as he took a step forward, a key turned in the lock, and into the room came Charity.

"Chary!" Adam said. There was a small spray of babies'-breath pinned to her light gray suit, and her black hair vas piled on top of her head, and held by silver combs; and at her ears, silver loop earrings, like gypsys', but she was not smiling, merely looking at Adam as though he were a bellhop or some other casual intruder. And again, Adam exclaimed, "Chary!" and began walking toward her.

All at once, she began to giggle, and the giggle grew into laughter, and Adam stood before her bewildered as she tossed her head back the way a man might, and laughed that very hard, wild, uncontrollable way there is of laughing.

"Oh my, migod," she managed, before another fit of the same type laughter, while Adam stood very embarrassed, yet distracted from his embarrassment slightly by the thought that something was different about Chary.

"You've changed," he said.

"I have, oh, Addie, my, migod!" and there seemed to be no end to her laughter.

Billy, who had come around to stand beside her, was even smiling, and for the barest few seconds Adam thought that here it was as he had always planned it, the three of them together, joking, old friends, and Adam grinned broadly, stroked his beard, his eyes twinkling at his friends. Ah, this is the way it should always have been, and would have been too had I ever caught up with you last fall... he said to them, "You know I've looked forward to this moment for eons!" And it dawned on him then why Chary looked different. She too had taken on some weight.

"Your added weight becomes you," said Adam.

She had turned to Billy and was telling him something about train times. Adam tried to hear, but she spoke too low.

"But wait a minute," Adam said, "We're not going to leave it at this, are we? Aren't we at least all going to have dinner tonight?"

"Out!" Billy said suddenly. He was pointing at the door with his finger, watching Adam carefully, waiting for Adam to go, of all things.

It must be a joke, and Adam laughed. "Down, boy!" he said, making his own joke. He smiled at Chary. "You really look good with that added weight. You ought to stay that way."

She put her hand to her mouth, palm in, as though she were going to catch something–a pit of some sort, or as though she might cough or sneeze, and Adam was slightly surprised to see she was simply laughing again–trying hard not to, but there you are–it was laughter, choked back. He wondered if she were herself.

"Why is Chary so silly? Is she doped up or something?"

Adam thought of the way Timmy used to giggle just as the sleeping pills took; the way Timmy would chuckle in his sleep.

"Come on, Addie!" and now Billy was actually pulling Adam along by the arm.

"Make him stop, Char!" Adam said.

"That's right, Adam. Ask a pregnant woman for help!" said Billy.

Pregnant. Chary was pregnant–that was the difference.

"It's still not too late, Chary," Adam said. "If you're not happy, it's my fault, and I'll still–" but he could not finish. He felt dizzy suddenly, very strange, and tired too. Gin always made him tired. "Let go, let go," his own voice sounded far away to him, but Billy took his hands off Adam. He said, "Go on now, Addie. We try to be nice, but it's way out of hand now."

"Yes," Adam said. "It is."

He remembered something Melnik had said to him. "You didn't get yourself into this mess because of that girl. You hardly know that girl. You can't fight an enemy by boxing with the shadow."

Billy was facing him then, and Adam staggered a bit as he moved toward him. He caught hold of Billy's shoulders, and it was in his mind to strike Billy, but instead, he began to try to tickle him.

"What the hell!" Billy shoved him away.

"I only wanted you to laugh," said Adam. He could see Charity's face over Billy's shoulder. The expression was grave now, she was frowning, and her eyes squinting, as though she must look very hard to believe what she saw.

Adam said, "Yes, it's me, Chary. It's Adam."

"Billy, let's get some help," she said.

They were both regarding him in a most peculiar way, as though there were actually something very wrong with him.

Adam held his forehead with his hand. "I–have to use your bathroom," he said.

"The bell–" Billy started to say, but it was too late already. Suddenly before he could reach anywhere, Adam was ill. Over the noise of his own vomiting, he could hear Billy cursing, violently, obscenely. Chary had run to the telephone. Adam began to cry and vomit at the same time. Billy only cared about his suitcases, and he was busy pulling them out of the way, but they were already soiled.

16

"From Venice, a postcard saying Chary had a boy, 6 lbs. There is no reason to suspect they would name it after me, and I did not even broach the possibility to Dorothy, but it does not seem unlikely."

FROM ADAM BLESSING'S JOURNAL

Adam glanced at his watch. She was already ten minutes late. Later and later getting off to her meetings every time Ernesto came by. It had been going on for a month. He had moved into Dorothy's small apartment on the Via Po, the day after Billy and Chary left Rome. Since then he had not touched liquor, not even so much as a glass of wine with his meals; and as he had promised Dorothy, he had not tried to communicate with Billy and Chary, though he knew the address of their apartment in Venice. Occasionally they sent Dorothy a card, and Adam thought how like Billy that was, to pretend a friendship with her, while he ignored Adam. Billy only did it to spite Adam, of that Adam was convinced, but he let Dorothy think what she wanted to.

"You should be glad they called me instead of the police," Dorothy had said to him once.

"But I have no reason to fear the police," Adam told her.

"You just don't get the point, Adam"–her answer.

It was Dorothy Schackleford who did not get the point. She believed everything Billy said, all about Adam making Chary afraid that night he had gone to their room at the Mediterraneo, all about Adam acting "strangely," every lie Billy told. Now she wanted to help Adam. Adam, she said, was an alcoholic. She had even tried to drag him to one of her "meetings." "You can't just wander around all day with nothing to do," she said; "once you admit you're an alcoholic, you're free, Adam. You can look for work, do something with your life"... Adam smiled to himself. He had plans. He let her go on thinking that he had inherited the *Stammbuch* from Mrs. Auerbach, that he was living off *that* money. He even tolerated her harangues about his lack of feeling. Adam did not feel anything, she said, not for anyone. What was the matter with Adam anyway?... He supposed she had still never gotten over being stood up by Adam on the evening of Mrs. Auerbach's service. Sometimes when she accused Adam of not even being grateful to Mrs. Auerbach for leaving him the *Stammbuch*, he felt like

shouting out the truth. Instead, he sat listening to her with a small grin tipping his lips. He could take it. He knew the score. He could see that before
very long, Dorothy Schackleford would turn against him too. Women had
always let Adam down in a way that made him look as though he had done
the wrong. More and more lately, he thought of the faceless woman
plopped down on the straight-back wooden chair in the kitchen of years-
ago: "And a lot *you* care!" she had said.... "And a lot *you* care!"

Dorothy Schackleford finally left for her meeting, not without admon-
ishing Adam for the hundredth time, "Not even a beer now, Adam. Nothing!"

"She really has love for you, Adam," said Ernesto.

"She wants to save me," Adam said. They chuckled and Ernesto said,
"Still–it is nice someone cares, ah?"

"*If* someone does," said Adam. "People have been known to marry people without caring for them, even have babies with them."

"That again!" Ernesto grunted. "Hey, let's go to the park! I have new
things to work out with you, Adam.""

"I wish we would do more than talk," Adam told him. "Isn't our place
built yet?"

"Adam, it is not America. You wait until you see poor little Civitavecchia.
Labor is cheap, but not plentiful."

"I want to see it," said Adam. "Why can't we go there and see it?"

Ernesto said, "In time. It will be a big surprise all at once. Then we'll tell
Dorothy all about it, too."

Sometimes when Adam was alone during the daytime, when he took
long walks through the Borghese Gardens, he fantasized that one day far-
off, Luther Schneider would visit Civitavecchia, even bring Timmy with
him. Adam would see that they got the best of everything. He would stop
by their table and chat with them. In some of Adam's fantasies, he would
hand Schneider an envelope which contained every single cent he owed
him, with interest besides. In others, he would hand Schneider a card
which said: ADAMO'S, Civitavecchia, Italy–Manager: Adam Blessing.
Owner: Luther Schneider.

Schneider would say: "You know, son, originally I expressed faith in you
simply because I feared for Timmy's safety. But now... Adam, I think of you
the same way I think of Timmy."

They would become devoted to one another, Schneider and Adam.

Schneider would say: "I love Timmy, but he's never been a real son to me,
poor little devil. *You* though, Adam–"

Strolling by the ilex trees in the Villa Borghese that evening, Ernesto seemed worried.

"Is something going wrong, Ernesto?"

"You are perceptive, Adam, one of the most perceptive people I have ever known. It was not my intention to burden you with more troubles."

"But, I haven't had to do any of the worrying, Ernesto. You've done everything!"

It was true. Ernesto had handled everything. From the very beginning, when Adam had proposed the club in Civitavecchia, it was Ernesto who had gotten an architect to draw up the plans, hassled with builders for a moderate price, gone back and forth to Civitavecchia to pick the land, and oversee the installation of the groundwork; and it was Ernesto who had handled the whole emergency with the equipment, when the workers were drilling for water. Had it not been for his friend, that emergency would have cost Adam ten times the amount. Ernesto's fiery ways, and his familiarity with the region and its people, had been a priceless asset. Ernesto had refused Adam's offer of a regular salary. He had been hurt by it. Since his father had recovered so rapidly from his illness, there was no more emergency, Ernesto pointed out, and he would live on his savings until the club was operating. Adam was accustomed to Ernesto's proud ways by now. As eager as he was to go to Civitavecchia with Ernesto and see the progress that had been made already, he understood Ernesto's reluctance to have Adam see anything before it was perfect. In the past two weeks, he had snapped a few pictures of the place under construction, but even these he was apologetic about. "You really can't tell how it will be," he would say. "I hate to even show you them, but I know your eagerness." Adam felt a thrill of accomplishment when he viewed the photographs. At last he was on his way to what Melnik had prescribed: a business of his own, and it would be a busy one at that.

"Adam, I worry. We are spending too much of your money."

"But that isn't so!"

"I feel bad about letting that rotten whore bribe you!"

"I–Forget that, Ernesto. A thousand dollars–that was cheap! Listen, I could have been taken for much more. Why won't you let me tell you about it?"

Ernesto shook his head. "No. I don't want to hear. I never should have taken you there in the first place. I feel bad about it."

We have so much to look forward to," said Adam. "I've forgotten all about that whore. Besides, I may not even have told her anything!"

"All the worse. I paid her your money for nothing then."

Adam said, "Ernesto, I don't care! I've forgotten it!"

"Now in Civitavecchia, more bad news."

"Your father?"

Ernesto sighed and shook his head. "No, Adam. it's the installation of the air-conditioning. The way it is now, the lines can't hold that much power. If we are going to have air-conditioning throughout Adamo's, we have to make arrangements for extra lines, to connect farther down. Otherwise we knock out everyone's electricity in the area."

"Is that all?" Adam laughed, and clapped his around his friend's shoulder. "I thought your father was taking a turn for the worse."

"I am a thrifty man, Adam."

"I know, but we have to put more money into it, that's all."

"I worry that we will run out."

"Dorothy's been talking to you," said Adam. "Isn't that true?"

He knew that whenever Dorothy could, behind his back, she discussed Adam with Ernesto. It had been Ernesto's idea to tell her that he was in Rome buying equipment for a new place on the coast–his folks' place. Dorothy was always comparing Adam with Ernesto; look how busy *he* is, Adam; and aren't you ashamed sometimes when Ernesto comes to visit and you see how hard *he's* worked all week?... Again, Adam would sit listening with the grin tipping his lips... he would hear Dorothy off in the other room of her apartment, whispering to Ernesto about Adam's need to be busy, about Adam's money becoming depleted day by day.... Several times it had become nearly unbearable, and he had begged Ernesto to let him tell Dorothy, but always Ernesto wanted things to be perfect.

"She tells me you imagine things, Adam. Oh, I know women, but I don't want you to pretend with me that you have more than you do."

"I can prove it," said Adam, "Let me prove it."

"No, no, I don't want any proof! I trust you. We're partners."

"Then what are you worried about?"

"I'm afraid you will be shocked by the amount we need next, Adam. I wonder if you realize how expensive these things are. Me, I'm experienced, even with a place as small as my family's–but you, Adam."

"Well?" said Adam. "How much?"

"Another $25,000," Ernesto answered.

Adam laughed. "So! I'll make a trip to New York! That amount I don't have with me, but I can fly to New York and back in less than a week. To tell you the truth, I wouldn't mind a trip. I think–"

"I could probably get the figure down," Ernesto said. "Say, $15,000."

"Oh yes, I have that left. Yes."

Ernesto slapped Adam's knee. "Good! Then you don't have to leave. I'll get him down, Adam. I can. I can make different arrangements."

"I don't mind a trip. Really, Ernesto!" The more Adam thought about a quick trip to New York, the more the idea appealed to him.

"No!" Ernesto said flatly.

"Why?"

"Because I need your advice, my friend. This is a crucial time. We are nearing completion."

"But it would only take me—"

"No, Adam!"

Adam was surprised at the sharp tone. He turned and looked at his friend's face.... But Ernesto smiled then, the large white smile which always reassured Adam: "Adam," said Ernesto, "I have a fear of planes and of friends on them. Now you will not have to fly in an airplane, and I am glad!"

The next day at breakfast, Adam read in a guidebook of a shop named Sirotta on Via Sistina. Among the various items the shop specialized in, the words "babies' bibs" had caught Adam's eye.

17

Vittorio Gelsi, 42, of 7 Via Monte Cenci was arrested this morning after a murder attempt. His wife, Maria, is in the hospital. Her condition is reported as critical. During an argument over money, Gelsi admitted stabbing her in the back. Tonia Gelsi, his sister, called police. A sometime "guide" for various tourist agencies, Gelsi was once fired by The Italian-Rome Scenic Tours Association for accepting money in advance from tourists for reservations in non-existent beach hotels in Ostia, Civitavecchia and Umbria. He served a three-year sentence for this offence, and several other, smaller terms for pickpocketing and soliciting as a pimp.

FROM THE ROME AMERICAN

The *carabiniere* smiled at Adam. "But he has admitted it, *Signore.*"

In Adam's hand were the photographs of Ernesto, the same he had seen in the newspaper, above the story of the murder attempt. Vittorio Gelsi, and after his name, a number.

The *carabiniere* said, "He has not take your money, I hope. He has take money from Americans before this thing."

"No," Adam lied.

"Why he call himself Ernesto to you? You call him Ernesto Leogrande? Is that he said his name is?"

"Vittorio Gelsi. The other name is–a joke. I know his name." Adam put the pictures on the officer's desk. "I want to help him. I am his friend."

"Pray for his wife, *Signore.* That will be most help."

"Well? Can I see him?"

"Not against his will, *Signore.* Prisoners have rights, too. He does not want to see you."

"He is embarrassed," said Adam. "I don't blame him. I still want to help him."

The officer shrugged. He smiled at Adam. "You can make a complaint if he has take your money."

"I don't want to make a complaint! Don't you see?"

"No." The *carabiniere* smiled again.

"If his wife is all right, will he be released?"

"He attempt murder, *Signore.*"

Adam sighed. "I will go see his wife."

"Si, *Signore.*"

"I will do all I can for him," said Adam.

"That is not the business of the *questúra*," said the police officer.

The questúra was in an old palazzo in the center of Rome. The walls were khaki-colored, and there was an institutional atmosphere, brightened by the handsomely uniformed *carabinieri* stationed at the outer doors. As Adam came into the heat outside, he saw Dorothy taking pictures of the *carabinieri*. She smiled and waved at him, and it irritated him that she was not upset. At dinner last night, she had said she was just glad Ernesto had not gotten his hands on the money of the Fellow's Foundation. He had mentioned a building in Umbria to her, ideal, he had told her, for a headquarters for the Fellow's. The government would lease it for very little; there were just a few things to be repaired, and Ernesto had promised to get an estimate for the Fellow's, and handle the negotiations.

Adam had said, "But even if he is a crook, don't you feel something for him?"

"Sorry for him," had been her answer. "In fact, I'm going to speak about him at our next session."

Dorothy knew nothing about the $25,000 Ernesto had taken from Adam. Nor about the additional $15,000 be had failed to collect from Adam before his arrest. That money, plus $5000 more was all Adam had left, other than the $10,000 in the safety deposit box in South Orange, New Jersey.

When Dorothy saw Adam, she waved and called to him, snapping his picture as he walked toward her.

"Did you see him?"

"No."

"This isn't going to make you start drinking, I hope."

"No."

"I have to be back at the office in half an hour. Adam, I wish you'd visit Fellow's. Just to see it. Not join it. Just see it."

"I have things to do."

"No gifts, Adam. Please, don't send any more gift to Venice."

"I didn't send *gifts!* I sent a gift. A baby-bib!"

"Returned."

"All right, they returned it. That was weeks ago, and it's all over. I don't mind telling you that I don't even think about Chary any more. Let her do as she pleases. I have too much on my mind now. A way to help Ernesto."

"You mean, Vittorio."

"Don't nag at me, Dorothy."

"Do you have something wrong with your eyes, Adam?"

"No."

"They look funny," she said. "Almost as though you were crying."

"Before I go to the hospital," said Adam, his head turned away from her so she could not see his eyes, "I'll stop by and pick up the mail at the apartment."

"Remember to call me if we hear from Shirley? I'm dying to know when she gets here."

"By now," said Adam, "she's probably dancing again."

Dorothy Schackleford was saying something about Shirley Spriggs having vowed not to dance for two years, and only one year was up, but for some reason, Adam was fighting back his tears with a greater urgency then, so that he was forced to cut short their conversation with the excuse that he needed a men's room, and that he would meet Dorothy at the Via Po apartment when she returned from work.

In the small *trattoría* where he found a men's room, Adam stayed to have lunch. He ordered *Zuppa di cozze,* and a mezzo-lítro of soáve. It was the first alcohol he had tasted since he had seen Billy and Chary, less the two months ago. Yesterday in Civitavecchia he had ordered a whisky in a place called Cucci's, but he had been unable to lift the glass, his hands were trembling so, his eyes filling with tears to a point where he felt people staring at him.

It was in Civitavecchia that he had finally begun to accept Ernesto's deception. Even after he saw Ernesto's picture in the paper, and went for the first time to the *questúra* to straighten out what he felt was an alarming case of mistaken identity, he was unconvinced that Ernesto had deceived him. He had gone to Civitavecchia a day later on the bus. As he rode along the old Via Aurelia, he smiled at the idea Ernesto had taken his money with no intention to ever build an Adamo's. Adamo's would be there, perhaps even finished (except for the air-conditioning, which he had never had the opportunity to pay Ernesto for). Despite Ernesto's wrongs, their dream of Adamo's in Civitavecchia was not among them.

There in Civitavecchia was the very building from the pictures Ernesto had shown Adam. Adam's heart had missed some beats at the sign: Cucci's... it was just remodeled, the waiter assured Adam, and Adam had sat out on the terrace waiting for his whisky, thinking of how often in his imagination he had sat on this same terrace, entertaining Luther Schneider, and Billy and Chary, laughing and talking on this same terrace.... Less than a week before he had come here to Civitavecchia, on one of Ernesto's and his walks through the Villa Borghese, Ernesto had told him that the terrace had been widened, that Adamo's would have the finest view of the sea in all Italy.

"You make me feel so happy, Ernesto," Adam had told him.

"Not *lèi*, Adam." Ernesto had seized Adam's wrist and pressed it with his palm. "*Tu*. We are friends. No longer *lèi,* but *tu.*"

When the waiter brought Adam the whisky on the terrace at Cucci's, Adam had remembered Ernesto's touching invitation to Adam to use the familiar form of address. He had left the whisky and run off, and since then at odd times, Adam would find his eyes filling up, as they had moment before coming to the *trattoria,* when he was leaving the *questúra* with Dorothy.

Adam poured his wine and began to eat his mussels.

When he finished lunch he would visit Ernesto's wife in the hospital. He would reason with her. It would do her no good if Ernesto were to go to prison again.

Adam remembered what the waiter at Cucci's had said: "I come from these parts, *Signore.* There has never been a family named Leogrande, nor one named Gelsi who run *the pensione* you ask about. That name, both of them, I can tell you is not of anyone around here."

And in Adam's mind had come the retort: "Not yet, but wait!"

For there was still time, still some money left.

"*Tu*. We are friends," Ernesto had said, and Adam felt forgiveness was the only obstacle in their way now. Adam would forgive him all, just as Ernesto had tacitly forgiven Adam for a crime he would not even allow Adam to confess to him.

18

August 5

Dear Billy and Chary,

I am writing this after a visit to a friend's wife. I am upset because she is dead, and it will cause my friend a great deal of trouble. There is no point in going into it all, since we are so out of touch, and no longer seem to know the same people. However, I think of you often, even though we are not as close as we once were. I am sorry that you did not like the baby's bib. I wish you had enclosed a note telling me what was wrong with it, as I want to exchange it for something you might like better. You are certainly hard people to buy gifts for! I never seem to get you something that pleases you.

Tonight from America a friend of Dorothy's is arriving named Shirley Spriggs. She is on her honeymoon with her husband Norman. This will keep us busy, but we always think of you two. I cannot tell you how happy I am that you are still married and everything is going well. I trust it is, or I would have heard otherwise. It is all right that you don't write because I know you are busy with the baby. Is it a boy, and if so, what did you name him? I am not fishing for compliments by that statement, because I can understand perfectly if you named him after either one of your fathers. My best to both of you and continued good wishes for a happy marriage. My best also to Mrs. Cadwallader when you see her.

Yours,
Adam.

August 6

Tonia tells me you are bother at the hospital and everyplace, come even here to the *questúra*. No money is owe you if you think that, and if you try to say there is money owe you, how do you prove? Stay away from my life.
Vittorio Gelsi.

August 8

Dear Billy and Chary,
I am writing this to you about Adam. He has started drinking again. He is very upset because a man who posed as his friend has turned out to be a crook, and now it seems, even a murderer. I do not want to bother you with this. I know you dislike Adam, and I can appreciate the reasons. It is just that lately I am worried about him to a point where I will do anything

I can to help him. I believe he has practically exhausted his money from the sale of the *Stammbuch,* and I am not disinclined to think this crook also got some of that money. Adam mentioned once that he was in a hospital. This is what I am writing you about. I know he writes to you, and I know Billy talked with him a bit while you were both in Rome. Did he mention the hospital, or the doctor? Either or both would help me. Last night he called some florist in New York long distance and begged to have a charge account reinstated. I don't know what any of this means, but as you can see, things here are not so good. If you know anything that might help me find out the name of the hospital, I would be grateful.

Here at Fellow's we are set up to handle mental illness as well as other problems, but Adam will have nothing to do with the organization. I used to think he was simply an alcoholic, but sometimes I wonder. My best to you both, and forgive this intrusion, but it's necessary.

Dorothy Schackleford.

The *carabiniere* smiled at Adam. "All right, *Signore.* He has consent. You wait and in a moment, you can see him."

Adam went and sat on a straw-bottomed chair opposite the police officer's desk. He had not had a drink in twenty-four hours, not since the fight with Dorothy over the fact he had found her letter to Billy and Chary, opened it and destroyed it after he read it. Well, he had expected Dorothy to turn on him; it was just a matter of time. He supposed Shirley and Norman had triggered it, and as he waited to see Ernesto, he promised himself he would not return to the Via Po until they were out of Rome for good. Dorothy had made reservations down the street at the *pensione* for them, and for the past four days, the pair were forever intruding on Adam. Norman had even tried to talk to Adam "man-to-man", as Norman put it, about Adam's drinking. The whole apartment had taken on the atmosphere of The Salvation Army, and Adam was tired of it. Last night Adam had suggested Norman take Shirley dancing, which was the occasion for a crying jag on Shirley's part, intermixed with sniffling memories of Ginger Klein's demise, and a threat to punch Adam in the nose from Norman.

Norman had even had the gall to ask Adam what his intentions were toward Dorothy.

"What are hers toward me?" Adam had answered him. "To betray me to my best friends?"

The *carabiniere* signaled to Adam to follow him, while another officer took his place at the desk. Adam went behind the *carabiniere* up a dirty, badly-lighted staircase. At a dark passage, down a narrow corridor, the *carabiniere* took a key from a chain attached to his uniform, and unlocked a door. In this room, in front of another closed door, sat a young policeman with his cap perched sideways on his mass of black curly hair.

"Signor Gelsi," said the *carabiniere.*

He turned to Adam with another of his cryptic smiles. "Any time you want to sign a *denuncio,"* he shrugged, "it might make you feel better, *Signore."* He tipped his hand to his cap, and walked out of the room. The policeman with the black curly hair pointed at a doorway, and Adam went inside. He sat on a bench and waited.

Friends come first, Adam thought, and he felt himself begin to choke up. When he saw Ernesto, he would say nothing about his shock at the knowledge that the woman in green from the whorehouse, was Ernesto's wife... nothing about Tonia, either, the brunette whore whom Adam had spent his time with, nothing about her angry denim; that she had taken a thousand dollars from Ernesto to keep quiet about Adam. Another of Ernesto's lies, Tonia had insisted at the hospital, and Adam realized that one thing Ernesto had told him *was* true. All of his family did speak English; Tonia told him in very plain English that Ernesto had first intended to blackmail him. The meaning of her words, anyway, was very plain.

"You were afraid you say something to me, no? You didn't not say anything, but Vittorio know you afraid. He would have blackmail you, but you give him the money without he do it!"

Adam was able to figure it out, trace the whole thing from the day he handed Ernesto the thousand to keep the brunette quiet; in the next breath he had mentioned going into business with Ernesto. Then Ernesto had dropped the subject of the brunette and what she knew. If it had not been the club at Civitavecchia, it would simply have been more blackmail. Adam sucked hard on the Gauloise to keep himself from feeling very sad. Outside the room he heard the police officer exchange words with another policeman, then in the doorway, Ernesto stood.

"Ernesto!" Adam walked across to him smiling, while the policeman with the curly hair shut the door, staring at them through the wire window.

"Don't call me that. You know that is not my name." Ernesto was sober-faced, and Adam thought he even looked angry.

"I want to help you." said Adam.

Ernesto rubbed at his hook nose, and let his hand drop to his side again. "I come to tell you leave me alone, and leave my sister alone! Leave Tonia alone!"

"I only told her what I told you. I want to help you!"

"She does not want me to be helped!"

"Then forget her, Ernesto. We'll figure a way out!"

"There is no way. The best way is you go. Leave us all alone. I come to tell you that."

"I don't want the money back. You think that?"

Ernesto glared at him, arms akimbo, rocking on his heels. "What money?"

"You don't trust me. You think I care about the money. I don't!"

"You are crazy!"

"Sit down, Ernesto. I have an idea. Listen, we could still build the place in Civitavecchia. I was there, Ernesto. I saw the place, and we could still–"

"Don't call me that! You are crazy." He turned and said something to the policeman at the window of the door. Adam did not understand more than the word "open."

"I have so much to tell you," said Adam, "Please. We can talk. I could open the place in Civitavecchia and we could run it together when you are free. We could–"

Ernesto spat on the floor. The Italian policeman shouted something at him and began opening the door.

"I have never been to Civitavecchia," said Ernesto, "and I will never go now. I have seen pictures though," he laughed, a laugh of derision. "I have a friend who is a brick-layer. He just finished a place called Cucci's, a do-over job. Did you see Cucci's?"

"Why do you want to hurt me, Ernesto?"

Ernesto said something to the guard who stood in the doorway, and the guard returned the remark with another, and an obscene gesture. Both Ernesto and the guard laughed.

"I remember when you told me the things about man's inhumanity to man," Adam said. "I don't believe you want to be cruel."

Ernesto started walking toward the door. "I don't care what you believe. I have my life not to care. I have my life what is left to sit in a cell and do nothing but not to care what you believe!"

"Are you blaming me? Is that it?" Adam pulled at his arm. "Are you blaming me?"

"Without you, and your money there would have been no need to fight her."

Adam's eyes were filled with tears. "But I only wanted to–" He could not think any longer what it was he had wanted to do.

"To have your fancy club, ah?" said Ernesto.

"But it isn't my fault! I came here to help you!"

"Help yourself to a jump in the Tiber!" Ernesto said. He was in the entranceway of the room when Adam caught his arm a second time and held on to it. "Remember the day in the Borghese? Remember, you said I should say *tu*. Not *lèi*, you said. We are friends."

Ernesto shook his arm free. "Let go! Crazy!"

"*Tu*," said Adam. "Ernesto, let me help you. Not *lèi*, you said, but *tu*." The tears were starting down his cheeks. "Wait, Ernesto, there's so much more I want to say!"

Ernesto stopped and looked back over his shoulder at Adam.

There was a crooked grin on his face, and the silver medal around his neck gleamed against the dim light of the low-watt bulb overhead.

"At least I am not you," said Ernesto; "I am a man at least!"

He spat a second time and made the same obscene gesture which the policeman had made a moment ago. Then he turned his back on Adam.

19

"...and this afternoon I am going to visit the grave of your wife. Do not be unhope-ful about the future. In order to make it easier for Dorothy, who is entertaining friends from America, I will be at this hotel for a while. You may write me here, but if you don't I will understand that it is because they probably don't allow it. I know you did not intend to hurt my feelings during our visit. It is not an easy posi-tion you are in..."

—A LETTER FROM ADAM BLESSING TO VITTORIO GELSI

The hotel was on the Via Vittorio Emanuele Orlando not far from the Mediterraneo. Adam was paying eight thousand lire for a double with bath, a deluxe rate, but he was glad to be away from the Via Po apartment. He posted the letter to Ernesto at the desk and walked out into a warm sunny day, not badly hung-over, not at all depressed. As he strolled along he looked for the familiar yellow sign with the telephone on it. There was one above a bar sign on the corner, and Adam ordered a whisky and asked the cashier for *a gettone* to make a call. He took his drink with him, dialed Dorothy's office number, and when she answered, Adam pressed the but-ton to let the slug drop into the box.

"Where are you, Adam?"

"In a bar."

"Where are you staying, Adam?"

"The Holy Father has asked me to share his quarters in the Vatican."

"I don't appreciate that, Adam. I don't appreciate any of it."

"Did I get any mail?"

She let out a sarcastic little laugh. "Stacks of it, Adam from all your friends. The florist in New York, the bartender in New York, Ernesto, Billy, Chary—I can't count all your mail."

"You're still mad, is that it?"

"Adam, I have to pay my phone bill. You called all over the world the other night. If Norman hadn't stopped you—"

"He's still around?"

"Of course he's still around. What do you think? Adam, he's a better friend than you know. They were supposed to go to Capri this week, and he's only staying because he's worried about you."

"I must be the most exciting thing that ever happened to Norman. Even more exciting than Shirley." Adam took a gulp from the whisky glass.

"Oh, Adam, you can't even stop drinking while you make a phone call. I can hear the glass."

"It's just wine."

"Norman was going to ask the police to help find you, if you didn't call today."

"The police have nothing on me," said Adam.

"Of course they haven't *got* anything on you! What kind of a way is that to talk! You were talking that way the other night! I don't know what you mean half the time any more! Adam, we're all very worried about you, that's all."

"I'm fine, Dorothy. Really. I really feel great!" He meant that. He felt tears in his eyes.

"Why don't you come back to the apartment?"

"When they go. Not before."

"Adam, I'll ask them not to stop by any more. Will you come back then?"

"It's the nagging I can't take," said Adam. "I haven't done such bad things." More tears. He turned his back on the bar so the old man behind it would not see his eyes.

"Where are you staying without luggage?"

"I have a new suitcase I bought."

"Oh, Adam, come back to the apartment."

"Yes," said Adam. "I want to. I want to pack everything.

"Pack?"

"I may have to go to Venice," said Adam. "Billy sounded worried the other night on the phone."

"Adam, he was worried about you."

"I know. I ought to reassure him."

"Come home, Adam, and we'll talk about it."

"You see, Dorothy," said Adam, "they could be having trouble with their marriage. There are some things you don't know, you see?"

"Adam... Just come home, will you?"

"I have to go to the Piazza Verano this afternoon. After that, maybe."

"The cemetery? Not the cemetery?"

"Ernesto's wife is there, Dorothy."

"What time are you going there?"

"Oh, after lunch, I suppose."

"All right, Adam."

"There's nothing to worry about," said Adam. "I just hate Norman."

"All right, Adam. I'll see you later then."

"Yes," Adam smiled. "Good-bye." He put the phone's arm back. There was a residue of tears in his eyes, which he brushed away with his fingertips. He swallowed the rest of his whisky and set off for the narrow old street north of Piazza Navona, the Via de Coronari.

The choice was between a silver salt cellar and an eighteenth century wood punch-ladle, with a worm handle and silver mounts. Adam stood in the antique shop trying to make up his mind. His book on silver was with the rest of his belongings on the Via Po, and while he was almost positive he would buy Luther Schneider the punch-ladle, he had some reservations. The punch-ladle was the more expensive gift, but the silver salt cellar was larger and looked less skimpy. Still, Schneider was more likely to have a salt cellar in his collection. Adam picked up one, then the other, ultimately choosing the punch-ladle. He left instructions for mailing, and enclosed the note he had written last night at the hotel. He had had to rewrite it this morning, for his hand had looked strangely unlike him, even though he allowed for the fact he was quite tight. It was a bewildering curiosity–last evening's handwriting sample. There were those odd breaks in the lower sections of his a's and o's. He had smiled to imagine such ominous traits in himself, and he had redone it with great care: "Greetings from The Eternal City with thanks for your faith in me." It was the first time he had ever put a message in with a gift for Schneider. He left it unsigned, but he felt a certain warm satisfaction at the thought that he had finally made a direct communication, as though somehow it gave more stature to his bond with Schneider. The clerk was smiling at Adam, bowing to him, being so very kind that Adam left the place with his eyes filled. There was a lot of good in the world, and as Adam crossed the street and headed toward the Piazza Navona, he realized he wanted to dine outdoors in the sun, where he could watch people, toast them with his wine in a secret sacrament, embracing absolute strangers and Billy, Chary, Ernesto... his friends... He thought suddenly of the nice clerk from the Gracie Branch Post Office back in New York City, the one to whom he had handed over the change-of-address slip, and to whom he had told the fib about Chary's moving. The clerk had such a friendly face. When Adam had gone back to the post office to reroute Chary's mail the second time, he had looked for that clerk in vain. Adam wished he knew his name. He would have liked to send him a post card, even though the clerk would probably not know who it was from. He would simply have liked to send him greetings from Rome. Tears again. Adam blinked them away. He turned onto the Via Guiseppe

Zanardelli, where he saw Passetto's, with the large summer terrace. He looked forward to a very happy luncheon there, and he had to stop a few feet from the entrance to get control of himself, to wipe his eyes.

A light rain began to fall as Adam was leaving Passetto's–a misty sort of precipitation with the sun still hot but screened by pinkish clouds. Adam had ordered an extra pot of coffee at the end of his meal, so that he no longer felt the gay euphoria he had while he was dining; instead, a not melancholy but more pensive feeling; serious, very serious now. A ton-sured monk passed him in the street, and Adam crossed himself–the first time in his life he had ever done it, but it seemed very natural. In the taxi on his way to the Piazza Verano he remembered his first trip to Rome, when he had ridden an elevator to the roof of St. Peter's Basilica. There were bits of saints' bones for sale there, along with the rosaries, guidebooks and Benedictine liqueurs. There were signs everywhere which warned "Do not spit," and Adam had thought at the time that it was comical for such signs to be there, but now he knew that it was very sad and he under-stood those signs. They were not there because people would spit, Adam decided, they were simply reminders that at any time, in any place, man could turn on you and foul you. Who was safe really, where was anyone safe from unkindness or vulgarity? Adam smiled. It no longer made him sad as it had in Passetto's when he remembered Ernesto's last words to him; it made him glad he could forgive Ernesto for another wrong, as he had for-given all his friends. Perhaps when he left the cemetery he would return to St. Peter's and buy a small sack of the saints' bones for Ernesto. Adam leaned back and closed his eyes, his neck rubbing against the leather seat, which was hot and sticky. He felt slightly dizzy, and he wondered if he could give in to the impulse momentarily to let his mind whirl, as though it were a separate part unconnected with his body, and it would whirl and spin, and even Adam would not be aware of it... just for a few slow sec-onds. Like a weight lifted, the end of great pressure... lightness, floating. Dancing.

"Signore! Per favore, Signore!"
Adam rubbed his eyes and sat up. The driver was pointing to an ornate procession in front of them. Black horses dressed in black plumes, a black hearse with a man on top wearing a Napoleonic hat.

"Here you get out, *Signore!*" said the driver, with a shrugging gesture to indicate his helplessness. "We are sticked!" he said.

Adam paid him. He waved a hand in answer to the driver's *"Grazie!"* and he walked along until he came to the outside gates of the cemetery. The short nap on the way had confused him slightly. He had the sensation of having dreamed a horrendous nightmare, but none of it could he remember. Just the feeling left from it–a pit in his stomach; his heart beating too fast. He began to smell the sickly odor of countless flowers which were set up on stalls lining the cemetery's outer gates. He waited while the black hearse passed through the gates; then he bought a bunch of lilies and went in the direction of the hearse.

Inside, the Piazza Verano was a world of marble, peopled by marble angels, marble children, marble adults. The living, like Adam, seemed to be intruders, and Adam noticed that many of them walked in the careful, almost apologetic manner of someone going through another person's house, without quite having his permission. Adam passed a marble house in front of which two small marble boys dressed in sailor suits exchanged a living rose. An inscription on a stone beside them said they had lived from 1860 until 1870. They were brothers: Tullio and Giusto.

Adam walked on, and the rain was still the same vaporish quality, with the heat muggy, the sun pushing its fire through the veil of pink clouds. At another marble house, Adam saw a marble woman holding out her hand, as though she were beckoning to him. He stopped and stared at her. He imagined that he saw a faint smile on her marble lips. He looked beyond her and into the house. There were chairs to sit on. There was an altar with a white lace-edged cloth, and on the cloth were frames containing photographs of children. A bowl of oranges. A prayer book. Tiny lights burned under images of the Virgin.

Adam went closer to the marble woman, to read her name on the tablet, but there was no name. He looked up again at her face and then she seemed to frown. He turned his back on her and hurried away, and he realized as he passed house after house, he would probably never find Ernesto's wife's mausoleum. He was not even sure there would be one so soon; sure only that the newspapers had announced her burial in the Piazza Verano.

At a corner, mounted under glass on a small tombstone, was the photograph of a young boy about thirteen. He was posed standing on a hill with his arms pulling a dancing kite, his hair tossed in the wind, his face laughing. He wore knickers and a white blouse, and on one leg his stocking had slipped down to his ankles, and there was a dog pulling at the stocking. Under the photograph was a name–one word–followed with an exclamation point: Mario!

Adam walked across to the tombstone and placed the flowers there.

"Mario," he said. He smiled and bent close to the photograph, "Is that your dog?" There were tears starting in his eyes, but he did not fight them and they blurred; a drop fell on the photograph. "I didn't have a dog," he said. "Mario, I didn't have a dog."

Two priests passed with large soup-tureen hats, babbling together in Italian, smiling. They glanced at Adam and glanced away.

"I'll buy a kite for Timmy, Mario," Adam said. "I'll tell him about you."

Adam straightened and backed away from the small tombstone. He gave a little wave at the photograph, smiling, the tears on his cheeks. As he started around the corner and down toward some lights on the ground in the distance, he remembered something about the dream he had on the way to the cemetery. He had been caught running down a narrow street with a knife in his hand. He remembered he was wearing the foulard and damask-tie silk dressing gown he had bought for Billy's wedding gift. The smiling *carabiniere* from the *questúra* was arresting him for murder. He remembered that he had protested that he had murdered no one, and the *carabiniere* had only shrugged. "There is no reason, but it might make you feel better, *Signore!*"

Adam stopped at a wrought-iron grating in front of him. It fenced off row upon row of concrete slabs, a hundred or more, with small bulbs by each one. The bulbs were about fifteen watts, only a quarter of them burning. Near the gate sat a fat old man in a little house nearly too small for him, the size of a ticket window. Outside the house were more lights fixed to a central switchboard which the man operated, and which connected with the lights that circled the concrete squares.

Adam looked at the man, and the man said, "Five lire."

"Why?" asked Adam in Italian. Adam wiped the tears from his face with his handkerchief, while the man said in Italian, "For the dead."

Adam shook his head. "I don't speak Italian well."

The fat man shrugged. He did not speak English.

"Why?" Adam tried again.

Behind him a voice said, "The lights are for the people who rest here."

He turned and faced one of the priests with the soup-tureen hats. In the priest's hands was a rosary. He had great coarse peasant hands, and a gold tooth in front of his mouth. "I speak English," he said unnecessarily. "Did you lose someone?"

"Not here," Adam said. "I'm a visitor."

"This is the *ossario*. The people are buried here."

"Where?"

"In the *ossario*. Excuse me. In those wells." He pointed at the fenced-in area. "For the poor, *Signore*. This is where the poor rest. They cannot afford tombs and land is scarce in Rome, so we put them in the earth ten years. Then when the time is up, the bones are dug up and they are buried here in a common grave."

Adam's eyes were blurred again from his tears. "Where are their friends who won't bury them?" he said. "Where?"

The priest looked at him a moment. Adam leaned into him. "Where are his friends?"

The priest stepped away from Adam. He was smiling. He said something to the fat man and the fat man shook his head and held his nose with his fingers. The priest nodded.

"I'm not drunk if you think that," said Adam.

"Perhaps not, *Signore,* but you have a smell of it."

The priest turned and moved away, handing the fat man some lire.

"Wait!" Adam called.

The priest turned, hanging back, and Adam hurried across to him.

"You have no right to treat me this way," said Adam.

"How did I treat you? I explained the *ossario* to you. I answered your questions."

"You told the man I was drunk."

"No," said the priest, "I said you had a liquor breath. No more."

"Why did you want to be unkind. You of all people! Isn't there enough unkindness in the world. Today at Passetto's I was snarled at because I accidentally knocked over a wine bottle, and now from a Father, this treatment!"

"*Signore,* I am a student priest, not a Father, and I have no time. Go back to your hotel and rest, *Signore.* Good day."

"Wait!" Adam said.

"Good day, *Signore!*" The priest walked fast, but Adam followed.

"Don't you know what's wrong? It's wrong to talk about people behind their backs!"

The priest did not look back. Adam continued following him. A woman kneeling by a marble statue of a nun looked up at Adam from her prayers, her rosary dangling in her hand.

Adam called to her: "He runs away from me! He is supposed to be a priest!"

"Listen!" Adam called after the priest. "I have a confession!"

He was hot and now slightly dizzy again. The priest was far ahead of him now, but again he shouted, "I have a confession to make to you. A crime! Wait!" He caught hold of a marble man, leaned on him, starting to sob. The rain was falling harder now. Adam stumbled as he moved on. He picked himself up again. The knees of his trousers were damp and dirty. The rain seemed to come more, and the pink color of the sky was turning to gray. Adam was very tired. He could not make it to the gates of the cemetery. He stopped again, and then again he saw the marble woman with her arms beckoning to him. He walked past her to the house behind her. His thirst was tremendous, and as he looked in through the window at the oranges on the altar, he thought of biting into one and sucking out the juice. When he tried the door, he found it locked.

"Please let me in," he whispered. He leaned his head against the door, felt the cool metal on his forehead. "Please let me in."

Behind him he heard someone shouting in Italian.

He let go of the door handle, and stumbled toward the marble woman. There was more shouting, and he saw people running toward him, people he seemed to recognize, but it was all a dream, wasn't it? He thought he heard Dorothy Schackleford's voice, but he fell to his knees without knowing if this were true. He put his head down on the cold marble slab beside the marble woman. "You don't have any name," he said to the cold marble Then he toppled over on his back in the wetness, his eyes barely able to see the marble woman's face through his tears. He blinked his eyes and looked up at the face, and there were no features there, just as there was no name on the slab beneath her.

"And a lot you care!" said the marble woman.

EPILOGUE

THE FELLOW'S FLYER
Fellow's Foundation, Rome Chapter

Amid the festivity of the Christmas Season, we pause to note with reluctance and sadness, that we are losing one of our most valuable and diligent Fellow's workers. Adam Blessing is sailing for New York on the "Leonardo da Vinci," December 19th. Our questions as to his future plans were answered in typical Adam fashion, with the simple and profound sentence: "My future is in the hands of Faith."

Adam Blessing has been with Fellow's a year in January, heading up our Alcoholics Anonymous Chapter. No one who has ever heard "our Adam" speak, can doubt how sorely we will miss him. His accounts of his recovery from a mental illness were an inspiration to all–his confidence, his very nearly spiritual enthusiasm for his work, will make it utterly impossible for anyone to take his place. He can be succeeded–yes, but there is no one quite like "our Adam."

We have grown to think of him as our special "Blessing," and our Treasury will be in mourning for a long time (as all Fellow's members know by now, Adam was an unparalleled fund-raiser!). New Yorkers are in for a treat at the Now Year's meeting of A.A., which will be an open meeting, and which "our Adam" will address. Remember the date well: January 30th, at 8:00 p.m. in Riverton Memorial Church on 5th Avenue and 90th Street.

We know Adam will be dropping in on another ex-Fellow's worker, Mrs. Wilson Neer, our own Dorothy Schackleford, who lives in Brooklyn Heights, New York. Dorothy was one of our leading lights for two years, heading up the Fellow's Children Center. Her cheerful smile and her hardy determination have been very much missed by all of us.

So, with our hearts full and our spirits inspired by Adam, we say *"Buon Natale,"* but never good-bye. And speaking for all of us, I would like to put it in a more personal vein... as Santayana once wrote: "I scarce know which part my greater be,/ What I keep of you, or you rob from me."

PART THREE

20

WIN WINS ROUND ONE THOUSAND-AND-ONE;
Manufacturer Ordered Out–For Peace

A temporary cessation of hostilities was arranged yesterday as wealthy manufacturer Luther V. Schneider agreed to move out of the Bucks County estate he has been occupying with estranged wife Win Griswold Schneider, former society beauty.

Lawyers for both sides in this knock-down-drag-out litigation agreed with Supreme Court Justice Paul Lindgren, that the battle line should be drawn back. Win and her millionaire husband have been living in the same $99,000 mansion on Lerch Road, Point Pleasant, Pennsylvania, and concentrating too much fire power in one area.

Schneider, who claims his wife's romance with the bottom of the bottle is jeopardizing their son's health, has agreed to move into the family apartment on East 91st Street in New York, temporarily. Win, who claims any diversion she might have, nowhere near matches Schneider's romance with his $100-a-week private secretary, is suing Schneider for separation. She asked $8000 monthly alimony, but agreed to accept $600 a week temporary alimony while regrouping her forces. Meanwhile, she will have full custody of the boy, Timothy Schneider, 11. Some two years ago this boy was the victim of a kidnapper, who has never been apprehended, largely due to the fact that Mr. Schneider refused to cooperate with authorities. The ransom money was given over to the kidnapper with no identifying marks on any of the bills, which reportedly added up to $100,000.

In Schneider's counter-affidavit he claimed his wife, at the time of the kidnapping, was concerned more about the amount of the ransom than about the safe return of her son. Schneider attributed the safe return to the fact he did not cooperate with local authorities or the F.B.I., but "trusted" the abductor. He does not trust his wife with their son, claiming she has often beaten the boy and ridiculed him for being "unbalanced."

Lindgren had adjourned Win's separation trial without setting a date. This was three months ago. Since that time, he said, Schneider's attorneys called him to report that Win had locked the child in a toolshed behind the house, in retaliation for "an unfounded conviction," that Schneider was see-ing Kate Weeks, his secretary, after office hours. Win's lawyers yesterday responded that the boy liked to play in the toolshed and that Schneider had maliciously misconstrued the game to mislead the court. The lawyers for Win Schneider added that Schneider's "gallivanting" with Miss Weeks was no secret to anyone. They said that Schneider had attacked their client, blackening her eye.

After listening to both attorneys in yesterday's Winter Court Session, Lindgren decided that, for the sake of the child, an armistice must be arranged, with Schneider's move the first step.

"Hello," said the voice.

"Hello."

There was a pause. Luther Schneider turned his swivel chair lightly to the left, facing his office windows. He said again, "Hello?" He glanced across his desk at Matt Flannery. "Do you think it's Timmy calling from the country?" he whispered, as though Flannery knew any better than he him-self knew. Flannery shook his head. "Don't get your hopes up, Lute." He had a faint smile of encouragement on his face. Sometimes when Win was out of the house Mrs. MacGivern allowed Timmy to phone.

Schneider said again, "Hello? Timmy?"

"No, it's not Timmy, Mr. Schneider."

"Who is it?"

"I have something important to talk over with you. It'll take a little time."

"Who are you?" Schneider said.

"A friend."

"Oh." Schneider looked across the desk at Matt and shrugged. Then he said into the phone's mouthpiece. "Just what are you calling about?" He was getting used to it. He had never realized before this litigation how many friends Win did not have. To date, six of her alleged friends had offered to make affidavits on his behalf. There was a small matter of money involved, naturally. Some of the other calls making the same offers were from former servants. Win had never had a way with the help, unless it was a way of turning even the most docile, third-floor, three-day-a-week servant into a raging, indignant threatening human soul, who quit only after the most unbelievable anathemas directed at Win. Three weeks ago a chauffeur in their employment for a year and a half, had called Schneider to offer to testify "free-of-charge, sir, that the bitch would as soon see your kid dead as see the sun come up the next morning."

REVIEW COPY

This book is published
and distributed
in the United States by
Stark House Press

For availability,
please refer to
Stark House Press
in all reviews and listings

STARK HOUSE PRESS
2200 O Street
Eureka, CA 95501
707-444-8768 (phone)
707-444-6600 (fax)
griffinskye@cox.net
www.starkhousepress.com

The voice on the telephone said: "You needn't sound angry. You did a favor for me, and I want to repay you, that's all."

"You'd better get to the point," said Luther Schneider. "I'm busy right now."

"Oh, you're not alone? I want to talk with you when you're alone."

"Good luck then," said Schneider. He saw Matt frowning at him from across the desk. He put his hand over the mouthpiece. "What?" he asked Matt. Matt said not to entirely discourage him.

"Can you call me later?" said Schneider to the telephone.

"Oh yes. I'm very patient, so don't worry."

"Try me in an hour," said Schneider.

He heard the click, the line went dead, and then the dial tone, and he set the phone arm back in its cradle.

"Another offer to defame the good character of your charming wife, hmm?" Matt Flannery blew on his glasses and wiped them with a corner of his handkerchief. "I wonder if *she* gets many offers."

"Probably thousands."

"Let's hope not one."

Flannery put his glasses back on. He picked up the thin onion sheets in front of him, leafing through them. "I'm on page 13, Lute, section 4."

Luther Schneider leaned back in his swivel chair, fondling his pipe while his lawyer began. "Section Four. On page 32 of her affidavit, Plaintiff states she was struck repeatedly by defendant on the night of September 16, and submits a doctor's report describing–"

Her neck. Schneider brushed a large hand through his gray hair and sighed. He had come close to strangling her that night. He had found her feeding Timmy whisky on a teaspoon to put him to sleep. A teaspoon won't hurt, she had said. Timmy was screaming, his face lobster-color; a teaspoon won't hurt his crazy head, for Christ's sake, she had said, falling in her drunkenness across Timmy

"...and vigorously deny that Plaintiff threatened her life then or at any other time," Matt Flannery continued, "and that pursuant to Section 309 of the Civil Practice Act–"

Luther Schneider remembered the Christmas a year ago, trimming the tree with Timmy downstairs. Win had come from upstairs, holding the whisky bottle by the neck, singing "I've Got A Lovely Bunch of Coconuts"–funny, how the mind remembered even the smallest details, like the song she sang then, and how he had stepped on a silvery-blue bulb on his way to her, trying to get her out of Timmy's sight before he saw she was naked. She wanted to know what the hell crazy kids knew about naked women anyway. "You're his mother–" yelling it; and Win yelling back just as loud: "I didn't give birth to that monster!"... "I'll kill you," he had said. Going around and around on the victrola–the Christmas carols: *Holy infant, mother and child;* Yes, I'll kill you, he had said. She laughed at him: "So you can be with her, Lute! Spawn another creep with her?"... Timmy watching everything, dressed in a pair of one-piece pajamas, standing under the tree: *Sleep in heavenly peace.*

Schneider only half-listened to Matt Flannery. He shut his eyes as though with that motion he could shut out the pictures in his mind's eye as well, the thousand snapshots there–the rewards, the punishments, take your choice; Kate leaning over in the morning to put her bra on, something that simple, recorded as well as Win in a rage at the doctor, the year Timmy was three and they knew for certain he was unbalanced, the blue vein that stuck out in her neck and her screaming: "The hospital gave us the wrong goddam baby, and you send this idiot back and tell them to find out where ours is!"... Kate and Timmy walking ahead of him the day they all went to the Central Park Zoo, the sudden sight of Timmy skipping, holding to Kate's hand . . as well as Timmy hiding behind the shower curtain in the upstairs bathroom of the house in Bucks County, five o'clock in the afternoon when Luther Schneider had come home early; telling Timmy, no, son, Mommy isn't after you with a knife. You dreamed it, son... lying to him... Schneider opened his eyes and looked across at Matt.

"I didn't hear you, Matt."

"I said, 'That's it.' Of course, I don't think any of it will stop Win or her lawyers, but it might impress the court, the parts about her mistreatment of Tim anyway... that's what we really want. Tim!"

Luther Schneider said, "For the time being, that's all. I'm going to marry Kate, Matt."

"First things first, Lute. Watch that damn temper of yours, if you want my opinion." Matt was stuffing papers into his briefcase, removing his glasses, and rubbing his eyes. "I mean it. Don't knock her around any more. Hell, you know I'd like to help you knock Win from here to the Battery, but it doesn't show up well in court, Lute."

"I don't want to knock her anywhere." Luther Schneider sighed.

"I know. She practically begs you to slug her. I know that. It's better you're apart for a while. Mrs. MacGivern will look out for Tim."

"I'm not really worried for the time being about him."

"Mrs. MacGivern's good with him, Lute."

"I know. She can handle Win when she has to, too."

Flannery got his overcoat from the leather couch in Schneider's office. "I'll be glad when Kate gets back here and things are normal again. I liked the way she used to take care of me. Get me into this thing and all," said Matt, sticking an arm in his overcoat sleeve. "She still in Bermuda?"

"Yes."

"A wonderful girl," said Flannery. "And that's an unqualified endorsement." He smiled and shook Schneider's hand, saying, "I know it's unsolicited too, but I like her, Lute, for the record, hmm?"

"Thanks," Schneider said.

"It's starting to snow out. Better not stay late." He waved and started out the door. Before it shut, he said, "Let me know if anything comes of that phone call, hear?"

"Another bum steer, probably," Schneider said.

Still, he waited at his desk for the telephone to ring. He was in the middle of a letter to Kate Weeks when the operator signaled an incoming outside call. He had made a rule that all incoming-outsides be put through on a direct wire. Matt's suggestion. Operators intimidate the real leads along with the phonies, Matt had said; we can't pick and choose; have to hear them all.

The voice said, "Can we talk privately for a while now?"

"Yes."

"I read in the papers about the troubles you've been having. I know you have to take precautions. Your wire could be tapped, I suppose."

Schneider said, "No melodramatics, hmmm? My wire is not tapped. Just get on with it."

"I'm sorry about all your trouble. I would have come home earlier if I had known. I read about it in Rome."

"Rome!" Schneider said.

"Oh, I know it wasn't in the foreign press. I got some back newspapers from another American. Scandal sheets, you know."

"And?"

"And I came home."

"Just to help me, hmm?"

"Yes."

"I see." Schneider shook his head and sighed, swinging his chair around to face the window and watch the snow falling.

"I'm sorry about all your trouble. Your wife has been very unkind. I hate unkindness."

"Are you a former friend of Win's or a former servant?" said Schneider.

"I'm your friend."

"Yes, of course... of course. Granted that, how did you know Win?"

"I didn't. I only saw her once. On the street. Near your place on Ninety-first."

"What is it you want Mr.–Mr.–"

"You wouldn't know my name, Mr. Schneider. I thought by now you might have guessed who I am."

Schneider rubbed his forehead with the palm of his left hand, an expression of exasperation on his lean countenance. "Well, I didn't guess. I'm sorry. I'm not good at guessing."

"I sent Timmy a tiny Basque fishing boat from Biarritz. I think that was the first gift. Oh, I know it's presumptuous to use the word gift– Schneider's eyes grew wide with amazement as he leaned forward, holding the phone even closer to his ear, as though it was impossible to believe what he was hearing. The Basque fishing boat from Biarritz, the cock-eyed red sail attached to it. It had arrived that fall when Win was having another of her "rests" at the Hartford Retreat. Schneider had made a note to ask her who they knew who might be vacationing in southern France. It had slipped his mind to ask her; the gift had been passed along to Timmy with no special significance attached to it... It had taken Luther Schneider over a year to put the puzzle together; another gift from Paris–this one for him, the helmetshaped silver cream jug. They had both been sent to the Ninety-first Street apartment. The jug he had not taken with him to the country. He had not mentioned it to Win either. It had arrived shortly after she had found out about Kate, and everything that arrived was reason for suspicion, every Christmas gift, birthday gift, letter, bill–it was nearly the worst period of their marriage. He had left it with the rest of his silver.... There was a food broker–Saperstein, or Sardonspore–some name like that, for whom he had once done a favor. Schneider had heard he was in Europe for General Foods. Perhaps be was the donor, Schneider had thought, but it was an unconvincing explanation. The jug was very expensive, well over $600.... The piece in the puzzle, which Schneider needed to solve the matter, arrived from Rome. The punch-ladle; the card with "greetings" and "thanks for your faith in me."... Then he knew. The silver salt spoons, the Basque cap for Timmy, the miniature Vatican City Swiss Guard–he knew who had sent all of them. Win would have had a lot of satisfaction in the knowledge that Timmy's kidnapper was again in touch with Schneider. She was the main one to say he would hear from him again. When Schneider had paid the ransom, it was Win in her shrill tones who promised: "This is just the beginning of what you're going to pay that fellow!"

"...none of the gifts would have been possible without your trust in me," the voice was saying, "and now I'm going to pay you back."

"You're going to *what?*"

"Repay you, Mr. Schneider. It was always my dream to repay you."

Schneider sat back against the leather swivel chair. "Repay me?" he said incredulously. He had not told anyone about the gifts being sent him. Against everyone's advice–Win's, of course–but also Matt's, his mother's, the F.B.I. agent's–against everyone's, he had kept his bargain with the kidnapper. He had purposely framed his response to the ransom note in a way intended to convince Timmy's abductor he would not turn on him. He had used words like "faith" and "integrity," appealing to him in a soft key, trying to reach him on whatever substrata level there was in his make-up which would respond to another human being's confidence in him. At the time he had thought of it as being like attempting to get some very fragile and infinitely precious object from the sticky hands of a recalcitrant child, approaching him inch-by-inch on tip-toe, afraid that one false move would send the object flying to destruc-tion.... He had tried to be ever so careful, and in the same way one does not ever fool some children, he had not tried to fool the man who had Timmy captive.... And it had worked. He had never regretted the way he had han-dled it. Long afterwards, when he realized it was this same fellow sending the gifts from abroad, his reasons for telling no one were striped half with fear that it would start a resurgence, half with a thin acceptance of the idea that the kidnapper felt remorse, gratitude, guilt–Schneider did not know what to call it. There was an ocean separating them. Schneider had simply let well enough alone.... He had not even told Kate about it, and he told Kate nearly everything, omitting only the raw details of his life in hell with Win. He was not a superstitious man, Luther Schneider, but he felt there was something frangible about the understanding which had passed between himself and the kidnapper, something that must keep it a covert thing; almost as though after all the time that had passed, if Schneider were to break his word, what would stop the kidnapper from finding some way to retaliate; this time, to harm Timmy?... Now he could only repeat his last words, "Repay me?" as though the most disbelieving, lip-service Catholic had suddenly been confronted with the vision of St. Peter saying: "You have kept faith and now I am here."

"Yes, that's right, Mr. Schneider. Where will you be, for example, tomor-row?"

"That's New Year's Eve," said Schneider.

"A perfect time to settle old debts, isn't it, sir?"

"I usually go to my mother's for the day *and* evening."

"Good. Tradition is a fine thing. I believe in tradition myself."

"Is this a joke? I have trouble believing this is—"

The voice laughed, "No, you have never had trouble believing. You believed in me sir. You never gave me away. You gave me great peace."

"I'm—gl-glad," Schneider managed.

"You sound as though you doubt me. I don't blame you. I'm sorry I cannot see you in person to thank you. I would like to shake your hand, Mr. Schneider. Thanks to you, I have been many places and seen many things. It has not all been easy for me; I have suffered too, and caused unhappiness to others. But I found my way finally. A whole new world opened up for me. A new field."

"A profitable field too," Schneider said. "It must be very profitable if you really mean that you're going to pay me back."

"It's not something I can explain on a telephone. Even in person, I wonder if I could explain it. It's very involved, you see."

"You got into some line abroad?" Schneider imagined telling Matt this. Matt was a lawyer first, of course. He could hear Matt's answer. "The man broke the law, Lute, and you didn't report his contact with you. You're an accessory! I don't care if he did pay you back!" Schneider was smiling all the more. Matt would damn near die once he got over being a lawyer.

"Yes, abroad. In Rome. It started in Rome, really."

"I see.... Well, Mr.—I don't know what to call you. Mr.—"

"I would tell you my name if I were sure you completely trusted me. Oh, I know you used to. When you had a reason to, you had faith. But you see, it's a funny thing about faith. Unless there is a good reason, one loses it."

"You're quite a philosopher."

"You've accomplished that for me. All my life I needed just one person to trust me. You did."

Schneider could think of nothing to say. He watched the snow. He could not stop imagining the look on Matt's face when he told him about this. Still, he could not quite believe it yet.

"I would like to tell you so many things," the voice said. "I can't. The things that have happened to me one doesn't sit down and discuss." There was a pause; Schneider heard a long sigh, then: "I will repay you tomorrow night."

"How do you intend to do this?"

"I can't say how. I wish I could. How or where, I can't say, but you will be paid in full. I can promise that. By midnight."

"My mother," Schneider said, "is very old. She has a weak heart. I–"

The voice cut in: "Don't worry. I won't be anywhere near your mother's."

Matt was picking Timmy up tomorrow morning, bringing him to Schneider's mother's home on Gramercy Park. Visiting privileges; Schneider thought they were the most sadistic words he had ever heard in any court.... The voice was reassuring him again; don't worry, it would be managed efficiently; no embarrassment to anyone. Schneider played with his pipe as he listened; thank you, the voice was saying again, and then again the part about having always dreamed of repaying him. Always. Thank you.

Schneider straightened up in his chair. "I want you to understand something," he said, "If this is any sort of joke, or trick, or an attempt to get more–"

"Please! Please!"

"Well, I want you to be damn sure I'm not putting up with anything else! Do you understand!"

"I forgive you for looking at it that way. How could you look at it any other way? I forgive you!"

"Thanks."

"Please, before I say good-bye, I'd like to hear a kinder tone. I know that's very brazen of me. After all, I have no reason to expect kindness from you, but I've grown to think of you as my friend. I've thought of you more or less as my benefactor. That's the word, all right–my benefactor."

Schneider said, "Happy New Year! Will that do?"

"Your tone sounds harsh still. Do you mean it?"

"If you mean what you're saying," said Schneider, "I mean what I'm saying."

"I swear by God," the voice said. "I swear it!"

Then before Schneider could think of a rejoinder, the voice said, "Good-bye, Mr. Schneider. You'll never hear from me again, but I'll never forget you. I like to think you'll never forget me."

"Maybe I won't," Luther Schneider said; and, as he heard the receiver click, he thought: maybe I really won't, and he had the same feeling he had had the night before Timmy's return, a certain blind confidence in something all the odds were against happening; almost like a rapport with a perfect stranger... and yet a stranger who knew better than Luther Schneider's most intimate friends, that the one thing Schneider had always wanted was an eighteenth century punch-ladle with a worm handle and silver mounts.

21

The Fellow's Foundation
240 Park Avenue
New York, New York

Dear Sirs:

At the request of an anonymous donor, we have been directed to present the New York Chapter of the Fellow's Foundation with the following check for $10,000. The donor specified that the announcement of this gift be made known at the open meeting of the Fellow's Alcoholics Anonymous Meeting on January 30th at 8:00 P.M. A certified check for that amount is attached to this letter.

> *Sincerely yours,*
> *A. K. Beardsley, Vice-President,*
> *South Orange Savings and Trust Company*
> *South Orange, New Jersey.*

"He wasn't that fat when I knew him," said Dorothy Schackleford Neer.

"So that's the great Adam," her husband said. He giggled, and a woman in the row in front of him turned around in her seat and damned him with her eyes. A hiss of "Shhh!" spread through the audience.

"Well, he wasn't!" said Dorothy Schackleford in a peeved whisper.

She had always made more of her friendship with Adam. She was always telling Wilson how she had nursed Adam through his breakdown, helped him become interested in the Fellow's Foundation, watched him progress from a wild ne'er-do-well to a dedicated worker, and ultimately parted from him, with a little Schackleford embroidery on the latter. Well, he *might* have asked her to marry him–it wasn't exactly a proven lie... Wilson was a few inches shorter than Dorothy, and without his glasses he could not see his own nose, but Dorothy thought of him as "a dear thing," and she was proud of the fact that he was one of the top engineers in Duco Oil Corporation. In April, they were going to Sumatra to live.

The speaker who had announced the $10,000 donation was pounding on the podium for order. There would be a hush momentarily, then a resurgence of the applause and chatter. The audience was as excited by the donation as they might have been if it were to be distributed among them in hundred-dollar bills. Behind the speaker, Adam stood, waiting to address the audience. He was enormous, Dorothy could not deny that. She wondered rather unkindly where on earth he bought his clothes, or did he have to have them made. His beard was even longer than it had been when she last saw him in Rome, and he looked much older than twenty-six.

Wilson leaned over and said: "He should have come a week earlier. He would have been the Santa Claus at the Christmas Party."

"Wil-son!" . . but she was not truly angry at the remark. She just hoped Wilson would be nice after the meeting when he met Adam. Wilson was not what Dorothy would describe as a sensitive person. She always thought engineers were not the type to be sensitive anyway. They were all slide rules and fix-things-down-in-the-basement. Once she had told Wilson how Adam had attempted to kill himself, after that Vittorio Gelsi's execution. She had tried to explain to Wilson that Adam felt responsible, even though he was not in the least responsible. For a while Adam had even believed *he* had murdered Gelsi's wife, and he had gone about saying he must repent. Bats in the belfry, Wilson had said, marbles in the attic, but that was Wilson for you.

The audience was quiet now, and Adam was stepping up to the podium. "I thought you said he was such a sporty dresser," Wilson whispered.

"Well, he was!"

The knees of Adam's pants were baggy, and there was no press in his suit. Worse, he wore a yellow shirt with a crooked green tie. Dorothy wished she had left Wilson home.

Adam had a hand on either side of the podium. He was leaning forward, staring out at the audience, waiting for silence. Finally, after several slow seconds in this pose, he straightened. His face was very grave, and when he spoke, his voice boomed out in the small church basement.

"My name is Adam Blessing. I am an alcoholic."

He paused and again looked at the audience. Dorothy attempted a faint smile when he looked in her direction. but if he recognized her, he showed no sign.

He said, "I used to hide behind a bottle for courage. I am not going to stand here and lie to you, and say I did not find the courage I needed, because I DID find it. I had a GREAT DEAL of courage when I drank. Drink gave me courage to pursue a very beautiful girl... My best friend's girl." There was a sprinkle of laughter from the audience. Adam Blessing waited for it to subside.

He began again, "Drink gave me courage to propose marriage to this girl....
Today, I am still a single man."

More laughter.

"I am also minus one best friend."

Laughter again.

"He was proposing all over the place," said Wilson.

"He exaggerates," Dorothy whispered back.

"Oh sure," Wilson said, "you were the only girl he ever proposed to, I
suppose."

"Drink," Adam boomed out, "gave me the courage to behave as a rich
man, when I was a poor man, gave me debts when I was debt-free, gave me
the courage to be a thief when I was honest. There is an awful lot of
courage in a fifth of whisky!"

Applause.

Adam Blessing's eyes were narrowed, now as he resumed: "Courage is
defined as that quality of the mind which enables one to meet danger and
difficulties with firmness. Dangers and difficulties, friends and Fellow's, not
delusions of dangers and difficulties, not imaginary dangers and difficulties,
but real ones. Liquid courage, the kind you find in a fifth of whisky, is one
of the best manufacturers of synthetic difficulties and dangers in the world
today! Is there courage in a fifth, oh yes, and plenty of it, but it's liquid!"

More applause. "Words, words, words," said Wilson. "I like it better
when girls speak and tell how they almost undressed in public when they
were drinking."

Adam Blessing said, "Some of us are people with little courage. If we are
alcoholics, we need to supplement our threads of courage with faith. How
do you have faith? Faith is contagious. You believe in me, and I'll believe in
you. We members of Alcoholics Anonymous have demonstrated that
credo to the fullest degree. I once looked up 'Faith' in the dictionary. I found
it defined as 'fidelity to one's promises.' Of course! Fidelity to one's promises! You trust me and I shall trust you. I will not ever forget you. If it seems
as though I am letting you down, it is not so. You are on my mind constantly. It is just a matter of time before I will be with you again. Faith!"

"What the devil is he talking about?" Wilson asked his wife. Some of the
audience were looking at one another with puzzled expressions. Dorothy
Schackleford Neer smiled, half with embarrassment, half with amusement.
Adam used to be called "The Preacher" in Rome when he first began with
Fellow's.

"I will leave you, but I will be back."

"A tiny nosegay to General MacArthur," Wilson snickered.

"You are always on my mind!"

"He would have been a great song-writer in the thirties," said Wilson.

"Tonight," Adam Blessing roared, "we heard of a donation of $10,000 to the New York Fellow's Chapter. What pure joy for the donor! Give, and you will be blessed!"

A few members of the audience were stifling smiles. There was a buzz of exchanged comments, shoulders shrugging with bemusement. Wilson gave his wife a questioning glance. "Is he all right?"

"He's just not organized," said Dorothy Schackleford, but she hoped he would not go on much longer. She glanced at her watch. The audience was very noisy now.

"Money cannot bring you peace, that is my message. Give it away! Peace is infidelity to one's promises, in the returning of another's faith in you, in the thought—no, the CONVICTION that faith can make you do ANY-THING! Love, MURDER, cry, laugh—"

"He looks like he's really crying himself," Wilson said.

"Oh God, I'm afraid he is."

"He is?"

"He needs a rest." Dorothy Schackleford covered her eyes with her hands, so she would not have to look at Adam.

Afterwards, he seemed all right. The chairman had interrupted him five or six minutes after Dorothy had stopped watching the podium. The chairman had said something about the meeting running overtime, and Adam, with the tears wet on his checks, had stepped aside without a protest. Dorothy and Wilson went up to him, and Adam hugged her with enthusiasm and shook Wilson's hand solemnly. They adjourned to a Schrafft's on Madison Avenue. Adam consumed two chocolate sundaes, and a piece of coconut layer cake. He asked Wilson about his work, and reminisced with Dorothy about members of the Fellow's in Rome. They were very nearly ready to leave when he brought up the names of Billy and Chary.

"Of course, I didn't expect a card at Christmas," he said, "but then again it might have arrived after I left. I might not have it yet."

"They're in Caracas," said Dorothy. "Billy's head of the Caracas office. We got a brief note from Chary on the back of their Christmas card. She's going to have another child."

"Caracas," Adam repeated.

"City of American-sponsored laundromats," said Wilson facetiously.

Adam seemed not to hear him.

He was playing with the cake crumbs on his plate, pushing them about with his fork. "I never knew what they named their boy."

"Ted."

"Oh... Theodore."

"Teddy, Chary calls him."

"I guess they didn't name him after anyone."

Dorothy could see the tears forming in Adam's eyes again.

She said, "What will you do now, Adam?"

"I've saved some money. I imagine I'll rest awhile."

"Good! "

"Rest, and eventually settle down somewhere," Adam said after the pause. "I have something to finish up here, and then–I'll settle down somewhere."

Dorothy picked up her gloves from the table. "It was good to see you again." Then she braved, "We liked your talk."

"I get worked up sometimes," Adam said softly. "It's as though everything builds up in me with such an urgency, I nearly explode."

"We better get on, Dorothy." Wilson was pushing back his chair.

"In Rome," said Adam, "I realized there was an obligation I must fulfill immediately. It upset me, the realization, but it brought me peace too. Perhaps it is the only true thing I'll ever do."

"Oh, you've done a lot of good in Rome, Adam. I heard all about it!"

"I'm very tired. Very tired... I'd like to settle down."

"We're walking as far as the subway, Adam."

"Go along. I'll have a glass of milk I think. Good night, Wilson."

"I love your beard, Adam." Dorothy was standing facing him, not quite sure the evening should end so flatly. But Wilson had made it very clear: *for the love of Pete, don't ask him back to the place!*

Adam said, "I'm going to shave it off tonight." He smiled. "It gets caught in the steering wheel."

"You have a car, Adam?" She could hear Wilson sighing behind her.

"I learned to drive in Rome, a month ago. I thought I might rent a car and practice."

She took his hand. "Good-bye, Adam. Let us hear from you."

"Good-bye and Happy New Year," he said. He dropped her hand and smiled. "It's nice, isn't it," he said, "to begin all over again?"

22

NOTICE

At three p. m. Mr. Blessing will visit The William Penn Lounge for another session in graphology. First Class Passengers only. On Tuesday and Thursday, he will be available at the same time in Lounge 2, for Tourist Passengers.

S.S. *Quaker City*
Philadelphia Line

Mr. Arlington Partidge of Rochester, New York, asked Mrs. Arlington Partidge if she was falling for that fat, phony slob or what?

"I'll be back in a minute," she answered, handing him her shuffleboard mallet. I just want to ask him one thing, Arl!"

She left her husband behind and hurried across to the deck rail where Mr. Blessing was standing, his arms behind his back, watching the sea.

"Hello there, Mr. Blessing." There was something almost saint-like about him, Mrs. Arlington Partidge often thought, and she did not mind it somehow that he showed no interest in who had spoken, but simply stayed in the same stance, touching his hand to his forehead in slight salute, without looking to see who it was he was greeting.

"It's Mrs. Partidge," said Mrs. Partidge, "Ethel Partidge, remember? My t-bars tend to slant downward; and I have those broad r's, remember?"

Mr. Blessing looked down at her. "Yes, I remember. You had very large handwriting, too."

"You really are something, Mr. Blessing! Memory like an elephant," she said. She thought when she said it that it was rather an unfortunate comparison. Mr. Blessing was so huge. "Yes, and you said I was an extrovert! Arl, my husband, tells me if I join just one more committee, he's going to wring my neck. I'm always doing sum'thin!"

"It is good to serve."

"Mr. Blessing, I feel like you know *all* my secrets. I mean, when you said that about my *m*, about the last stroke of my *m*, remember?"

"The fact that it was more angular than the other?"

"Wow-boy! You do remember everything! Well, yes, that's what I mean. I mean, I doubt that my own husband knows I'm a little neurotic."

"Mrs. Partidge, I did not say you were a little neurotic. I said it could be a sign of that, or it could simply indicate a desire for self-assertion."

"I mean, what would *you* think of a woman who sits around wondering what it would be like to have dinner with Dave Garroway. I don't mean just wonder, either, I mean set the table in my mind and everything, right down to what color linen napkins. Now!"

Mr. Blessing said, "I don't know who Dave Garroway is, Mrs. Partidge, and anyway, I really can't talk now. I'm thinking."

"Lord, you mean you're analyzing in your mind? I interrupted you analyzing in your mind?"

"It's quite all right. It was a brief interruption."

"Forgive me, Mr. Blessing. I'll just run right along and not bother you with another word. I had no idea you were doing *that*. Please excuse me."

At dinner that night Mrs. Partidge told Claire Cottersley-Smith how she had come upon Mr. Blessing that afternoon when he was analyzing in his mind. Claire Cottersley-Smith said that was nothing, wait until she told Ethel what Al had to say when he got back to their stateroom last night. Claire said, "Al said, 'well, I had a talk with your boyfriend, Claire,' and Al said they stood on deck for nearly twenty minutes passing the time of day. Al said his guess was Mr. Blessing was a defrocked priest. Mr. Blessing talked a great deal about Rome, Al said, and Al said Mr. Blessing had a misty look in his eye."

"Well, that's the very same look we've seen two or three times. Like he was crying!"

"Exactly," said Claire Cottersley-Smith, "and if you ask me Al is right. Ever notice how he avoids women? Well, he's shy! He was a priest, and he's not used to women!"

"He's like a man without a friend in the world," Ethel Partidge said. "It makes me want to die inside, does it you?"

"Yes," said Claire... "A de-frocked priest! Imagine! Reduced to fortune-telling on a cruise boat!"

"Graphology, Claire! It's more scientific. You should know what he told me about my *m*'s."

Claire Cottersley-Smith was more interested in Mr. Blessing than in Ethel Partidge's *m*'s. After the old Jerry Lewis movie in the William Penn Lounge, she nagged her husband into trying to have a second conversation with Mr. Blessing. "Ask him," she said, "if he knows Latin. That'll clinch it!"

She and Ethel Partidge nursed green Stingers in the bar with Arlington Partidge, who was slightly miffed at the fact Al Cottersley-Smith had established contact with the mysterious Mr. Blessing, and not he.

"One day your Mr. Blessing will simply drop dead of a heart attack," Mr.

Arlington Partidge said. He was extremely thin, and he never allowed Ethel to say that he was skinny.

"I like a lot of meat on a man," Claire Cottersley-Smith said.

After both women had had a third green Stinger and were right at that point of giggling hilariously at anything Arlington Partidge said, as long as it was not funny, Al appeared.

"Not a priest," he said sitting down. "Order me a whisky."

"Why not a priest?" his wife said.

"Well, we were having this talk about people who take these cruises, see? I say people get along in years, kids grow up, get through college and all that, and folks decide to spend a little money on themselves for a change, go away, see some sights."

"Yes? Yes? Go on."

"I need a whisky... well, he says to me that it's too bad money is so important to people. He says to me it used to be important to him, but he found out it wasn't and then he says something I damn near died at." He signaled the waiter for a whisky.

"What?" said Claire and Ethel together.

"He said he came into a great deal of money only a few years ago. A great deal, he said, repeating it, you know, like it was a million dollars or something? Well, this is the part that kills me.... He said he gave it all away, every nickle of it except for a small amount he had already spent selfishly on himself. He said he gave it all away to a worthy charity, and then he found peace!"

On Wednesday Ethel Partidge reported to Claire Cottersley-Smith that in a brief conversation with Mr. Blessing she learned this was the first time he had ever worked on a cruise boat, that he was not going to do it after the boat docked, that he had no "regular line."

On Thursday Claire Cottersley-Smith reported to Ethel Partidge that Al said Mr. Blessing spoke with Al for a half an hour on Faith and Loyalty, and Al saw real tears in Mr. Blessing's eyes, and Al was back to his original belief that Mr. Blessing was some kind of defrocked priest.

"Al said he said he had once done a terrible thing, but it was a beautiful thing too because it was necessary and true."

"A woman!" Ethel Partidge said. "Oh, gaw, he got involved with a woman!"

"That's what I think and that's what Al thinks. He messed around with some woman!"

"What kind of woman would let a priest mess around with her? Would you?"

"I don't know," Ethel Partidge said. "I might... if it was one of those terrible passions, I might not be able to stop!"

"It'll haunt him the rest of his days. I told Al that at breakfast. The rest of his days."

"How come he said he'd found peace, if he got himself defrocked for messing around with a woman?"

That night Arlington Partidge came into dinner beaming like a Cheshire cat.

"You would all be interested in something that just happened to me," he said. "In the radio room."

"Oh, Arly, don't play games!"

"Your shipboard Romeo was writing a cablegram. I just happened to see it over his shoulder. I just happened," Arlington Partidge announced in a triumphant tone, "to jot down its contents."

Ethel, Al, and Claire all made a dive for the slip of paper he set on the center of the table.

ARRIVING SATURDAY ABOARD S.S. QUAKER CITY. MY WANDERING IS AT AN END. I AM READY TO SETTLE PERMANENTLY. NOT WITH YOU NECESSARILY, BUT NEAR YOU CERTAINLY, TO HELP YOU FOREVER IN ANY WAY I CAN. BRING BABY TO MEET BOAT. WE WILL ALL BE REUNITED AT LAST.

"A baby!" said Claire Partidge.

"Who did he send the cable to. Did you see her name?"

"No," Arlington Partidge said, "he had not filled that in when I saw it."

Friday was spent with Ethel and Claire sitting about on the shuffleboard deck, reconstructing how they imagined it had happened. Ethel favored the idea a young girl came to confess a slight sin to him, and he led her on to greater sin. Ethel said it could just as easily have happened to her, if she were single, say, and on this very cruise; it could just as easily have begun with her casual mention of her *m*'s to him, that day on deck when he was analyzing in his mind.

Claire favored the idea, that he had become involved with a fast whore, but she agreed with Claire that it most likely began in a confession box.

Arlington Partidge and Albert Cottersley-Smith, when asked their opinion, chorused that they were very nearly bored silly with the mere thought of Mr. Blessing, and on Friday night they stayed up long after their wives had gone to bed, drinking whisky and discussing the matter.

Saturday the S.S. "Quaker City" docked on time, on the dot of noon. Up until then the morning had been spent in frantic fashion by both the Partidges and the Cottersley-Smiths, who were not weathered travelers, and were anxious with thoughts of things they forgot to pack, mislaid passports, and the exchange of adieus and addresses with other passengers. They all decided to have a drink together at a bar near the wharf, as a farewell gesture, and it was while they were deciding on the bar to meet in that they got a last glimpse of Mr. Blessing.

"Look!" Ethel Partidge gasped. "He's coming down the ramp now, see? Carrying his duffle, the lower ramp, see?"

"His woman should be meeting him," said her husband.

"Oh gaw, you mean we'll see her. Meeting her right out in open, hah? Oh, gaw, Arly, hold my hand!"

The Partidges and the Cottersley-Smiths looked after the enormous figure. They saw his hand raise suddenly, then they watched while he flagged his arm wildly. He was smiling and laughing, and it was the first time any of them could remember him doing either. But there was neither a young virginal type waiting on the wharf for Mr. Blessing, nor was there a more experienced-looking type waiting for him. In fact, a woman was not meeting Mr. Blessing at all.

Standing in the square with his legs apart and his hands on his hips–a straw hat resting back slightly on his head (as though he had pushed it back in anger or disgust) was a man. He was dressed immaculately in a white linen jacket with navy-colored linen pants, white shoes, and a red twill silk tie which was almost the same shade as his hair. Mr. Blessing was rushing toward him; a grin cut across his whole huge face, his free arm reaching out to the man. The man was alone. He did not see Mr. Blessing at first, but when he did see him, there came over his countenance one of the sourest expressions that the Arlington Partidges and the Albert Cottersley-Smiths had ever seen. It made the warm Caracas sun seem suddenly, unbelievably chilly.

EPILOGUE

From *The New York Daily Journal*–
                    WHO WAS WIN'S MURDERER?

Many people did not like Win Schneider. When the police interviewed close friends and servants of the dead woman, their list of suspects ran to two pages. There were many who might have done the deed.

Two months ago she was found strangled in the bedroom of the $99,000 home on Lerch Road in Bucks County, Pennsylvania, and the police are still trying to discover who was the one person who hated her enough to kill her. She was murdered shortly after noon on December 31, New Year's Eve day. The housekeeper was marketing in New Hope, and young Timmy Schneider was on his way to visit with his grandmother and father in New York. The Schneiders were estranged. Luther V. Schneider, President of Waverly Foods, was at his mother's house at the estimated murder-time.

There were many rumors. Talk of a fat man in a rented car being seen in the vicinity, as well as suspicions that a bitter former chauffeur had taken revenge on his ex-employer. A dazed Puerto Rican suffering from a mental illness confessed to the crime, and a brother of the murdered woman made the statement that he might have done it himself, if he had ever found time.

It was a greatly publicized case, certainly the most colorful crime in a decade.

While the murder itself was not particularly, unusual, most of the people involved in the known circumstances of the case, are unusual. Luther Schneider is a millionaire. His son, Timmy, was once kidnapped and returned after Schneider paid a ransom of $100,000. The Schneider vs Schneider court battles still leave judges and lawyers involved in the litigation, with red ears. The murdered woman, the former Win Griswold, was a society beauty of some twenty years back. The Griswold family is well known to Eastern society circles.

WHO was Win's murderer? Who dropped the receipt near her body, the only tangible clue there is in the case, a simple piece of ordinary receipt-book paper, marked across it: PAID IN FULL?

THE END

.

Alone at Night

by Vin Packer

*"When you're alone in the middle of the night and
you wake like someone hit you on the head,
You've had a cream of a nightmare dream, and
you've got the hoo-ha's coming to you...*
T. S. ELIOT

1

For one stunning half-second, as Slater walked through the snowy night toward Boyson's Cafe, he thought he saw the Cloward boy on East Genesee Street. Usually, it was Carrie's face he thought he saw in the crowd; it was Carrie looking out the window of a bus, or looking up from some table behind him, as he studied his reflection in a mirror, or in his nightmares–Carrie, the cigarette dangling from her lips, the slight tip to those lips, almost a smile of amusement, but really a thin little leer: *you won't get away with it, Slater.*

I am; you're dead... but still, telling himself that at such times, never quite took away the sliver of terror, at the unreal nearness of Carrie. Hallucinations... but still.

Only last week he had sent off a Christmas card to Cloward, at the penitentiary. If I can ever help you, he had dictated a little note to be enclosed... and O Mr. Burr, Miss Rae had looked up from her dictation with misty eyes which worshipped him, O Mr. Burr, to still forgive that boy, him–wrecking your life that way, drunk and O sir, you could teach us all about Christian forgiving!

Suddenly, as Slater Burr stepped inside Boyson's, shaking the snow from his gray-checked cap, he knew he could not face Jen's relatives that night. He could not face another of Chris' lectures about Jen's life being ruined, nor the nervous frivolity of exchanging gifts by the tree, nor everyone's asking him what the latest was about the plant... The latest was, he was losing the plant–Burr Manufacturing was going down the drain. Slater put his coat across his lap and ordered a martini. This time he saw Carrie's face reflected in his own eyes as be looked into the bar mirror; two tiny Carrie faces, two tiny cigarettes with their smoke spiraling up in his corneas; one saying, *'You're not a success without me, and you never were.'...* And the other? The same: *you won't get away with it, Slater.*

I've been getting away with it for eight years, Carrie. He picked up the martini and walked across to the phone booth. He dialed the McKenzies.

"Merry Christmas to all, and a Happy New Year!" Chris answered. That was Slater's brother-in-law in a nutshell: Mr. Goody Two Shoes, spilling over with good will and do good. Chris McKenzie, head of P.T.A., S.P.C.A., and last but O God never least, the Kantogee County Chapter of A.A.... Mr. Wonderful, spokesman for The Nearly Damned, available and declamatory any Friday evening in the basement of The First Presbyterian Church: My name is Chris McKenzie, and I'm an Alcoholic.

Slater said into the mouthpiece: "My name is Alcoholic, and I'm a Slater Burr."

"Very amusing, Slater... We've been waiting for you."

"Boozing it up over there, as usual, Chris?"

"I think you ought to search your heart and discover the reason you have to be so defensive, Slater."

"I'm just having a nice defensive ice-cold martini, very dry, with a defensive twist of lemon," said Slater. He parodied a singing commercial: "Remem-ber how great, all-that- booze use-to-taste? Martinis–still do!"

"Did the meeting go badly, Slater? Is that it?"

"You're all dying to know, aren't you, Chris?"

"Jen was wondering, is all."

"Well put Jen on," said Slater, "and by the way, Chris."

"Yes?"

"I was in Cayuta Trust this morning. Old man Caxton seemed concerned about Jen. I wonder if you think that's any of his business?"

"I didn't say anything to Caxton."

"Right after he expressed his concern, he told me his dog had been sick last week. He told me what a fine vet you were."

"You've been drinking, Slater. You wouldn't make those insinuations, if you hadn't had a few."

"Yes, we're all out of control but you, Chris. You just let me worry about Jen's drinking, and my drinking."

"This is no way to talk tonight, Slater."

"It's the Christmas spirit, Chris-mess. Let me speak with Jen."

"She's across the hall at the neighbors. You'll have to hold on."

Slater glanced at his watch while he waited. Eight o'clock. The stores in Cayuta, New York, were open until nine on Christmas Eve. That was a lifesaver; he still had a few more things to get Jen. Things he could not afford. Caxton had been his last hope, and Caxton had flatly refused a loan for Burr Company. It was just too risky a proposition, with the new zoning proposal... perhaps some other bank, one out-of-town. And by the way, how was Mrs. Burr ("young Mrs. Burr", folks in Cayuta called Jen) how was young Mrs. Burr? He had heard–

"Heard what?" Slater had not been willing to let the thought trail away.

"O nothing." Caxton sang-song back, "We all think she's such a pretty little thing, that's all, and hope she's well."

Just across from Boyson's, was the downtown employment office for Leydecker Electric. Slater could see it through the pane of the phone booth, which faced Genesee Street. Even though it was Christmas Eve, and snowing furiously outside, there was a line in front of the office. Slater knew that if he were to go out and cross the street, he would find some of his own men in that line.

There were only a few industries in Cayuta. In addition to L.E., there was a macaroni plant, a shoe company, and The Slater Burr Manufacturing Company. The latter was the oldest drop forge factory in the country. It produced forgings for other industries, from automotive, to agricultural, to locomotive. The Stewart family had owned it for more than a hundred years until Nelson Stewart died, when Slater took control. He gave the company his name; he even changed the name of the Stewart-owned office building on East Genesee to The Burr Building. Even Nelson Stewart's only heir had had Slater's name: Carrie Stewart Burr, the late Mrs. Burr, killed (long sighs, sad eyes rolled toward heaven) by the drunken Cloward boy... Slater took a sip from his martini, waiting there in the phone booth. I'm getting away with it, Carrie; it's Leydecker I'm fighting, not you, and not Cloward. He folded open the door of the phone booth and signaled for another drink. Then he fed the phone's box nickels, at the operator's time call.

Jen's voice was interspersed with the sound of the money ringing.

"What took you so long?" Slater asked.

"I was in the next apartment... with *drinkers.* Chris and Lena and assorted relatives are drinking ginger ale by the tree in the living room."

"I don't want to come over. Can I skip it? Meet you home?"

"You can do anything you want to do, darling. I'm bored to tears, and I'd love an excuse."

"I have a few things to get. Then I'll meet you home."

"I wish we could go to Europe," Jen said, and Slater knew then she was a little high; high, and back on going abroad forever, live on the Left Bank, on nothing–a loaf of bread, cheese, wine; what-do-we-need, we have each other. All right, all right, but not tonight, Jen, he thought; no patience tonight.

"If Leydecker keeps at it, we may go there... in rags."

"Wonderful!"

Slater felt his impatience quicken. Mrs. Burr spends quite a lot on clothes, sir, says Miss Rae; Miss Rae says, Mrs. Burr spent $508.15 last month, sir, and this month–

"Things are lousy, Jen," Slater said. "I'm not in a gay mood."

"How was it?"

"Bad." He imitated Leydecker's voice, "It is the *duty* of local leaders of industry to improve their properties, to appeal to local bankers, *if* necessary, for funds to enhance... Oh, well, it was that way."

"Chris said you saw Caxton."

"Refused," Slater said. "A flat refusal."

"But last summer Caxton said–"

Slater sighed. "Last summer, darling, L.E. was on the skids, and I was the fair-haired boy."

Only last summer, Caxton's kindly green eyes had looked up approvingly at the city council meeting, shining while Slater shined: "Don't think like losers!" Slater had shone, "Mr. Leydecker's attempts to get new industry in here are like attempts to get rich old strangers to change their wills in your favor! We're in the heart of the Finger Lakes, and we need to sell ourselves as a tourist attraction–sell our lakes, sell Cayuta, but don't sell it down the river to outside industry!"

"Winner" and "loser" were words Slater pounded in at council meetings, pounded in with his fist on the table, his eyes flashing, huge and powerful, compared to little Kenneth Leydecker, Jr., balding and prim, his frightened eyes peeping out through his gold-edged rimless glasses.

Slater was the winner, hands down, in his perpetual battle with Leydecker. All of Leydecker's proposals–for a new municipal airport to attract industry, for a new zoning law which would force the Burr plant from its center-town location, for this improvement and that one, were fought by Slater in council meetings, and defeated.

Slater had only to remind Cayutians what had happened during the war years, when Leydecker Electric expanded via Stamford-Clyde, an outside industry, which shared contracts and labor with L.E., then pulled away leaving L.E. over-expanded and under-contracted, and leaving Cayuta an official "depressed area." He had only to call attention to the fact that Burr Manufacturing Company, built with local capital and local brains, had never employed any but local people.

Then, late last summer, the wind shifted. Oil wealth, a construction boom, and high temperatures in Kuwait, a Persian oil sheikdom, all worked in Kenneth Leydecker's favor. He won a contract to produce 30,000 air conditioners for export to Kuwait. Leydecker Electric, for so long floundering and fishing for new industry, was on its feet. The wage scale in Cayuta for factory workers was up–up and beyond what Slater Burr could afford–and the town felt a new hum, an upsurge in spirit: L.E. was working nights, as well as double day shifts. Kenneth Leydecker no longer looked like a loser, and the Burr plant in center town, began looking exactly as Leydecker always said it did: like an eyesore.

Jen said, "How about the zoning proposal?"

"I'm afraid it'll go through, Jen."

"Did you give them the arguments against it?"

"My arguments sound pretty thin lately."

"Did you tell them it'd put B.M.C. out of business?"

"That's not news to anyone, Jen, and it wasn't news to Leydecker tonight that I can't swing a bank loan. He's on the board of Cayuta Trust; he knows what he's doing."

"I'm sorry you sound blue, darling." And that was so like Jen, like her to tell him she was sorry, just as she might tell someone at the club she was sorry he had lost at tennis.

"All right, I'll meet you home."

"I'm so pleased! I was so bored, Slater! They're all talking about bomb shelters over here. Is that all America can think about?"

He supposed he was in for another evening of Europe versus America. Jen had spent two years in France, nine years ago. Life's highlight for Jen, Slater thought derisively; what she would remember when she was an old woman. And Slater? Carrie's face in the bottom of his martini glass now: *No, she won't remember her real highlight, Slater; it's between you and me.*

"They're your relatives, Jenny," Slater sighed.

"I never said they weren't. They bore, bore, bore me! I wish we could go to Europe, Slater."

"I know... I wish it too."

"And they're all eating! Peanuts, doughnuts, potato chips, just filling their faces. The fat Americans!"

"Okay, okay," Slater said tiredly; could he count 20 men through the windows, across at Leydecker's? 30? "God hate America."

"Well, *I* do get bored, darling."

"It's hard for an oriental like yourself to adjust," said Slater.

Jen giggled. "I may be an American, darling, but I'm not dead. Everyone here's so dead!"

"I'll meet you at home, Jenny."

"Pick up some champagne, darling."

Live on the Left Bank on nothing, a loaf of bread, cheese–

He said, "I thought we weren't going to make anything special out of this commercial proposition–*American* Christmas."

"We're exchanging gifts. We might as well have some champagne."

"Shall I get a tree? They're selling white plastic trees in Woolworth's."

"Yes, be sure to," Jen giggled again. "God, don't you wish we were in a little French cafe near the Seine, sipping wine quietly."

"Don't kid yourself, Jenny. That little French cafe would be just as hammed up with Christmas decorations as Boyson's Cafe here on Genesee Street."

"But everything would be written in French, so I'd forgive it."

"Joyeux Noël," Slater said. "Bonne nuit."

"I'll see you at home, darling."

"Au revoir," said Slater Burr.

2

Rich Boyson sat on a stool in the rear of his restaurant, waiting for Slater Burr to come out of the phone booth. Rich was not a localite in the true sense of the word. He had moved to Cayuta fourteen years ago, when B.M.C. was still the Stewart Company, and Leydecker Electric, affiliated with Stamford-Clyde, was the big industry in town... Even in those days, Leydecker and Slater Burr were fierce enemies, and Rich's customers had soon filled him in on the reason.

It was hard for Rich to imagine Slater poor, or working in the shipping department at Stewart–hard to think of him as a gangling kid without even a high school education, impossible to think of him as Fran Burr. (He had changed his name, after his marriage to Carrie.) But he was that, and he had been called Fran Burr, right through his teens.

It was not difficult to imagine Kenneth Leydecker's father keeping Slater's father on a foreman's salary, while he adopted all Roy Burr's ideas for switches and connectors to improve L.E. equipment. Roy Burr had died of cancer at 48, his savings spent on his dying, the family in debt at his burial... No, if Kenneth Leydecker was a chip off the old block, it was not hard to imagine that... And anyway, that happened all the time. Rich's own father had been a chemist, and Rich would like to have all the money his father's ideas had netted Canadaigua Foods... but Slater Burr poor?

Slater looked like the kind born to money. He was a good six four, one of those huge men with coal black hair and large dark eyes, sure and cool, with his checked caps and sports cars, and the distance between himself and other men, that made Rich call him Mr. Burr. He could walk into Rich's place in khaki pants and a T-shirt, and still there would be something about him to tell Rich he was better-off than most of Rich's customers. Not many of the better-off class came into Boyson's, but Slater and Jen did, always by themselves. They were the kind Rich liked, the kind who really enjoyed their drinks, sat at the bar sipping martinis and talking as though they were two youngsters who had just met... The fact was, Jen Burr was a youngster, compared to Slater, but Rich sometimes thought of them as no different from the university kids, who came over weekends from Syracuse or Cornell... Together, they were like kids. Alone, Slater was friendly, but not a talker, not one to sit on a stool looking around either; quiet, studying the mirror, a real loner.

The only thing Rich Boyson could remember about Carrie Burr was that she walked around Cayuta in pants, always with a cigarette dangling from her mouth. She was not a drinker, and during their marriage, Slater seldom came into Boyson's, except for cigarettes and a fast one at the bar. No one really knew Carrie. She had gone to school outside Cayuta all her life, and she had married Slater the first summer she was home from college. She was tall like Slater, with the same pitch-black hair, which spilled to her shoulders, straight and shining, and her face was not pleasant, because she seldom smiled, but it was a good face, Rich remembered... just very solemn, with brown eyes that seemed to look through a person.

But Jen! Jen was like Slater's buddy. Rich thought of it as having a wife who was a pal, as well as someone to cook the meals and raise the kids. Rich's own wife was married to the Motorola television set in their bedroom. Oh, she had had her little fling years back, and Rich had broken Al Secora's ribs because of it... but now her fling was played out on a 19" screen, marked out a week ahead on the *TV Guide*. When Rich got home at night and started to gossip about people who had been in the place, Francie could hardly tear her eyes from the Tonight Show. It worked out that Rich told her all about people like Slater and Jen, while she didn't listen, then she told him all about Johnny Carson and Zsa Zsa Gabor, while he didn't listen. Then side-by-side they went to sleep, each one feeling bighearted about putting up with the other's drivel.

Sometimes Rich Boyson got fed up and told himself that if he were married to someone like Jen Burr... well, and he had to laugh... well, he would not be Rich Boyson, was all. He might be rich, but not Rich Boyson... He guessed Jen McKenzie Burr was the most beautiful woman in Cayuta, New York–hell, in the whole of Kantogee County! She was a little, very thin woman, with long yellow hair that hung straight and silk-like, skin like ivory, round deep blue eyes, dimples, and a snub nose. Rich thought of her as a little doll; that's what she was, a little doll, full of fire and what-for, and she could drink big Slater Burr under an oversized banquet table.

When Slater came out of the phone booth, Rich walked up to the front of the bar and pounded him on the back.

"Merry Christmas, Mr. Burr. Can I give you one on the house, for the Yuletide?"

"Thanks, Rich, but I've got last-minute shopping to do."

"Wish Mrs. Burr a Merry Christmas for me."

"O we'll be in during the holidays."

"Say, Mr. Burr," Rich said. "Know who came in here to use the phone today?"

"Someone who doesn't drink?"

Rich Boyson laughed; he stretched out the laughter. He had almost put his foot in it. He had just started to blurt it out, when somewhere in the middle, he had checked himself. God knows Slater Burr would find out somehow, if he did not know already, but Rich Boyson was not going to be the bearer of bad news. It was none of his business; he prided himself on staying out of other people's business, and for all Francie heard of his nightly gossip, he was clean when it came to keeping things to himself.

He intended to let his question get lost in his own laughter, then to shuffle away—fast.

But Slater Burr said, "*Who* was in using the phone?"

"Santa Claus!" said Rich Boyson, trying to sound as though he believed in the joke. It fell predictably flat and embarrassing between Burr and himself.

Burr responded with a thin snort, and swallowed down his martini. He swung his big legs off the barstool, and reached for his black wool cap on the counter.

"Seeing you, Rich," said Slater Burr.

Rich Boyson watched him push through the revolving door.

Santa Claus, he thought disgustedly, as he made his way back to his office... But still, he knew it was better saying that, than saying Buzzy Cloward was back in Cayuta... large as life and free as a bird—eight years later, using Boyson's pay phone, with his bags set on the floor outside the booth.

3

It was ten-thirty before the excitement died down. Its death left an uneasy embarrassment. The red and green Christmas lights blinked on and off on the small plastic tree set on the window sill of the apartment. The radio on the table played *O Holy Night,* and Selma Cloward, seated opposite her father and her brother, in the living room, glanced at her simulated diamond wrist watch. Her thoughts were spilling in every direction– getting to mass, what to do now Buzzy was back, and then on Oliver Percy, on why he would unbutton his shirt that way, just sit there with his shirt unbuttoned–period.

She said, "If you want to come to mass with us, Buzzy, it'd probably be all right, but you wouldn't have much fun, all girls and–"

"No, thanks, Sel."

His refusal made her glad she had asked. For the past hour she had wondered if she should chance the invitation. She was not attending mass with five other Ayres salesclerks, as she had pretended. She was going alone, and afterwards to Boyson's, and somewhere along the line she hoped to connect with Oliver Percy.

Selma Cloward was 30, three years older than Buzzy, and still unmarried. It was on her mind how Buzzy's return would affect her relationship with Percy. He was new to Cayuta, the new personnel director at Leydecker Electric. She had never mentioned Buzzy to him. He was a plump man in his late thirties, with a round apple-cheeked face, and bright blue eyes behind heavy black-shell glasses. A few weeks ago in Boyson's, when she was having the usual drinks with the crowd after work, he had come in, and they had struck up this conversation about winter. Right away, she had liked him, and nights she hung back when the other Ayres girls went on home, and they had drinks together. He was very much the gentleman, neat as a pin and one to order his scotch by brand. Martin's V.O., he always said, and his bills were never crumpled or old, but spanking new ones, as though he had just come from the bank.

Then last night he had asked her to his place for a drink. They had both had a lot to drink, and Selma had already decided on the stairs going up to his apartment that she would let him make love to her. She realized he was very drunk when they got inside. He had tripped against his table, and stumbled against the refrigerator when he got the drinks. They had three drinks while sitting on the couch, and on the fourth, Oliver Percy took off his coat, his tie, and unbuttoned his shirt. He pulled his shirt open and said, "There!" Then he took off his glasses.

"Well, you are quite well built!" Selma had said, for lack of anything else to say.

Oliver Percy responded: "I don't want you to think I did this because I don't think you're a nice girl. You are a nice girl."

So they sat there that way through another drink, Oliver Percy with his shirt open, Selma Cloward wondering what it all meant. At eleven o'clock he called a taxi for her, led her carefully down the stairs, and said, "Don't feel bad tomorrow. You're a good girl."

Well, drink did strange things to people, was all. Buzzy was proof of that. Selma Cloward loved Buzzy more than she had ever loved either parent, but she never fooled herself that Buzzy was not trouble. Long before he had ever met the Leydecker girl, he was making his way. As a youngster his idols were the Italian numbers men from the 2nd Ward, and he would run their errands for them, but late in his teens Slater Burr became his idol, and he picked out Laura Leydecker to make his way by new means.

Selma had grown accustomed to having her brother "away". His letters from prison were filled with talk of parole, but she had not counted on it. The truth was, she had counted on never having to worry about Buzzy returning to Cayuta. In prison he had worked in the kitchen, and taken correspondence courses. Selma had figured that when he got out, he would get a job somewhere miles away. In her mind's eye, she had seen herself one day years off, taking a train to visit him. She had imagined him older, gray-haired, stoop-shouldered, thin... meek, somehow.

It was true that he seemed more serious (glum was closer) and older, but his hair was the same fire red, combed in the elaborate pompadour he had affected eight years ago, and his gray eyes were solemn, but striped with a certain distant bravado, as though he were waiting for something to happen which would restore the cocky gleam there in the eyes of his photograph, on the mantle. He wore a light-colored sports coat with dark pants, and a jaunty, black-and-white striped floppy bow tie, loafers and red wool socks. He still had that habit of combing his hair every five minutes, then playing with the comb, twanging its teeth with his fingers.

He did have a job; he could not have been paroled without one, but to Selma Cloward's way of thinking, it was a very strange job for Buzzy. He was going to be a secretary to a man named Guy Gilbert, while Gilbert wrote a book... Way in the back of Selma Cloward's mind was the hazy suspicion that Buzzy might have broken out of Brinkenhoff... Still, he had written about this Gilbert, a newspaperman who had taken an interest in him. He was carrying matches from the Algonquin Hotel, where he had stayed last night with Gilbert. Gilbert had bought him the sports jacket and slacks. Gilbert had given him money for Christmas gifts, and in a week, when Gilbert came back from Florida, Buzzy was going to New York to work for him.

Maybe it was all the way Buzzy said, but The Whole Thing made Selma nervous, and for the first time since he had called from Boyson's, Selma Cloward was able to admit to herself that she wished he had not come back... Not when she was just getting to know Oliver Percy... just beginning to wonder how S.C.P. would look embroidered on the scarlet bath towels in her Hope Chest.

"Want some more wine, son?" Milton Cloward reached down beside the davenport and picked up the jug of grape wine. He poured some into Buzzy's glass.

"Thanks, pop."

"Wine don't hurt. Goes down smooth, don't it? It's not like the hard stuff. Now, you can hardly feel a thing, can you, son?"

"No, I can't feel anything."

"Not dizzy or anything, is that right?"

"I feel fine, pop."

Milton Cloward's way of showing intoxication was to get dizzy, a moment before he passed out. He seldom drank, only on holidays. He did not understand men who became wild and crazy when they drank, but he knew that it happened, and he blamed Alcohol for all Buzzy's troubles.

At ten-thirty that Christmas Eve, he was beginning to wonder if the wine had been a good idea. After all...

He said again, "You can hardly feel a thing, can you, son?"

"I'm really okay, dad."

"Yes," his father went back to the subject they had been discussing, "Cayuta's changing all right. Used to be the Stewart Building was the cat's meow with an elevator and one operator. But we got a team of six now, working two shifts, right up to eight at night, and nine on Fridays."

Milton Cloward was Starter of the elevator men. He was not a janitor, but off-duty hours he kept an eye out, like a night-watchman, which earned him the right to have this small apartment on the Burr Building's second floor. He could never get used to calling it The Burr Building; he had worked Car 1 when it was Nelson Stewart's place, and there were no other elevator men... Now The Burr Building belonged to Cayuta Trust. Slater Burr had lost it to the bank last year. Before he signed the papers, Slater Burr made sure Milton Cloward kept his apartment there; in the midst of all his troubles, Slater Burr thought of Milton Cloward. Another man–his wife run down by Milton Cloward's son, might have put the family out years ago, but Slater Burr was different from other men... Milton Cloward could remember when he was Fran Burr, a kid too big and busy for his age, and he supposed that was what made Slater different from other men, and he never had trouble remembering he wasn't Fran any more, but Slater–to Milt Cloward, Mr. Burr.

Selma Cloward said, "I'll say things have changed. Oliver Percy says we'll get more industry now, things are looking up."

"Oh yeah," her father said, "there's talk General Electric might move here, 'ploy about 300 men. Buy-build-boost Cayuta! See all the banners and signs saying that, Buzz?"

"Yes. It was the first thing I noticed on my way from Syracuse."

"It's hitting Mr. Burr hard, though. I hate to see that."

"He's paying slave wages down to his place, pop! It's about time he got it. Oliver Percy says he pays slave wages."

"Now, Sel, I told you that kind of talk ain't necessary."

"It *isn't* necessary, pop, but it's true. You can make more in the yarn department at Ayres, than you can make down to Burr's."

"Well, he needs to fix his place up. Repairs cost."

"He isn't fixing anything, Oliver Percy says."

"She just don't like Slater Burr's wife," said Milton Cloward. "You know Mr. Burr remarried?"

"Yes, I remember Selma writing."

"Married Jen McKenzie. Brother's a vet here now. Now, maybe she's a little hoity-toity, but she's a young–"

"A lit-tle hoity-toity!" Selma cut in. "A lit-tle hoity-toity! Har-de, har, har, har! She comes into Ayres like she was Miss Queen of England, and I can tell you I'd rather wait on Miss Queen of England, than on young Mrs. Burr, any old day of the week! She talks as if she lived in Paris, France, up 'till last Tuesday! 'Miss!' she says, 'I'm looking for a little envelope blouse, something to show off a seed-pearl choker. I saw one in Paris in shrimp-pink, which I adored!'... Oh, I can tell you, she's just what I need saunter-ing down the aisle on a Monday morning! And I hear she drinks like a fish too!"

"Now, now, Sel," Milton Cloward wagged his large hand back and forth, "that's just their way, rich folks. But I want to tell you, Buzzy," his face took on a serious expression, "Mr. Burr's been decent about everything. Do you know from time-to-time he asks about you?"

"He sent a Christmas card a week ago. Sent one every year."

"You see! Now, I don't want to go into all of That, but I just want the record straight. Slater Burr is a decent man, been decent about everything!"

"And Mr. Leydecker?" said Buzzy Cloward.

"Don't see him, s'all."

Selma said, "You know damn well you see him, pop, and he don't speak. For all I know, one day he'll put a bug in Oliver Percy's ear, and it'll be curtains for me."

Milton Cloward looked up at the clock on the mantle. "Holy Mackrel!" he said. "You see the time? It's quarter to eleven." He got up and reached for the jug of wine, carrying it to the kitchen. "I got to get going," he said.

Selma told her brother: "He don't speak to pop, and he don't speak to me."

"And Laura?" Buzzy Cloward finally said.

"She's a re-cluse."

"What do you mean, Sel?"

"A re-cluse. That's what everyone calls her. I don't know what it means. She don't come out."

"I know what a recluse is, but what do you mean she doesn't come out? She doesn't ever come out?"

"Un-uh. Never."

"That just doesn't make sense! Do you mean she doesn't go places, do things? Movies? I know she didn't go to college, after all. You wrote me that in one of your first letters, but–"

Selma said, "Buzzy, Laura Leydecker hasn't left that house in years!"

Buzzy just sat there, staring at his sister with a look of amazement. Selma Cloward looked away. She stood up, glancing again at her watch. She said, "Earl Leonard gave me this for my birthday last year. You remember Earl?"

"Yes. Sort of."

"We was going hot and heavy for awhile. I mean, it looked like the Real Thing... Then he got transferred, when the Wright Plant left Cayuta... That's what happens. We get a new industry and new men, two–three years ... then pfffft!"

"What's the matter with Laura?" said Buzzy.

"Only thing I hear is rumors. She's crazy, she's sick–nobody knows the truth... I got to meet the girls, Buzzy. If we don't get there early, then we have to stand."

"Somebody ought to know the truth."

"Look, Buzzy, want my advice? Stay out of it! She sure isn't up there on the hill pining away for you, so just stay out of it! Want my advice, she's flipped her lid or something–I don't know. She's a recluse."

"It's been eight years. Eight years. It still affects her?"

"What affects her I don't know anything about, but my advice is, look what it done to you, Buzzy!"

"I haven't had such a bad time of it, Sel. Meeting Guy Gilbert was the biggest break in my life... No, I haven't done badly. It's just that, it wasn't fair. If I could only explain–just to myself, Sel–why Leydecker lied about giving me the keys to his car that night... then... then I'd forget the whole thing."

"I know you always said that, Buzz, about Leydecker giving you the keys to his car... but I been thinking about it for eight years, thinking about it and watching Mr. Leydecker prance around Cayuta, and it just don't seem like he'd be the kind to give his keys to a drunken kid he hated."

"I think he wanted me to kill myself, so I wouldn't marry Laura."

"Buzzy, that still don't explain how you got into Slater Burr's car. If Leydecker gave you his keys, you would have been in Leydecker's car... Naw, Buzzy, it don't add up. You was drunk, Buzzy... There I go again, saying you was. Oliver's always correcting me. Live around pop, my education goes down the drain... You should have heard Earl Leonard talk. Remember?"

"No, I don't think I really knew him."

"Maybe that's right. It was '58 or '59. Yeah, you wouldn't have known him. Well–pffft, like I said. But he was a talker. Propinquity, he says: that's why we fell in love, he says. It was propinquity. I looked it up and it means nearness. I always wondered if he felt so near to me, why he didn't ask me to go to Rochester, when the Wright plant moved. But he didn't. Anyways," she said, "I got this watch from him. And now... there's this new man. Oliver Percy. Oh, he's a gentleman... intellectual type."

"A recluse," Buzzy Cloward said. "I remember her hair. You know, Sel, in prison you read a lot. An awful lot. There's not much else to do. I even read poetry, if you can imagine. I remember this one about this farmer, married a girl who didn't want to sleep with him."

"What'd he marry her for?"

"I don't know... He did. Anyway, he used to lie awake nights and miss her, you know?"

"He had a legal right. He could have gone to court."

"Well, he didn't. He just missed her. And there was this stanza, I remem-

ber." Buzzy Cloward sat up straight, looking down at his hands as he recited:

> She sleeps up in the attic there
> Alone poor maid. 'Tis but a stair
> Between us. Oh, my God, the down,
> The soft young down of her, the brown
> The brown of her–her eyes, her hair, her hair!

He coughed self-consciously, reached for his wine glass, and took a long
swallow. His sister was embarrassed too, and she coughed and murmured
"... the way the cookie crumbles, I guess."

Buzzy said, "Between you and me, maybe I was never really in love with
her, but I used to remember that. Her hair. That line: 'The brown of her–
her eyes, her hair, her hair!' "

Selma said, "Well, her hair was her best feature."

"Yes."

"Laura Leydecker's hair was her very best feature. Other than that, she
was peculiar."

"Not that peculiar. She was sick a lot. Shy too."

"Well, now she's a re-cluse."

"We used to have good times. I never minded the way she was."

"It's the way the cookie crumbles, Buzzy... I got that expression from Earl.
He was a great one for expressions."

Milton Cloward walked into the living room wearing his overcoat, carrying his hat. "We better push on, Sel."

"I'll get my coat, pop."

"You understand don't you, son? I wouldn't leave you alone on Christmas Eve, but I didn't plan on you. Didn't even know you was coming."

"It's okay, pop, honest! I'm tired too."

"You just pull out that hide-a-bed... You know how it works? They had
them things before you went up, didn't they?"

"Yes, pop."

"I didn't mean to say it like that."

"It's all right. I was 'sent up.' There's nothing wrong with calling a spade
a spade, pop."

"And you understand about tonight?"

"Sure. Of course!"

"You see, Olinski's new on the job. Heck, he didn't have nothing steady working for him for years, you know? Watchman this place, parking lot attendant that place, sort of a drifter. Now, he's got something steady, something regular and decent. I put him on Car 2, right before the holidays. That's the most important, gets the most traffic. Should have seen his face, son! Well, when Olinski asks me to drop in on the festivities at his place tonight, was about a week ago. I didn't think I'd have much to do, so I said yes."

"I know, dad. I really want to get some sleep."

"Means a lot to Olinski to have the Starter show up to his place, you know?"

"Sure."

"Heck, all we'd do is sit around and sip and get dizzy. Be in no shape to open our presents tomorrow morning."

"Have a good time, pop."

"I put the wine away, Buzzy, but I don't want you to think I mind if you have another little one. Christmas Eve and all. But you know, too much isn't good no matter if it's whiskey or beer or wine."

"Don't worry, pop, I've had enough."

"I wasn't worried. Don't get that idea. You wouldn't make the same mistake twice, not after what you been through. Isn't that right?"

"Right."

"So you just feel free to do what you feel like. I don't think you feel like going out or anything, do you?"

"No, I told you. Thanks. I'm going to bed."

"Well, okay, son. It's your home. You treat it like your home."

"C'mon," Selma Cloward called from the hallway, "or I'll be late and have to stand, pop!"

4

"'I do not want to be intimate with people. Why did I come here to a small town?'... Know who said that, Slater?"

Jen Burr wore a big, jackety lime-green cardigan, over white wool pants. She was barefoot, stretched out on her back, on the thick gold carpet in their living room. There was a black velvet pillow under her blonde head; her legs were crossed, and one hand held a champagne glass half-full; the other, a long cigarette holder carved from ivory. She smoked Gauloises, a French cigarette. The smoke spiraled up between Slater and her. He was lying on his stomach, on the eight-foot salmon-colored velvet couch, his glass of champagne resting on the rug by the couch leg. He wore white boxer shorts, nothing else. The room was dimly lit by the Solar lamp on Slater's kneehole desk; in the background Booker Little's trumpet sounded softly on the hi-fi.

Slater said, "Who said it?"

"Sherwood Anderson said it."

"It's profound," Slater said. "I wonder how he ever thought of it."

Jen giggled. "I love you, Slater Burr."

"Je t'adore," Slater said.

"You make it sound like 'shut the door.'"

"What time is it?"

"Eleven-ten P.M. Christmas Eve. Merry X . . Do you know how Sherwood Anderson died, darling?"

"Nope."

"He choked on a toothpick."

"Hmm."

"Isn't that a typical ending for an American writer?"

"I'm sure we had a few who coughed themselves to death with consumption, in the grand European tradition."

"Are you in a mood tonight?"

"A mood for what?"

"A mood ... You know. Depressed?"

"Not particularly."

"Good... God, I love Max Roach."

Slater said, "Who the hell is Max Roach?"

"He's playing the drums and vibes. Hear him?"

"Um hmm."

"I saw Stan Getz in Paris, just about ten years ago tonight. Lord, I remember that night! If anyone had ever told me that night, that I'd be living in Cayuta, New York now, I'd have jumped in the Seine."

Slater said, "Darling, when you die—no matter what year or where, I'm going to have engraved on your tombstone, born Buffalo, New York 1929, died Paris, France, 1952."

"That's not very nice."

"Don't make it into something now; it's just a joke. Just a weak little joke."

"I'm not dead—it's this town."

"Sometimes you talk as though I personally dragged you away from Paris by the hair, and brought you here."

"Slater, I never blame you. You're the only one who's alive in the whole damn town! I knew that the minute I saw you. I saw you across the room that night, and I honest-to-God fell in love with the back of your head!"

"I wish to hell we could get out of this town too, Jen. You know that, don't you?"

"I don't see why we can't. With Leydecker squeezing you this way, I don't see why we don't just sell out and get out!"

Slater hauled himself up from the couch. "Want more champagne, or have we had enough?"

"Please, darling."

He reached down for her glass. "I wouldn't get more than peanuts for the place, the condition it's in. And if the new zoning proposal goes through, I couldn't sell it even for peanuts. I'd have to merge with some company already set up, work for them. I'm 47 years old, and the only thing I know a damn about is the forging business. I'd be lucky to be a foreman in a merger. Burr would just be a subsidiary business. No one's crying for a 47-year-old executive whose own place went bust!"

"But we aren't bust, darling!"

"Jen, we're damn close. People are really beginning to listen to Leydecker. Any more industry in here, I'll be out of business. I lost 10 men last week to L.E.... If a new industry doesn't do it, the zoning proposal will. Leydecker's beginning to pick up votes, and I mean—fast!"

"Oh, you've always beat out Leydecker, darling, and you will again. I wish we were in Paris... right now."

"I won't beat out Leydecker. He's foxier than I thought."

"Besides hating you, darling, what does he want all these changes for? He's got his new contract. Why isn't he satisfied?"

"For one thing, how many sheikdoms are going to be wanting air-conditioners? He's got to worry about what happens after this job. Some of the industry he's scouting might use his plant... Hell, if I can just get a loan somewhere, I can fix up our place, get a status quo on the zoning, and find a subsidiary line for Burr... But–it's like dreaming. If it wasn't for Leydecker, I'd get all three, but he's boxed me in. He's scheming day and night... It used to be, a strike down at the plant meant money lost, and I'd fight to prevent it. Now, I'm torn. The more labor problems we have, the more unattractive Cayuta is to industry scouts. I'm getting so I'm tempted to cause a strike. I'm getting–"

"Sentimental over me, darling?... Come on, honey, it's Christmas Eve. Hush! I didn't mean to start it all up again."

Slater said, "It doesn't start and stop at your command, I'm afraid."

"Let's have another drink."

"I'm on my way for more right now. I don't know if we need more, but here goes."

"Since when have we cared if we *need* more?"

"All right, okay, more champagne, coming up."

"And no more shop talk, hmm?"

"No more shop talk," Slater said.

Jen McKenzie had initially come to Cayuta for a few months' visit with her brother. Chris was a veterinarian, who used to practice in Buffalo, New York. He moved to Cayuta after a scandal over the fact that he was selling, for medical experiments, the pets which clients brought him to "put to sleep." The near ruin resulting from the scandal had a sobering effect on Chris, whose very name in the same sentence with "sober" was a novelty. Chris joined Alcoholics Anonymous, and the Society For The Prevention of Cruelty to Animals. The toughest and most scraggly old cat handed over by a client, was put to sleep as delicately as one handled long-stemmed crystal, and anti-vivisection became Chris McKenzie's middle name.

Whatever thread of rebellion there was left in Chris by summer 1954 squirmed uneasily around his sister in the presence of Slater Burr. He had been the one to introduce them, on a June night at the country club.

"Who's that large man with his back to me, Chris?"

"Slater Burr."

"And the woman?"

"Carrie, his wife."

"*She's* his wife?"

"Yes."

"Good God, I saw her earlier in the Ladies. I took her for a lesbian."

"Well, she's not, and don't shout that word around the club."

"Introduce me... to him, I mean."

It began then.

Chris did not know it then, and Lena never knew it. Maybe no one at The Kantogee Country Club knew it that night, but Jen and Slater.

Slater told her later... a few days later as they parked in his Jaguar up at Blood Neck Point, on Cayuta Lake: "I fell in love with you instantaneously, Jen. Was it that way for you too?"

"Faster than that," Jen had answered.

A month from that night, Chris came into the guest room where Jen was finishing dressing.

"Going out again?"

"And again, and again."

"I know who it is, Jen. It's trouble, believe me."

"I can't help it, Chris," she had told him frankly. "I don't know how to stop."

The Booker Little record rejected itself, and Eric Dolphy's alto sax began a lazy exploration of "Stormy Weather." Jen Burr rolled over on her stomach and lit another Gauloise.

"What are you smiling about?" Slater said, coming in with the champagne glasses.

"I was remembering a night at Blood Neck Point."

"Any one in particular?"

"The first one."

"The night poor Secora got beat up for making time with Francie Boyson."

"That's right, we saw them there. They were leaving when we were driving in. You said 'Good God, that's my foreman with Rich Boyson's wife.' I didn't know how funny it was then. I was just afraid it'd be our first and last night."

"Boyson broke a couple of his ribs... You'd never think Rich was anything but easy-going. Tonight, I think he was drunk. He offered to buy me a drink, and said something about Santa Claus coming in this afternoon to use the phone."

"Our first night," Jen said, "and you said you fell in love with me instantaneously."

"Do you remember what was playing on the radio?"

"Doggie in the Window."

"Right!" Slater grinned down at her as he gave her the champagne. "I must have that doggie in the window."

"And I was thinking–I must have that Slater Burr."

"You had him."

"Not quite, darling, not at all quite."

He went back and flopped on the couch.

She said, "Slater? If things hadn't turned out the way they did, what do you think you'd be doing tonight?"

"What do you want to hear, Jen? That I'd be up in bed laying Carrie?"

"Why do you get so angry? You get angry whenever I bring it up."

"There's no need to bring it up. Why must we talk about Carrie?"

"Because we never have. It's been eight years. It seems to me enough time has elapsed so–"

"So that we can go into the intimate details of my marriage with Carrie?"

"I didn't mean just that, but that's a start, at least."

"A start to what? A fight? Every time you drink–"

"No, Slater, you know that's not fair. Not every time I drink. Hardly ever. But Carrie was–so damn unlike someone you'd marry. I could understand if it had been for money, but–"

"But it wasn't."

"I know. You've said it enough."

"I'm not in a mood to tell you what Carrie was like in bed, and that's what you're fishing for, Jen."

"There probably wasn't any bed."

"Then there probably isn't anything for me to say on the subject."

"I wish you'd just talk about her. You still feel guilty, Slater, that's what I'm getting at. Just because we wished her dead, and she died, you feel guilty."

"I did not wish her dead, goddam it! I wanted you, and I didn't want her, but I did not wish her dead, Jenny!"

Slater sat up and scratched a match to light a cigarette. "I wished her dead! That's one hell of a nice topic for Christmas Eve!"

"Should we save it for December 26th, or the day after Easter, or the day after Thanksgiving, or the day after Mother's Day, or–"

"Stop it, Jenny!" Slater shouted. "You're drunk, and you want a fight. You're bored, and you want a good fight!"

"If it takes a fight to make you discuss it with me, then let's fight. Turn up Eric Dolphy and we'll shout over it, if you want, but let's discuss it!"

"Eric Dolphy, Eric Dolphy, somebody or other Roach! I'll say this for you,

Jen, you don't miss one goddam beat of the music. We could be blown sky-
high by the bomb, and you'd know whether it was Charles Mingus playing at the time, or Thelonious Monk!"

"Carrie wasn't killed, Slater! You didn't kill her and whatever-his-name-
was Cloward didn't kill her. She jumped in front of that car!"

Slater sighed. "Whatever-his-name-was Cloward would be happy to
hear that," said Slater. "Why don't we wire Brinkenhoff, or whatever-the-
name-is prison, and give him the news."

"Oh, you know the name of the prison. When I was in the office Tuesday, Miss Rae said, "Isn't Mr. Burr wonderful? Every year he sends that
boy a card to the penitentiary!'... isn't that just wonderful!"

"So what? What do you want to make of that?"

Jen sat up and shook her Gauloise at Slater, knocking its long ash off on
the rug: "Guilt! You're so guilty you identify with that drunken kid! You
wished Carrie dead, and you feel as though you killed her, and not that kid.
Well, I don't think anyone killed her. She couldn't stand losing you! It was
suicide!"

Slater laughed. "Oh, God, you must be out of your mind, Jen!"

"I say she jumped in front of that car!"

"Out of your mind!" Slater laughed again. He tipped his glass over, breaking it, sweeping the glass aside on the table.

"And you pay penance! That's why Burr Company is failing! You're
afraid to be successful without her!"

"Balls, Jen!"

"You're letting the place slip through your fingers, because you have to
pay penance for something you didn't even do! You can't let go of your
guilt! That's why we're stuck here, you have to pay penance for Carrie's
death!"

"Jen, shut up!" Slater was on his feet.

"You'd think you ran over her, the way you act! Penance!"

In a long, sudden step, Slater Burr crossed to her. His large hand cracked
down across her jaw; the slap rang out like a lash. Her champagne glass
tumbled over on the rug. She fell backwards, her hands covering her face.

For a moment, nothing but the lazy bleating of the saxophone filled the
room. Then Slater dropped to his knees beside her.

He said softly, "Jenny?"

He pulled her up.

"I don't want you to touch me," she said.

Slater took his hands away.

"Slater, that's the first time you've ever hit me."

"I'm sorry."

"You know why I don't want you to touch me?"

"I don't blame you," he said.

"No, it isn't that... I don't want you to touch me, because I want you to touch me. I don't care what you do, if you'll touch me. Do you see what that's like, Slater? I hate it!"

"We've both had a lot to drink." He knelt so that her legs were between his. He leaned in to her and kissed her mouth.

She put his hands up to the buttons of her cardigan.

"I'm so in love with you, Slater."

"That's the way I feel about you." He undid the buttons, reached his hand behind her sweater to the clasp of her brassiere, and undid that.

After a while, he said, "Who's on the trombone?"

"Jimmy Knepper."

"I knew you'd know, even now."

"I love you, Slater. I just love you."

"Move to the couch? Rug's wet. Champagne."

"No."

The phone rang out and Slater groaned.

"Never mind it," she said, "Never mind, darling."

"Why do you wear pants? Complicate things."

"Why do you?" She looped her thumb around the elastic on his boxers. "Off!"

Slater chuckled. "I do not want to be intimate with people. Why did I ever come here to a small woman... Know who said that, Jen?"

"Slater Burr said that." Jen sighed.

5

There was no answer.

Donald Cloward put the phone's arm back in its cradle.

He did not think of himself as "Buzzy" any longer. When Selma and his father called him by that name, it registered in the same nominal way most things about his old life did.

His memory of that life was very sharp, except for those few hours on the night of August 30, 1954. In prison he had relived his years like some-one reading and rereading a novel, finding new things, re-examining old ones—viewing his life in a detached way, as a reader views a character in a novel, knows everything he can about the character, but feels no flesh-and-blood intimacy with him.

He stood up and ran a comb through his hair, while he studied his reflec-tion in a mirror. He remembered once Slater Burr snapping at him: "Stop combing your hair!" and he thought of it then, and stuck the comb back in the rear pocket of his trousers. He was amazed to learn that the memory was still so sharp, that the inner punch of apprehension, still vivid... Today, he might have said flatly: "Why?"—he wasn't sure—but at the time he had felt as though be were stealing something, picking his nose—something, and Slater Burr had found him out.

Cloward walked across to the window of his father's apartment and looked out. Across the way the tower clock on top of the Cayuta Trust: 11:20 P.M.... In a way, he was thankful Slater Burr had not answered the telephone. It was late; what if he had awakened him? At the same time, he felt the urgency of making contact with Slater Burr... of starting the busi-ness he had come to Cayuta to accomplish.

East Genesee Street was lit by Christmas neons, and slushy now with a wet snow. NOEL chimed out from the bank's tower, and Cloward could see people in the streets rushing to church, to Boyson's, to The Mohawk Hotel Bar, to their homes and their relatives' homes.

Since leaving Brinkenhoff, he had felt as though he had been erased from life. He existed, but there was no life he was involved in himself; he was simply involved in other people's, as he encountered them, and not missed at the end of the encounter. He thought of last night at the Algonquin with Guy, the long torture of sitting there while Guy talked endlessly about Priscilla. Cloward had never even met this woman, never would, now she had run out on Guy, but he knew it was not the last time he would hear about her, just as last night was not the first time. The stories were the same. Guy repeated them, as though each time they were every bit as fascinating to Cloward, as they were to Guy. Hours dragged by. Cloward tried every tack to keep himself interested, and to believe he was a part of this man's life. Cloward asked questions about her, suggested answers to Guy's questions to himself, listened, listened, but each tack was futile. He was not even in the room; Guy was talking to himself: "My Cilly" this, "My Cilly" that... just as he talked about his work, with the same selfish force that believed Cloward had no life but through Guy Gilbert.

Cloward and Guy Gilbert had first met, a few weeks after Cloward had sent his recipe for Brinkenhoff Bouillabaisse, to the *New York Journal Times* Cooking Contest. Brinkenhoff Penitentiary began easing its regime at the time Cloward was sent there. There was a new warden, a more permissive attitude toward correction.

Cloward was assigned to the kitchen, a fact that irked him in the beginning. It was where the dullards were put to work. He borrowed cookbooks from the library. If he kept within the penitentiary budget, the warden permitted some innovations and experimentations with the food. Cloward had set out to impress the warden. He had perfected a soup made from fish and vegetables, copying the word "bouillabaisse" from a book which described a similar dish. When he read in the newspaper about the contest, he was sure he could seduce some outside interest to supplement the warden's interest in him.

He was not surprised when the newspaper's editor saw a story possibility in Brinkenhoff Bouillabaisse. Guy Gilbert, a reporter of human interest pieces, was sent to interview Cloward. Gilbert wanted to do a study of the Brinkenhoff correction system as well.

So it began, with Cloward believing he could use Gilbert. When Gilbert helped him with his parole, Cloward congratulated himself. He accepted Guy's offer for work...

Only in the past three days, since he was out of Brinkenhoff, did he realize Guy was using him, as a buffer against an immense loneliness, and as a sounding board.

The scene on East Genesee aggravated Cloward's feeling of anonymity. Next to the Cayuta Trust was The Clark Building. Eight years ago, on a hot afternoon in July, he had gone there with Laura Leydecker, to look at apartments. They were to be married at Second Presbyterian Church that September—never mind what Kenneth Leydecker thought of it any more. They had kept their bargain, waited one year.

Buzzy Cloward was nineteen that summer. He had gone through crazy years of wild-and-nervous carrying on. In those years, Slater Burr still owned the building where Buzzy lived, and Milton Cloward more than once spoke to Slater of Buzzy's wildness.

"If you speak to him," he would tell Slater Burr, "I think he'd listen to you. Tell him he'll never get nowhere, rate he's going."

And Slater Burr in those days, big and full of fun, easygoing and always warm with Buzzy, would take the boy aside and say in a stern voice: "Your father wants me to speak to you, Cloward."

"Yes, sir?"

"Well, I'm going to do just that!" still stern... Then, with a wink, "Hello, Buzz!" and he would pound Buzzy's back, chuckle and be off.

Buzzy Cloward in those days had been The One at Industrial High, which was not the same as being The One at Cayuta High, where college was the next step, and where girls of Laura Leydecker's class strolled through the halls with neat young men in jackets and ties, discussing This and That, not at all self-consciously.

The One at Industrial High wore work pants and denim shirts, put Alka-Seltzer in ink wells to the wild guffaws of other unruly boys (all boys), went to shop drunk on beer, and started sawdust fights from the shavings on the school floor, careened through the halls shouting and whistling, swallowing wine by lockers, flunking and repeating, and off-hours, stealing hub caps from cars, running errands for the numbers men, seducing older women' (girls in their early twenties who worked at Stamford-Clyde-Leydecker Electric), hanging around the pool halls and bowling alley... restless, attention-seeking, handsome in a rash, merry-and-worthless way... And always, the underlying gloom and fear of After Graduation, of girls who were not like Selma, but different and better, of running an elevator, or working at S.C.L.E., or wasting.

And sometimes, when he saw Slater Burr's sports car flip up to the entranceway of The Burr Building, saw Slater hop out, rich looking and unharassed, as though in all the world there would be nothing a Slater Burr might think to wish for, were he allowed just one wish, Buzzy would watch him momentarily with wonder: what could it be like to be him?... And Slater would wave at him and call his name—he always did—and for a moment, just an inch of infinitesimal time, Buzzy Cloward would be a part of that world which was Slater's, and he would feel the blood circulating gaily in his veins, feel some of the magic rubbing off on him, and a bounce to his step when he walked.

In his last year at Industrial, on East Genesee Street, at an Armistice Day parade, he saw a girl in the doorway of the Ayres Building. He was with Ted Chayka, both high on beer, and he stopped to look at her. Her back was to him, and her shoulders were shaking, as though she were crying, and down her back, long soft brown hair, and she was wearing high heels and stockings.

"That woman's in trouble," he told Ted.

"It's not a woman. It's the Leydecker girl. She always wears those heels."

"She's crying, isn't she?"

"C'mon, she's balmy. I heard she was balmy."

But he left Ted, buoyed by beer and impulse, went up to her and asked what was the matter.

"I have an earache."

"My name is Buzzy Cloward. I'm an earache specialist."

"You know who I am, don't you, or you wouldn't have come to make fun of me?"

"No, I'm not making fun. I wanted to help you." And it was funny how easy he found words which sounded solemn and sincere, for part of him was standing off enjoying his composure and ease. He was an actor. "What you need is to sit down some place, rest a minute."

"Not in Murray's," she said.

He knew Murray's; it was where the Cayuta High kids hung out. He never went there.

"Tannemaker's," he said. "Do you want to have a coffee at Tannemaker's?"

She was not really pretty, but there was something winning about her. A vulnerability, and an intensity that seemed to know about it. Her hands were white as snow, fragile hands with long fingers, and a delicate look to her small, thin body as though she were made of porcelain. No make-up at all on her face, but these very clear green eyes, and lips a natural red... and tiny clean pearls at her neck.

She said, in that slow and well-spoken way of hers, "I don't think you've been drinking coffee," with just the barest trace of a smile.

"I will though, at Tannemaker's."

"You don't have to," she said.

"Your name is Laura, isn't it?"

"I suppose you've heard all about me. "

"I'd like to."

How easy it was, and it never had been with a girl, except Selma, factory girls... not Kenneth Leydecker's girl or her kind.

In Tannemaker's he drank another beer, while she had coffee. Again, he stood off at one side watching himself there in the booth with her–the actor. For the first time in his life he wanted to change. Not for her, exactly, but he grinned at her, and he talked to her and made her laugh. He did not mind her strangeness. It was there, he could not miss it–not a balmy strangeness as Ted Chayka had inferred, but the feeling she was not following all the conversation. She seemed preoccupied and sometimes he knew she was not listening to him, and when she did listen to him, she took what he was saying very literally.

"I've had earaches myself," he had said at one point. "They're no fun."

"Fun?" said she.

"I mean, they hurt."

"Oh, I see... In yours, was there an inflammation of the drumhead?"

"I don't remember."

"I think I have myringitis right now."

"What's that, for Pete's sake?"

"Inflammation of the drumhead," she said.

He saw her often after that, usually at Tannemaker's in the beginning, and then, wherever they could manage. He was as odd to her as she was to him, but between them there was an imponderable rapport. She read poetry to him, and he, in turn, spoke words to her she had never believed were in the English language, and if he took her with a violence that showed his intense fury at her father, who called him "dirt"; she cried his name with trembling joy and spoke afterwards of his gentleness. They amazed one another, and there was that to bridge their differences.

At nineteen Buzzy Cloward was the first high school graduate the Cloward family had ever had. He was a manager of Woolworth's on Grant Street, earning $60 a week. He had a light suit and two dark ones in his closet, loafers, and thirteen neckties. He had stood up to the President of Leydecker Electric, and told him he intended to marry his daughter. He had been threatened by Leydecker, lectured by him, begged, pleaded with, scorned by him, and ultimately Leydecker had bargained. They were to wait a year.

It was a year which left Laura and Buzzy exalted and doped on the excitement they were able to create in one another. Marriage, with its license for all the more unfathomable-to-them opening of their senses and sensuous exploration, seemed to be the millennium. Laura was afraid she would die before that September, or that Buzzy would, or that the whole

world would just blow up. The actor waited, patiently, pleased with himself and half-hating the actor, because he did love her, and told himself that
over and over, watching for the change in Kenneth Leydecker's eyes, for
the moment Leydecker would believe it, for the acceptance from him.

That day when they went to The Clark Building, there was still no
change in her father.

Before they left the house, Buzzy said to him: "We're apartment hunting
this afternoon, sir."

"I know what you're hunting, young man. Not apartments."

The superintendent was busy placing Fourth of July banners on the face
of the building. He gave Buzzy the key to 4-F (furnished; $52 a month) and
they both took the four flights by twos, by now both geared to Opportunity's magical and unpredictable way of presenting itself... Afterwards,
Laura said, "I think sometimes it's all an illusion. 'All is illusion till the morning bars, Slip from the levels of the Eastern Gate. Night is too young, O
friend! day is too near!'... Don't you feel that way, darling?"

"I only worry about your father," Buzzy had answered.

It was funny how the mind remembered little details, sounds and smells,
so that it could summon them to life with the moment: and in prison, for
Donald Cloward, that moment she said that, and he answered her, he was
walking down the stairs of The Clark Building, and the tin guard on one
step was loose, the stairway dark, smelling of lixivium and coffee perking
somewhere, and from the street below a bus groaned. He remembered he
had thought: This place is a worse hole than the place I live in now. He had
thought of the spacious rooms in the Leydecker house on Highland Hill,
the rugs and stuffed chairs and gold mirrors, room after room. And there
was a roach on the stairway which he stepped over, so as not to kill. *Not
yet, Leydecker; if I give you time, you'll come my way.*

"Don't worry about my father," Laura Leydecker had said. "He's resigned
to it now... Oh, I do love this place—our first home, never mind it's tacky, I
do love this place!"

Then, the glare of the sun as they reached the street; their eyes squinting
in the new brightness, and the smell of paint on the clothes of the superintendent, as they returned the key. He was carrying a red, white, and blue
puff-banner.

"Took your time about it," he said; he had winked.

"It was not a nasty tone of voice, I didn't think," Laura had said as they
walked away from there. Then: "It was very good for me that time. Was it
for you?"

It was another victory; God, he had given Leydecker a pounding! But, "Yes, very good, Laura," and he took her hand possessively.

Donald Cloward walked away from the window. He sat down on the hide-a-bed, and lit a cigarette.

In a moment he would feel the hands on his shoulders again. He shut his eyes. He could smell August, taste whiskey, and in the darkness he tried to see whose hands those were on him there in the night.

6

He had never been to The Kantogee Country Club before that night, the 30th of August.

The club was set on Cayuta Hill, high up over Blood Neck Point, at the lake. It was a low-hung, rambling structure, with a red star attached to its roof. Selma's crowd, and others in Cayuta, called it "The Kremlin."

Kenneth Leydecker had suggested the evening–his first amiable move–and he had driven them there in his Chrysler. On the way, it seemed to go well, though Laura was very nervous, and Leydecker quiet, until the car approached the hill.

"The points of those stars are symbols, Donald," Leydecker said then. "Symbols, all four. They represent Character, Community Spirit, Culture, and Christianity."

Buzzy smiled to himself, remembering another way it had been put; he had heard it many times:

> Character meaning born rich and look down
> Community Spirit meaning pay low wages, own the town,
> Culture meaning buy nice clothes, drink good booze,
> Christianity meaning for God's sake, keep out Jews!

But sour grapes was not a part of Buzzy Cloward's mood that night. He said simply, "That's very interesting, sir."

"'The desire of the moth for the star,'" Laura said dreamily, "'Of the night for the morrow, the devotion to something afar.' "

"I don't know where you get all those thoughts, Laura," said Buzzy. "Do you, Mr. Leydecker?"

"That particular thought came from Shelley," Leydecker said. "All Laura's thoughts come from books. Laura reads all the time; too much of the time. I'd hoped she'd go on to college, and get some direction, learn to channel her intellectual capacities."

Laura said, "I have the oddest feeling of fluctuation in my ankle."

"You do?" Buzzy said.

"Yes... Look at all the crowds of cars. There must be 100 people here."

"Saturday night," said Leydecker. "You haven't been here in a long, long, time, Laura."

"I never enjoy myself here."

"We'll have a good time, Laura," Buzzy said. "Is your ankle hurting you?"

"It doesn't *hurt...* I don't read all the time either."

"I'm reading John Steinbeck's *Sweet Thursday* right now," Buzzy lied. Selma had it out from the Ayres Lending Library.

Mr. Leydecker pulled in at the parking area. Buzzy saw Slater Burr's Jaguar and said, "Slater Burr's here."

"Are you an admirer of Slater Burr, Donald?" said Leydecker.

"Oh yes, we're good friends."

"It doesn't surprise me."

"Sir?"

"I said, it doesn't surprise me."

Laura said, "I wish we weren't here. I would much rather have gone to a motion picture."

"Well, we're here," Leydecker said.

Buzzy had rented a white dinner jacket from De Lucca's on South Street, worn the trousers to his navy blue suit, with a navy blue tie and white shirt; black shoes, bought especially for the occasion. Kenneth Leydecker never looked at his daughter's fiance, without Buzzy's knowing instantly something in particular was wrong. Everything in general was wrong about the prospective son-in-law of Kenneth Leydecker, but each time they came face-to-face, there was the particular, always new... always clear in the beady eyes behind the bold-edged rimless glasses.

Leydecker said, "An ordinary suit would have done, Donald."

This conversation, while Laura was in the Ladies, to look at her ankle.

"Everyone is wearing white coats, sir. I thought–"

"Not with navy trousers from a navy suit."

Then Leydecker said, "What are you drinking, Donald?"

"Oh–" and for a moment he could think only of beer; he drank nothing but beer.

"Ginger ale and whiskey, I would guess," Leydecker said. "I believe that's what you people like."

"My people don't drink," Cloward lied; Selma always ordered rye and ginger ale. How did Leydecker know that?

"I don't mean your family. Your kind. Your class, Donald. I don't have to mince words with you. The people here tonight, yes, look around–these people are not your people."

"I know some of them."

"Slater Burr, perhaps, yes. Like finds like, no matter."

"I don't understand. You mean, because Mr. Burr was poor once, and I'm... not rich either."

"You're not poor, hmm?"

"No, sir. And I finished high school."

"You don't see anything else similar about *Mr.* Burr and you?"

"What?" said Buzzy. "What do you want me to see?"

"Take a good look at Mrs. Burr. Does she seem very beautiful, or gay, very popular? She's over there, at the table near the door. Look at her."

Buzzy had never seen her so dressed-up. She seemed ill-at-ease in the gown, and the inevitable cigarette hanging from her lips was out of place. She wore a large leather-strap wrist watch on her arm that seemed out of place as well. She was by herself, watching the dancers in the center of the room, with a certain bored air, as though she were wasting her time and resentful of the fact. But Buzzy had always liked her; he had never thought she was any different from anyone else—richer, and not as well-dressed as women with her money, but he had never pondered it.

He said, "What's the matter with her?"

"She's being used, I'd say. Ask yourself why a man like Slater Burr married her. When you have the answer to that one, ask yourself why he's so obsessed with seeing that his name replaces her maiden name—on every-thing—even on the building you live in."

"I see... and you think I'm that way?"

"I don't *think* it."

"Well, Laura and I don't want anything from you. We've never asked anything from you yet."

"And don't."

"Thank you for the drink, sir." Buzzy poured the rye into the ginger ale, then wished he had drunk it straight, though he was not sure why he wished it. He did not like the taste of whiskey, and he was unaccustomed to drinking it.

"It's the last thing I'll buy you, the last thing I'll give you. The first and last. I want that clear."

"I don't expect anything."

"Ho! Ho!"

"I don't."

"Wait until Laura's doctor bills come... You know, don't you, that among other things, Laura is a hypochondriac?"

"Maybe you've made her one, sir."

"We're discussing effect, not cause. Laura is a very complicated person. She's different from other girls her age, and she always was. You know she's different."

"We've been all through this, Mr. Leydecker."

"If you loved her–if–you'd let her have the chance to go to college, where her mind can be developed properly, and appreciated. She's very sensitive, a very nervous girl. You won't be able to handle her. You're nowhere near knowing her yet... Just wait. Watch her this evening, around other people. You'll see how well you know her."

Leydecker's bald head glistened in the light as he peered up at Buzzy Cloward. His small, bitter mouth was turned to a slant as he spoke, and he seemed to Buzzy like a weird, little angry bird, who wanted to peck out Buzzy's eyes.

"I know you hate me," the Actor said, "but I'll show you I'm not what you think I am."

"I don't hate you. I loathe you," Leydecker answered quietly.

"I don't care. I'm going to marry Laura." But his knees were weak, as they always were in a confrontation with Laura's father. The palms of his hands were wet, and he felt breathless as he stood there.

When Laura joined them, her father acted as though there had been no harsh words spoken. During the first dance, Buzzy said, "Well, he was at me again."

"Father is persistent. It's one of his major characteristics."

"He said he loathed me."

"It's so crowded here. I hope I'm not getting synovitis of the ankle joint."

"Where do you learn all those medical terms?"

"I just know them. I like to know what's wrong when I feel ill."

They danced the whole set, to "Hernando's Hideaway" and "Hey, There", "I Love Paris" and "Young at Heart". At the end of the set, Laura went back to the Ladies. There were many couples there their age, but when they waved at her (Buzzy knew none of them) she seemed embarrassed.

"Let's meet some of them, talk to them," said Buzzy.

"No. They don't really like me. I want to look at my ankle, besides."

He was not disappointed. He felt a strange exhilaration growing among the crowd of young people near the west wall, where they all sat in a gang. It was as though they were all witnesses to some imminent accident, waiting for it on their front-row folding chairs, holding drinks to tide them through the count-off.

A few times, meeting some of them had been unavoidable–in the lobby

of The Palace or on the street, and always it was their amused counte-
nances against the confusion of Laura, and a sullen defenselessness in
Buzzy, so that Buzzy went away with the feeling that he and Laura were
paired-off left-overs in life, mavericks of the town.

Buzzy wandered to the bar while Laura was gone, and drank rye without the ginger ale, a few shots. He saw Kenneth Leydecker, little and smug,
standing at a table talking with the people seated there, rocking back and
forth on his heels. He decided he would get Laura back in Leydecker's car
when she came out; let The Kantogee Country Club go to hell! He would
control her–he knew how to control her perhaps better than he knew anything else–and he thought of his hands on her, his mastery, the way her
body went through every pace he put it to, the soft feel of it answering his
commands, and then having her, after a long time, controlling her until *he*
was ready... until *he* said so.

He had another drink when the set started, and Laura was still in the
Ladies. He wandered back to the Men's. He combed his hair and washed
his hands, feeling the Negro attendant's eyes studying him–his clothes.
What did a nigger know anyway, but he felt a panic. Then, as he was dry-
ing his hands on the towel the Negro handed him, Slater Burr walked in.

"Hello, Mr. Burr!"

"Buzzy. "

"Nice to see you here!"

"How are you?"

"You know I'm getting married."

"So I hear."

"The Leydeckers. I mean, Laura."

"Yes." Slater turned on the faucet.

Buzzy took out his comb. He began to comb his hair, standing beside
Slater Burr. He said, "We're being married in September."

"Umm hmm."

"We're going to ask you to our wedding."

"Fine."

"It's at Second Presbyterian Church. I don't know how big it will be yet.
We have a lot of plans to make. Were you married at Second Presbyterian
Church, Mr. Burr?"

"No."

"Well, Mr. Leydecker suggested it. I don't know how big it will be yet.
We have to go over everything. I was telling Ken tonight, we want it just
right." The "Ken" surprised Buzzy as he said it, and he was thinking per-

haps he was just a little high. Then suddenly Slater Burr snapped, "Stop combing your hair!"

He stared at Slater Burr. Slater looked away from him, flipped a coin at the attendant, and walked out the door.

"I was just combing my hair," Buzzy said to the attendant. "Just combing my hair."

The attendant shrugged, and began rearranging the bottles of aspirin and hair tonic on his white glass tray.

Buzzy wandered back into the bar and ordered another shot. Slowly, all the while he was thinking over Slater Burr's flare-up, thinking over how he would get Laura back in the car, and how he was becoming just a little, very little high, he became very drunk.

It was not an unruly intoxication, not like the wild noise of wine drunk down by the lockers at Industrial High. It was a quiet, moody drunkenness, in which his words came out thick and lisping, and his coordination went off; he dropped a glass, knocked over an ashtray. He was aware at one point of Laura.

"I'm almost positive now that it's synovitis of the ankle joint."

He was aware of voices telling Laura he was in no condition... and at one point, aware of Chris McKenzie offering to drive them both home... and then, aware of telling Laura *she* could go, if she wanted to.

"I'm afraid I'm ill and must."

He stood at the bar and felt better, and soon, he felt he had a second wind.

Mr. Leydecker said he did the right thing, letting Laura go.

He smiled down at Leydecker, and he had a drink with Leydecker. The hands of the clock above the bar whirled when he looked up there, and he grinned and told Leydecker time was flying, time was flying.

"You ought to go home."

"I know. I know."

"You can take my car."

"Oh thank you, very much obliged."

They stood in the lot, near a tree in the shadows, with Leydecker's arm around his shoulder. Leydecker was on tiptoe to accomplish it. Little Laura Leydecker's father; little roach he had not stepped on; little bird with button eyes–peck, peckpeck.

"Wait a minute. The keys. Is the way clear? No sense walking around so drunk, for everyone to see."

"Thank you very kindly, old sir."

"Not at all."

"See you around, old bird, and many, many thanks."

He sat behind the wheel. "Get in there!" to the keys... Singing, "Hey, there, you with your nose in the air. Love nev-ver made a fool–"

Somewhere then... sometime then... hands on his shoulders.

Ultimately–screaming.

"It's Mrs. Burr!"

Buzzy Cloward stared up at a million winking stars, whirling in a black August sky.

Then he looked down, and there were more little lights–a strange dash-board, needles, buttons, levers... A Jaguar.

"She was run over!" a voice shouting again. "Oh, Jesus Christ, she isn't moving!"

II.

With his fingers, Donald Cloward squashed the cigarette in the ashtray. He stretched out on the hide-a-bed.

Once–a year ago? two?, he had talked about it with Guy.

"Guy, I know damn well someone took me from the Chrysler to the Jag. Those hands on my shoulder are as clear as–"

"Why didn't you remember it at the time?"

"Guy, I was scared! I just fell apart! I'd murdered someone!"

"Spilt Milk Department. Anyway, you still drove the car," Guy had answered. "It'd still be manslaughter... Your concern is getting out of Brinkenhoff. I think I can expedite things, but I can't do it, if you brood over August 30, 1954!"

"All right... I'll concentrate on my typing and shorthand, and maybe next month, the warden will let me study dressmaking."

"If dressmaking will help you qualify for a job as my secretary, you're damn right you'll study dressmaking!"

"Okay, Guy."

"Just forget the whole business."

"Okay, I will."

But he didn't, and he wouldn't... not until after his talk with Slater Burr.

7

"Hello? Hello? Good morning, sir?"

Kenneth Leydecker opened his eyes. There was a crack of light from the hall. Just outside his bedroom door, Mrs. Basso's shadow.

"A moment, please."

Leydecker scrambled out of the large double bed, and scampered across the chilly carpet to the Martha Washington chair. He took his blue-and-gray striped robe from its back, and wiggled into it. He was a small man, who often bought suits from the Ayres Boy's Department—size 16, usually—a thin, balding man, squinting for his eyeglasses now, finding them on the bedside table. Once he had them on, he got back under the covers, propped his pillows against the scrolled headboard, and leaned back with his hands folded on his lap.

"Come in, please," said Mr. Leydecker.

He was not a man accustomed to having his breakfast in bed. He liked to breakfast in the dining room, while reading yesterday's *New York Times;* then, on the dot of eight-forty, leave his home for Leydecker Electric, stay there as late as possible.

On holidays, he was acutely aware of his loneliness; he was lost and restless and nearly always teary-eyed.

Mrs. Basso carried a huge silver tray to the bedtable.

"Merry Christmas, sir."

"Merry Christmas to you, Mrs. Basso."

"The sun's out, and it's a nice bright day, after yesterday's wet. I'll pull the blinds for you, sir, and there's more Christmas cards on your tray there, beside your paper."

"Thank you."

"That makes 172 Christmas cards came for you and Miss Laura, so far, sir."

"So far? I should think this would be the end of it."

"Oh well, there's often two or three that'll straggle in the day after, and the day after that too."

"At least someone's paying attention to them."

"Oh, now, I think Miss Laura looks at them. I think sometimes when no one's around, Miss Laura looks at them, sir."

"Did she have her breakfast yet?"

"She was down early, same as always. There were dishes in the sink when I got here this morning."

Leydecker eased the tray over onto his lap, and put the napkin across his chest. "Mrs. Basso," he said, "there's something you'd better know."

"Yes, sir?"

"The Cloward boy is back."

"I know that, sir. My son told me last night. He saw him walking up East Genesee Street yesterday, carrying his bags to The Burr Building."

"Umm hmmm, well, I don't know what we can expect."

"No, sir, I don't either."

"Well," and Leydecker let out a long sigh, "well, Mrs. Basso, we'll just wait and see. Merry Christmas again."

"Yes, sir, and thank you for my envelope."

She went out the door, closing it behind her.

Leydecker worked at his soft-boiled eggs. Usually, on holidays, he stayed in his room, or downstairs in his study, avoiding the kitchen and second bathroom, and the hallway to the back stairs–Laura's ambit... In the beginning, he had done it out of sadness, kindness, and embarrassment, but now with the passing of the years, he did it to spite her, for he realized whatever brief and bitter encounter they had in the house was a source of perverse satisfaction to her. She would say the most wicked things to him, laughing out at his reaction, in her high-pitched tones of near hysteria, as though she were parodying all the scenes of madness she had ever seen at the movies, before her voluntary seclusion. Sometimes Kenneth Leydecker wished she *had* gone truly mad, but the wish filled him with contrition and self-accusation, for he was ready to accept the blame for Laura; if not blame, responsibility.

He could not blame himself for his intense reaction to Min Brister Leydecker's death. He had been raptly dedicated to Laura's mother; her death, when Laura was ten, had left him not only immensely bereaved, but simply inconsolable. He could find no sense to his wife's sudden death, nor any justification; there was only grief, and the numb acceptance of reality. As time wore on, he was aware of Laura, but he put her off. Mrs. Basso looked after her; he drowned himself in work, pleased and tortured himself with memories of Min, and Laura grew up. By the time he tore himself from the past and took an interest in her, she was behaving like some distant cousin his own age, with her spinsterly mannerisms and outfits, her imaginary ailments, and her nearly morbid addiction to reading. She was sixteen then.

Once he asked, "Laura, why is it that you don't wear saddle shoes, skirts and sweaters? Don't the other girls at High dress that way?"

"Yes, they do. I get a chill without stockings, and there is no support in those shoes, father. They're younger than I am too, you know, in their viewpoint. But I admire them; they seem very gay, filled with alacrity."

"Don't you ever mix with them?"

"I'm bound to, father. We have classes together. We're not close, though. They think I'm odd, and I suspect I am, from their point of view."

At such times he would think again of her mother, the same way he used to think of the dead as a small boy... as though she were just invisible now, but very much present and watching all of it. Often, alone in his room, he would weep and whisper, "But what can I do about it, Min? What? Show me!," as though the dead could show someone how to live.

He had an idea that college would be the answer for Laura. She was terribly bright, and he knew from his own college days at Princeton that the most incredible eccentrics often bloomed into astonishingly well-liked individuals. Radcliffe, he had always heard, was very successful with women like Laura, who were brilliant and withdrawn. He had once dated a girl from Radcliffe, who was now a leading physicist. She had married a Harvard scientist, and she was not nearly as well-endowed as Laura was physically. She had stuttered so badly, it was painful to hold a conversation with her; still she was very popular, voted something or other in her class, Leydecker could never remember what.

He had mentioned Radcliffe to Laura. She had seemed most enthusiastic... That was to have been the answer, and he had put her off again, suspecting least of all that a Donald Cloward would intervene.

Leydecker sighed and buttered his toast. At some point on this Christmas Day, he would have to go to Laura, and tell her Cloward was back.

Kenneth Leydecker had always thought of himself as a Christian man, and hating another human being was incompatible with that thought. But he had meant it when he had told the Cloward boy that he loathed him, and he had meant for Cloward to kill himself the night he gave him the keys to his Chrysler. If he had not killed himself, Leydecker would have prosecuted him for auto theft.

Again, because he thought of himself as a Christian man (even as he walked back into the clubhouse that night, leaving Fate to decide Cloward's course) he believed that a Divine Power had interceded. Somehow Cloward had decided on a flashier car for his departure from The Kantogee Country Club (just give their kind an inch), and Carrie Burr had paid for his drunken audacity. Leydecker reasoned The Divine Power did not cause Carrie's death; it simply put Cloward's sort in perspective, removed any tinge of guilt from Leydecker.

When Cloward insisted to the police that Leydecker gave him his keys, Leydecker accepted the indisputable Scheme of Things, and lied. What would it have profited Cloward, had Leydecker admitted it? It would not bring Slater Burr's wife back to life; it would simply have involved Kenneth Leydecker unnecessarily.

Blood will tell; Min had always said that.

So it did; the Chrysler was not good enough for a Donald Cloward.

And then, it should have been that everything would go back to normal, to the way it was before that fluke meeting of his daughter with Cloward. Laura should have gone on to Radcliffe... to marriage... to the things a girl of Laura's background went on to. Never mind her bad start; it would have all been ironed out at college.

Leydecker squeezed the tears brimming in his eyes, and wiped them away with his napkin. Long, long ago in the old days, on Christmas morning, it used to be that Min and he would sleep no later than seven o'clock, when Laura would bound into the room, golden-haired and laughing, and tugging at their blankets to go down to the tree... Even after Min's death, there was always some polite and pleasant formality by the tree on Christmas; then breakfast afterwards... On her own, four or five years ago, Mrs. Basso had started coming in on holidays to serve him breakfast. It was the same time she had started her embarrassing habit of counting the Christmas cards, as if to say 172 people still cared, when the truth was: who did?

Leydecker got out of bed and put the tray on the bedtable. On his desk, by the window overlooking Highland Hill, were the files of the Boost Cayuta Committee, and the zoning proposal he was to edit, before presentation to the City Council. At least his presence counted somewhere. He was nearly sure of General Electric now. If everything else around him was suspended in some sort of lethargic limbo, the city of Cayuta would not suffer the same dilemma. It would die if it did, just as it had been dying before L.E. got the contract from Kuwait. It took a long time for a city to die, and in the meantime, while Slater Burr dazzled city officials with his eloquence, and the dreams of turning Cayuta into a summer tourist resort, Burr Manufacturing Company realized a nice profit. He paid low wages and put nothing back into the company. Even the Cayuta Fire Department was afraid to declare all the flagrant violations in the plant, for fear it would set the city in a deeper economic recession, with a shut-down of one of the few existing industries.

Kenneth Leydecker was his father's son, same as Burr had old Roy Burr
in him. Leydecker could remember Slater's father, and the sniveling notes
he wrote apologizing for days he missed work, like a child carrying a note
to school after a day's absence. Roy Burr had been a pasty-faced, groveling
man, too old for his years, always suffering from a cold and fits of lethargy,
a huge, clumsy fellow with hairless arms and weak pouting lips, with a brilliant spark to his brain, imprisoned by the doughy layers of irresolution. His
inventions were visionary, save for two which L.E. used to their advantage,
and it was an incredible and imponderable discrepancy that this half-heart-
ed, fidgety fellow had been capable of concocting any useful thing. It had
been to Kenneth Leydecker, Sr.'s credit that he kept him on the payroll. He
was of no use during a work day, off sleeping behind crates, watery-eyed
from his colds and too much sleep, shuffling and apologetic, seemingly with
only one wish: to die, and he had accomplished that at a premature age.

Ostensibly, Slater Burr was his opposite, a go-getter, wide-awake and
angry as Roy Burr was docile, but the blood told as it always does, mani-
festing itself in a different and more lethal way. Leydecker had only to
watch Slater Burr make up to Nelson Stewart, observe the subtle changes,
beginning with his changing his name from Fran to Slater... then on down
to his marriage with Carrie, his weak-egoed transfer of his name to Stewart-owned properties, his flashy accoutrements, and ultimately with Carrie's death and his marriage to a silly girl half his age, the gradual self-ab-
sorption... the drinking, and the deterioration of the Burr plant, the-hell-
with-it slough-off of a whole city, behind a facade of concern... He was, in
the end, as weak and irresponsible as his father had been; worse than Roy
Burr, because he was a schemer and his weakness had vitality.

Well, and Kenneth Leydecker tucked his handkerchief back in his robe,
with a testy gesture of resolution, he would rid Cayuta of Slater Burr, the
same as he would rid a place of vermin. Slater Burr was just as noxious as
vermin, to Leydecker's way of thinking, and sometimes Leydecker believed
that if Fate had not dealt with Laura in the strange way it had, it could have
easily been Donald Cloward he would be fighting now... And if Cloward's
return meant he was to have two battles on his hands, then he would fight
both of them!

Kenneth Leydecker dressed, studying himself in the full-length mirror
attached to the back of his closet door. He was small and inconsequential-
looking; his reflection mocked his resolution, but his jaw, his eyes behind
the rimless glasses, the fists of his hands, and the tiny squared shoulders
were determined. For he was his father's son, and Kenneth Leydecker, Sr.,

just as frail-looking physically, every bit as ineffectual in his appearance, had been a paragon of strength!

When he opened the door, and went down the long hallway, his step began to lose its quickness. His heart took a dive. From the banister, he could see the tree in the parlor, which Mrs. Basso trimmed every year, and he felt Min watching. He felt the fullness behind his eyes... the same old thing. But he pulled himself up to his full five-three, nervously wiped his mouth with the back of his hand as he paused before Laura's door, and then he knocked.

He heard the sounds of her television, as she turned it up at the knocking. Another movie.

He knocked again.

Louder, chaotic.

As he opened the door, the room was dark, but the moment he stepped inside, she snapped on the very bright overhead light. She was sitting on the bed, in slacks and a blouse, barefooted, wearing one of the Robin-Hood caps on her head. At the sight of him, she doffed it, in her usual exaggerated greeting, and dropped it on her lap. There was just a fuzz on her head; less than on his own.

"Please turn down the television," he said.

"You're standing very near to the set, father. You do it."

He walked across and turned the knob, lowering the sound.

With the remote control button, fixed to her bedtable, she raised it again, and laughed. "We must learn to meet Life's little obstacles with courage!"

"I have something to say to you, Laura."

"Oh, and is it Merry Christmas, father?" She laughed again.

"Donald Cloward is back in Cayuta," he said flatly.

She turned off the sound. She sat quite still, looking at her father, the shock registering slowly in her eyes. She was surrounded by the usual dozens of books and magazines on the bed, and by the small box of clay. On the bureau across from her, were scores of small clay dolls, all wearing brown wigs, made from the hair of her own wigs.

Kenneth Leydecker had, years ago, hired a woman to come to their home from Albany, New York, to fit Laura with a wig. She had come after a series of specialists had convinced him, that while there was no physical cause for Laura's loss of hair, the psychological cases were just as stubborn and hopeless.

Mrs. Tweed, the woman from Albany, referred to the wig as a "transformation."

"Oh, you'd be surprised how many women have to wear transforma-tions, and no one suspects!" she had said. "Movie stars come to me by the dozens; cafe society, debutantes... why we had a little eleven-year-old girl last month, poor dear, not a hair on–"

And while she talked, matching strands to the fuzz left, explaining how to have a transformation dry-cleaned, and how to set one, saying "your transformation" this and "your transformation" that, Laura listened with no expression on her face. Mrs. Tweed worked four days, staying all the while at The Mohawk Hotel ("Don't worry, my line is top-secret, same as the F.B.I.") and at the end, she fitted Laura for two transformations, and pre-sented her with three of the felt Robin-Hood caps, one in lime, one in bright royal blue, the third in scarlet. "For use when you're by yourself, or when you sleep," she explained. "The elastic inside holds them in place. It's fun to wear them at a jaunty little angle, and they come in all colors. I'll leave the catalog."

That was that... Laura never wore the wigs... She had already stopped going out of the house, long before the arrival of Mrs. Tweed. She would not even cover her head with a scarf for a breath of air in her own yard, and she did nothing to change things.

She stayed in her room, mostly, and if she left it, it was to eat in the kitchen during Mrs. Basso's absence, or to sneak a book from the library, off the living room. She had not set foot outside the house in seven and a half years, since the furtive trips to clinics outside Cayuta, with her father.

The few confidantes Kenneth Leydecker had were sworn to secrecy; and Mrs. Basso was... That was that.

"Donald Cloward is back, Laura," Leydecker repeated.

"Was he here?"

"No."

"Well, he's out. Free. So are the birds, father. It's hardly my concern."

"I just thought that you ought to know."

"Are you disappointed, father? Had you hoped he would die in prison?"

"To use your words, it's hardly my concern."

"It really isn't any more, is it? You haven't a worry in the world. Every-thing is in God's hands. Well, I just wonder what the hell God did with my hair, father! Do you suppose he gave it to some good little angel?"

"God had nothing to do with that."

"Yes, his mercy endureth forever... I bet you thank Him because there's no chance now of my seeing Buzzy, even if I wanted to. Do you thank Him, father?"

"Laura... Laura, I never thanked God for a misfortune."

"Well, give yourself time, father. Perhaps when you're kneeling down this very Christmas night, a little prayer will slip out. 'Dear God, all knowing and just, thank you that Laura is bald as an eagle, and not married to Buzzy Cloward, with whom she copulated in evil bliss and–' "

"Laura! That's blasphemy! Nasty-tongued blasphemy!... I did not come in here to gloat! What if the phone should ring, and suddenly you should find yourself speaking with him! You answer the phone sometimes! I came in here to prevent embarrassment for you!"

"Oh, I'm not surprised. You've always been considerate and attentive."

"I'm sorry if you can't see it that way."

"Why, if you hadn't been so terribly thoughtful and considerate, and kind, and attentive, there might be a whole family of little Clowards running around downstairs by the Christmas tree now, instead of Mrs. Basso. Oh, thank your lucky stars, father! It's much better this way, isn't it?"

"Laura, I–"

"Because we *would* have had a big family, father! Buzzy and I were naturals, father! Did I ever tell you we were naturals?"

"Very well, Laura, if you're going to start *that* talk, then there's nothing more I can say."

He turned and started out the door.

"At least I won't die a virgin, father... Put out the light, as you leave, please. I only put on the overhead light in *your* honor, father, so you can have a good look at me."

He flicked the light button with his finger.

"And a Merry Christmas to all!" said Laura Leydecker, as he shut the door.

8

"I think he probably has Blue Eye, Miss–Miss–" Chris McKenzie fumbled for her name.

"Miss Sontag, Dr. McKenzie. Mona Sontag. I work in the office at Burr. Secretarial." She pushed her empty glass forward on the mahogany bar, and Jitz Walsh put it under a beer jet to fill it.

"Well, I'm sure it's Blue Eye. Is the cornea a bluish white?"

"Sort of. Yes, and the white of his eye is all red. Poor little dog. We named him Burr. My mother did." She giggled, and turned to Slater. "No offense. I just been working there so long and all."

"No offense," Slater agreed.

It was late Christmas afternoon, near four. Most of the lake places closed in the winter, but Walsh's Place bragged: OPEN YEAR ROUND, EVERY DAY.

Jen and Lena were filling the jukebox with quarters, and while Miss Sontag solicited medical advice from Slater's brother-in-law, Slater sipped scotch, and tried not to get into conversation with the fellow a few stools to his left. His name was Secora, and he too worked for Slater, had worked for him as far back as World War II, when the plant was making precision forgings for airplanes and warships, and Nelson Stewart was still alive.

That day after Slater and Jen had their first rendezvous at Blood Neck Point (where they had seen Secora drive off with Rich Boyson's wife as they drove in to park) Secora had called to report his ribs were broken in an accident. Eventually, Slater learned Rich Boyson was the accident, but at the time he had shrugged it off without connecting the two incidents. He had ordered Miss Rae to keep Secora on the payroll during his long recovery, a gesture he would have shown any long-term employee. Secora returned months later with a chummy display of gratitude, which took the form of slapping Slater's back during Slater's rounds of the plant, and a few times, an invitation for a beer at the bar across from the plant, refused by Slater. Time passed and Secora's attitude changed; he was thick with the union leaders in the plant, less friendly, and Slater felt, slightly bitter at the bad times B.M.C. was realizing. That afternoon, Secora was bent on fond reminiscences of Nelson Stewart and "the old days," and Slater sensed he was working himself up to a fight, despite his euphoric air.

Secora was saying, "Those were the days! Say, Mr. Burr, did we win four Army-Navy "E" awards or five?"

"Five," said Slater.

"I was just starting in at B.M.C. then. 'Course, then it was Stewart Company."

"Umm hmm."

"We could sure use another war," said Secora, "or another industry in this town."

Slater got off the barstool, as Chris McKenzie was advising Miss Sontag to bathe her dog's eye with warm two per cent boric-acid solution, several times a day. It had been Jen's idea to come to Walsh's Place and bring her brother and Lena, to make up for Slater's absence at their home last night. Jen liked to "slum," liked crummy little bars like this one and Boyson's. Slater realized she enjoyed the attention she received from the people in those bars, enjoyed having them watch her... and perhaps envy her. That was part of Jen, part of her youngness and her restlessness.

He went back near the jukebox and caught a hold of her, waltzing her around the small space with an exaggerated aplomb. McKenzie's wife drifted back to the bar.

"Hey, Slater, it's a Twist, not a Waltz." Jen laughed.

"Only one knows the difference is Chris. He's the only one drinking ginger ale."

"Be nice to him, though, hmm? It's Christmas."

"Oh, I'll be darling to him."

"Having a good time?"

"Divine, Jenny, a divine time!"

Jen grinned up at him. "I know. But we have to make some effort with them, once a year anyway... and it's more fun out here, than in their place. Lena doesn't think so. 'Jen,' she said to me, 'you and Slater pick the lowest places. I mean, the people here.' "

"Too close to home."

"Don't I know it! Do you know she used to date Jitz Walsh?"

For awhile, they danced without talking. Slater's mind was back on Leydecker. The latest was that Leydecker had called an emergency meeting of the zoning board for next Tuesday. He was determined to push through his proposal. G.E. was ready to scout Cayuta some time in the spring, and it was Leydecker's thought that by then, a demolition crew might already have in progress the removal of the Burr plant. A park could take its place—a beautiful park, for public use, landscaped and lovely, in center town. The mayor had called Slater that morning to tell him about the meeting. The Cayuta Macaroni plant was owned by the mayor's brother, who wanted a new industry kept out just as badly as Slater did. It was an indisputable fact that Slater's plant was not only an eyesore, but also a source of labor disputes and unrest–another bad mark for the city. No company wanted to move in on trouble, but if the zoning proposal were passed, the trouble would be removed.

The mayor had said, "We've got to appeal on the basis that B.M.C. is a local business, and no city progresses by putting its own people out and letting in outsiders... Now, that's the approach, but it'll take a lot of fast talk, and you've got to work on a loan and promise great improvements via it. I can't fight, Slater. I'm in no position to, and it'd look bad if my brother fought, so it's up to you! You've got to stop Leydecker!"

"A penny?" Jen said.

"Oh, I was just thinking about..." Slater began, but stopped short. The door had opened and closed, and Donald Cloward stood by the cigarette machine, at the entrance to Walsh's.

"What's the matter, Slater?" Jen said. "See a ghost?"... Then she saw him too.

For a moment, he watched Slater and Jen; then, when they saw him, he gave a slight nod, and went across to sit by Secora.

"The Cloward boy!" Jen said. "My God in heaven! What's he doing out?"

"I don't know."

They kept on dancing, watching while Cloward ordered a beer, and Lena McKenzie moved away from him. Chris nodded at him, and Secora punched him in the arm with a big grin and asked him when he got sprung. Cloward's face went red with embarrassment. Again, he glanced over his shoulder at Jen and Slater.

"Let's say hello to him, Slater."

"What for?"

"What do you send him Christmas cards for? To be nice."

"Oh, hell–nice!"

"He keeps looking at us, Slater. Let's!"

She took the lead, and Slater followed.

Cloward stood up and made a jerky little bow. "Hello. You're–" and for a moment the words stuck in his throat. "You're–Mrs. Burr."

"Yes. How are you?"

"Oh, I'm all right, thanks." Then–and there seemed to be some special significance attached to the greeting and the look in Cloward's eyes, be said to Slater, "Hello there, Mr. Burr. I'm glad to see you again."

"Buzzy."

Secora was watching the whole moment with open curiosity, turning on the stool, and staring at the trio. Chris McKenzie was noticing out of the corner of his eye, still talking about antibiotic treatment for Blue Eye in a dog. Lena was lurking behind her husband, and Jitz Walsh had turned on the water in the bar sink full force, and was rattling glasses busily and nervously. The only one disinterested seemed to be Miss Sontag, who was trying to get Chris to help her remember the word "terramycin."

Jen said, "Are you home for good now?"

"No, ma'am. Just for a few days. I'm going to work in New York City, I think." He looked back at Slater, standing behind Jen.

"Oh, I envy you!" said Jen. "I adore New York!"

Cloward picked up his beer glass, and before he swallowed, tipped it slightly in Jen's direction. "Well, Merry Christmas."

"Merry Christmas to you... is it Fuzzy?"

"Buzzy... I'm called Donald nowadays."

"Donald. Merry Christmas, Donald."

Slater excused himself and went back into the Men's. He leaned against the sink, pausing to collect his thoughts. He was just a little tight, but he knew he should have been more effusive, should have pumped the boy's arm in the old gesture of bygones-be-bygones... was that right?

The shock at seeing Cloward so suddenly had thrown him off. He should have feigned the attitude of forgiveness, just as he always went out of his way to ask old man Cloward how Donald was, and to send the Christmas cards each year. He remembered the stumbling, remorseful letter Cloward had sent from Brinkenhoff the first year, and the agonized expression on Cloward's face when Slater confronted him on the night of August 30th. The events of the night began to whirl through Slater's brain, beginning with Carrie saying:

II.

"Actually, I was thinking of a way to increase the velocity of the power hammer, on the Rolli machine."

They were standing near the parking lot at The Kantogee Country Club, off to the right, on the bank, where there was a sudden drop to the highway.

He had seen her leave the clubhouse, while he was at the bar talking with Jen. Jen was telling him that it was hopeless; she was making arrangements

to go back to Paris to work, and he was trying to keep his voice down, trying, without moving his lips, to tell Jen he loved her, his eyes looking away
from her as though it were merely a quiet conversation, not the desperate
intense moment it was, when he saw Carrie leave. He saw her face in profile, the cigarette in her mouth, the hunched-over posture he had found so
endearing and sad, so long ago, her awkward walk in the long dress (her
awkwardness too, he had always found dear and winning) and the solemn
paleness of her face. She was furious, he knew; liable to take the car and
go, if she were in such a mood, and it would cause gossip, inspire Jen to go
ahead all the quicker with her departure plans... so he had excused himself
from Jen and followed Carrie. When he caught up with her, he asked her
if everything were all right. She gave him her usual shrug, looking off in the
direction of the lake, not speaking to him. Then he had said: "What are you
thinking?"

It was her usual answer too, to any attempt on his part to probe her mind.
She considered her evasiveness a part of her immense control; it was Carrie's conceit that she never raised her voice, spoke an angry word, or discussed anything which bothered her, other than something like increasing
a power hammer's velocity.

There were times when she would weep, but she would always have
some strange explanation for it: her desk in the solarium was in the wrong
place, or her cactus plant was dead (she was a specialist in cacti), and then
she would do something about it, move the desk, bury the dead cactus, and
the tears would be gone as suddenly as they had come... and the iron control back, the stiff expression on her face, the spring of vitality in her
movements, as she drove herself through a day.

When Slater had first met Carrie, she was home on vacation from college. Slater was managing the Stewart Company plant, and Carrie had
appeared one afternoon by herself to look over the machinery. Mechanics
fascinated her; and her attitude, as Slater showed her about, was very
much like a man's, poking and fooling with this part, adjusting that one,
inquiring in her technical way about the use of the lever on one machine,
or the roller on another. She wore fly-front pants and a white shirt, rolled
to the elbows, showing firm-muscled white arms, and her stride as she
went through the plant was long and sure, and over the shirt she wore a
suede tunic, a pack of cigarettes stuck in one pocket of the tunic. Her face
was marvelously handsome; a tinge of pink lipstick on very wide lips, deep
brown eyes, a good nose, and black eyelashes, long and dark in contrast to
the fair and perfect skin. As Slater had watched her, his heartbeat was deep

and powerful; it seemed to him like some thrilling secret that her soft woman's breasts must be buttoned up in the shirt, covered with the suede tunic, that all of her softness and tender flesh in hiding that way was all the more intriguing and lovely than girls who showed themselves more daringly, as if to offer for approval what she took for granted and covered. So he told himself, and his blood burned. His excitement at that first encounter was at a pitch that stayed through all the other meetings with her. And he liked the way she was so natural on her tours through the plant, and the way the men liked her, not one of them fresh or disrespectful to Miss Carrie. He would hear them talk about her afterwards, all the talk admiring and amiable, as though she were a woman who cut through the vulgar and unnecessary underbrush of male-female differences, and class differences, and was simply liked for herself; not the way it should be with every woman, but the way it was around Carrie: her special individuality.

There had never been a single doubt in Slater's mind that Carrie was a fascinating woman; his marriage had endured for the sole reason she was so fascinating, but she was not vulnerable as he had once imagined when he was younger and had thought of the soft white breasts behind the tunic, white and unseen, waiting to be awakened; nor was she sad and needing protection, behind the facade of surety. She was a force, to whatever end, she was one.

That night in August, wearing the pink-and-white dotted chiffon she looked uncomfortable in, there was the same quality of wistful awkwardness and defenselessness, but Slater saw through the mask. He said quite flatly, "Carrie, you know very well about Jen and me, don't you?"

"Yes," she answered.

"Carrie, I'm going to say something that has to be said, much as you hate this kind of personal discussion. I'm very deeply in love with Jen."

"I'm not surprised," she said, not at all abashed. A slice of orange moon in the summer sky showed a placid, cool look on her face. She dropped her cigarette butt on the gravel and erased its hot ash with the tip of her evening slipper. From her beaded bag, she took another cigarette, ignoring Slater's fumbling for his lighter, and lit the cigarette with her own.

Slater said, "Is that all you have to say... that it doesn't surprise you?"

"Yes... That, and that I'd like to go home. Incidentally, Slater, the Cloward boy is back there in Kenneth Leydecker's car. He's very intoxicated. I saw Leydecker give him the keys. Leydecker must be out of his mind. The boy can't drive in his condition. We'd better drop him on our way."

"Carrie," Slater said, "don't skip over this one. Not this one!"

"I'm not skipping over it. I heard you."

"And you have no reaction to the fact I love someone else?"

She gave him a polite smile. "I don't really believe in love. It's a convenient word, one of those words which can force chaos into a more traditional pattern, at least ostensibly."

"I want to talk about it, Carrie, not around it–about it. I don't know what all this crap means... convenience and chaos! What does all that crap mean?"

She said, "If a man says he's deeply in love with someone, it gives him a more traditional license to behave as he intends to anyway."

"And when I was in love with you?"

"You intended to marry me, didn't you?" said Carrie. "It wouldn't have been easy for you to marry me, without saying that you were in love. I didn't require your avowal of love, but you required it of yourself. It was easier for you to believe it, or at least to say it, whether you believed it or not."

"I loved you when I married you, Carrie."

"We don't have to get psychosemantic about it. We're married, and that's that."

"You used to say you loved me."

"You wanted to hear it, Slater. You used to remark how awkward I seemed saying it... No, I was never comfortable with the word 'love'; you were right."

Slater said, "Then what did you marry me for?"

"I thought we would be good together, that simple."

"Good how? In bed?" Slater gave a bitter chuckle.

"I'm sorry if bed was a disappointment. I know I didn't place much emphasis on it, but I never refused you, Slater."

"There's more to it than not refusing me, Carrie."

"I don't doubt it, but there never was for me. Either way, it never seemed a problem to me."

"You could take it, or leave it alone."

"Yes."

Then she said, "It doesn't come as a surprise to you, Slater. We've been married 14 years, so don't act as though this is the moment of truth, simply because it's never been discussed between us... I'm quite serious about the hammer on the Rolli. I want to draw up some plans, speak with Secora on Monday. Will you drive me home now?"

"Some goddamned marriage!"

"I doubt that anyone's is perfect."

"I doubt it too, Carrie, but now I want a little more than what we have."

"You've found ways before, to have more than what we have."

"You knew about the other women too?"

"I presumed something like that went on during your trips."

"Did you know about Caxton's niece? That went on right under your nose, here in Cayuta."

"Yes. I received one of those nasty anonymous phone calls that fall."

"And you didn't give a damn?"

"I haven't been unhappy with you, put it that way, Slater."

"You should have been, if you'd had feelings."

She took a drag on her cigarette: the smoke spiraled up between them, and she said: "I should have objected, I suppose, when you decided to replace father's name with yours on the company. Oh, everyone said I should. Lawyers, bankers. Why, the Stewart Company is a tradition, everyone said: it's always been the Stewart Company. I realized that it was-n't that important to me, but it seemed important to you... I let it happen... I feel the same way about your women."

Slater said, "What is important to you?"

"Father was. The Burr Company is. Having a child was, when we were involved in that... There are certain things I wasn't made for, I suspect. I couldn't carry a child beyond the third month, and I was never taken with bed... I suppose I live day-to-day, Slater. I like to work, and I'm not dis-pleased with our life, except during these analyses of it."

"Carrie," Slater said, "I want a divorce. I want to marry Jen."

"When we were young," she said, "you came to me with the idea of changing your name from Francis to Slater."

"Slater was my middle name," he said. "A lot of men take their middle name."

"All right, but let me finish . . At the time, I thought it was a silly notion. You were very intent on it, though, remember?"

"Francis is a hell of a name for a man!"

"I don't think it would have bothered a *man*. But you were a boy, really, twenty-four, twenty-five... a boy. I thought at the time what a lot of trou-ble it would be–changing it on the checking account, legal papers, so forth . to say nothing of getting people used to it... Well, it wasn't going to be trouble for me. I said to go ahead, if you wanted to, and you did. It worked out fine. I don't think anyone in Cayuta calls you Francis now."

"What has this got to do with a divorce, Carrie?"

"My yardstick has always been how much trouble it would cause me. A divorce would upset my whole life, Slater, and I don't want one."

Slater said, "Do you know I could kill you right now? I could honest-to-God kill you."

"No, Slater, that's something you can't make yourself believe just because you say the words. You're letting off hot air, that's all. Most of this discussion is; most discussions are.

"You wouldn't know anything about hot, Carrie."

"I know about you. I know a little about hot, too. I know that hot doesn't stop and figure things out, as you do. Hot–love–whatever you want to call it, takes what it wants. There's nothing to stop hot from running off with a Jennifer McKenzie, anytime he's ready. Oh, he'd have to give up a lot, but isn't hot, love–whatever you want to call it–irrational?... Hot takes what it wants, and it keeps what it wants, Slater. I know a little about it. I don't go in for labelling things, but I know about things, a whole lot more than you do... Now, take me home, and bring the Cloward boy. He's too drunk to drive."

"I'll take you home, all right!" He was shaking with fury, shaking and holding himself back from simply walking over and knocking her backward, down into the highway, a drop that was far enough to kill anyone... even Carrie, hard and tough as she was.

"And bring the Cloward boy."

"The hell with the Cloward boy!"

"He could be you, Slater, years ago."

"Meaning what, Carrie?"

"Meaning stop hiding behind words. You were the same kind of kid he is... wide-eyed at the rich, always with the comb in your back pocket ready to preen, dreaming of driving the kind of car you're driving tonight, chasing after some maverick daughter of a rich man, calling it love... and then fourteen years later, surprised that it all didn't turn out like Paramount Pictures... surprised that there's responsibility attached, and then you can't just walk out as easily as you walked in!"

"Goddam you, Carrie," Slater said, "Goddam you!... I loved you when I married you. I was in love with you!"

"Get the car, Slater, and bring him," she said. "I'll wait here."

He crossed the gravel drive with the fury ready to snap his brain. As he went by the rows of parked cars, he heard the strains of "Hey, There," from the clubhouse, and he heard a voice singing lazily in the August night: "...love nev-ver made a fool of you, you used to be soooo wise, you–"

He stopped by Kenneth Leydecker's Chrysler. Behind the wheel was the Cloward boy, his head leaning against the window, his mouth hanging open, singing foolishly. The key was on in the ignition, with it, the car lights.

Slater reached across the boy and turned off the key, the lights.

"Thank you very much, old bird, but I better be moving along, Mr. Ley-decker, sir, old bird."

"C'mon Cloward! Ass!"

"Hey there, you with your nose in the air, love–" the boy sang; he was too drunk to understand anything.

Slater put his hands on his shoulders and pulled him from the car. He walked him across to the Jaguar, put him in the front seat.

He turned on his headlights when he got in on the other side. Straight ahead, on the bank, the pink-and-white dotted chiffon showed in the moon-light, the long white arm, the incongruous leather strap of her wrist watch. Beside him in the Jaguar, the Cloward boy leaned into him, kept up his in-toxicated singing, stopping and starting up again, his words thick and slurred, head dangling.

"Just shut up!" Slater yelled. His anger at Carrie was wild in his voice, and he wished now that he had gone back into the clubhouse to tell Jen good night, to tell her he would work something out; he wouldn't lose her. He imagined her waiting for him, watching through the crowds for him, won-dering where he was.

He felt like just scaring the hell out of Carrie, roaring the Jag up with a near miss, so she would have to jump out of the way. He gunned the motor forward, headed right for her, and in the slow second before he swung to avoid hitting her, he imagined her jumping back and falling down the bank to the highway, a straight-line drop-off. The sudden thud of Carrie's body against his grill amazed him. He slammed on the brakes and jumped out. The chiffon was already soaking with blood, and Carrie's face–the eyes lus-terless like those of a fish at the end of a hook–stared up at him.

He did not touch her, but instead, began to run. He ran up the side yard, for some reason toward the lights of the club kitchen, acting on a stupid impulse to get water, to wash out the blood, wipe away the incident... just clean it all away. Then he stumbled and fell to his knees, and in the dark-ness on his knees, he could hear someone shouting.

"It's Mrs. Burr!"

He pulled himself to his feet.

"Oh, Jesus Christ, she was run over! She isn't moving."

This time he began running back toward the Jaguar, as though he had not been anywhere near it... as though he were running from the clubhouse.

He saw two men standing by his car, pulling the Cloward boy from behind the wheel where he had slumped when Slater had jumped out.

9

The door of the Men's in Walsh's Place opened and closed, and Slater Burr looked across at Cloward.

"I'm sorry to barge in on you," said Cloward, "but I wanted to talk with you. I called you last night around eleven, and three or four times today."

"How are you, Buzzy?"

"I don't go by that name much, any more, Mr. Burr. Donald."

"You wanted to talk to me?"

"Yes... It's not a very pleasant subject, and I'm sorry for that, on Christmas Day."

"Well?"

"And thank you for the Christmas card. For all of them."

"All right."

"I wanted to talk to you about–the accident that night."

"I should think you'd want to forget it. I've forgotten it," said Slater, "and I should think you'd want to... Are you out of Brinkenhoff for good now?"

"They don't give vacations, Mr. Burr... Yes, I'm out."

"I'm glad of it, Donald. It was very unfortunate–the whole thing. If you don't mind," and he started the motions of leaving, "I'd like to keep it forgotten."

Cloward touched the sleeve of his jacket. "Wait! Listen a minute. I've had a lot of time to think about that night, to go over everything, Mr. Burr."

"And?"

"Every time I went over it, one thing stuck in my mind. One thing. Someone moved me, Mr. Burr. I was sitting in Leydecker's car, and someone moved me."

"Donald, at the time, you said Leydecker gave you the keys to his car. You said you must have just wandered over to mine afterwards. Leydecker denied giving you the keys, and you didn't have his keys when you were found in my car... I think it's all best forgotten."

Cloward said, "Please listen to me, Mr. Burr... I know he gave me the keys. I know I was in his car, last I remember."

"Why do you want to go over and over it, Donald? It doesn't change your position any." Slater started toward the door. "Forget it!"

"In *your* eyes, it would, Mr. Burr. What if you knew that Leydecker put me in your car, sir? What if you knew that Kenneth Leydecker put me in your Jaguar, not so I'd run down Mrs. Burr, but so I'd run off the bank your car was facing! Mr. Burr, I couldn't have seen that sharp turn, drunk as I was! I would have gone straight down to the highway. I almost did, didn't I?"

Slater Burr's hand dropped from the doorknob. He turned around and looked at Donald Cloward.

Cloward said, "I want you to know I didn't steal your car. I never would have—not your car... For whatever reason he had, sir, Kenneth Leydecker put me in your car. I know damn well he did!"

10

After Donald Cloward followed Slater Burr into the Men's, Chris and
Lena McKenzie began dancing. Jitz Walsh started a conversation with Jen
Burr about his European travels during the war, and Mona Sontag carried
her beer down to the other end of the bar, rejoining her date.

"Welcome back," said Albert Secora, "or are you just slumming for a few
minutes?"

"I was having a very nice conversation with the doctor."

"The doctor! If he's a doctor, I'm an astronaut."

"A veterinarian is a doctor, Al." She pronounced it vet-ah-naran. "Maybe
not an M.D. but..."

"A V.D. maybe, Mona?" Secora guffawed at his little joke. "Yeah, a V.D....
in charge of syph and gon. And I'm an astronaut... Hey, did you hear the
joke about the astronaut?" She was watching the McKenzies dance, and he
had to poke her arm to get her attention. She looked down at her sleeve
and his fingers there, as though a garbage man had his hands on her. It infu-
riated him, but he went right on with what he was saying.

"Hey, Mona? Knock. Knock."

"All right!," she said tiredly. "Who's there?"

"Astronaut."

"Astronaut who," she said in a bored voice.

"Astronaut what your country can do for you, but what you can do for
your country!" He gave a loud snort. Mona merely sighed peevishly. She
said, "I don't think it's nice to make fun of the President of The United
States of America."

"Oh, for Pete's sake!"

"Well, it isn't. You just don't have respect."

"You don't mean for the President, you mean for Slater Burr."

"I heard you talking to him, Albert, all about how good the old days were,
when Mr. Stewart was running the place."

"So what?"

"He knew what you were getting at. He moved away from you, didn't
he?"

"What the heck do I care what he does, for Pete's sake! You know how
long I'll be working for him, when G.E. gets here–about two seconds."

Mona Sontag said, "When I go out with someone on Christmas Day, the

very most important day in the year practically, I expect the certain someone to behave like a grown-up man!... Did I whine around about work? Big
people don't like it, Albert. They come in to relax like anybody else, and
they don't like their employees sitting around griping."

"*Big* people! Oh, wow! *Big* people!"

"Well, he owns the place where we work, doesn't he? Lock, stock and
barrel!"

"I suppose it's all right for you to sit up there and get free medical advice
from that horse doctor, though, ha, Mona?."

"A man enjoys discussing his work. I was having a very nice conversation with the doctor."

"Well, I was discussing Slater Burr's work, wasn't I?"

"He knew what you were getting at. He moved away from you, didn't
he? He went off and danced with his wife!"

"Was he supposed to ask me for a dance, Mona?"

"He did it to get away from you."

"Heck with it!"

He sipped his beer silently for awhile; then Mona got around to the subject she was dying to talk about. She waited long enough for the edge to be
off their testy conversation, and she said, in a conciliatory tone: "What I
wonder, is what's going on in the Men's right now."

"Same thing going on in the Women's, Mona, only in one place they're
standing up, and in the other they're sitting down."

Secora wondered too, but he was still smarting at her words.

"On Christmas Day... of all the disgusting remarks... And that's another
thing. Albert, that's another thing. Did you notice that I paid absolutely no
attention to the drama taking place down at this end of the bar? I paid no
attention, just went right on with my conversation with the doctor."

"If you weren't paying attention, how did you know there was a drama
taking place?"

"What I mean. Albert, is that I didn't gawk at them."

"Aren't you wonderful, though!"

"You gawked! Gawked right up at them!... I was just as surprised as you
were to see Donald Cloward walk in here, but I paid no attention."

"I bet you don't perspire, either, Mona. I bet you don't ever have to blow
your nose, or clean under your nails, or any of the things we human beings
indulge in, ha, Mona?"

"I don't gawk!"

"Well, Merry Christmas, Mona. You can just bet your neck that I'm delighted I socked ten ninety-eight into that brooch I gave you!"

"You want it back, Albert?"

"Heck with it! *Big* people!... I could tell you a few things about Mr. Big in the can there! If he's so big. why doesn't he have the price for a motel when he wants to make out, or a hotel even!"

"Referring to what exactly?"

"Referring," Albert Secora said, "to a night I saw him up at Blood Neck, in his car, with Jen Burr, before she was Jen Burr!"

"You kidding me? They didn't even give each other the time of day, until his wife was killed."

"Heck they didn't. Me and a certain party, who shall remain nameless, as she is married to someone else, saw them up there. Parking. Couple of months after she first hit town."

Mona Sontag shoved her beer glass forward on the bar top to signal a refill. She said, "Honest to God?"

"Honest to God... Now, if he's such a Mr. Big, Mona, why didn't he hire a motel, or even a hotel? He was up there same as I was, and for the same reason."

"You sure?"

"Just as sure as I am that he kept me on the payroll three months while I was sick, so I wouldn't mouth it around!"

"What do you mean, Albert?"

"Well, I had an accident next day. I had a fall and broke some ribs. You think he'd a kept me on three months, unless he had a good reason? He didn't want me mouthing around what I saw."

"G'wan!"

"You don't remember the time I was sick three months?"

"I never paid any attention to you. I was engaged to be married to Wally Herman at the time."

"Well, he kept me on, so's I wouldn't mouth it around."

"I bet you did anyway."

"Naw, hell, whatta I care what he does! He was laying Mitzi Caxton once, years and years back too!"

Jitz Walsh walked back and took Mona Sontag's glass, put it under the beer jet; then refilled Secora's too.

"There's a lot of things goes on in this town," said Secora. "For instance that high-and-mighty wife of the so-called doctor. She used to hang around up to Farley's Lake with Jitz here. Years before Chris McKenzie moved to Cayuta."

"Oh, I know that."

"She acts like she never seen him before now. I was noticing when she come in. 'Hello, Lena,' he says, and she says, 'Ha-lo, there,' real snippy like. Ha-lo there... like she never even heard of Farley's Lake."

"Well, I never heard that Slater Burr was hanging around with Jen McKenzie before they were married."

"Oh, yeah... Yeah, I was floored and so was Francie, when we saw them drive in at Blood Neck."

"Not Francie Boyson."

"We used to get together, time to time."

"Rich Boyson's fat slob of a wife?"

"Eight years ago she was fat in the right places."

"God, Francie Boyson! I should think anyone could do better than that!"

"She suits him, don't she? Suits Rich, and he owns his own place, which is more than anyone you go out with owns!"

"Including you."

Secora was going to answer her, but then the door of the Men's opened, and out came Slater Burr and Donald Cloward. Burr had his arm around Cloward's shoulders.

Beside Secora, Mona sucked in her breath.

Secora said, "Well, well, well, lookit that. They're old buddies all of a sudden."

"Don't you start anything, Al."

"Start anything? What the heck am I going to start, for Pete's sake?"

"Well, don't gawk and butt in. You know."

"I do *not* know! What am I? Some kind of a horse's ass? I know how to conduct myself, same as you."

"It's your hostile attitude I worry about. You know what hostile means?"

"No, Miss Webster's Dictionary and Encyclopedia, I'm stupid or something, for Pete's sake!"

"Just be nice, Albert."

"I am nice! You don't give me credit for knowing the alphabet!"

Slater Burr led Cloward to the bar. "Hey, Jitz!" he called out. "Let's set 'em up here, fellow... What're you drinking, Buzzy?"

11

The night Jen told Chris McKenzie she was marrying Slater Burr, they had this conversation:

"I can't say I'm happy, Jen."

"I'm not asking you to be, but you could hope that I'll be happy."

"You're 22, and he's 40."

"39."

"All right, 39. It's the same thing."

"What do you have against him, besides the fact we were having an affair before Carrie was killed?"

"Nothing against him, Jen. It's just that you don't know what you're getting into. He's more complicated than you know. Carrie Burr was complicated too. They suited one another."

"She never liked the same things Slater did, never."

"But she knew what he liked and let him have it. She knew how to manage him. She knew him like a book. You don't."

Jen had laughed. "She didn't know Slater at all, not at all."

"Don't be foolish, Jen. They were married 14 years. What I mean is, she kept him jumping."

"You make him sound like a little dog who jumps through a hoop for his trainer."

"Maybe that's the way it was. Don't be so sure you can make him happy. He's a grown man, and you're a child in more ways than age."

"You think I'll bore him?"

"It's possible you'll bore each other after awhile."

"And then, Chris?"

"I don't know," he had answered.

Now he knew. Night after night, drinking as they did, he knew.

Others in Cayuta knew as well as Chris knew. Only last week when Elmo Caxton brought his dog in with Harder's gland, the subject had come up.

"How's your sister"–Caxton.

"Well, I hope she's all right," Chris had said.

"They seem to get out a lot, seem very lively," Claxton had remarked.

"Slater Burr does too much drinking," Chris had told Caxton. "It worries me. He doesn't worry me, but my sister could just as easily go the way I did."

"Runs in families, does it?"

"Well, now, I'm not saying that. No, that's not a fact, but..."

"Pretty thing like her. Too bad," Caxton had ended the conversation.

No, it wasn't just Chris who knew, never mind Lena's complaint that Chris was obsessed with the subject of alcoholism. Give Lena enough rope and... well, look at her right now, Chris thought as he stood in Walsh's Place. She had gone past her limit three beers ago. She was down by the jukebox, performing a little dance solo, her glass in her hand, singing softly to herself.

It was Slater, though, who irritated Chris the most. He was very high, encouraging Cloward to elaborate on his flimsy theory of what had happened the night Carrie was killed. Everyone in Walsh's Place was listening; by now, making no pretense of it, even joining in–the way Secora was, agreeing with all of it, and telling Slater everything Slater said was right. Jen was very intoxicated too, mothering Cloward, smoothing his hair and calling him "poor baby" (both of them, not a year apart in age) and Miss Sontag was watching the proceedings through bleary, half-shut eyes, saying over and over, "I ought to report Mr. Leydecker to Father Gianonni. He's a priest; he'd know what to do."

Slater, of course, was buying the drinks.

" 'Nother round," Slater told Jitz, "... and he actually said he hated you, Buzzy?"

"He said he loathed me," Cloward answered. "Said it right out, ah?"

"That's why I got so drunk, I think. I was upset. I'd never been to the club, never been out with him and Laura that way."

"And he gave you the keys, drunk as you were?"

"Yes. Laura had gone on. Mr. McKenzie here–he took Laura home. She was sick, something was wrong with her ankle." Cloward looked at Chris for confirmation. Chris shrugged his assent. He remembered taking Laura Leydecker home, remembered her complaint that she had synovitis of the ankle. He remembered too that Leydecker had seemed almost eager for his daughter to drive with them; he had wanted to stay on, which was peculiar enough, for a man who rarely went to the club, whose friends never went there. Maybe Leydecker had said all the things Cloward claimed, and maybe he did give Cloward his keys, and hope Cloward would kill himself. What did it change? Cloward still wound up behind the wheel of Slater's Jaguar, no matter the circumstances: it was still manslaughter, clear cut... And if it made Leydecker look bad, it did not make him a murderer now, nor even an accessory. Water over the dam; that was what most drunken conversation concerned itself with. Try to tell that to a drunk.

Still, it was wrong of Slater to encourage this sort of talk in public; it was the sort of vulgar shenanigans all drunks became involved in, and were sorry for the next day.

Chris said, "Slater, we really ought to push along."

"Go ahead. They out of ginger ale or something? Jitz? You out of ginger ale?"

Secora laughed hardily at the remark, and clapped his hand on Slater's shoulder. "You're a beaut, Mr. Burr!"

"Slater," Chris tried again, "we came in your car."

"Well, take the bus back, Carrie Nation. Buzzy, here, came out on the bus. Came looking for me. Clear his name. Like any man!"

Jitz Walsh set up another round of drinks, another ginger ale for Chris. Lena was sitting down in a chair now, near the jukebox, cooing to herself. Chris left her drink on the bar.

"I know Leydecker personally!" Secora said. "He's always butting into union meetings. I know him personally! Always blabbing about new industry. What the hell we need it for? We got The Cayuta Macaroni Company and Burr Manufacturing, ha, Mr. Burr? Shoe plant, and whatthehell!"

"That's right, Secora," said Slater. He put his hands on Cloward's lapels. "Buzzy here'd like to work for me. He's got an offer in New York working for a newspaperman, but he'd rather work for me."

"I feel lost in New York," said Cloward. "I dunno. The fellow I'm supposed to work for is carrying the torch for some girl. I get tired of hearing it. This is my home, here."

"Sure," Slater said. "And if what you say is true, if Leydecker put you in my car, well, now, hell! Hell, you got a gripe coming!"

Jen said, "I don't think you even ran into her. I think she jumped in front of..."

Slater cut her off. "Oh now, Jen. Crap! Jen! People knew Carrie better 'n that."

"Well, Slater, I..."

"The important thing is that Leydecker was out to get Buzzy! Now, I personally believe Buzzy! I think Leydecker did put him in my car. My car was pointed right at the drop-off."

Secora said, "Leydecker coulda pulled off the emergency and started the car rolling even."

"No," Cloward shook his head. "I hit her too hard. She could have jumped out of the way, Al, if I'd been rolling."

"Maybe she didn't want to jump out of the way," said Jen.

"Oh, now, Jenny! Now nobody gets killed with a car coming at them on a slow roll. Now, hell, you don't know anything about it! Why, at the time you were so daffy over Horace Dryden you couldn't see your nose on your face." Slater laughed and tickled her under the chin. "Good old Horace!" he said. "Fell in love with him when you saw the back of his neck! You all know that? Old Horace the Bore-ass was Jen's big moment that summer. Up at Blood Neck Point with him till the roosters crowed."

"Slater! Oh, Slater," and Jen laughed then. She sang, "I must have that doggie in the window, the one..."

"With the fleas in his hair," sang Slater.

Secora let out another whoop of delight at Slater, and said, "Why shore, shore enough, old Blood Neck!" He feigned a playful sock at Slater's jaw. Slater looked uncomfortable. He downed his whiskey, while Secora turned to Mona Sontag and said, "How'm I doing? Am I nice or hows-stile?"

"I'm tired, Albert."

"Well, now, just when I'm having me some fun, you're tired."

"I can't help it... all this beer."

"Heck, Mona, it's Christmas Day!"

"I was going to church this evening."

Donald Cloward leaned into Slater. "I didn't come back to make trouble for Laura's father, Mr. Burr. I just want a start. I can't see myself in New York City."

"Sure, well, we'll talk about it," Slater said.

Mona Sontag murmured: "I ought to tell Father Gianonni about Mr. Ley-decker. A priest knows what to do."

"Be funny," said Secora, "if Leydecker was driving the Jag himself."

Cloward said, "That wouldn't make much sense, Al. I don't think he'd just take Mr. Burr's car. He was nowhere near there either."

"He coulda run for it, left you there. Why wouldn't he, if he wanted you out of the way?"

"I don't think so... No," said Cloward.

Slater Burr said, "Secora, why don't you take Miss Sontag home? She's had it!"

Secora ignored the remark. "D'yah drive a Jag a lot, Buzzy, 'fore that night?"

"It was my first and last time."

"The one and only time, for Pete's sake? Heck, they're a little complicat-ed. I don't think a drunk could figure it out, never been in one. Not figure it out and get all that speed up for a short distance... Now, I, myself, once drove a Jag. S'got an English shift, you know, more forward speeds than ours. I had to sit there awhile and figure it out, and I was dead sober."

"Any bright person could figure it out in a second, Secora," said Slater. "You better take Miss Sontag home, Mister. She's falling asleep."

"I ain't bright, or something?"

"I didn't say that... I just think you'd better take her home."

"I think I just did it instinctively," Cloward said.

"A Jag? It isn't like our cars, not the '54 ones. Course some of them are now. I'm talking about the old ones, Mr. Burr. I had trouble the day I tried one, was nine, maybe ten years ago."

"Tired, Albert," said Mona Sontag.

"She'll get a second wind," Secora told everyone. He turned back to Donald Cloward. "You didn't even have a trial, did you?"

"No... But..." Cloward was frowning.

Slater Burr said, "Take her home, Secora!"

"What's the matter with you, Mr. Burr? Leydecker could have been driving your car, couldn't he? Keys were left in it, weren't they?"

"Right now," said Slater, "I'm thinking of Miss Sontag. A gentleman takes a lady home when she's had enough!"

"Sla-ter," Jen touched his arm, spoke softly. "Not so rough... Go a little easy, darling."

"Thank you ver-ree much, Mr. Burr," said Mona Sontag. "He isn't gentleman."

"The heck I'm not! I spent ten ninety-eight on a..."

Slater had him by the arm now, and was taking him to the door of Walsh's Place. Chris McKenzie got off his stool and helped Mona Sontag.

"He isn't gentleman," Mona Sontag said.

"You don't have any right to do this to me, Mr. Burr!" Secora said.

"You horned in on the little party, now horn out!" Slater answered. He gave him a shove out the door, and Mona Sontag caught his arm and dragged along with him.

For a moment, the pair stopped in the drive outside Walsh's Place, and Chris McKenzie could see Secora's face, red and angry.

"You were pretty rough on him, Slater," Jen said.

McKenzie watched while the pair got into Secora's old Chevrolet. "They're all right now. They're leaving," he said. "We ought to go too."

"One on the house first," Jitz Walsh smiled.

"Well, not for Lena," said Chris. Lena could not drink any more if Walsh had taken one across to her. She was sitting down by the jukebox with her head on the table.

"You're a fine one, you are," Jen giggled, "talking about taking ladies home. Look at Lena."

"Lena didn't ask to go home," said Slater. He turned to Donald Cloward. "Secora was butting in. This sort of discussion shouldn't he open to public debate in a barroom."

A fine time to think of that, Chris McKenzie told himself.

12

Carrie Burr had never laughed much, but when she had, the laughter burst like an explosion–whoom! Slater could hear them in his mind, one after the other now, while he faced Cloward in his living room.

"No kidding, Mr. Burr," said Cloward, "I never thought of it before. Not until Secora said it."

"Secora is a know-nothing, Buzzy!"... All right, and there went another; oh, a know-nothing, is he, ummm, Slater, and ha! ha! ha! Whoom! Whoom! Whoom!

Jen said, "He's not our favorite person. He's one of the union leaders at the plant, Donald. I was surprised to hear him speak out against Leydeck-er that way. Leydecker's very thick with those union people, isn't he, dar-ling? He's always speaking up for them at B.B.B.C. meetings."

"B.B.B.C.?"

"Buy, Build, Boost Cayuta," said Slater. "This is a hell of a town to want to settle in right now, Buzzy. Whole place is on the skids."

You are, you mean–Whoom!... But Slater smiled, relaxed looking, legs stretched out, big and easy-going, "Yeah, Secora talks through his hat! His kind tilts the way the wind blows, and the wind was blowing in the direc-tion of free drinks this afternoon."

Cloward's short, freckled hands were playing with a comb, running their nails through its teeth and twanging them; his eyes slightly glazed from drink. "Still," he said, "I never thought of the fact I'd never driven a Jag before."

"It is interesting," Jen said.

"Jen, get dinner!"

"What?"

"I'm sorry," said Slater. "I'm just hungry. We all are."

"O-kay, but watch your tone of voice, or the cook will quit."

He watched her walk across the room toward the kitchen. And if she were to know the truth, what would she say or do? He knew what Car-rie would have done under the same circumstances; she would have turned him in, graciously, of course, and emphatically; Carrie had been a woman of Character. But Jen? Ah, and he laughed inside, he knew. "We can hide out in Europe, Slater." It would represent another chance to get abroad... Maybe not. It was hard to know anyone any more, hard to know himself, and why it was he could sit there facing Cloward after Cloward's eight years in prison, and think only of two things about him: that he wished to God Cloward would put his comb away, and that he would have to get Cloward out of Cayuta, and fast.

It had all gone too far. In the beginning, Slater had thought it might be amusing–even useful–to have Cloward's theory on Leydecker's involve-ment in the accident go the gossip rounds in Cayuta. The idea of Leydeck-er thinking his daughter was too good for an honest working man would turn a lot of people of Secora's ilk against Leydecker... and it would sift through, reach others too. It would also renew everyone's interest in, and speculations about, Leydecker's daughter. That mystery had blown over in the past few years; eventually people simply accepted odd facts, the same as they accepted the fact that Horace Dryden's mother was a kleptomani-ac, and Paul Ayres never touched money without wearing gloves, and Father Gianonni of St. Anthony's was a lush.

Slater had imagined some slight diversion from the idea of Kenneth Ley-decker as the community's hope and rescuer... a little gossip to sidetrack the notion. He had even toyed, for the briefest moment, with hiring Cloward. To ease his conscience? No, he crossed that one off; he had gone beyond con-science a long time ago. In as far as he was now, he had become stout enough to throw off the chill of a bad conscience almost at once... But if he had hired Cloward, it would make him look as good as it made Leydecker look bad. An act of charity, forgiveness... It had seemed just that simple to Slater at Walsh's Place. Even though Cloward had not a shred of evidence against Leydecker in the manslaughter charge, it would start tongues wagging, that was all.

Then goddam punk Secora put his mouth in! There had not even been a suggestion that anyone could have been behind the wheel but Cloward, until Secora's dull brain sparked for the first time in his life.

Cloward sat opposite Slater in the Windsor chair, quite drunk now. They had all had a few more at Walsh's Place, before Lena fell on her face, and then they had mixed martinis here at home. In a way, Slater gave Cloward credit for picking up Secora's lead and not making anything out of it, but he did not like the fact Cloward dwelled on the matter, nor the fact Cloward wanted to stay in Cayuta. He was glad of this chance to straight-en out his thinking and put it back on the wrong track.

Now Cloward was back on the subject of getting his newspaper friend interested in Secora's theory.

"Guy's real quick," Cloward was saying. "Things that take me all day to figure out, Guy figures out in seconds."

"What's he say to your theory of being put into my Jag by someone?"

"Well, you see, Mr. Burr, I never went into it too much with him. Guy used to say it was irrelevant. Irrevelant... because I still drove the car that killed her."

"He's right, Buzz."

"But if Leydecker were driving the Jaguar..."

"Wait a minute, Buzz... Now, listen to me."

"Yes, sir?"

"I personally hate Leydecker. He's causing me plenty of trouble. There's a new zoning law he's pushing and..."

"And he stole your father's ideas, or his father did. I remember my dad always saying that."

"Yes. Well, that's my point. There are a lot of reasons I don't like Leydecker. I'd be the first to want to prove what you say is true. Not just because I hate Leydecker. Buzz, but because, after all, my wife was killed in that accident."

"Yes, sir... I see."

"It's just a flimsy theory all the way around. You know Leydecker."

"Yes."

"He might give you his keys and hope you'd kill yourself, but as for Kenneth Leydecker taking a chance like that... Come on, use your head."

"Yes, I can see where it'd be unlikely."

"Leydecker wouldn't risk everything, and Buzz," Slater let out a small laugh, "he wouldn't have killed Carrie. He always liked Carrie! The whole idea is just bull, Buzz. Bull!"

"I guess you're right. It's far-fetched."

"You want to concentrate on your future, not your past."

"But you said yourself that Leydecker might very well have moved me to your car, sir. I wouldn't have taken your car, not yours!"

Slater said, "And that may be. And I believe you, Buzz. I think I believe you... But it doesn't help you now."

"Where you're concerned, it does."

"Yes. I'm ready to buy your theory, and it puts a different light on things, though I never felt angry at you. You were drunk. I've been drunk too."

"I'd really like to work for you, sir. I don't feel right in New York. I'd start anywhere, at any salary. I know it could be arranged... Sir, I don't want to be a secretary. What kind of a job is that for a man?"

"Okay," Slater said, "but wait a damn minute. It'll take time to arrange that through the parole board, right?"

"Right. It will take some time."

"And I've got to work out some problems... So why don't you go to New York, and work for this fellow for a time, and then I'll send for you."

"That would be just great, Mr. Burr!"

"I'd have to write your parole board and so forth."

"Yes, Sir!"

"And in the meantime, I wouldn't shoot off my mouth to this newspaper fellow about your plans. You let me handle it."

"Don't worry, Mr. Burr."

"It might take a little time, but we'll do it, Buzz. Now, that's a promise."

"Thank you, Mr. Burr."

"And the sooner you go to New York, the better."

"Why is that, sir?"

"Well, if it looks as though you're back here to make trouble, Leydecker might get into it. He could write your parole board just as well. Gossip gets around. God knows what Secora is saying right now."

"I see what you mean... But I'm not supposed to leave until the end of the week."

"We might arrange it so you can leave earlier."

"Where would I go?"

"Hell, Buzzy, you been cooped up a long time! How about a hotel, money for some shows... have a little freedom. You won't get it around here."

Slater got up and walked across with the martini pitcher, poured Cloward another drink. A euphoria was rising in him now, dissolving the edge of panic he had felt earlier. No more whooms in his head; *I am getting away with it, Carrie,* and he ruffled Buzzy's hair, "We'll work things out," and he began to feel all right again.

Buzzy Cloward said, "One thing, though..."

"What's that, Buzz?"

"Well, I keep wondering about Laura, about what happened to her."

II.

At ten o'clock, Kenneth Leydecker, his green celluloid eyeshade fixed to his brow, sat at his tambour desk in his study, rereading the speech he had composed for Thursday's meeting of the B.B.B.C., "...and to attract industry we must have lower rates of interest for financing it. The State of Pennsylvania will go as low as two per cent, whereas New York requires at least five and a half per cent. Furthermore..."

The ringing of the telephone surprised him. He looked at the telephone as though there had been some mistake, but on the second ring, he picked it up.

"Hello?"

"I would like to speak to Laura."

"Laura is in bed at this hour," he said.

He heard the click on the line, and knew that Laura was on the extension upstairs. He had known this call was inevitable, but he had not been prepared... now with Laura listening, he felt shaky and apprehensive.

Donald Cloward said, "It's only ten o'clock."

"Nevertheless, Laura is in bed."

"What's the matter with her, Mr. Leydecker? You know who this is."

"Yes, I do know who it is."

"I want to know what's the matter with Laura. Is she a prisoner or something?"

"I think that's your status, much more than it is Laura's."

"That was my status. Now I want to know Laura's!"

"She wants nothing to do with you, Donald."

"I'd like to hear her tell me that... I want to hear her tell me that she's all right."

"I'm afraid that's impossible."

"Why?"

"Why? Because it is!"

"I'm not trying to start anything up again, Mr. Leydecker. I'm going away soon, but I want to know if Laura's all right."

"She is all right. Now, there's nothing more to say, Cloward."

"I want to talk to her. When can I call her?"

"If you call here again, I'll call the police. Donald, I don't want you to bother us again!"

"I just want to talk to her! I've got to know if she's all right."

"You'll have to take my word for it."

"The same way I took your word about the car keys, Mr. Leydecker?"

Kenneth Leydecker dropped the phone into its receiver. He waited a moment, then picked it up again, and got a dial tone. He was relieved. Laura had hung up at the same time.

13

In the car, Jen Burr tried to make him feel better about it.

"We've all done things like that, Don."

"I shouldn't have called there. I don't know what got into me. I was sit-ting there by myself in the living room, and suddenly I remembered her phone number. I just thought I'd try seeing how she was."

"You get a good night's sleep, and everything will be all right in the morn-ing. You're still a little tipsy. Things always look worse."

It was something she told herself, as well as Cloward.

She had been left with no alternative but to drive Cloward home. While Cloward was phoning Laura Leydecker in the living room, she and Slater had been arguing in the kitchen. It was her own fault for nagging Slater. She had begun with a complaint about his remark at Walsh's Place, that she had been to Blood Neck with Horace Dryden (lecherous creep!), and it had ended with her telling Slater he was behaving like some sort of criminal, covering his tracks, lying, then this new idea to spirit Donald off to New York City tomorrow, unbeknownst to anyone.

She should have been perceptive enough to realize that Cloward's return was dredging up all the mucky guilt and self-recriminations Slater carried around inside him. Lord, last night she had gotten a close enough look at it, Slater slapping her that way. She should learn to leave it all alone, let Slater work it out himself, however he chose to do it.

Slater had gone up to bed angry at her. Another First, she thought sadly; last night a sock in the jaw, tonight going to bed in a huff. They never had those kinds of quarrels, never. There was not a thing in the world which could happen between them, that their bodies near each other could not diminish in seconds... Yet tonight, she had gone into the bedroom to get the keys to the car, leaned over Slater and touched his shoulder: "I'm taking Donald home, darling."... "Do as you please, darling," he had answered sarcastically... And for a horrible few moments as she went down the stairs, she had the feeling he missed Carrie, and that Slater and she were all wrong together; why hadn't she known that all these years? Why hadn't she lis-tened to Chris? He had warned her Slater was too complicated. Carrie knew how to handle him.

"I did everything wrong tonight," Donald Cloward said beside her.

"You're not the only one."

"Now I have Mr. Burr angry at me."

"He was angry at me, Donald. He's under a lot of pressure, and sometimes I forget that."

"I don't see why he didn't tell me good night. It's as though he knew I'd called Leydecker."

"No, he didn't know it. And I won't tell him tomorrow. It was a quarrel we had, in the kitchen. It didn't have anything to do with you."

But I'll be glad when you're gone, Jen thought... Maybe she and Slater ought to cut out the drinking; maybe Chris was right: it made good things bad, bad things worse. Sometimes Chris' corny clichés hit their mark. Ah, but God, not Slater and her, there wasn't anything wrong there. It was the goddam town and goddam Leydecker, and now the Cloward boy coming back like this. Still, she felt sorry for Donald Cloward. He had told her about his newspaper friend and the long hours spent listening to him pour out his troubles, while Donald sat feeling no one wanted to hear his, and that there was no one.

She said, "We've all had too much to drink."

"You certainly can hold it, Mrs. Burr."

"I shouldn't be driving. I can feel my drinks."

"I shouldn't have let you bring me home. I should have called a cab."

Jen said, "They take hours to get to our place."

"Or a bus, or something."

"A bus!" Jen laughed. "The buses don't run after five o'clock in Cayuta any more... People either have cars, or they're too poor to go out."

"Yes, it's all changed... Buy, build, boost–Cayuta! But it feels like home, you know?"

"You're lucky to be leaving. I wish we were."

"I'll be back though. Unless Mr. Burr's mad at me now."

"He has no reason to be mad at you, Donald. Get it out of your head."

"I shouldn't have called Laura, but I wish I could just see her. I don't love her. I don't think I love her. Maybe I never did. It's hard to say. But I'd like to know what's wrong, why she never comes out any more."

"Donald, you're driving me crazy with that noise you're making with the comb."

"I'm sorry." He put it back in his pocket. "It's a habit. I know it's irritating. I saw Mr. Burr look at me back at your place once. I was doing the same thing, and I could see in his eyes he was disgusted... I have to watch myself. I've been away so long, I'm not used to people. I forget... For awhile there, back at your place, I realized I was talking too much about–the other Mrs. Burr."

"What do you mean?"

"I was just saying how much I liked her. He acted sort of angry, you know what I mean? I realized it must have stirred up a lot of old memories for him. It must have hurt him. No offense, or anything, but it must have been hard for him to remember the other Mrs. Burr. I've got to watch myself."

"What did you think of her, Donald?"

"She was always swell. I mean, everyone liked her. Mr. Burr worshipped her, I guess. I shouldn't have brought up her name so much."

"Don't feel guilty about it, Donald. Maybe he doesn't like to think about her, but it wasn't all the way you thought."

"I guess I shouldn't even be talking about it now. I'm too drunk... But I did like Mrs. Burr."

Jen felt a tiny dart of anger, just a sliver, enough to make herself say, "What was so great about her?"

"She was kind."

"Oh, kind... Sure. Just between you and me and the proverbial lamp-post, Donald, she was a bitch!"

"Of course, I didn't know her well, but..."

"Carrie Burr was far from kind. They were never happy, so just put your mind to rest on that score."

"I always thought they were."

"Everyone did," said Jen, turning on to Genesee Street. "But it wasn't so. If she hadn't been killed, Slater would have divorced her."

"Really, Mrs. Burr?"

"Really... It's bad enough to have her life on your conscience, but don't have their happy marriage on your conscience too. It just wasn't a happy marriage."

"Are you sure?"

"Yes, I'm sure, Donald... And I'm sure you didn't do any harm calling the Leydeckers either. So sleep well tonight."

"You're great, Mrs. Burr. I mean, you understand what it's like to feel–oh well, crummy."

"Yes, I know what it's like... Poor Slater, he's felt pretty crummy for a long time, and I'm afraid I haven't been much help."

"I think you're both wonderful people, Mrs. Burr!"

"Thanks... We like you too, Donald... Well, here we are."

"I wonder if Mr. Leydecker will tell Laura I called?"

"The best thing is to forget all about the Leydeckers."

"I know that," he said. "It's just that I wonder about Laura. I guess it's the drinks."

"It always is... No, you get a good night's sleep."

"Mr. Burr said I was to come out to your place tomorrow. We'd figure things out."

"Then I'll see you tomorrow."

He got out of the car and then ducked his head inside for a moment. "You've been just swell, Mrs. Burr!"

"Sweet dreams," said Jen.

"Thank you, ma'am."

He slammed the door shut and watched her car turn on Capitol Street. Then he started towards the entranceway of The Burr Building. He glanced at his wrist watch, pausing a moment in the wet street, looking across at The Clark Building. After a second or more, he turned away from the entranceway, down Genesee, weaving a little from left to right, but going rapidly.

14

When she had been very young, when her mother was still alive, in the years and years before Buzzy Cloward, she used to sit around the back porch steps with Peony Stubbs and Betty Jean Means, solemnly debating a preference between losing her hearing, or going blind.

"I'd rather be deaf any old day of the week!" she would insist. "If I were to go blind, I'd wish I were dead!"

And Peony would declare that she would wish she were dead if she could not hear, and Betty Jean Means, stuck on horror stories of World War II, told by an older brother, would ask them both what they thought of being "basket cases." Wasn't that worse than going deaf or blind?

Laura Leydecker often thought of those days and that particular theme, when she went nightly down the back stairs to fix her snack before the 11:15 late show on television. She turned on as few lights as she could. There were no near neighbors on Highland Hill. Not near enough to see from their windows into the Leydeckers'. But the thought was always there that someone might look in, see her through the straw blinds in the kitchen, the same way she could see the outlines of the pine trees and hydrangea bushes outside. She crept around in an old robe of her father's; the wig made her flesh creep, she never wore it, someone else's hair, like someone's hand sewed on; no, let any busybodies think it was him raiding the icebox; him whom she hated... and she thought how much better it would have been, had blindness struck than this unimaginable thing. This Thing was somehow shameful, laughable, as she had always been laughable, really, oh, she knew that... but blind... Blind she could have gone to one of those schools for the sightless, entered their world and stayed among them... and she had fantasies of that being what had happened. Sometimes she would shut her eyes going up the back stairs and see how easy it was to maneuver... Or in her room, she would sometimes turn off the sound on the television set, watch it and think of being deaf.

Both alternatives were better. To be the way she was, was to be Betty Jean Means' "basket case." The irony of those discussions and those days (O how hysterically and gleefully she had laughed when her mother sang the song about the ball being over, and Mary taking out her false teeth, her false eye, taking off her wig!) was renewed nearly every day.

No amount of newspaper clips left under her door by her father, telling of wigs being The Fashion, could do war with the bitter fact she would rather die than let it be known. God, Fate was like Dreams the way it chose just the right thing for you, so brilliantly and cruelly selective in its choice... wouldn't you know *that* would happen to Laura Leydecker, ha ha's down the tunnel of her imagination, wouldn't you just know it would be something like *that!*... And in her bureau drawer, the gold-back brushes of her mother, and gold-edged combs to mock her.

She had tried; tried everything every doctor told her, and long after she had stopped seeing doctors, stopped mourning the loss of Buzzy, stopped everything but living in the world of her room, there was nothing to change things. Only in dreams was it any different, and that was nearly every night. The same, the same: the whole thing had simply never happened. There she was! Walking down Highland Hill, brown hair spilling to her shoulders, blowing ever so lightly in the breeze: *blown hair is sweet, over the mouth blown.*

Settling before the set again that night, at eleven-fifteen, she saw her reflection opposite the bed, in the mirror, while she ate the turkey, taken from the refrigerator downstairs. She looked to herself like some wild creature, gnawing a bone; and on purpose, she exaggerated her performance, contorting her features, ugly and crazy, all the while remembering the sound of his voice on the telephone an hour ago: *I want to hear her tell me that she's all right.*

Oh yes, fine.

"Really?"

"Yes, glorious, Buzzy!"

"Just as good as the last time?" he had murmured, his mouth warm and moist at her ear. *"Or better?"*

"The best and happiest moments of the happiest and best!"

"You say beautiful things all the time, don't you? Shakespeare and things."

"That was Shelley. You know it's usually Shelley. It was from his 'Defence of Poetry'. "

"But those are words. I make you feel them, don't I?"

"Oh, yes! You do!"

It was hot that July afternoon, and he was very tan, his bronze-colored arms and legs and shoulders wet from lovemaking, but not heavy on her; he never once was. The lightest thing in the world was the loved one's body. He stayed that way smoking a cigarette, giving her a drag, touching the wetness of her hair at her forehead with his freckled fingers, kissing her gently at first and then with the renewed passion that was always there, the hard hanging-on of one to the other.

"*Darling, do be careful. We have to dress. The man will be wondering what happened to us.*"

"*I wonder if he'll keep this same crummy bed in here after we move in?*"

" '*Bed of crimson joy, and dark secret love.*' "

"*Shelley.*"

"*No, not that time. Blake.*"

"*It's still a crummy bed.*"

"*I love this place!*"

And she had. She had closed her eyes in the few slow seconds of silence between them, and thought of memorizing it: this feeling of herself under him, the two of them wet and loving, so that there seemed to be no sensation but their joy. On the stairway as they left, she had said: "I think sometimes it's all an illusion. '*All is illusion till the morning bars, Slip from the levels of the Eastern Gate. Night is too young, O friend! day is too near!*'... Don't you feel that way, darling?"

There was a tin guard loose on one step, the stairway dark, smelling of mustiness, coffee cooking, and the noise below of traffic in the street. She thought how beautiful it was that soon she would know every step of the stairs, every crack in the plaster, every detail of their home, and the sound of him on those steps coming up to number four at a day's end, waiting for that sound: how beautiful... And there was a roach running down the stairway, frightened and blind and ugly looking, and he had stepped over it, not wanting to kill it; that was him.

"I only worry about your father," he had said.

She put aside her plate of food and leaned back against the pillows. She closed her eyes and tried to remember what it had felt like, but her mind fastened on the bizarreness of herself under any man now. She opened her eyes. On the television screen a woman in tights, carrying a fan, was performing a seductive dance before a man sitting at a table, holding a drink, leering at her.

The woman was singing:

> "Do you know what it means?
> To miss New Orleans,
> When that's where you left your heart?"

She remembered an afternoon years back at Cayuta Lake, when a boy named Ted Chayka had looked that way at her. Chayka had gone to Industrial High with Buzzy; he was a big unruly fellow who fished off the pier at the lake and drank beer out of cans, always eyeing the girls who came to swim there. Buzzy had told him to stop staring at Laura; there had been a fist fight, and Buzzy had cut his eye. At home later, Laura had fixed a band-age to the cut, and her father had walked in the kitchen then, home from work. He had been unmoved by the story. As though Buzzy were not present, he had said, "If you'd been at the pier with a decent boy to begin with, Chayka wouldn't have bothered you at all. You were with someone of his own class. That was the reason you were treated in such a manner!"

Bed of crimson joy, and dark secret love.

She remembered... an afternoon in summer, at the clearing in Hunter's Woods, the shelf fungus they had broken off a tree to write their names on, beside them on the ground; the lavender joe-pye weed near the spot Buzzy had lain his shirt, and the red-start warbling above them in the catalpa tree, while Buzzy undid the buttons of her blouse. And their eyes! The way they were looking at one another then, looking right into one anoth-er, as though eyes could touch the parts of a person, burrow right into the heart and hold it securely; keep it that way forever, in one long look like that, and then...

Laura Leydecker sat up in bed suddenly. She reached for the control panel of the television. She shut off the sound, listening. She heard the noise on her window pane, as though someone were throwing pebbles at it from down on the ground. Quickly, she turned off the set, and pulled the lamp chain. She sat in the darkness.

Again.

She stole out of bed and crept across, pulling up a slat of the Venetian blind.

By the light of the street lamp in front of the Leydecker home, she saw him.

He was standing beside the Engelmann's spruce, in the side yard. He was looking up at her window, and now, he reached down again, tossing a scat-tering more of gravel, some of it hitting the pane lightly, the rest, the wood-en frame of the house.

Momentarily she watched, without moving, staying to the side of her window. Then, when he did it again, she reached out her hand, up under the blind, and raised the window a few inches. She got down on her knees, peeping out at him through the bottom slats of the blind.

She heard him call her name softly.

She was trembling now; again he called, "Laura? Laura?"

Her voice broke when she answered him. "Go away!"

Her lips rubbed against the cold plastic slat, as she forced her words out, softly as she could manage.

"Laura, is it you?"

"Yes. Go away."

"I have to see you! I called your father tonight, but he wouldn't let me talk to you. I want to know if you're all right."

"Yes, but go away, please."

"Will you see me tomorrow?"

"I can't."

"Why? What's wrong with you, anyway?"

"I'm—ill."

"What's wrong?"

"It's ... a form of alopecia."

"What? I can't hear you."

"I don't want to tell you. Please go."

"Can I come back tomorrow night?"

"No."

"Please! Let me come tomorrow night. I can be here any time you say, meet you down by the back porch, the way we used to. Please!"

"Go now, Buzzy!"

"Yes, you'll meet me tomorrow."

"Go now, or father will..."

"Tomorrow," he said, "nine-thirty tomorrow night. Okay?"

"Yes," she said. She began to feel weak and sick. "I'll be here at nine-thir-ty!"

She waited long enough to be sure he had gone. She saw him walk away, saw his red hair under the street lamp, as he turned down Highland Hill, and then she sank back on her haunches and held her hand to her mouth, heaving up nothing but retching agony from deep inside.

II.

In the dream, Kenneth Leydecker was explaining the reformulation of the zoning rules, at a luncheon. He was standing on the podium in the large dining room at The Mohawk Hotel, looking out at the faces of his audience, seeing now Paul Ayres, now Elmo Caxton, now... a light, a very bright light, just as he was stating the new boundaries, a glaring light suddenly... and then he was awake.

"Laura!" He jerked himself up, his eyes blinking, his hands fumbling for his glasses.

"Father, you have to go to Buzzy and talk to him."

"I have to do nothing of the kind, Laura! I certainly do not have to do anything of the kind... Now what's this all about?" adjusting his spectacles on his ears and nose. Her eyes were bloodshot and tearful, her mouth quivering. She stood bare-headed, wearing his old robe and her pajamas under it, barefoot... suddenly pathetic-looking, worse than he could remember, the defiance gone out of her. He had always hated the defiance, but now that it was replaced with this hopeless despair, he realized how much easier it had been for him the other way.

"Laura," he said, "I know you heard the telephone call."

"You have to see him, father. You have to go and see him. I want you to do that for me."

"What good would that do? What would it accomplish? Laura, put your mind at ease. He won't come here."

"He just left here, father."

"He did *what?*"

"He was outside my window just now."

"I'm going to call the police." Leydecker's hand reached across for the telephone. Her hand stopped his.

"Father, please listen to me. I beg you to listen to me. For once!"

"Well, Laura?"

"He'll come back again. He will, father, no matter if you call the police or not."

"Don't you worry. The police can take care of him."

"Father, don't you understand? I don't want him taken care of that way. Haven't you done enough to Buzzy?"

"I did nothing to Donald Cloward, Laura. He did it to himself."

"The same way I did it to myself, is that it, father?"

"Laura, please. *Please,* Laura! Do you think I enjoy seeing you this way? Laura, if I could do *anything*–anything to help you, don't you know that I'd do it?"

"Would you, father?"

"Certainly!"

"Will you go see Buzzy? Will you go and tell him that I have an illness? Just tell him that I have an illness, father. You don't have to be specific! You can think of something. Tell him I have an illness that has changed me, and that I'm embarrassed to see him, or talk to him on the telephone... Father, if you did it in a nice way, he'd believe you."

"Laura, Laura, the police would see to it that..."

She shouted, "I don't want the police to do it, father! You do it!"

Tears formed in Kenneth Leydecker's eyes. He took off his glasses and wiped at his eyes with his fingers. "If you want that... then..."

"I want it, father."

"Very well, but..."

"Will you do it tomorrow? Tomorrow morning?"

"He had no right to come here." Leydecker sighed. "No right at all."

"I'm asking you, father, *will you do it?*"

"I said I would... He actually *came* here?"

"I was sick after... sick right on the floor of my bedroom. I could hardly walk in here."

"He just left?"

"I told you, father, he was just here!"

"All right," said Leydecker. "All right. I'll take care of it. You'd better take a pill, Laura."

"I shall, father."

"Yes, take a pill. You need some sleep."

"I wonder if anyone in the world gets as much sleep a I do," she said, walking out the door.

The moment the door was shut behind her, Leydecker took the telephone to his lap. He dialed the three digits which would ring the police.

15

"Who was it?" Nancy said.

"I'm afraid I have to leave early," Ted Chayka answered, as he walked back into the living room. On the floor beside her chair there were half-a-dozen red-stained Kleenexes wadded up and tossed there. There was the acrid, sickly-sweet smell of Milday Nail Polish Remover. Nancy's lap was peppered with tiny red peelings, nail size. This was her habit at night, to peel off as many of the red shells as she could from her fingers; then finish the removal of her nail polish with a liquid, on those nails she could not peel... Christmas night was no exception. The tree was lit on the T.V. top, a testimony to the holidays, and there were tie boxes and jewelry boxes there—their gifts to one another, and strands of tinsel were draped around the ears of the T.V. indoor antenna, but it was still just another day. Chayka was due at work at eleven-thirty, an hour away, and Nancy was probably fussing over in her mind, whether to watch the late show featuring Tyrone Power, or the mystery movie.

"Early? How come?"

He said, "That was Rich Boyson on the phone. My cousin's down to his place with a bag on."

"So let him. What's it to you?"

"It's Christmas night," said Chayka, depressed at the dullness of his voice, and at the irony of his own unnecessary announcement: *it's Christmas night,* "Rich doesn't want it spoiled for the customers."

"Is your cousin the only one who celebrates the holidays by getting a bag on? What's Rich Boyson in business for anyway?"

But she was not arguing because she cared that he had to leave an hour early; Nancy was just running off at the mouth again, about nothing at all.

Chayka said, "I guess things are out of hand... Anyway, I said I'd stop in."

"There's a play coming on at ten-thirty, so I'll watch that, I guess."

"I'm sorry," Chayka lied. "I have to go, though."

"So—go," with a shrug of her shoulder.

"Want a can of beer from the icebox, while I'm up?"

"No, I want one from the oven."

"No sense being nasty, Nancy."

"Come on, Ted, I was kidding, for God's sake. Kidding, s'all."

"I guess I'm jumpy. I'll get you a beer."

"I don't know what's wrong with you lately, Ted."

"I don't know either," he said. "Nerves, I guess."

But he knew very well what was wrong. He thought about it while he got Nancy her beer, and then while he dressed in his blue patrolman's uniform–his shoes polished to a high shine, the crease in his pants sharp, the new black hatband on his cap, clean... the shield polished. He thought about it while he drove his old Plymouth down to Boyson's.

What was wrong was that he had changed.

He had been married seven years to Nancy, and during those seven years, he had changed from a hoarse-voiced, shiftless, drunk-every-weekend garage mechanic, to a solemn and sober member of the Cayuta Police Department. He had become something, and becoming that, he had realized there was more to go. He wanted ultimately to be a Police Lieutenant, a detective... but not just that... He wanted to be a happy and respectable citizen, Someone, as well as Something. He wanted to love his wife and have her kids... and there was Nancy every night, same as always, same as seven years ago, slopping around in her bedroom slippers, peeling off her polish, dropping her Kleenexes and her stockings and her empty beer cans wherever she had a mind to–going at Life with all the zest of a "before ad" for Geritol.

To make matters worse, it was all gone between them, as bad now as it had been wonderful in their teens, when they could not even wait out a movie in the darkness of the theater–not even a good movie, because every fiber of their being demanded more than the hand-holding, the furtive, futile groping: More and Everything.

Now, whenever he mounted her, he felt a sick, sinking loss, a feeling that invariably lent him enough anger to compensate for the emotion of passion, and it was a violent thing between them, quick and thankless. She received no pleasure; she did not have to tell him that, and she never did, in words. They never spoke about it... But it was there–in their mutual embarrassment at love scenes on T.V., in the child they could not conceive, in her "kidding" and his "nerves", and in the indifferent way of the passage of their years of married life.

"It's Christmas night."

"So–go."

It could not continue; if it did, the seven years of studying and working and getting-and-taking advice... and succeeding, step-by-step going ahead, would all be for nothing.

It was not Nancy's fault that he had changed (God knows the drunken nights she had tolerated before Chris McKenzie came into their life to change him!) but it was not his fault either, that now he wanted more and better. And the more be wanted it, the better he wanted it to be, the worse it became between them. For a month he been unable to touch her–even to touch her, to try. Gone, and in its wake, a zero.

As he parked the Plymouth before Boyson's, he heard himself, in his mind, telling Chris about it, asking Chris about it. Tomorrow morning, when he was off-duty, he would go for coffee with Chris, air it–the whole thing... or it would drive him crazy, drive him back to the bottom of the bottle, where he used to look for solutions. Where there were none.

Rich Boyson was hovering near the entranceway of the bar, waiting for Chayka.

"Hi, Ted," he said. "My golly, I'm sorry, but..."

"Don't be, Rich!" Chayka told him. "Where is he?"

"Down at the end. I don't like what he's saying. I got to protect my good customers."

"Dirty mouth?"

"That I could handle myself, Ted. He's throwing around some pretty big names, not saying very nice things either."

"Okay, Rich."

Chayka walked back carrying his cap, nodding to this one and that one, and to Vincent, the bartender. When he came to the last stool at the bar, he said, "Hello, Al."

"Well, well, well! Himself!"

"You here all alone tonight?"

"Mona don't hold her drinks any better than you used to. I took her home. We was up to Jitz's place, at the lake."

"How about drinking up, Al?"

"Wha for?... Listen, you heard the joke about the astronaut. Knock. Knock."

"You've had enough, fellow. I'll give you a lift home."

"I got my Chevy outside."

"You're a little bagged to drive, Cousin."

"Yeah, yeah, well–so arrest me."

"I'll give you a lift instead."

"Let me finish first. I got half a beer... I got news too. News that ought to interest a policeman."

"Some other time, hmmm?"

"I was out with your sponsor s'afternoon, Ted. Isn't that what you alcoholics call your wet nurse? Yep! Me and Mona was drinking up to Jitz's place with the horse doctor and his wife, and Slater Burr and his *current* wife... and–get this, Cousin... And Donald Cloward."

Chayka studied Al Secora's cloddish features with contempt. The empty eyes, dulled by alcohol, shot with red, the thick mouth edged with beer foam, the brown hair mussed and lacquered with hair oil. Secora seemed to personify what Chayka himself had been called years back: that dumb Polack. And Chayka knew, knew as well as he knew that Secora would spill on himself half the rest of his drink, that handled a few inches this side of Rough, Secora would start a fight.

"Give me a ginger ale, Vincent," he said, and then, to reassure Rich's bartender, "A fast one for the road. Then we have to shove off."

"Yeah, I was honored to be amongst the big people, s'afternoon, Cousin. And I put a few twos together, for a four. A Police Department four."

Vincent shoved a glass of ginger ale down the countertop, and Ted Chayka picked it up, picked up Secora's glass and beer bottle with it. "Let's sit at a booth, Al. You can tell me all about it."

"I'm not kidding, Ted. I may be gassed, but I'm telling the truth."

They sat down across from one another.

"What truth?" Ted asked.

"I figured out that Slater Burr killed Carrie Burr, that's what truth."

"Sure. And I'm Milton Berle."

"No, no, you listen to me, Cousin. I figured it out. Donald Cloward remembers being moved from Leydecker's car to Slater Burr's. Someone moved him. He remembers that. He thinks it was Leydecker!"

"Un huh... What else?" said Chayka tiredly.

"Well, Slater Burr went along with it. He went right along with it, Cousin, up to a point. He says, 'Sure, Donald, Leydecker was out to get you.' He went right along with it, up until I brought up the fact a Jaguar isn't all that easy to operate, if you're gassed and you never operated a Jag before."

"It all makes a lot of sense, Al. Now how about working on your beer."

"You listen to me, Police Department!"

"I'm all ears."

"I'm telling you that Donald Cloward never drove a Jag. If he'd pleaded innocent and had a trial, any lawyer woulda fixed on that little point. He nev-ver drove a Jag... But that's about all Slater Burr ever did drive, and it was Slater Burr's Jag, and Slater wanted Carrie Burr out of the way, so he could marry the horse doctor's sister!"

"That's a hell of a stupid thing to say, and you know it, Al!"

"Oh, I know it, ha? Listen, I saw them together–Jen McKenzie and Slater Burr, couple months before Mrs. Burr was killed. They was up to Blood Neck making out, same night I was up there with Francie. 'Member? Whatta you think I was kept on the payroll for when my ribs was busted? So I wouldn't squawk! That's what for!"

"What if they were there? That doesn't prove he'd murder his wife, even if he were having an affair with Jen Burr then."

"It'd establish a motive, though... es-tab-lish a motive, as they say on the T.V."

Secora slopped beer down the front of his shirt, and Chayka was relieved to see there was only an inch left in the bottle.

Chayka said, "Why don't you just worry about yourself, Al?"

"Because I don't have anything to worry about! And I'm tired of being pushed around!"

"Who's pushing you around?"

"Slater Burr pushed me the hell out of Jitz's place! He knew I was getting wise."

"Oh, sure. He has a lot to fear from you."

"Well, doesn't he? You ever think how much weight I throw around with the unions down to his place?"

"You're going to announce to the unions that he's a murderer, is that it? Oh, that's going to fix Mr. Burr, that is."

"Just don't say he's got nothing to fear from me! He can afford another strike like I can afford to lay that broad he murdered his wife to marry!"

"Al," said Chayka, "listen to me now. You got a bag on and you feel your oats. But tomorrow you're going to wake up and feel like a goddam ass, shooting your mouth off down here this way."

"Crap, I am!"

"You know how it always is, the next day."

"Do you? Any more? Since you become Jesus Christ?"

"Al," Chayka forced a smile, "let me take you home now. You're beat! You could use some sleep. Work day tomorrow, you know."

"Slave day."

"Sure, well, how about it? I'll drive you up to your place, and tomorrow you can pick up your car... You know what a drunken driving rap means? A couple hundred bucks, and no license for a few months. Where would you be then?... And you'll get picked up, Al. There are extra men out tonight looking for someone to arrest. End of the month. You know how it is."

"You lousy cops would arrest your mothers. You mother-arresting cops!" He guffawed at his joke and drained the bottle of beer.

"C'mon, Cousin."

"Okay, but tomorrow isn't going to change today, and my two plus two equals four."

"We can talk about it tomorrow."

"It was Cloward got me on to it. Cloward was up there spouting like a goddam whale... all about how he remembers being moved from Leydeck- er's car to the Jag."

"Sure," Chayka said, helping his cousin out of the booth, "we'll talk about it tomorrow."

"Don't worry," said Al Secora, "I'm going to do plenty of talking about it tomorrow."

After he dropped him off, Chayka drove toward the station. If there were any way he could simply rub out Secora's kind, like a man rubbing out a roach under his shoe, he would do it. He was very familiar with all the nuances of the dumb punk putting in his nine-to-five, and nothing else; then hanging around beered up and belligerent at men who contributed a lot more than screwing bolts on by the clock. It was the Secoras, whose only responsibility outside a day's work was to keep their flies zipped up in public and pay their taxes grudgingly, who sat around scorning The Rich. Without The Rich, they'd be back rubbing stones together for fire, but it never penetrated their thick brains that men of responsibility and industry made it possible for them to loaf away their lives.

That was how Ted Chayka saw it, and he knew all the nuances. The bor- rowed glory of being at Jitz's place with Slater Burr's crowd, the drunken resentment at the fact he was one of them then, but not one of them... then the building up of his wobbly ego, by tearing them down... All in the glori- ous haze of alcohol, where the possibility of Slater Burr murdering his first wife was every bit as probable as Al Secora being the new Sherlock Holmes.

And tomorrow, Al Secora would talk about it. That was what angered Chayka. It would create nasty gossip in Cayuta among Secora's kind, and it would spread. Because there were a lot of people jealous of the Burrs, blaming Slater Burr for Cayuta's ubiquitous business problems, blaming anyone big enough to put the blame on, the same as Nancy blamed the Burrs or the Ayres or the Leydeckers for anything from an early winter to a two-cent rise on butter.

Chayka parked his Plymouth in the lot behind the station and stepped over the mud puddles on his way to the door. When he had coffee with Chris tomorrow morning, he would tell him what Secora had been shout-ing around Boyson's... let Chris hear it from Ted first... let Chris know where Al Secora stood with Ted Chayka; cousins was the end of it, cousins was the only fact to their relationship... and damn that fact!

The loudspeaker on the wall beside the coatroom droned: "Calling Car 7, in the third district... at Genesee and Maple, automobile accident ... at South Corner on ..."

"Ted?"

Chayka turned around and faced the desk Lieutenant.

"Don't bother taking off your coat. I'm putting you at it a few minutes early tonight."

"Sure... What is it?"

"Do you know Donald Cloward?"

"Sure."

"You know what he looks like, I mean?"

"I went to school with him."

"Good. He's been up bothering old man Leydecker. We just got a call. Leydecker says he left on foot, ten minutes or so. Check Highland Hill, then follow down Genesee to The Burr Building. He's probably some-where along that route."

"Who's driving?"

"Leogrande," the Lieutenant said. "He's out front with the motor going. Waiting. He wasn't sure he could identify him."

"I can," said Chayka, beading for the main entrance, "I used to hang around with him. Heard he was back."

16

He often dreamed of Carrie. He never remembered the dreams, but he would awaken as he did in the gray light of six that morning, and feel her presence like a heavy veil of gloom enveloping him. And at those times, he would turn his head and see Jen beside him in the bed, and a wonderous relief would sweep through him, and reality would seem like found money, a clean bill of health from the doctor, a thing he did not want to do that he discovered he did not have to do.

He sighed and smiled, rested his large hand on the soft silk gown cover-ing her thigh. He lay there with his eyes open, listening to a wet winter snow dribble in the tin drain trough, outside the bedroom window.

Random remembrances of Carrie wandered uneasily and sketchily through his thoughts, and fixed, finally, on their honeymoon night up in the Adirondacks. Throughout dinner at the main lodge Carrie had indulged in her usual shop talk, as though the day were no different from any other, and afterwards, over brandy, when Slater leaned forward and said softly: "Let's go back to our cabin now. You know how I love you, don't you, Car-rie?" She had looked across the table and answered, "I suppose we'd better get at it." Very seriously. Slater had laughed at her way of putting it: poor, solemn Carrie, but she seemed annoyed at his laughter. He had paid the check, and the walk back through the woods was slow and silent. He had known, from the stiffness of her embraces before their marriage, that it would require patience on his part; he had imagined she was shy and em-barrassed beside him, as they went toward their cabin; he had thought ahead of ways to make it easier for her. On a pretense of checking over the car, he would spend time away from the cabin while she undressed. He had given instructions to the lodge to have a bottle of champagne on ice in the cabin. Little, predictable touches to facilitate their lovemaking.

Once inside, almost the moment Slater turned on the lights, Carrie began to undress. She did it matter-of-factly, the cigarette dangling from her lips, chattering away about a rotation bolt on a roller as she folded her slip and hung up her dress, and then, naked, she turned to Slater, who had begun to undress as well.

She said, "I don't think I'll be much good at this sort of thing "

She sat on the bed waiting for him. Her body was white and beautiful, slender and tall and small-breasted, and at the same time that Slater felt desire mounting in him he felt some loss, as though a sun were bright but not warm, as though the intriguing mystery of Carrie was simply not there: she really was what she was, no more; nor pretended to be more: it had all been in his eyes.

Still, she had received him easily, not gratefully, nor excitedly, but naturally, and afterwards she had lit a cigarette and begun talking of other things again.

He had said, "Did you feel something when we made love, Carrie?"

"Of course," she had smiled, one of her rare smiles, the polite one.

"Do you love me?" he had asked, feeling slightly foolish and surprised to hear himself ask her that.

"Yes."

Then he had said, "Was it the first time for you, Carrie? I couldn't tell."

"No."

"I'd never thought of that before, that you'd been to bed with a man before I met you."

"I think most girls have these days."

"Did you love him?"

"He was a blind date in college. I was quite drunk. I don't think I even knew his last name."

"Anyone else?"

"Slater, you're like a schoolboy... But no, no one else."

"You're a strange girl, Carrie."

"Why do you say that?"

"You seem to just take everything in your stride."

She had answered, "I try to."

So it went, so it went... and ultimately Slater took things in his stride as well, accepted her ways and their life, at times even thanked God it was devoid of petty quarrels and disorder. He was free to do most anything he wanted to, and he indulged himself in his freedom, and felt none of the contrition other men in his circumstances suffered, and if there were something missing between Carrie and himself, there was something there too which was missing in other couples: a certain calm, call it, a pattern which gave harmony and the peace of resignation to things as they are, and things seemed all right.

Until Jen.

Meeting Jen was like discovering a sixth sense in himself–a whole new faculty for feeling life. Before Jen, he had never even come close. He had never had a glimpse of the myriad shades of gaiety and solemnity which love could arouse, and he could look at her and touch her, and tell her about it, and she did that with him too. Both of them did, right from the start. His marriage then seemed like a long, complaisant prison sentence, with Jen as an unexpected reprieve. Every motion he went through with Carrie, he contrasted to his time with Jen, and he knew for certain that his marriage was unbearable any longer.

Carrie's death did not leave him remorseful. He was at first shocked at his own ease in the situation, and there were high euphoric sensations of having controlled his own destiny, without a pang of guilt, and it was easy too, to feel mere disinterest in Donald Cloward, almost as though by disposing of him, he had disposed of his own falsehoods to himself, and broken away from them. He became philosophic and insensitive to inner predictable impulses to be guilt-tinged and morbid, and he took life with Jen as though it were a prize for his sovereignty over such impulses.

He was rarely unhappy. When he was, he could not explain it to himself. It would come over him all of a sudden... maybe while he was out drinking beer at a lake place with Jen on a weekend, seeing himself in the mirror behind the bar, watching momentarily with fascination while his arm raised and lowered, the beer tipped into his mouth and there... was that good? He would feel depression start, prelude to a glimmering of crazy chaos: the plant going to pot; he would soon be 40; every weekend morning, a hangover; on and on—chaos without meaning, and Carrie's face then in the feeble rays of illusion, always smiling when she never had alive, smiling and smoking, and waiting for him to get his.... Maybe that way it came over him, and sometimes in other ways.

Once he had taken his secretary, Miss Rae, for a ride before he dropped her off at her home. It was autumn, and it was just an impulse. He long ago told himself he never had a kindly impulse; it was simply bare impulse, no explanation, but then they were driving to Hunter's Woods, and she was saying "O look at those leaves, and colors!"... He got out with her; he always kept a pistol in the glove compartment of his car. He liked to shoot from time to time, at cardboard targets he put to trees; sometimes at rats by the pier at the lake. An exercise, or a sport, from time to time. He shot at a tree, a tin can, a fence, and Miss Rae giggled and tittered beside him, and when he looked at her once, he saw her face flushed with happiness, and then she told him something her brother had said last week when he was visiting her. A bird had fallen into the pond in her back yard. O, she loved birds, don't misunderstand, and she was not laughing at the bird, but at what her brother said then. And she had been forced to stop in the midst of her story, while tears of mad laughter rolled down her cheeks. "My brother said, my broth–" and he had waited while more laughter frustrated her, thrilled her, then finally, "My brother said: 'Bird overboard!'" Then she had shaken with more fits of laughter, and the depression had begun rolling his way again, he could feel it coming at him. He drove her home. She got out of the car and said, "This has honestly been the most delightful afternoon I've ever spent, Mr. Burr!"

And on the way home, he had felt like taking the pistol from his glove compartment and shooting it through his brain.

He could not explain it. It was just there, and not very often, but intense when it was, like an incubus riding him in his sleep.

That morning he was close to it, but it was explainable that morning. Cloward's return had marred his sovereignty, intruded on it, and Carrie had come to his dreams to taunt him, worse for the fact he could not remember the dream. He watched Jen sleeping beside him, remembering last night's quarrel. He felt alone, and just as afraid as he always felt on the fringes of the depression. Someday it would come and not go. Then he would lose to it, and the inner doubts would grow and be big enough to throw off his control.

He wanted Jen then; desire spilled through him, as though he were clutching at all he could count on that had flesh and blood and heart. Quietly he moved over and pulled the covers back gently, touching the silk of her gown near her thighs, lifting the gown, putting his lips there. When she stirred, she touched his hair, murmured "darling," and finally, raised him up by the shoulders to her mouth, so that their mouths were pressed together in the last long finale.

He had gotten away; he felt himself come back, steady, steady.

"What a beautiful way to wake up, Slater."

His voice was even, the same. Good! "Yes," he said, "are you cold?"

"Hardly."

"Do you want a cigarette?"

"I think I'd like some more sleep."

"Okay," he said, "I think I'll have one . . in the den."

"You can have one here, darling. I don't care."

"No, I'm too awake." He got up and straightened his pajamas, reached for his robe and slippers.

As he started out of the room, she said, "Slater?"

"What?"

"Thank you."

"Thank you," he said.

II.

Chayka took a cup of coffee back to the cell in the overnight lock-up. He turned the key in the door and walked across to the cot.

"Buzzy?"

Cloward rolled over and stared up at him. "Where am I?"

"Don't get excited. You're in jail."

"Oh, Gee-zus! Gee-zus!" Cloward sat bolt upright, rubbing his eyes, fixing his clothes.

Chayka set the coffee down on the stool beside the cot. "There aren't any charges," said Chayka. "It's all right, believe me."

"I vaguely remember... I was walking along Pine Avenue, wasn't I? You're a policeman, Ted?"

"Umm hmm. Surprise of the century, hmm? Yeah. I picked you up with Ernie Leogrande. Remember Ernie?"

"Sort of. Not well... I was at the Leydeckers, was that it?"

"The old man phoned in a complaint. He didn't want to press charges, or anything like that."

"What'd I do, anyway? I talked with Laura for a couple of seconds. I wasn't even in the house!"

"Well, he doesn't want you on his property. He says she doesn't want you there either."

"A lot he knows."

"Look," Chayka sat down beside him on the cot, "you're not planning to stay in Cayuta. Last night you said you were cutting out, going to work in New York. If that's right, I'd just stay away from the Leydeckers, if I were you. Stay away from them, and don't talk about them, Buzzy. Open old wounds, is all... People have forgotten all about that."

"I know," Cloward sighed.

"I fixed things for you at home, too. I didn't think you'd want your old man in on this... so I called up Selma. I told her you were going to ride around with me."

"What did she say?"

"She said when were you going to get any sleep... I said you weren't sleepy. Being home was exciting, and you were wide awake."

"Thanks, Ted."

"I always liked you, Buzzy. You were trying to straighten up and fly right, way back when I was still drinking beer out at the pier and working down to Pat's Garage... I remember you socked me once, when I got fresh with

Laura. 'Member that?"

"Yes. Thanks, Ted. I can't use any trouble."

"I began seeing the light a little while after you got sent up. I straightened myself out, with the help of Chris McKenzie, and–here I am."

"I saw McKenzie yesterday. At Walsh's Place."

"I know. That's another thing, Buzz... talking about what happened that night. I mean, at a place like Jitz's... It stirs things up, you know?"

"I know... How'd you hear about it?"

"My cousin. Al Secora. You know what Al's like. He's a flap-jaw, a sore-head."

"Well, I wasn't pouring out my troubles to him. I was talking with Mr. Burr, and he was butting in."

"Yeah, that's like him... but it's still no good to talk about all of it."

"I know. I got high."

"You on parole?"

"Yes."

"You're not even supposed to drink, are you?"

"No."

"You see, Buzzy, you just ask for trouble."

"You're right... I just had something to say to Mr. Burr. Something that's been bothering me for a long time. I just wanted to tell him about it."

"I heard a little about it. My advice is to forget it."

"Then... I was pretty drunk, I guess... I wanted to know about Laura. Ted, do you know anything about her? My sister says she's a recluse."

"Nobody ever sees Laura."

"Why? What's wrong with her?"

Chayka shook his head. "Your guess is as good as mine. I think she's a little balmy, you know? She always was a little balmy, Buzz."

"I can't understand it, though. She was going to college, I thought."

"For awhile, after you were sent up, she used to be around. I used to see her. Saw her once at the movies... But a few months later, you didn't see her around at all. I heard she was going to go to college, and for awhile we all thought she had... Then the rumors started she was up at the house on Highland Hill all the time. Just not coming out. I don't know."

"Ted," Cloward said, putting the coffee mug back on the stool, "I don't want to bother Mr. Leydecker. I have my own thoughts about him, but I don't want to get involved with him... I'd just like to see Laura once."

"Don't do it, Buzzy. He can make plenty of trouble for you. Plenty! You're on parole! If you go near there again, he'll get his back up. He made it clear he doesn't want you on his property."

Cloward sighed. "She wanted me to meet her tonight. Nine-thirty."

"I'm telling you, Buzzy, you could ruin everything for yourself."

"I don't know what to do... I just don't know."

"Call her up and tell her you can't make it, if you want, but don't go there."

"I know you're right. Mr. Burr wouldn't have anything to do with me any more, if he knew this." Buzzy took a sip of the coffee. "He's going to help me. I think I'm going to work for him."

"Yeah, you were talking about it last night in the car."

"Maybe I'm not worth his help. I don't know. Maybe I ought to stay out of Cayuta for good."

"Let me call Laura, Buzz. I'll tell her you can't come. Be better if I do it, in case Leydecker answers. If he answers, I'll just say you gave your word to me you wouldn't go near there again, and he could tell her... Simple. Doesn't implicate her or you and if you are coming back to live here, I wouldn't have Leydecker for an enemy."

"Any more than he is now, you mean... I guess that's best."

"You haven't got it in for Leydecker, have you?"

"No. No, I guess not. I know I don't. I just want to forget it."

"That's best. It really is."

"Okay."

"Stay out of bars around here too, and keep your mouth shut, Buzz. Play it safe, until Mr. Burr gets it all fixed."

"Yes. Can I just walk out of here?"

"Now? Sure! I'm off duty, and I can run you home."

"You don't have to do that."

Chayka said, "It's not any trouble. I'm going up to see Chris McKenzie, and I go right past The Burr Building."

III.

The broadbacked figure drest in blue and green
Enchanted the maytime with an antique flute.
Blown hair is sweet, brown hair over the mouth blown
Lilac and brown hair;
Distraction, music of the flute, stops and steps of the
      mind over the third stair,
Fading, fading...

"What does it mean?"

"I don't know, Laura."

"Why did we come here?"

"To put my shirt by the lavender joe-pye weed."

"Why did you read that to me? What does it mean?"

He smiled and pulled her down, touched her blouse smiling, looked into her eyes; "Blown hair is sweet... over the mouth blown."

"Do you love me, Buzzy?"

He began to smile more, to laugh.

"Why are you laughing?"

He was laughing very hard, laughing with his hands cupping his mouth, mean laughing, the joke on her. He managed to say again, "Blown hair is sweet... over the mouth," but

he was convulsed and could not finish.

"You *know!*"

"Yes. Yes, of course!"

She got up and ran, tripping over the shelf fungus with the D.C., L.L. carved on its face, and down through Hunter's Woods, naked and crying, with the crowds in between the trees, pointing, laughing the way he did.

She awakened to find Mrs. Basso's huge arms around her shoulders, her face crushed against Mrs. Basso's immense bosom.

"There, there, there."

She pulled away, and saw the book of Eliot poems on top of the pillow on her bed, where she had fallen asleep early this morning reading "Ash Wednesday." "Fading, fading, strength beyond hope and despair, climbing the third stair..."

"It's all right now," Mrs. Basso said. "Oh, Laura, honey, it's all, all right."

"All right, is it?" and she began to scream.

17

Chris McKenzie slammed down the phone angrily. "That's all the thanks I get!" he said.

Lena was getting another glass of water at the sink, swallowing down more aspirin. She said, "Chris, the trouble is you boil everything down to drinking. You could have told Jen the gossip without the sermon about drinking thrown in. Everything doesn't boil down to drink!"

"Everything that has you running back and forth for water and aspirin this morning boils down to it, Lena."

"So I got a hangover... Hang out the flag!... Tell me what Chayka said about him and Nancy."

She sat down at the kitchen table and poured more coffee. She had heard everything Chayka had said about Secora's accusations against Slater, but that was a lot of blue mud. What she wanted to know was more about the problems Ted Chayka had with Nancy. Chris had given her the eye when Chayka started in on *that.* She had gone on into the living room, as she knew he wanted her to, and turned on the television. Still, she had been able to catch some of it, enough to be very titillated.

Chris said, "If I were to tell you that there was some truth to part of what Chayka was saying, what would you say then?"

"What part?"

"The part about Jen being mixed up with Slater *before* Carrie's death."

"How mixed with him? Sleeping together?"

"Uh huh. Sleeping together."

"And you knew it."

"Yes. All those times she was pretending to be out with Horace Dryden and the others, it was Slater. The whole summer, it was him."

"Holy Cow! Did Carrie know it?"

"I don't think so. If she did, she knew it the way she knew everything about Slater... she just passed over it. I don't know if she knew it or not."

"Well, how'd Al Secora know it?"

"I don't know that either. I don't know very much about this whole thing, but it's nasty gossip to be going around... Of course, Slater'll ignore it. Just go on drinking–the hell with it. But it'll hurt him, and it'll hurt Jen too."

Lena said, "I don't see that at all. You just found yourself another excuse to hit Slater about his drinking, s'all."

"One day he'll show up at one of our meetings. It's awfully hard to admit you're an alcoholic!"

"Yeah," Lena said, "but you make up for it later. Later it's all you can talk about."

"I talk about other things... Blue Eye, Chiggers, Rabies..."

"Distemper, Housebreaking, Worms," Lena finished the list. They both laughed.

Chris said, "Seriously though, it's nasty gossip."

"No one will give it a second thought, if you ask me. Oh, sure, they'll believe Slater and Jen were having an affair–that wouldn't surprise anyone who knew Slater, but this other stuff–it's silly."

"I agree, but I thought Jen should know what's being said."

Tell me what Chayka said about Nancy."

"It wasn't all that important. They have problems."

"I can't imagine wanting to sleep with Nancy Chayka."

"You're probably not her type either, Lena."

"Is there another woman?"

"I think it's just the Seven Year Itch. He's lost interest. You know, Ted's a bright guy, and she's not exactly the high I.Q. type."

"Rubbish, Chris! Ted was Industrial High. Ten years ago he didn't know Q was in the alphabet."

"Well, he knows it now. That's my point. He's matured."

"Just because he joined AA?"

"Don't ride it too hard, Lena."

"All right, but the fact is, Nancy Chayka is a slob. She's let herself go."

The phone rang at that point and Lena said, "Doctor, my little dog is shivering and singing 'My Old Kentucky Home'. Does it mean anything?"

Chris said, "See if they pick it up at the hospital."

The phone stopped ringing, and Chris said, "They've got it... Slater never would have married Jen if Carrie hadn't been killed."

"It's her hair," said Lena. "I don't think Nancy Chayka's been to a beauty parlor in ten..."

Then the buzzer from the Animal Hospital signified the phone call was a personal one.

Chris got up and lifted the phone's arm from its wall bracket.

Slater Burr's voice said, "I've had it with you, Christ"

"Slater?"

"Yes, Slater! I mean, this newest piece of slander is goddamned laughable!"

The look on Chris' face clued Lena to run into the bedroom and pick up the extension.

Chris said, "It isn't something I made up. I just thought Jen should know."

"I'm not only an alcoholic, I'm a murderer!"

"I just told Jen what Secora was yelling around Boyson's place last night, that's all. I thought Jen should know what yesterday's drinking expedition led to."

"I'm a murderer! Oh, that's a hot one, Chris!"

"I didn't say it. Needless to say, I discount it, but..."

"Oh, you'd love to believe that! You'd love to! Jesus Christ, what is wrong with you, Chris? You get Jen all excited just because we had a little fun at Walsh's Place yesterday, and your wife fell on her face!"

"Leave me out of it!" Lena's voice chimed in from the extension.

"Then stay the hell out of it!"

"Yes, Lena," said Chris, "stay out of it!"

"He brought me into it! So I did fall on my face–you weren't so great yourself, Slater Burr!"

"Le-na!" Chris shouted. "Hang up the phone!"

"The next time you get any bright ideas about me," Slater said, "just tell them to me and leave Jen out of it!"

"She happens to be my sister, Slater."

"We'll be more than happy to leave you both alone," Lena McKenzie said.

There was a click.

Chris said, "Slater?"

"He hung up," said Lena.

"Look, Miss Busy-Body, did you have to butt in?"

"My dog has fleas!" Lena sang out, "Doctor McKenzie? My dog has... "

"Oh, for God's sake, Lena!" He dropped the phone and went back and sat at the kitchen table.

When Lena waltzed in, he said, "You should have stayed out of it!"

"Boy, was his dander up!"

"I know," said Chris. "It's funny, because Jen just laughed off the whole thing."

"She probably had a delayed reaction."

"I know Jen better than that. She wasn't at all excited. I never thought Slater would think twice about it. I thought Jen might, but not him... Well, that's the thanks I get."

Lena sat down and picked up her cup of coffee. After a moment she said,

"When was the last time they slept together?"

"Now how the hell would I know that, Lena! My sister doesn't..."

"No. I mean Nancy and Ted," Lena McKenzie said.

II.

Selma was already at work when Donald Cloward got back to the apart-ment. His father took a coffee break and sat with Cloward at the table in the living room.

"The thing about Olinski," Milton Cloward was saying, "is that he wants to please me. Now, a lot of fellows run the thing without thinking. Just another job to a lot of fellows. But Olinski remembers little pointers I give him, like Keller Insurance on seven, likes to have the operator ask a pas-senger getting off 'You going to Keller?' Then point out the office to any-one going there, you know, son?"

"Yes, pop, I know."

"You see, Keller is just around the corner to the left, and people miss it. Sometimes just go right back down. Could lose business that way... But Olinski always remembers to ask, 'You going to Keller?'... I put him on Car 2, you know, right before the holidays."

"You told me, pop."

"He looks up to me. It's only natural to feel something for The Starter, but Olinski don't just think of me as boss. He's got a real notion to please me, you know, son?"

"Sure, pop "

"That's why I went to his place Christmas Eve. You shoulda seen his face when I come in the door, son, he..."

Cloward sat there half-listening, with a loneliness all through him now. He was very tired, physically tired, and tired too of his father's perpetual talk about the job and Olinski. He realized the same thing he knew when he sat listening to Guy: he was not in the picture at all. His only hope was Slater Burr, and last night he had almost destroyed that with his drunken visit to Laura Leydecker. He had to prove to Slater that he was a different person from the dumb kid eight years back, quick and ambitious and through with his past; that was his one chance, convincing Slater Burr of that.

He had no interest in being Guy Gilbert's secretary; the very idea of being a secretary repelled him. Nor did he have any enthusiasm about working in a huge city where he would count for nothing, with his prison record and his lack of education. But working for Mr. Burr he could climb fast, exactly as Mr. Burr had done, working for Nelson Stewart.

In prison for a year he had had a cell mate who was keen on psychology. He used to discuss with him the fact Slater Burr sent a Christmas card every year.

His cell mate had said, "Maybe this Burr wished his wife dead."

"What sense would that make?"

"A lot. You did what he might have done himself, so in a way he's grateful to you, because you saved him from doing it. It's not unusual."

"He was crazy about her."

"You never know, Don... Then too, lots of breaks a guy gets here, he gets from the people he did the most damage to on the outside. I've seen it happen. I knew a murderer once, his only visits at the end were from the victim's sister. It makes some people feel big as hell to forgive. They feel like little gods!"

Cloward did not accept the theory because he was not sure he understood it, but he never lost the idea that when he got out he would at least straighten out one fact: he was sure he had not stolen Slater Burr's car that night. It was like an obsession with him. He went over and over the conversation he would have with Mr. Burr, and he did not pretend to himself that it was all he wanted. He never lost the hope that Slater Burr might say, "We have a place for you in the plant, Buzzy, if you want it."

Once or twice, he even imagined Leydecker making the same offer; Leydecker saying, "All right, you and I know I gave you the keys, and you and I know that at the last minute I moved you to Slater Burr's car, hoping you'd hit the drop-off. I'm ready to make it up to you."

But that was a fantasy, no thread of likelihood there. Leydecker had no sympathy for Cloward's kind; Slater Burr, on the other hand, was cut from the same cloth. If Nelson Stewart had been a snob, Slater Burr could easily have been in Donald Cloward's shoes. There was the difference, to Cloward's mind.

Now it was beginning to work out, wasn't it? If he could just keep hold of himself, watch impulses, and drinking that inspired them... keep hold, and play everything exactly as Slater Burr had told him to... But in the back of his thoughts that morning was the fear Slater Burr would get wind of what he had done last night, after Mrs. Burr dropped him off, or that he would simply change his mind... that something like that would go wrong.

His father said, "Well, son, I best be getting back."

He looked at the old man. He wanted to be a lot more than Milton Cloward, a lot more than a male secretary too.

"I think I'll sleep," he said.

"Did you have an exciting night with Ted?"

"Sort of."

"We was worried when you didn't come home for so long. Of course, we knew better than to think you'd get in any trouble, but..."

"I saw some old friends, was all."

He felt the urge to tell his father he had been with the Burrs. He wondered if his father would react with anything but worry that his son would get into trouble again; it all came down to that... No, he would wait.

"I never thought Ted Chayka'd make anything of himself, but it goes to show you... How long you staying on, son?"

He felt like saying don't worry, pop, I'll get out of your way as fast as I can.

"A day or two. I'm not sure yet."

"We're glad to have you."

"Thanks pop."

"After all, this is your home."

"Yes."

"I best be getting back, or Olinski will be The Starter before I know it! Got to keep my eye on Olinski," his father chuckled.

III.

Anyone else might have taken the rest of the day off, or waited until the union took action, but Mona Sontag could only think in terms of finding a new job immediately. She had already missed her first Christmas Club payment, and with Burr sick, and the terramycin Dr. McKenzie had advised, so expensive, her dismissal that noon had rocked her into a panic. Behind the panic was: *I told you so, Mona.*

In a way she did not even wonder why she was fired. She was the sort of person who gave money to the Cancer Fund out of fear that refusal to contribute would lead to cancer... Over and over yesterday, she had told herself two things: don't get mixed up with people you're not in a class with, and don't give in to Albert Secora just because he bought you such an expensive present... She had not listened to herself on either count. She had gone right on drinking with the Burrs and the McKenzies up at Jitz's, and when Al took her home, she had let him do it on the couch in her parlor. She had brushed her doubts and rules aside, and now she was paying for it.

The personnel director at Leydecker Electric studied her application form.

He said, "Ten years at Burr Manufacturing Company?"

"Ten years," said Mona Sontag.

"And you were fired just like that? For no reason?"

"The reason given," said Mona Sontag, "was that the office was over-staffed." God punished, was all. *But I will punish you according to the fruit of your doings, saith the Lord.*

"Right at Christmas time," Mr. Percy, the personnel man said, "and right in the middle of the day... That seems strange."

"I was given two weeks severance pay," Mona Sontag said, to emphasize that if she had done something very wrong, she would have been let go without pay, as Linda Hadley had been let go, for stealing from petty cash.

"Were you the only one let go?"

"The only one from the office," she hedged. It made no sense to feel shame at being fired along with Al, but she felt shame anyway, because of letting him do it last night... all so shoddy, there on the couch in her parlor, drunk. There was no point in trying to figure out Slater Burr's reasoning. She had been too drunk to remember what had taken place in the latter part of the afternoon, at Jitz's, and she no longer cared. God had punished, and now she needed a new job.

"Then others were fired, in the plant?"

"I heard some talk about it, but I can't say for sure."

"Miss Sontag," Mr. Percy said, "would you mind very much waiting here a moment?"

Mona Sontag gave him a defeated smile, a shrug. "I got all day."

Some holidays these were turning out to be! Burr with the Blue Eye, and herself cheapened and out of a job. *I told you so, Mona,* she thought, while she waited for Mr. Percy to return.

18

Min's solemn eyes watched from the leather frame on his desk, as Kenneth Leydecker finished his telephone conversation with Mrs. Basso.

"The doctor gave her some tranquilizers," said Mrs. Basso, "and they've quieted her down, sir, but she wants to be sure you talked with the Cloward boy, as you promised."

"That's all taken care of," he said. Min's eyes seemed to sharpen with disappointment at the lie, and Leydecker looked away from her face, and down at the report on his desk. "... the probable sales volume will be more than $9,000,000 for the company this year compared with $4,250,000 last year." He said into the phone's mouthpiece: "This is a very busy time for me, but I'd come home if it'd help, Mrs. Basso."

"No, sir, I think it'd make everything worse. I think the girl wants to be alone, is what I think. His coming back like this has started it all up again, sir."

"I know... I know... Did Doctor Yates say anything else?"

"Just to keep her doped up until things pass over, sir."

"Is she eating, at least?"

"Nothing, sir."

"I see... Well, you've done all you can, Mrs. Basso, and I appreciate it."

"I'm sorry, sir. It's such a shame."

"Yes," Leydecker said, "call me if there's anything important."

He hung up, and looked back at Min's photograph. "It wouldn't have done any good to talk to the boy!" he said aloud to her. "The police know how to..." his voice trailed off, and he shook his small body from his thoughts, shuffled through his papers, and gave Leydecker Electric and The City of Cayuta his attention... At least the day had brought one good, positive thing Kenneth Leydecker's way. In the morning mail, a letter from The Ithaca Lock Corporation. They were highly interested in Leydecker's very confidential proposal for a merger with Burr Manufacturing Company. Their plant outside Ithaca was amply equipped to accommodate a merger, and their tentative estimate was much more than Slater Burr could hope for from any other concern. If Leydecker could squeeze Burr out via the zoning proposal, Burr would have no choice but to accept I.L.C.'s offer. It was a coup for Leydecker, no doubt of that; quite different from leaving Burr with no alternative, which would make Leydecker look like the villain... He would rid Cayuta of its foremost eyesore in center town, enhance Cayuta to G.E., then work for Leydecker Electric's merger with G.E.... Very neat and sound, but there would be plenty of careful work on Leydecker's part.

Leydecker had already warned Oliver Percy not to hire any more employees from Burr Manufacturing Company. A representative from I.L.C. was arriving in Cayuta next week, all on the sly, to look over Burr Company. Leydecker wanted no labor disputes there... everything in order. No one wanted to buy anyone else's bitter draft. Burr Company was worth little enough, without the added distraction of labor trouble. Even though that would not affect I.L.C. after a merger, it looked bad.

After Burr and The Cayuta Macaroni Company were gone, Cayuta would be a decent city. The day was past when a small city could exist on its home-grown industry; all the big money was on the outside. The thing was, to pull it in, and that was what Kenneth Leydecker intended to do—pull it in! The trouble with Slater Burr's kind was that they did not want to work for anyone else; they were living back in the forties, when there was a war and war contracts... The trouble with small cities categorized as "depressed areas" was they did not gang up on the Slater Burrs—force them to act... Well, Kenneth Leydecker would do it for Cayuta, and Kenneth Leydecker would come out just as nicely as Cayuta would.

He picked up the inter-office phone at a buzz, and listened to Oliver Percy.

"Send her up," he said. "I'll talk to her myself."

And that was part of it too... reaching everyone, big and little alike, having time for a secretary named Miss Sontag, the same as for Hamilton Carruth, from Ithaca Lock.

II.

"Oh, you're just drunk!" Francie Boyson said. "How'd you get so drunk in the middle of the day?"

She wished he would hang up. She was sitting in the banister-back arm chair with a glass of beer and an egg-and-olive at her elbow, trying to follow *Search For Tomorrow* on the television at the same time she talked to him. Thank God it was Rich's day to buy the week's meat for the restaurant, and he was downtown doing just that right now.

"Well, did we or did we not see them up at Blood Neck making out? Just answer me that, Francie."

"What're you doing drunk and talking all over about that? That's over and done with. I been true to Rich ever since then, and I don't like it being dragged in, after all this time!"

"Francie, if I told you that you might be a murder witness some day, in a murder trial, what'd you say to that?"

"I'd say you was having more of your drunken pipe dreams, is what I'd say!" But she put down her glass of Buds riser, leaned across, and turned down the sound on the set.

"This is no pipe dream, Francie! I'm collecting evidence!"

"Oh, yeah? I'm collecting stamps!"

"Slater Burr murdered Carrie Burr, to marry Jen Mc Kenzie... Now! How does that set with you, Francie?"

"Get outa here!" Francie Boyson said. Then she turned the set off altogether. "Get outa here!" she repeated, eager... waiting for Al Secora to continue.

III.

At noon, Walter Olinski had a three-hour break before he was back on Car 2. Sometimes he went home, ate lunch and lounged around the house; other times, he took the bus up to the P.W.V. club, drank some beer and played the pinballs. Today he had done the latter, and instantly, as he walked in the door, he regretted it.

It was The Club's fault, for letting non-members come there, just because they were Polish, and The Club needed the money. Al Secora was no war veteran! Walter Olinski had fought in The First World War, and he resented the way outsiders like Secora came into the P.W.V. and threw their weight around, as though they'd broken the Hindenburg line single-handed!

What irked Olinski even more, as he strolled into the bar, was the fact Secora was sounding off about Milt Cloward's kid.

Milt Cloward was a Prince, one of the greatest guys Olinski had ever come across, and while Olinski did not hear everything Secora was saying, he did hear Secora say, "And Buzzy Cloward will get it next! Me and Mona got fired, and there's no telling what Slater Burr will do to Buzzy Cloward!"

"Yeah, yeah," Brushkin, the bartender was humoring him, "but I'd sober up before I made any more phone calls, Al."

"Gimme some more dimes," Secora said. "Next I'm calling Cloward. Don't think he's not going to get the axe from Slater Burr!"

Olinski said quietly, "That's all you know."

"What's that mean?" Secora said, turning to face him.

"Mr. Burr is very fond of that boy, for your information."

"Sure, pop, and you won the second battle of the Marne. We heard all about it."

"Donald Cloward is going to make something out of himself," said Olinski. "More than you'll do... not even a member here."

"He'll make something out of himself if Slater Burr don't get him first. C'mon, Brushy, gimme some more dimes. I'm collecting myself some evidence."

Olinski said, "Mr. Burr has asked Donald Cloward to stay at his place. I happen to know that for a fact."

"He's *what?*"

"Milt told me right before I went off. He was real proud because Mr. Burr's taking an interest in Donald. Him and Mrs. Burr asked the boy up to their place to stay. Your talk don't amount to nothing, never did. You don't belong here at the P.W.V."

Secora said, "You got shell-shock, old man. Don't know what you're talking about any more."

"Oh, I know what I'm talking about. Milt told me right before I went off. 'Whatta you think of that, Olinski,' he says, 'Slater Burr's taking a personal interest in Donald'... Well, I says, I think that's swell! And that's what I do think. You just want to make trouble, Albert Secora."

"What's this about them moving Buzzy in?" Secora said.

"Surprise you that there are decent people, Albert?" Olinski said back. Then he turned away from Secora, and went back toward The Trophy Room, where he could have a beer and look through the magazines in peace.

IV.

"But Mr. Leydecker," said Oliver Percy. "I don't have any idea where he'd be. I don't relate to his sort at all."

"Did you call Boyson's?"

"Of course. It was the first place I called, sir. Then I called Walsh's Place, and O'Conners, and the pool hall."

"And his home?"

"No answer."

"He wouldn't still be hanging around Burr Company?"

"I tried there too, sir... It seems to me, sir, that we can hardly be accused of unfair employment practices if we hire people Mr. Burr has fired!"

"I don't care how it seems to you, Oliver! Don't hire anyone from Burr Company. Miss Sontag said just the two of them were let go for no reason. Now, I don't like the looks of it."

"He's fired people before, sir... She had very dirty fingernails."

"Oliver, Al Secora is big in the union at B.M.C., and she's worked there for ten years! Firing them both in the middle of the day doesn't make sense! It sounds to me like Slater Burr is building for a strike! Otherwise, there's no sense to it."

"Why would he want a strike?"

"Someone might have tipped him off about I.L.C.... I don't know why he wants one, but he's asking for one, that's clear!"

"Yes, sir... I'll keep trying to locate Secora, Mr. Leydecker, but I truly don't relate to his sort at all!"

"You'd better start relating to his sort! His sort is what we have to deal with! I can convince Secora, if I can get my hands on him. He's pliable, and he doesn't like Slater Burr."

"Could Secora stop a strike?"

"He could if he just said he didn't want the job anyway. The union won't fight for a man who doesn't want the job, and I'll see to it that Secora won't need the job. We won't hire him... his name won't be on our payroll, but we'll take care of him," Kenneth Leydecker said, "if you just *find* him, before he ruins everything!"

V.

Everything had gone so well that morning... right until Chris called.

It had been the first time, in a long time, that Slater had made love to her twice. He had awakened her that way; then he had come back an hour later. He had loved her very slowly and well. There was something poignant and special about it... sometimes there was, and the second time had been one of those times... Afterward, they had smoked cigarettes, the bedsheet covering them, the first circle of morning sun spotting their pillow.

"I must have dreamed of Carrie," Slater had said. "I felt low when I first woke up."

"It's Donald Cloward being back."

"I suppose... That was stupid yesterday, bringing him here–getting involved with him at Walsh's."

"Do you think there's anything to his story?"

"No. I was humoring him along."

"And the job you promised to get him?"

"More of the same. But in the den I was thinking," Slater said, "I think I'll give him some money, get him out of my hair and back to New York."

"Yes... Is he coming for dinner tonight?"

"The hell with it! I'll tell him to come to my office and give him the money. He can get the sleeper tonight."

"We'll have dinner alone."

"I'd like that," said Slater.

Chris had called while Slater was showering. What he told her made Jen laugh. God, what next, would people think of to say about Slater!

Jen had said, "Was I supposed to be off hiding in the bushes, like Carole Tregoff, Chris? Just think what a sensation it'll be in Cayuta! Another Finch trial!"

"Jen, it isn't funny! I know there's nothing to it, but it's nasty gossip. Prepare yourself."

"I'm ready to swear in court that Slater and I fell in love the second we laid eyes on one another! And if the Cloward boy hadn't done in Carrie, well, we might very well have! Okay?"

She had felt very pleased, lying there in bed, full of Slater, full of him and glad to announce possession of him, right from the start.

She had a smile on her face. She felt high and gay, superior to Chris's world of if-you-knew-what-people-were-saying, and drink-will-be-his-downfall. While she let Chris babble on in his old maid's tone of portentous anxiety, she planned to go down and make a Bloody Mary for Slater, have it ready for him when he came out of the shower. He was a magnificent man; his magnificence was stamped all over her; God, she bet not another woman anywhere felt as Jen Burr felt right then!

When Slater came from the shower with a towel around him, a grin cut across his face as she handed him the drink.

"Happy this morning," she said, "and get ready for a good laugh, darling." And then... all hell had broken loose.

She had never seen Slater act that way before; it was as though something had snapped in him.

He had called Chris back, and the house had shaken with his shouting.

He had refused breakfast, hurried into his clothes, and gone off to work in the station wagon, hardly saying anything to her.

After she pulled herself together, she was able to realize that her suspicions were accurate, right to the letter. Slater *did* feel guilty about Carrie's death; it was not just a sore point, it was a malignancy.

Around eleven o'clock, he called to apologize. He sounded more like himself, but there was still a peppering of hysteria in what he said. He had talked to Cloward. Cloward was coming to dinner that evening, and Slater was putting him on the sleeper to New York at eleven P.M.

"Don't mention it to Chris," he said, "or to anyone."

"Very hush-hush, hmmm?"

"Goddam it, Jen, that silly tone in your voice is irritating! I'm trying to get something done about this thing!"

"You're not really concerned about the talk, are you, Slater?"

"I just want Cloward out of here!"

It was best all the way around. As Jen drove the Jaguar to pick up Donald Cloward, she realized that. It was what the boy wanted and it was best for Slater too. There had been enough pressure on Slater these past few months; Cloward's return was the catalyst to a minor crack-up in Slater... because what else could it be called?

Jen turned onto Genesee Street, and stopped before The Burr Building. She watched while Donald Cloward came out, carrying his bags, his father hovering in the background, waving at Jen, smiling.

Jen heard Cloward say, "See you later, pop."

While Cloward put his bags in the jump seat, Jen said, "You're not angry with one another, Don?"

"No, not at all."

"I just wondered... the way you said 'goodbye'."

"He thinks I'm going to spend a few days with you, before I leave for New York. He doesn't know I'm taking the sleeper tonight. I thought I'd write him a letter when I got to your place. If I try to tell him, he'll just feel bad that he didn't make me welcome, or something. Both him and Selma... Mr. Burr said it was better this way, to write a letter."

Jen said, "Do you want to drive, Donald?"

"Gee, sure!"

He came around to the left side of the car and got in.

"It's great of you and Mr. Burr to do this for me," he said... Then, for a few moments, he sat working with the shift, to figure it out, before he could make the Jaguar go.

19

The luminous dial on the alarm clock by the bed read four-twenty. Ted Chayka rolled over on his side and thought about his dream. It had been the same old one. In it, he always failed the police examinations and had to go back to Pat's Garage and beg for his old job.

"Don't try to be what you're not," Pat always said, at the end, and Chayka always woke up, just as Pat's grease-stained hand reached out to touch him.

There was a faint odor of stale beer in the room. Chayka did not have to guess where it came from. Nancy had left one of her ubiquitous empty cans beside the bed last night. This morning, when Ted came into the bedroom to go to sleep, he had found the bed unmade, as usual, and covered with last night's newspapers, the *TV Guide,* and more nail-polish peelings.

He thought of his talk with Chris that morning. He had complained to Chris about the way Nancy did that—peeled off her polish that way, and Chris had said it was a nervous sign. Probably Nancy was as nervous as Ted was, Chris had said. What they both needed was a long candid talk together.

While Nancy and he ate breakfast, before he had come in to sleep, he had tried.

"Nance," he had said, "what do you think about us?"

"What do you mean?"

"I mean, do you think we're as good together as we used to be?"

"In bed, or what?"

"In every way," Chayka said. "In *every* way, Nancy."

Nancy had answered: "You been itching for a fight all week, Ted, so you might as well get it off your chest! What's the matter? You still burned because I didn't send your uniform to the cleaners last Tuesday?"

He had dropped it there. A long candid talk with Nancy was as likely as hot snow or cold fire; he might as well have a long candid talk with the kitchen sink... Then, it occurred to Ted Chayka that there was someone else he was supposed to have a talk with... someone else, and finally, he remembered. He was to call the Leydeckers, tell whoever answered, that Buzzy Cloward was not coming by there again.

Chayka reached for the phone, and started to dial, when he heard Nancy's voice on the wire.

"....wouldn't surprise me," she was saying, "nothing would about Slater Burr. But do you know for sure, Francie?"

"Well, I happen to know first hand they was having an affair, summer of 1954, but I can't say how I know. I just know for sure."

"I'm not surprised," said Nancy. "But how'd the Cloward boy get in the car?"

"I heard he was put in the car. Slater Burr put him in it!"

Oh, for the love of Christ! Chayka banged the phone down and got out of bed. He put his trousers on over his shorts and reached for his shirt on the back of the chair. Then be slid into his socks and shoes and went into the living room.

"Hang up that phone!" he said.

Nancy said, "Count Dracula is awake! I gotta hang up, Francie."

When she put down the phone, Chayka said, "That's nice gossip! Dammit, Nancy, I want you to cut it out!"

"For your information, Ted, Francie Boyson called *me*. I didn't call her!"

"What the hell is wrong with you anyway, Nancy? Don't you know the Burrs can sue for that kind of talk?"

"Are they tapping everyone's wires now? That wouldn't surprise me! Where you going?"

"Out." Chayka grabbed his coat and scarf from the hook in the ball.

"It's all over town anyways. They going to sue the whole city of Cayuta?"

"You believe that gossip, and next you'll believe the earth is flat!"

"Where are you taking yourself off to, middle of the afternoon?"

"I have an errand," he said.

There was no sense chancing Nancy's overhearing a call to the Leydeckers. God alone knew what she would make of that!

II.

Mona Sontag was mad at Father Gianonni. She had said her Act of Contrition and the Hail Marys, but she left St. Anthony's angrily. Father Gianonni had yawned during her confession. That was a man for you–just yawn it off, same way Al Secora just pushed her back on the couch right there in the parlor. Never mind making it nice, taking it seriously. One damn man was just like another. God was already punishing her, and if a priest was not going to take the sin seriously, he was not going to have it in his power to forgive her. The mumbo-jumbo would not get her off the hook, not if the priest had no interest. Half of it was up to the priest. At the end of the confession, when he had said, "Pray for me, my child," she had felt like saying back, "Oh yeah? Why should I do *you* any favors?"... But she had said a prayer for him, a very quick one, since she was not a type to take chances with Fate.

Mr. Leydecker had been very nice about all of it, but he was not about to hire her. Big as life out front of Leydecker Electric was a sign saying "Office Help Needed," but he was not about to hire Mona Sontag. All that talk about not hiring help from another industry in Cayuta was just clap-trap... and since when... since when! Leydecker Electric had even hired Linda Hadley, a known thief!... But not Mona Sontag!

All Mona could think of was that Al must have really fixed them, the last hour at Jitz's place. She had a lot of trouble remembering anything about that time; she had not really come to until Al was fumbling with her clothes in the parlor. Oh, God, and the things he had done too–things no man had ever done to Mona Sontag, and there weren't *that* many men in the first place. She had never been punished this much before, and she could not blame God!

"I didn't know, God," she said to herself as she walked down Capitol Street. "How was I to know he was some kind of pervert!"

Ah, but that was no excuse. No excuse. She let him, was all, and now she was like a piece of dirt.

At Acme Drugs, she stopped to buy terramycin for poor Burr. She was nearly in tears now, thinking of Burr with the Blue Eye, and herself in the state she was in: "*...and I detest my sins above every evil, because they displease Thee.*"... The thing was, how *long* were they going to displease Him?

She waited for the druggist to get her the medicine, and then she found herself staring at the phone booth, back by the soda fountain. She looked up at the big clock–four-thirty, and she thought to herself: *He* wouldn't be home yet. I could just say, Mrs. Burr, ma'am, I'm sorry about yesterday...

That was all... I'm sorry about yesterday. If God and the priests weren't going to help her, she would have to help herself. While she fumbled in her change purse for a dime, she took it back about God not helping her; it was-n't fair, and it wasn't very safe to think along those lines. No, God was okay... and there was a dime. The trouble with Father Gianonni was he drank all the communion wine, and was half-asleep most of the time, as a result.

Bravely, she walked back and shut herself inside.

"Hello?"

"Hello, Mrs. Burr?"

"Yes."

"This is Mona Sontag, from Walsh's Place. I mean, from yesterday at Walsh's Place. Remember?"

"Oh yes, Mona, how are you?"

"I'm fine... I'm not fine, exactly. I'm sorry, Mrs. Burr, ma'am, about yesterday."

"Mona, we were all celebrating Christmas. You have nothing to be sorry about."

"Well, I don't remember it very well."

"Mona, we were all in the same condition. There's no reason to feel badly."

The tears gathered in Mona's eyes then. She said, "I been ten years with B.M.C., ma'am. My dog is even named Burr. I just–don't know what to say, but if I did something yesterday to cause..." and her voice broke, and she fished in her coat pocket for a tissue.

"Cause what, Mona?"

"Cause Mr. Burr to fire me, ma'am."

"Mr. Burr *fired* you?"

"He said the office was overstaffed, but Mrs. Burr, there's work enough there for ten girls."

"I don't understand. Are you sure that was the reason?"

"No, ma'am, because he fired Al Secora too, so I thought..."

"I see."

"I thought it was something I did yesterday, or Al."

"Mona," Mrs. Burr said gently, "let me talk to Mr. Burr when he comes in."

"I tried to get another job, but..."

"You're upset now, Mona. You just forget about it until I talk with Mr. Burr. Then I'll call you, tonight, at your home. All right?"

"All right, Mrs. Burr."

There was a click, and Mona Sontag said a feeble, futile "goodbye" to the dial tone, hung up, and let herself out the booth.

III.

Only last night, Oliver Percy had said he should have a raise, for all Kenneth Leydecker was expecting of him lately. He had not said it to Kenneth Leydecker; he would prefer to forget the person to whom he had said it, but even if there had been a bit of braggartry in his long harangue over a glass of sherry late, late last night, this afternoon was proof enough his complaint was justified... Here it was five-thirty already, but forget all about *that;* look who he was here in center town traffic with!

Finally, he had located him at the Polish War Veterans Club. He was to deliver him to Leydecker Electric, where Leydecker was waiting to talk with him... Well, that would be a pretty talk, you can bank on that! In *his* condition!... They were driving through downtown traffic, and it was no easy task to steer, with Secora clapping his arms on Oliver Percy's shoulders and breathing his foul breath in Percy's furious face!

"Tell you what, buddy," Secora was saying, "we're gonna have a strike *and* a trial, hah?... Oh, ask not what Slater Burr can do to you, but what you can do to Slater Burr! Hah? J.F.K.... Hah?... Hey–knock, knock!" Secora rapped Oliver Percy's shoulder with his knuckle. "Knock, knock!" he repeated.

"Please!" said Percy, "this is five o'clock traffic."

I'm hardly a Personnel Director, Percy had said, only last night, *my title should be Executive Confidant!*

"You know what I did last night, Mr. Percy-O? First time I ever did it to a woman, see. You gotta be a little boozed up, see. I–"

"I *don't* care to hear about it, thank you!"

"Well, ain't that the old nose-in-air fer you!"

"I'm trying to drive this car safely."

"Someone ought to pin a rose on you for that, Percy. Hey, knock, knock!"

"Will you stop punching me, please?"

Percy swung the car over to the curb, near L.E.'s downtown hiring center. Somehow, he was supposed to propel this person up to Kenneth Leydecker's office!

"Who's there? Astronaut," Secora was talking to himself, "astronaut if Slater Burr killed his wife, but ask what your country can do for you!"

"Oh, shush! Shush!" Oliver Percy shrieked, and by now, the five o'clock crowds were thick in front of the place... gradually, a few here, a few there, turning to stare.

It was an immense embarrassment for Oliver Percy even to be seen in the company of Secora; after all, he could *hardly* turn to the onlookers and say, "This is all part of my duties, you understand!"

Percy felt sudden relief when he saw Ted Chayka walking toward the car.

IV.

"...So we come, to the end, of a per-fect day," Miss Rae sang to herself as she covered the typewriter and dropped her pencils in the white mug on her desk, just outside Mr. Burr's office... A bit of irony at day's end, she mused... per-fect day, indeed! Perfectly preposterous!... Ah, and the dear lamb in there so sorry about all of it now... How many times had he buzzed her to see if she had gotten hold of Mona Sontag yet!

"Don't worry, sir," she told him each time, dear heart, don't worry, "I'll locate her. She's probably in some cafe."

"Keep trying Secora too, Miss Rae. Tell them both it was a mistake."

Yes, lambie, and we all make them. "Yes, sir," she had answered.

Well, she would certainly have enough to fill a page or two in her diary this evening.

She planned the beginning: "I knew instantly that something was wrong when he walked in this morning. His dear blue eyes were sunk deep in..."

The door of the reception room swung open, and a young man in a leather jacket stood there, a cigarette dangling from his lips. Well, if it isn't Marlon Brando, Miss Rae said to herself. She liked her little mind jokes. The obituary of her daydreams read: 'Behind the spinsterish facade of Millicent Marvin Rae, was a rollicking good humor, and a quick and full heart.'

She said to the young man, "The office is closed."

"I want to see Slater Burr."

"If wishes were horses," Miss Rae answered, "beggars might ride."

"Is he still here, or isn't he?"

"He is. But you have no appointment, and if it's employment you're seeking, the employment office is on the first floor, to the right of the door as you enter, and *it* will be open at 8:30 in the morning."

"I'll wait for him to come out." The young man sat down in one of the leather chairs.

Miss Rae said, "This office is closed, young man."

"Has he got someone in there with him?"

"That is none of your business."

"Uh huh. Well, I'll wait, Miss, if you don't mind. I'll just sit here quietly and wait for him to come out."

"It won't get you anywhere... What do you want with Mr. Burr anyway?"

"That is none of your business, Miss. I'll wait."

"Wait. You won't bother me," said Miss Rae.

But it did bother her, which was one reason she did not pick up the inter-office and tell Mr. Burr he was there. Heaven knows what the young man wanted, but Miss Rae knew Mr. Burr would probably tell her to just go along, he'd take care of it. Then she would miss her ride home with him... *Dear, dear* heart, our time together is so fleeting–moments stolen from the years in inches... Ah lamb, and tonight he needed her, so upset and all, his cherished brow furrowed in frowns and worries. There, there, it's not that bad.

"We all get out of sorts, sir," she had planned to say, as he drove her down Genesee Street. "And I've seldom seen you lose your temper so. You were due. We're all due a day like that, sir."

And he would say, "What about you, though, Miss Rae... in all the years I've known you, you've never once..."

"Ah, never mind an old maid, sir. But I have my days too, sir." Days near you, lamb.

The young man said, "When's he usually come out?"

"Oh, this time sometimes, sometimes later... sometimes six, and sometimes seven."

"Tell him I'm waiting then. Tell him that."

"I can't disturb him, young man. Those are my orders."

"Do *you* hang around until he leaves?"

Always... waiting, hoping: *Miss Rae, can I drop you?* . . She said, "I do my work. When my work is done, I go home."

Tonight, after the evening ritual–the cooking dinner, sweeping, bathing, preparing clothes for the next day, then: the diary, writing in it at her desk, in her nightie and robe, with her hair pinned in rags: "Today, he must have had a fight with her. There's no other explanation. Two people were fired. I never saw him in such a rage."

Marlon Brando was stubbing out his cigarette impatiently. Just go on! Just leave! She said, "I think he'll be very late today, young man," but her words were punctuated by the opening of his door.

The young man stood up. "Mr. Burr? Mr. Slater Burr?"

"Yes."

"I'd like to talk with you, Mr. Burr."

"What about?"

That's a lamb; don't give him the time of day; O I'm waiting, see me, dear?

"It's personal, if you don't mind..." looking now in Miss Rae's direction. She went right on putting away her things, ostensibly oblivious, and he would say: "Anything you have to say can be said in front of Miss Rae."

Slater Burr said, "Miss Rae?"

"Yes, sir?"

"Why don't you just run along now. Why, it's after five-thirty!"

Sometimes, though, it was after six, remember? And I was always here, lamb, and today when you need reassurance, I wanted to...

"Yes, sir, I'm leaving now," said Millicent Rae.

20

"All right," said Slater Burr, "fifty dollars, but how the hell do *you* know Oliver Percy?"

"That's my business. I just want to get out of this town. You hand over the money, and I'll say my little spiel, and we'll call it even, okay?"

"Thirty, forty, fifty," Slater counted out the bills and slapped them to Miss Rae's desk. "All right, I'm waiting."

"Percy claims this fellow he works for has it in for you."

"That's not news. But what about I.L.C.?"

"Percy says this fellow–Limedecker, or whatever it is, has plans to get I.L.C. to come and see your plant. Bid on it. All on the sly, you understand. L.E. wants to merge with G.E. They hope they can get you out with the zoning plan, force it so you have to sell to I.L.C. Percy says the Industrial Development Committee won't be sympathetic with you if you get an offer from I.L.C., and your likelihood of swinging a loan in these parts will be unlikely, if you know what I mean, if you got an offer from I.L.C.... That make sense?"

"Yes, it makes sense," said Slater Burr.

"Percy says Leydecker will stop at nothing to get you out! He says it's like an obsession with him, getting you out of town!"

"Is that it?"

"Yes. Do I get my fifty now?"

Slater pointed to the money, and the young man scooped it up.

"Is this the way you live?" Slater said.

"It's the way I earn travelling expenses sometimes, when I'm stuck in a small town like this. I head for the Y.M.C.A., sort of a home office."

"And that's where you met Oliver Percy?"

"He goes there to–swim," the young man snickered.

"You don't look queer," Slater Burr said. "I'm not. *Me* queer? Would you take me for a faggot?"

"I don't know what I'd take you for," said Slater, buttoning his coat, "but I know I'd a hell of a lot rather be taken for queer than taken for you!"

Whoom! Carrie's explosive laughter; oh, Mr. High and Mighty, is evil so offensive to your delicate sensitivities? And he laughed inwardly at himself, waiting until the young man was gone; how coolly he had said those words: I'd a hell of a lot rather... Whoom! Whoom!

But Fate was often an unsuspecting ally. He knew it as he picked the phone off its cradle and made the call to Miss Rae; let there be a strike over Sontag and Secora, it was all part of the scheme of things; only Miss Rae knew better, knew that he had fired them in a clap of fury, and he would tell her they were not to be rehired, she was not to try and reach them. Her telephone did not answer; when he got home, he would call her again.

And when he got home, he knew even more how easily Fate often cooperated. In the kitchen he made himself a martini, waiting for Jen to finish her tirade.

"...makes you look guilty, that's what I'm concerned about–firing them that way, all over asinine gossip!" she said.

He said, "Jenny, how well do you know me?"

"I'm beginning to wonder."

"Do you *ever* listen when I talk about business?"

"Slater, it has nothing to do with..."

"Just listen to me, Jenny. Please?" a little smile playing at his lips. "I fired them because I want a strike! I couldn't just fire two people for no reason; it'd *look* as though I wanted a strike. Jenny, I chose them because it'll seem as though anger motivated me... Oh, I'll be forced to rehire them, no doubt of that, but for awhile there'll be plenty of trouble at the plant."

"What do you mean?"

And he told her about Leydecker and Ithaca Lock. He watched while her expression changed from one of anxiety to one of admiration, then love, in the softness of her eyes, the release of her full lips from their tightness, the beautiful, soft countenance of calm.

"Now do you see?" he said.

"But you were angry when you left this morning. I'd never seen you so angry."

"Yes. I collected my thoughts in the car, on the way to the office... You see, Jenny, everything works out."... Whoom!... Well, Carrie, it does; look-it me, hmmm? He said to Jen, "Is Cloward in the living room?"

"Yes... Slater, I'm sorry."

"Oh, God, don't apologize! Business is complicated, Jenny."

"You had me scared. For awhile I was even..."

"Even what?"

She laughed. "Oh, well... I let Donald drive, coming out here?"

"Yes?"

"He had trouble starting the car–the shift, you know?"

"And for awhile you began to think I was the bogy man, hmm?"

"It did frighten me a little. On top of that, Miss Sontag calling, and everything."

"Yes, well, he probably had trouble with the shift the night he killed Carrie too... You know, Jenny, I think you're right. I'm not much on parlor psychology, never liked it, but I think you're right. I probably did feel some guilt about Carrie's death. I suppose it's only natural."

"Of course, it is, darling."

"Yes, well, I'll be glad when Cloward's out of here."

"And so will I! Slater, I love you."

"Je t'adore."

"It still always sounds like 'shut the door' when you say it."

"I wish we could go upstairs and shut the bedroom door."

"Take a raincheck, will you? For about eleven-thirty to night?"

"You're on."

"Slater, I feel so much better! Oh, darling!"

And it was fine between them again; the Martini just right too; a giddy glow of euphoria all through Slater Burr, with the explosive sounds of Carrie's laughter far, far in the background.

II.

"I'm sorry about my cousin, sir," said Ted Chayka. "I took him to his place, and I got my wife to go over there, keep him home for the night."

"Yes, that's best. I want to do what's best for the town, do you understand me, Chayka?"

"I certainly do, Mr. Leydecker."

"Your cousin has quite an imagination."

"You mean the stuff about Slater Burr killing his wife?"

"Yes."

"I don't blame Mr. Burr for firing him."

"It wasn't because of Secora's idiotic talk, Ted. It's a bit more complicated. Slater Burr is above that... No, I trace it all to Oliver Percy."

"*What*, sir?"

"It's too involved. But you see Percy is a braggart. He gets puffed up with importance... Now, he dates Donald Cloward's sister. He's told me a few times that he takes her out... I think he's been telling her my business, showing off the fact he's in on many very personal and discreet business relations... I think he told her, and she told her brother, and word got back to Burr through the Cloward boy."

Chayka did not understand, but be nodded as though he did.

Leydecker said, "It was very nice of you to come here and deliver

Cloward's message... I'm sorry you got involved in all this other business."

"Oh, that's all right, sir."

"I know a policeman doesn't make much, and I'm happy to reimburse you for your time."

"Please, Mr. Leydecker, I wouldn't think of it."

"I want to reimburse you... and there's something else."

"I don't want any money from you, sir."

"Never mind protesting, Ted... I want to give you something. And," Ley-decker looked at his wrist watch, "it's quarter to eight now... I want you to do something else for me."

"Certainly, sir."

"Secora claims Cloward is at Slater Burr's."

"Yes, sir."

"I want you to call there and tell Cloward that I'd like to talk with him. Here in my office. At nine-thirty tonight. Tell him personally. Tell him it's about Laura."

"Yes, sir. I'll do that."

"You see, Chayka, my daughter is very ill. I can't trust Cloward. I can't know for sure he won't go to my house tonight and upset her."

"I think I can promise you he won't."

"Think isn't good enough. I don't want him near my house."

"I see."

"I'm going to tell Cloward in plain English that he'll find himself in plen-ty of trouble, if he goes near my house. Oh, I'm going to be nice to him. I want to check out Percy through him too, confirm my suspicions on that count... The important thing is that Cloward comes here at nine-thirty."

"I'll call him right now, sir."

"I'd appreciate that," Leydecker said. "And something else, Chayka. You don't go on duty until eleven or so, do you?"

"No."

"I'd like you to go by my house about nine-thirty, just in case there's any slip-up, do you see? I'll give you $50."

"That isn't necess–"

"Never mind protesting, Ted. I like you. I think you're going to amount to something!"

"Thank you, Mr. Leydecker. I certainly want to. I'll call Cloward right now, sir."

III.

Yes, lamb, I'll take care of everything, GRanite 2846, for the hundredth
time, but O lamb, I don't care.

"Hello?"

"Mr. Secora?"

"Yeah."

"Mr. Secora, this is Miss Rae, Mr. Burr's secretary."

"How's it hanging?"

"What?"

She could hear laughter in the background; Oh, Al, she could hear, what
a thing to say!

He was guffawing as he spoke, "You'll understand it in your next life,
Miss Rae, when you come back a man." More laughter.

"Mr. Secora?"

"Yeah, what's up? To what do I owe this crappy honor?" But *she* could
take the abuse; for you, lamb, *anything!*

She said, "Mr. Burr is sorry. You still have your job, Mr. Secora. It was
just a little fit of temper."

"Oh, just a little fit of temper, hah?"

"That's all," she said cheerily. "We all have them. But you will be paid for
today, and you still have your job."

"Miss Rae?"

"Yes?"

"When you go to work tomorrow, you tell your Mr. Burr that he can
shove his job! You tell him that he can take his fucking job and–" Miss Rae
clamped down the phone's arm, shaking, her ears burning with the obscen-
ities Albert Secora had begun to shout.

IV.

"I don't get it, Buzzy," said Slater Burr. "Why would Chayka give you a
message from Leydecker?"

They were all sitting at the dining room table. Jen Burr had answered the
phone, and called Cloward away from the table. Cloward poked at his
lemon pie and shrugged. "I guess he just ran into Leydecker, Mr. Burr."...
Above all, he was not going to be trapped into a confession of last night's
drunken folly. Not just when everything was going along smoothly.

"I just don't get it! Chayka's a policeman. What's Leydecker calling in a policeman for?"

"Ted and I went to Industrial High together, Mr. Burr. I think Mr. Leydecker probably remembers that, and thought we'd be running into each other."

If he did not keep the appointment with Leydecker, there was a chance Leydecker would call the Burrs himself, perhaps spill the whole story; then Slater Burr would know he was still foolish and back in the past... There was another reason he wanted to meet with Leydecker... not just curiosity about Laura, but back to the old fantasy. *"You and I both know the truth, Donald, and I'm ready to make it up to you."...* Let all of them make it up to him, if they wanted to. Let them all feel big as hell to forgive Donald Cloward; big little gods, *let* them!

Slater Burr said, "Forget it! That's my advice–forget it!"

"Mr. Burr?"

"What?"

"I want to see him. The train doesn't go until eleven. I could still see him and catch the train. What would it hurt?"

Jen Burr said, "I'd be curious to know what he wants."

"Oh, the hell with it! He's got a policeman in on it, he probably wants trouble for you, Buzz!"

He could not tell Slater Burr how Ted got in on it, without giving it away. Ted had said "He's not going to make trouble for you, Buzz–honest he isn't. He just wants to talk to you."

Cloward said, "He's not going to make trouble for me."

"How can you be so sure, Buzz?" said Slater Burr. "Remember, you're on parole."

"But I didn't do anything," Cloward lied. He looked hard at Jen, hoping she would not give away the fact he had phoned the Leydeckers last night.

Jen Burr said, "He'd still make his train, Slater. Maybe he wants to tell Donald what happened to Laura. I wouldn't mind knowing that myself!"

"Listen!" Slater Burr was shouting. "You asked for my help, Buzz! Now you want me to help you! I told you to stay away from the Leydeckers! I'll put you on the 11 o'clock and that's that!"

"I said I'd be there, Mr. Burr. I want to go."

"What'll it harm, Slater?" Jen said.

V.

He watched Jen light a Gauloise, put it in her mouth and begin clearing the table, with the cigarette dangling there from her lips. He could hear more whooms! and he shut them out with effort, trying now to think through the haze of alcohol and the noise of china rattling as Jen stacked the plates. Jen never walked around with a cigarette hanging from her mouth, and what was a policeman calling Buzzy Cloward for, to deliver a message from Leydecker; cockeyed; he had to think straight, just for a few more hours. He could offer to drive Buzzy to the Leydeckers, take the back road, pull the choke out and flood the engine; invent motor trouble... Delay it... How long could he do that?... Or, when he got Buzzy in the car, he could reason with him, frighten him with remembrances of the past, and how Leydecker hated him... That was okay... a drink somewhere, get the kid loaded. That was okay. He would have to handle it just right. Whoom!... and Jen with the cigarette that way, as though for an instant of time, Carrie had gotten inside her, was pushing her to encourage Cloward to meet with Leydecker... But what did Leydecker want?... Secora had gone to him, told him the story; Leydecker wanted to hear more, wanted Ted Chayka to hear more... If Buzzy Cloward just skipped out, his story would not hold up... just hot air. Leydecker and Chayka would see that.

Jen said, "Slater, what are you frowning about?" "Was I?"

Cloward said, "Mr. Leydecker probably just wants to warn me not to go near Laura."

Jen winked at Cloward, as though she and Cloward had some little secret all their own. "I think so too," she said. "I think that's all he wants."

And the most impossible, crazy ideas began spinning through Slater's mind: a trap was being set for him. Jen had seen that the kid could not operate the Jaguar immediately; Jen was in on it. Whoom! and again.

Slater said, "Have a brandy, Buzz. We'll have some brandy."

"There isn't time," said Jen. "It's eight o'clock. Donald will want to wash up!"

"What?" Slater looked at her, as though she were the enemy there with the Gauloise hanging off her lips. "Not *time?* It's an hour and a half away!"

"I think Mrs. Burr means that I shouldn't drink, sir."

Jen smiled at him. "Ummm hmmm."

What the hell was going on! And the whooms came like distant thunder, and through it all the phone ringing again... ringing, ringing, and Jen saying, "Get it, Donald, hmmm? It's right behind you."

21

"That was fun!" said Nancy Chayka. "You're fun, Al. Ted's turned into a namby-pamby."

"If I'd gotten Slater Burr, I was just going to tell him: fuck your job! You ain't going to buy me off with your job, not any more!"

"S'afternoon, Al, Francie Boyson tells me the whole story, see? But she doesn't say how *she* knows, see? 'I can't say how I know,' she says, 'but I know.' "

"Sure, she knows. We was hunting the same kinda thing in the same hunting ground as Slater Burr and Jen McKenzie. Boy, I don't know why the bells didn't ring a long time ago, when Mrs. Burr got killed."

Nancy Chayka peeled off another nail, sitting there on the couch beside Albert Secora, in his apartment. She said, "What'd the Cloward kid say?"

"Well, I says, who is this, and he says this is Donald Cloward, see?"

"Yeah, I heard *that*."

"So, I says, If I was you, Cloward, I'd get the hell out of that place before Slater Burr kills you too, I says."

"I know, I heard *that*."

"I says, You're a sitting duck, Buzzy! It was Slater Burr driving that car, I says, and nobody else. I figured it out, I says, and I hit it right, because I got fired today for what I know, and then he tried to rehire me, Buzz. Oh, the heat's on him, Buzz! I says, He don't want to help you, he wants you out of town. You just happened to come near the truth yesterday, only not near enough."

"Yeah, well, what'd he say?"

"He didn't say nothing. I says, Are you listening? and he says, 'Yes.' "

"Then?"

"Then I just told him. I says, Slater Burr and his dear whore wife was sleeping around *before* that so-called accident, and he wanted the first Mrs. Burr out of his life. I just told him. *You* heard me."

"What'd he say?"

"Nothing. He just hung up."

"Just hung up, hah?"

"Yeah... Hey, I had enough coffee. Let's have a drink."

"I'm supposed to baby-sit with you. You're not supposed to drink."

"Oh yeah? Sez who?" he laughed, putting his hand on her arm. He ran it down her arm to her skirt.

"You're fun," she said.

"Yeah, and I think we can have us some fun, Nancy. Get us a little snort, sort of oil us up for some fun."

22

He knew in an instant that it was true, an instant that closed the gap between doubt and knowing, while Slater Burr came around to get inside the car where he was sitting, still unsure, until he realized what song Slater Burr was humming. *Hey there, you with the stars in your eyes.*

Fear began to sift down from his brain in fine sands, then became heavy pressure, and wave after wave of it swept through him, while Slater Burr started the engine.

Slater Burr said, "What was that phone call all about anyway, the last one?"

"I told you. I couldn't understand. A drunk or something."

"But you said 'yes' at one point. What'd you say 'yes' to?" They turned down the drive, and soon they would be alone in the night.

"Someone, whoever it was, said– I don't remember. Something about it being the wrong number. Yes, they asked me if they had the wrong number."

"They?"

"He did."

"Who, Buzz?"

"I don't know. Honestly."

"I see." And again, the song; only now he was whistling it. They cut across the black road leading from the Burr house, onto a side road... not the highway, which would take them right into Cayuta.

Slater Burr said, "What're you so nervous about?"

"I'm not."

"Playing with your comb that way."

"Oh, that's just a habit. I'm sorry."

"Nothing to be nervous about, Buzzy."

"Yes, sir."

They drove along in silence. He kept whistling the song. Cloward was perspiring now, his clothes soaked. Then the engine sputtered.

Slater Burr said, "Oh, oh."

"Something wrong?" Cloward managed.

"I better stop and have a look at the motor."

"Yes, sir."

"Hope we don't run into trouble out here. It's so damn far from anything."

He stopped the car and got out.

While he was looking under the hood, Cloward reached for a cigarette. It would be impossible to run. He could never run fast enough; Slater Burr could catch him. He fumbled for a match, but found none in his pockets. He snapped open the glove compartment and saw the gun. Quickly, he took the gun. He could think of nothing to do with it, and he saw Slater Burr walking back to the car, so he sat on it.

"I'm afraid we have some motor trouble. It might take awhile to fix it."

"Yes, sir."

"What's the matter with you?"

"What do you mean?"

"Your hand's shaking."

"I don't know. I–"

"What is it, Buzzy?"

He threw the cigarette out the window, eased his hands back by the seat of his trousers.

Slater Burr said, "What the hell's the matter with you?"

His right hand gripped the gun firmly, and he pulled his hand out from under him and pointed the gun at Slater Burr.

"*What the devil?*"

"You take me into town, Mr. Burr. I'll kill you, if you don't."

"I told you the car's in trouble. Now, don't be a fool!"

"I'll kill you, Mr. Burr," Cloward repeated. "You're not going to kill me."

"Buzzy, I don't want to..." and he moved toward Cloward, and Cloward felt his hands on his shoulders again, familiar... and his finger squeezed the trigger.

23

"*That's all the facts when you come to brass tacks,*" Mrs. Basso read, "*Birth and–*' Laura, I really think this is not a very *nice* poem!"

"It was your idea to read to me, Mrs. Basso," Laura sighed.

"Well, I never suggested this sort of reading!"

"Then stop reading to me. Go home."

"I was just waiting until your pills took and you got sleepy."

"*Birth and copulation and death,*" Laura Leydecker recited. "*I've been born and once is enough....* Is the word copulation offensive, Mrs. Basso?"

"The entire poem is offensive, Laura." Mrs. Basso flicked through the pages. "*You've had a cream of a nightmare dream, and you've got the hoo-ha's coming to you. Hoo Hoo Hoo...* It's not even poetry. I don't like it at all!"

"Why don't you just go home, Mrs. Basso."

"You know the whole thing by heart anyway."

"So I do."

"Why should I read it to you? Really, Laura, you ought to try to pull yourself together. Your poor father is frantic."

"Then go down to L.E. and sit with him, Mrs. Basso."

"And you haven't eaten..."

"No, and I won't eat until you go home... It's nine o'clock."

"Oh, I'm leaving, have no fear of that. I just hoped your pills would take before I left."

Laura Leydecker said, "You don't like me at all, do you, Mrs. Basso?"

"I love you, Laura, and my heart goes out to you, but you don't try. A girl like you, wasting away here, making those grotesque clay dolls, and watching the television until your eyes are red... Reading this sort of book!... You need to get out!"

"And be laughed at, Mrs. Basso? Be ridiculed?"

"Mrs. John F. Kennedy wears a wig when she goes to parties. I read it in the newspaper."

"Well, I don't feel like becoming the town spectacle, Mrs. Basso. I had enough of that when I was younger. At least this way, nobody knows what to laugh at. I hope they think I've taken to the bottle!"

"What an awful thing to say, Laura."

"Would you rather be a drunk or bald, Mrs. Basso?"

"Why, when Jack Paar was on the Tonight Show, he'd even brag he had a hairpiece," Mrs. Basso said.

"Mrs. Basso, I'm tired."

"Your pills are working. Thank heaven!"

"I'm not just tired that way. I'm tired of all this talk about all these celebrities who have wigs. I don't care to hear any more of it. If I have to hear any more of it, you'll have to hear my kind of talk. Do you understand me?"

"Don't start your disgusting talk with me, Laura. Bad enough you read this trash... this T.S. Eliot, without your talk too."

"Give me my book back, and go home, please."

"That's exactly what I intend to do, Laura."

Laura Leydecker sank her head back into the soft pillows and waited while she heard Mrs. Basso's footsteps descending on the back stairs. Then the rattle of the garbage can, as she took the brown paper bag from it for deposit in the bin outside, on her way from the Leydeckers... then the shutting of the kitchen door.

A drowsiness fought her hunger, and she lay there for awhile, until hunger won over. She got up and slipped on the old robe, went down the long hallway, and down the stairs.

Whatever the pills were she had taken, they were more effective than the others, over which she had built a certain immunity, so that it took three, sometimes four to put her to sleep. These sleeping pills had tranquilizers mixed in.

I love tranquil solitude, and such society, as is quiet, ah but fuck tranquillity, she thought, and she thought all the other words he had ever taught her, and put them in legion against tranquillity; ah God, fuck tranquillity, and she looked in the icebox for something there to eat.

She did not even turn on the kitchen light, because fuck the kitchen light, as well, and all light. She had read somewhere that even the blind turned on the lights in their homes, to better appease those with sight, to seem more like them... well, that had not been her luck, to seem like anyone, but a bald old crow, and she gave a little laugh, a little tipsy laugh–that was what those pills did to her, and by the light of the icebox she found a brick of cheese. She left the door open on the refrigerator, holding it with her leg, gnawing on the cheese, a bald old mouse, alone in the night, *life goes on forever like the gnawing of a mouse...* but it seemed then suddenly, very suddenly, that Edna St. Vincent Millay was terribly, terribly wrong: life did not go on forever: life had an end, and Laura Leydecker realized it, so quickly, and so suddenly, that she barely touched her fingers around to her back, after the crack of a gun, after the beginnings of blood warm down her flesh; life did not go on forever, for in an instant the mouse was dead.

24

He fired three times to be certain.

He watched while Leydecker slumped to the kitchen floor; he had hit him clean and accurately.

Quickly, he wiped his prints from the gun, and with his gloves, placed the gun back in Cloward's hand, easing out the stick he had put in its place, while he drove Cloward's corpse to the Leydecker house.

Cloward's body was slumped across the porch, where Slater had dragged him, the hole in his head still oozing blood, which was smeared across Slater's overcoat.

He had not wanted to kill Cloward; the gun had gone off in their struggle for possession of it. If he had not killed him, he would be dead, that was certain.

There was not even time to figure everything out, but he felt a certain thrill at his own quick thinking, and his thoughts were still spinning, weaving the story, coming in bullet-like succession. Cloward had insisted on keeping his appointment with Leydecker. Slater had noticed a certain sullenness as he drove him to Leydecker's. No, he had not even been aware of Cloward taking the gun from his glove compartment; he always carried the gun, target practice... and Slater could see himself standing in the police station, logical and concerned, he had always liked the kid, sent him a Christmas card every year; yes, he would say, he was at my house for dinner... Jen and I... and then, starting down the walk as he went over all of it, he realized he would be put to the test sooner than he had planned... much sooner... Now!

"Mr. Burr?"

"Yes... Is it *you*, Chayka?"

They came into the circle of light from the street lamp, at the side of Leydecker's house.

Chayka was out of breath. "I heard a gun. I came running. I was just at the corner."

"It's too late," Slater said. *Whoom!* But he stayed steady, facing Chayka, letting the pieces fit into place. There, it was coming out, his words, clearly, not a shred of hesitation. "I'm afraid it's just too late."

"What happened?"

"Donald Cloward was at my house tonight. He had an appointment with

Mr. Leydecker and–" but Chayka did not wait for him to finish. He ran toward the house.

Another lucky break. Slater thought of the blood in his car. He would have to get rid of the blood, and he hurried toward the car, realizing even as he went through the motions, that he could not wipe it away. He would have to explain it away. That was it. Let me just explain; let me just pull myself together and explain... and he leaned against his car, his heart banging against his chest, those crazy, mocking explosions of laughter aggravating his thoughts; oh God, let me just explain it... But there you were, Ted Chayka was walking toward him again, and he felt his nerves rev up, felt himself take hold.

"It's too late, isn't it?" he said. There was a sliver's chance, of course, that Leydecker was still alive... but that sliver was removed with Ted's answer.

"Yes... too late. Do you want to tell me about it, Mr. Burr?"

"Certainly," Slater said. "I suppose you were to be here at nine-thirty too, hmm?"

"Yes. I was supposed to be here."

"Well, you're right on time... Unfortunately we were early."

"What happened, Mr. Burr?"

"Donald Cloward had this appointment with Leydecker. You know that. I think you delivered the message."

"Yes."

"Well, Cloward got nervous. I thought it was nervousness. He wanted to be a little early, he said. Kept asking me if my car could go any faster, you know?" the words were pouring out, easy, natural, and Chayka stood there watching him respectfully, listening. "I let him out. I thought he was a little sullen. I thought I'd wait for a minute and see how things went... Then maybe I'd get a fast one at Rich Boyson's, and come back for him, if things seemed all right."

"Yes... Well, we better start on to the police station. You can tell me about it in the car," Chayka said. "We have to make a report."

"Certainly. I'm glad to cooperate. There's blood in my car. After Cloward killed Leydecker, he came running out to me. I said, 'Donald, you have to turn yourself in. I can't help you.' They'd had some sort of argument." That was bad... the part about blood on Cloward. There were ways of testing blood; that was a mistake. But if the police believed him, would they bother to check? Whoom again; all right, but wait... wait and watch me work this.

Chayka said, "We can take my car. I parked it around the corner."

"Just leave mine here, hmm?"

"I think that's best."

"Certainly... Anything to cooperate."... Jen... He could call Jen; tell her to pick up the car, wash it with ammonia... no, don't ask questions; go and get it... meanwhile, he would cooperate.

They walked toward the head of Highland Hill. Chayka said, "Then Cloward killed Leydecker, is that it?"

"Yes... Then he killed himself. I couldn't stop him. He ran from my car, back to the porch. He killed himself."

"I see."

"He shot him through the window." God, he had almost forgotten that; good, he had remembered... No, oh, God, it was full of holes. Let me think. Whoom! Whoom!, and in the street light's amber glow, Carrie's face, smoke spiraling up, curling around the leer on her face like a snake coiling to spring out at him.

Chayka said, "I made a call to the police."

"They had a fight, you see. Leydecker ordered him out of the house, or something. I couldn't understand the kid–he was so hysterical. But I heard them shouting at one another in there."

"I see... My car's over there."

"He shot him through the window, on his way out of the house. I don't know what was said between them. Did you have any idea what it was all about?"

"No," said Chayka.

"I told him that he'd have to turn himself in... Well, I guess he took that way out–shooting himself... He ran back, and I heard the gun go off again."

"Make sure your door's closed, Mr. Burr," Chayka said.

"Well, Ted," said Slater Burr, "it's pretty horrible, isn't it? Are there any questions you want to ask?"

"No... I'm off-duty."

"What did Leydecker want with the kid?"

"I think he just wanted to make sure Buzzy stayed away from Laura."

"Then that's probably what the fight was about."

"Umm hmm."

They turned onto Genesee, a silence between them for several long minutes, while Slater tried to think it through; no, it was best not to send Jen for the car. Leave the car; if they believed him...

He said, "It sounds pretty unbelievable, doesn't it, Ted?"

"It's a strange world, Mr. Burr."

Good! "Yes, a strange world... You never know what will happen next... Poor kid, though, I feel sorry for him. I even feel sorry for Leydecker, and you know," a brave little chuckle, "we never got along, Ted. I mean, we weren't good friends."

"I know that."

"But I wouldn't wish him anything like this. Shot in the back that way." Oh my God, that was dumb! Whoom! Dumb! He said, "Donald told me he shot him in the back."

"Umm hmm, well... It's a strange world."

He began to get a weak feeling as they pulled in at the police station... a suspicious air of calm enveloped the place as he walked in with Chayka. Chayka pointed to a chair and asked him to wait a moment. He sat down, blood all over his overcoat; explain *that* by saying he had run back at the gunshot, pulled Cloward to him, hoping the kid was still alive; why every year I sent him a Christmas card–whoom! and now he heard a man's voice curt with anger. "...don't just leave two bodies and come running with..." and he caught no more. Mumbling and another angry sound... Slater Burr waited. Then his face broke into a grin. Lieutenant Cheever! He knew Cheever very well; he used to buy Cheever drinks, take him across to Rich Boyson's when Cheever stopped by the plant. Cheever was okay; good!

He stood up and smiled at Cheever. "Hello, Lieutenant."

"Hello, Mr. Burr. I hear there's been some trouble."

"Yes. It's terrible!... There was this shouting argument between Leydecker and Cloward, and... has Ted filled you in? There was this really..."

Cheever interrupted. "Let's go into my office," he said.

Slater said, "Yes. Yes, I can help clear the whole thing up, I think."

"You say you heard Leydecker and Cloward shouting?"

"I should have interceded, but..."

"To the left," Lieutenant Cheever directed him.

Slater smiled at the lieutenant. It was reassuring to see Cheever, out of it all to see so familiar a face, one he could count on for sympathy, understanding; I thought the world of that kid... no, not too exaggerated. He had killed Carrie, remember, *that kid*.... Watch me work it, Carrie, he thought, and as Cheever beckoned him toward his office, Slater felt a tickle of elation: oh he'd come through, he would... he *would*.

Then from the far end of the station, a figure hurrying through the door, scrambling like a cat with its tail on fire, toward Slater and the Lieutenant, and Slater stared at another familiar face, oh very, very familiar... The face of Kenneth Leydecker.

That was the biggest whoom of them all.

THE END

THE NOVELS OF VIN PACKER
by Jon L. Breen

Today, any type of mystery novel from the toughest to the coziest might be published first in paperback. The paperback original of the nineteen-fifties, however, was almost entirely a hardboiled, masculine domain, directed at a male audience and created by male writers. Not until the contemporary gothic trend of the sixties and seventies did female-oriented mystery fiction become a major factor in original softcover form. There is at least one exception, however, to the overwhelming maleness of the major paperback original writers of the fifties: Vin Packer, who is unique among the most successful paperback writers of the decade in other ways as well.

Vin Packer was born Marijane Meaker in Auburn, New York, in 1927. Though she has used her birth name as a byline occasionally, notably on the novel *Shockproof Sydney Skate* (1972), the bulk of her work has appeared pseudonymously. Her best-known pen name is M. E. Kerr, which she has used for a highly successful and honored group of young adult novels, beginning with *Dinky Hocker Shoots Smack* (1972).

M. E. Kerr's autobiography, *Me Me Me Me Me* (Harper and Row, 1983), discusses her early life through her sale of a short story (under the name Laura Winston) to *Ladies' Home Journal* in 1951. The book is addressed to the readers of her young adult novels and refers frequently to characters she used in the M. E. Kerr titles, but there are occasional references to her work as Vin Packer, including her possibly unique reason for entering the suspense field: "solely because I'd heard that *The New York Times'* mystery columnist, Anthony Boucher, would review paperbacks. Encouraged by his reviews of my work, I stayed in the field about ten years before going on to hardcover under my own name, Meaker" (page 212).

As the quote above suggests, Packer's original impulse as a novelist was not building either puzzles or suspense. Very few of her books can accurately be called detective or mystery stories, though they are certainly crime novels. Most are not even suspense tales in the conventional sense. Rather, they are straight novels that happen to concern a crime, and usually the action consists of the events leading up to the crime, with the emphasis on the criminal's motivation. Once the crime has taken place, the novel is virtually over. The investigation rarely plays a major part.

A number of elements recur again and again in Packer's fiction. One of the most pervasive is the troubled adolescent character. Though many of the later novels deal entirely with adults, equally troubled, the interest in the problems of youth that would inspire the M. E. Kerr books is quite obvious in the early Packers. Her ability to get inside the heads of children and teenagers, realistically reflecting their problems and attitudes, is comparable to Stephen King's. More than once, the central character is an adolescent male being raised by a widowed or divorced mother, with a well-meaning but ineffectual family friend attempting to serve as father substitute.

Another recurring element is homosexuality. Under the name Ann Aldrich, Packer wrote paperback Lesbian novels, a surprisingly viable subgenre in the fifties, though there was no comparable market for sympathetic stories of male homosexuality, at least from mainstream publishers. Some of the Packer novels have specifically gay subject matter, and references to homosexuality, veiled and direct, are numerous even in those that do not.

References to college days are frequent, with much attention to the initiation and rushing rites of fraternities and sororities. Many characters share Packer's background at the University of Missouri, specifically its vaunted journalism school.

Packer often employs quotations from popular song lyrics (oddly, never with a copyright notice) and poetry, sometimes original. The novels are always *au courant,* filled with topical references to news events, motion picture and television personalities, and concerns of the day.

Finally, and most significantly, Packer's novels are totally devoid of either heroes or villains. Virtually everyone is troubled, mixed up, or deluded at best, psychotic at worst. No one is totally okay, and nearly every character has at least some redeeming qualities. Packer specializes in psychopathic killers of varying types, and her treatment of them is never simplistic. Indeed, her absolute refusal to provide easy answers to psychological or social problems is one of the qualities that most endeared her to the critic she originally sought to impress, Anthony Boucher.

Come Destroy Me (1954) was not the first Vin Packer novel. Gold Medal, the publisher of all but one of Packer's paperback originals, lists three earlier books opposite the title page. *Spring Fire,* a Lesbian-themed book published in 1952, was her first major success and perhaps her most famous single title of the period. Also listed are *Dark Intruder* (1952) and *Look Back on Love* (1953), both of which are identified as crime fiction in Allen J. Hubin's bibliography, *Crime Fiction, 1749-1980.* But *Come Destroy Me* was the first of her books to be reviewed by Boucher and the earliest I have examined for this article. It sets a pattern for many of the Packer suspense novels to come. Only from the publisher's cover blurb and the chapter epigraphs would the reader know until very late in the story that the book was a crime novel. Packer is interested in exploring the roots of violent crime, and most of the novel is concerned with setting up the circumstances that eventually lead to murder.

The setting of *Come Destroy Me* is Azrael, Vermont, in the Green Mountains. Sixteen-year-old Charlie Wright is a quiet library habitue, a brilliant, Harvard-bound student who is constantly teased by his college-age sister Evie. Most prominent older male figure in the fatherless household is irritating lawyer-widower Russel Lofton, who is mildly courting Charlie's mother, Emily. Epigraphs from trial testimony and psychiatric reports let us know that Charlie will kill, but the suspense lies in whom, how, and why. Although the reader knows Charlie will do murder, he initially doesn't seem all that much more troubled and confused than most adolescents, and therein lies much of the case history's fascination.

Object of Charlie's sexual fantasy is book dealer Jill Latham. Their first meeting foreshadows the classic coming-of-age movie *Summer of '42,* though this meeting is considerably less innocent on both sides. Jill is an odd-mannered heavy drinker with affected speech patterns, very much like a Tennessee Williams character.

Boucher was immediately impressed. As he would later, he praised Packer's reluctance to offer easy answers–"she never quite answers her own questions with any pat psychiatric diagram." The novel is "well and subtly written, with acutely overhead [sic] dialogue, full-length characterizations in brief compass, and excerpts from hearings that capture the exact flavor of authentic transcripts" (*New York Times Book Review,* 7 March, 1954, page 27).

Whisper His Sin (1954), though very different in cast and milieu, follows a similar pattern. New Yorker Ferris Sullivan–a poetry reader, personally fastidious, a "hopeless eccentric"–arrives at Jackson University in Virginia. He is clearly homosexual, though the term is waltzed around in the first part of the novel. His mother has tried throughout his life to erase those "tendencies," also seen in his Uncle Arnold. At Jackson, senior Paul Lasher becomes Ferris's protector and the wealthy Carter Fryman IV his chief tormentor. Again, the chapter epigraphs foreshadow the crime to come, though the questions of who will be killer and who victim are more ambiguous. (As is often the case, Gold Medal's blurb tells far too much.)

The treatment of homosexuality in the novel is fascinating, since the author is apparently trying to satisfy the moral qualms of the public and depict gays sympathetically at the same time. Lasher, a closet homosexual who wants to be "double gaited," takes Sullivan to a gay party at a New York apartment, then is angry when Sullivan, for the first time in his life not an outsider, fits in with this world all too well. The host is a Capote-ish outward queen known as Rug (because people walk all over him). At the party, the discussion of the homosexual and his options in a straight society becomes franker. Of the guests, only a Merchant Marine, a very minor character, seems well-adjusted to his sexual identity, so this is not what the present-day gay community would be likely to hail as a "positive" depiction. Still, in a mass market 1954 paperback, the scene seems far ahead of its time.

Packer appealed to Anthony Boucher's keen interest in true crime cases. His review identified the murder with a "startling recent New York parricide" and described the book as "a forceful and tragic novel of college life, homosexuality (handled with a surprising combination of good taste and explicitness), and the bitter after-the-fact relationship between collaborators in murder" (*NYTBR*, 31 October, 1954, page 39).

Following two more novels of troubled youth, *The Thrill Kids* (1955) and *The Young and the Violent* (1956), both centered in New York, Packer published the first of two novels concerned with race relations in the deep South.

In the opening pages of *Dark Don't Catch Me* (1956), Harlem youth Millard Post is sent unwillingly to Paradise, Georgia. His grandmother is reported to be dying, and his father can't get off work to make the trip. As Millard travels south, and is gradually introduced to the horrors and inconsistencies of Jim Crow, we are filled in on the explosive situation that awaits him, all revolving around the household of wealthy landholder Thad Hooper: his long-dead twin sister, his sexy wife, his children, his black servants, and his white friends and neighbors, who are all busy debating the implications of Brown versus the Board of Education of Topeka, the Supreme Court decision mandating school integration. More than anything else, however, the large cast of black and white characters is obsessed with and motivated by one thing: sex.

This time, all the specific foreshadowing of crime is in the cover copy rather than the text. Even more than its predecessors, this is a straight novel for most of the distance. Like all Packer's work, the novel is ambiguous and lacking in easy answers, but it is less successful than *Come Destroy Me* or *Whisper His Sin*. The reader has the feeling that the eventual crime and its aftermath could have been treated in greater detail–indeed, the story could support a book twice the length. It could have been an interesting example of the Big Trial novel, but legal proceedings were usually employed by Packer only in her chapter headings.

The overemphasis on sex brought the first mildly negative notice from Anthony Boucher, who found the book "dominated and distorted by an obsession with sex so powerful as to make John O'Hara's view of life seem somewhat bowdlerized." Packer made the root of "the entire Problem of the South... purely sexual in origin" (*NYTBR,* 21 December, 1956, page 12). The anonymous reviewer in *The Saint Detective Magazine,* which reviewed paperback original novels in a monthly feature called "The Saint's Ratings," awarded the novel two halos (the next to highest rating) but groused that the novel "tries to take the 'color problem' into a barely modernized Uncle Tom's Cabin. Outstanding craftsmanship is wasted on what any Southerner will recognize as strictly Yankee plumbing" (June 1957, page 111). Both reviews referred to the story's origin in a recent real-life case, pegged by Boucher the "wolf-whistle" case.

3 Day Terror (1957) has several similarities to its predecessor, being set in a small southern town (Bastrop, Alabama), also faced with the imminent integration of its schools and also visited by someone from New York. Dee Benjamin, who once had a celebrated local romance with editor Jack Chadwick, now returns from the North a divorcee. Stranger Richard Buddy is in town to campaign against school integration. His racist tracts consist of a chilling burlesque of songs from *My Fair Lady.* The novel continues the previous book's theme: that virtually all the racial troubles in the South are based on lust and sexual fear. Again, the body of the book is a build-up to a violent finish, but a less criminous one than in the earlier novels. Boucher did not review the book, and the *Saint's* rater awarded only one halo, while introducing similar caveats: "We fail to recognize too clearly Vin Packer's South and her Southern dialect seems to have a faint ring of the north in it. The story itself seems at times to get as confused as the lives of the people who tread not too ably through it" (December 1957, page 101).

The novel is clearly not one of Packer's best, but it contains the kind of social observation that makes the least of her work worthy of attention, as when politico Troy Porter discourses on the requirements for a southern politician: "Even God himself had to produce a son to get some respect down here, and a good politician's got to do a hell of a lot more. He's got to go to church, and he'd better have gone to war. He's got to have a wife, kids, a dog and a low-priced car. He can't get caught sinning, but he better seem capable of it" (page 27).

Packer's next novel, *5:45 to Suburbia* (1958), seems to be guiding the reader to a shock ending that never happens. Though listed with Packer's crime novels in Hubin's bibliography, it really isn't a crime novel at all but rather a combination of two fifties bestseller genres: the executive-suite novel and the adultery novel. Despite the title, there is very little about life in the suburbs. Main character is 50-year-old publishing executive Charlie Gibson, who objects to his company's new Confidential-type scandal magazine, yet unnamed but called Vile around the office. We meet Charlie on his fiftieth birthday, then flash back to earlier birthdays, beginning with his eighteenth when he was a student at the University of Missouri. A former classmate, now a TV commentator, is scheduled for expose in Vile concerning an old pederasty charge.

Another 1958 book, *The Evil Friendship*, is definitely criminous, fictionalizing New Zealand's Parker-Hulme case of four years before. In his review, Boucher characterized the case as a Lesbian Loeb-Leopold and pronounced Packer "as relentlessly tough-minded as any of the best 'hard-boiled' writers" (*NYTBR*, 7 September, 1958, page 28).

The Twisted Ones (1959) may be the finest of Packer's novels. The narrative alternates the lives of three troubled youths: Brock Brown, 15, handsome, puritanical New Yorker, a compulsive thief subject to blinding headaches; Charles Berrey, 8, a precocious New Jersey boy who is a big-money quiz show contestant; and Reginald Whittier, 19, a shy stutterer, mother-dominated with a friend-of-the-family father substitute. Parents in Packer novels are full of well-meant but excruciatingly harmful advice. Whittier's mother exhorts him, "Be a bush if you can't be a tree!"

All three boys have serious problems, though Brock is the most obviously disturbed, and in the closing chapters all three commit murder. Though the trio of well-drawn central characters never meet, they are linked by Packer in inventive ways, and a simplistic *Time*-style epilogue about Memorial day murders by members of the "shook-up" generation ironically brings them together at the end.

Though the novel was written before the quiz scandals hit, the quiz-show sequences in *The Twisted Ones* provide a good example of Packer's ability to use the events that define the times in a way that is successful both artistically and commercially. Her next novel, *The Girl on the Best Seller List* (1960), was inspired by another phenomenon of the day: Grace Metalious and her best-selling novel of small-town scandal, *Peyton Place*. In this novel, Packer flirts with the whodunit form for the first time, as several residents of Cayuta, New York, have good reason to contemplate the murder of novelist Gloria Whealdon, author of the best-selling *roman à clef, Population 12,360.* What makes the subject matter especially interesting is that Packer, though obviously a more serious and admirable writer than the fictional Whealdon (and probably the real-life Metalious), admits to drawing freely on real people and experiences for her own fiction. Typically, the expected crime occurs very late in the book. Though Packer answers the question of who committed the crime, there is a fine irony in the solution.

Both *Twisted Ones* and *Girl on the Best Seller List* have a character named Dr. Mannerheim. His first name changes from Clyde to Jay, but in each case he is a Ph.D. who practices or wants to practice psychology. Clyde has an art history doctorate but teaches psychology at Brock Brown's school. Jay actually practices psychology, but much is made of the fact that he is not a "real" doctor, and there is some question whether his bills can be taken as income-tax deductions. In a later Packer novel, *Something in the Shadows,* there is a reference to still another Dr. Mannerheim, though he never appears in the story. Prolific writers for the pulps and paperback originals often repeated character names out of haste and carelessness, but Packer never strikes the reader as a careless writer. She seems to know exactly what she is doing in using Dr. Mannerheims in three books, though what significance the name has for her is grist for a deeper study than this one.

The author's choice of character names is often intriguing. She would return to the title character's name in *The Damnation of Adam Blessing* (1960) for the main character in one of her M. E. Kerr novels, *The Son of Someone Famous* (1974). *Adam Blessing* drew another admiring review from Boucher, who wrote that Packer, "consistently the most sensitive and illuminating writer of paperback originals, is at her perceptive best" in "a full-scale and disquieting portrait of a psychopath" (*NYTBR*, February 1961, page 51).

In what may seem an extreme example of drawing on real life, Packer uses her own real surname for the main character in *Something in the Shadows* (1961). Folklorist Joseph Meaker (yet another former University of Missouri student) has moved to a Pennsylvania farm with wife Maggie, who is employed in advertising in New York. Joseph is a confirmed, indeed extreme animal-lover, and when his cat Ishmael is run over by a doctor's Mercedes, Joseph begins to plot revenge. His plans take an odd course when he insists that he and Maggie befriend Dr. and Mrs. Hart, inviting them to dinner. The story is more like a standard suspense novel than most of Packer's, the reader suspecting that Meaker will murder but not knowing whom or how. The crime comes earlier in the book than usual, though still in the second half. Maggie's occupation provides the vehicle for some advertising parodies, notably a soft-sell cigarette commercial. ("Ladies and gentlemen, Pick cigarettes bring you three minutes of uninterrupted silence .... The public is tired of noisy commercials. They're irritating," page 20). Early in the novel, Joseph receives a letter from a Hungarian woman and former left-wing activist he knew at Missouri. The real-life origin of this character can be seen in the author's relationship with a Hungarian man, described in *Me Me Me Me Me*.

The writer Packer is most often compared to by reviewers is John O'Hara. That the influence is a real one is suggested by the O'Hara parody contained in *Something in the Shadows,* where one character imagines some O'Hara dialogue.

Indeed, Anthony Boucher, in reviewing Packer's next novel, *Intimate Victims* (1962), credits her "eye and ear for nice distinctions of culture and usage as acute as those of... O'Hara and Nancy Mitford" (*NYTBR,* II November, 1962, page 52). Reviewing the novel in tandem with Ross Macdonald's *The Zebra-Striped Hearse,* he finds in Packer "an almost comparable amount of meat," high praise indeed considering Boucher's view of Macdonald. A closer comparison in the crime/suspense field might be Patricia Highsmith, as the relationship between main characters Robert Bowser and Harvey Plangman has something of a *Strangers on a Train* flavor. For once, a crime appears at the very beginning of the book. The treasurer of an investment firm, Bowser has embezzled over $100,000, and he is planning his imminent escape to Brazil when, through an unfortunate stroke of fate, he inadvertently trades jackets and wallets with Plangman in a service-station restroom. Obsessive social climber Plangman, a pitiful collector of brand names and foreign phrases who is one of Packer's most memorable characters, finds the evidence of Bowser's plans and takes the opportunity for an odd and elaborate blackmail plan: Bowser must take Plangman's place as superintendent of a boardinghouse near the University of Missouri, while providing him evidence by mail on which clothes to wear, brands to buy, and dishes to cook while futilely courting a rich man's daughter. Of course, the scheme will culminate in murder, but again who will murder whom is left to the end of the book.

Alone at Night (1963) is Vin Packer's last novel for Gold Medal. In fact, only two more novels under the pseudonym would appear, one a hardcover. Once again, the setting is Cayuta, New York, in the Finger Lakes. This novel may represent Packer's closest approach to a detective story, albeit an inverted one. Buzzy Cloward went to prison for causing the death of Carrie Burr, running her down while drunk and driving her husband's car. Now he returns to Cayuta, where Carrie's husband Slater Burr has remarried. The reader soon comes to suspect that Cloward may not be guilty, but any whodunit element is short-lived: Slater is the person really responsible. Awkward questions begin to arise–how, for example, could the drunken Cloward immediately figure out how to drive Burr's difficult and unfamiliar Jaguar?–and the novel's suspense lies in how (or whether) Burr will ultimately be found out.

The last Packer paperback original is better, though still not in a class with the best books of the fifties and early sixties. *The Hare in March* (Signet, 1966), like several of the novels from Gold Medal, is given a cover blurb that emphasizes its trendiness: "A shattering novel about the college boys and girls who fly high on violence, sex, and L.S.D." As usual, it is far less conventional and predictable than the blurb might suggest. The first chapter suggests a traditional mystery, as two Far Point, New York cops on patrol discover a dead girl next to a spaced-out college boy in a car at the local lover's lane. But the novel then flashes back to the events leading up to the crime, in a pattern like that in Packer's earliest books, albeit some-what more complex in plot. The scene is Far Point College, where L.S.D. is used in a fraternity hazing. Undersized Arnold Hagerman is a chilling fig-ure in the grand tradition of Packer psychopaths. That Packer kept her fin-ger on the pulse of the times is indicated by her topical references–Vietnam protest (still fairly early in 1966), Timothy Leary, camp, and a couple of names that remain quite current today: Ronald Reagan and Cher.

Following one more novel, the hardcover astrology comedy *Don't Rely on Gemini* (Delacorte, 1969), the Packer byline was retired. In 1972, with the first M. E. Kerr book, the author almost immediately attained a firm place among the most celebrated authors of young adult "problem" novels. Few if any of the Kerrs could be classified as mystery and suspense, until the most recent one, *Fell* (1987), which is not only a mystery but introduces an element that could not be more foreign to the world of Vin Packer: a series detective!

M. E. Kerr's continued fame seems secure. But her alter ego Vin Packer is one of many authors of suspense fiction who are unjustly forgotten and deserve revival. She was a big seller in the fifties–the back cover of *Dark Don't Catch Me* is already claiming 4-1/2 million copies sold–and Boucher considered her one of the best crime novelists of her day, regardless of for-mat. A rereading of her novels today bears out his opinion.

If you enjoyed this book, you might enjoy the following from

Stark House Press